INHERITING TROUBLE

DAWN SMITH

ALSO BY DAWN SMITH

INHERITING REDEMPTION

This is a work of fiction. Names, characters, places, and incidents are products of the author's imagination or are used fictitiously and are not to be construed as real. Any resemblance to actual events, locales, organizations, or persons, living or dead, is entirely coincidental.

Copyright © 2020 by Dawn Smith
All rights reserved.
ISBN: 978-0-9850871-3-5
Library of Congress Control Number:2019913576
ebook ISBN: 978-0-9850871-2-8

Published by Dawn Smith
Learn more at: dawnsmithmysteries.com

Cover, illustrations and layout by Ben Gilliand
Learn more at: bgvisual.com

Printed in the United States of America

ACKNOWLEDGEMENTS

Thanks to pre-readers Lori Livingston, Sunny Gilliand and Laura Brown. Thank you to Jane Ryder and Lindsay Guzzardo at The Editorial Department and to Joie Gibson at Wiser Words Editing. Any mistakes in this book are the author's. Thanks to Ben Gilliand for the wonderful artwork.

ABOUT THE AUTHOR

Dawn Smith lives in Texas with her husband JW, and Rumor the spoiled cat. She can be reached through her website www.dawnsmithmysteries.com.

For my sister, Lori Livingston.
Your encouragement and love help me daily.
Gone too soon, but forever in my heart.
Enjoy riding those horses in heaven.

The righteous shall inherit the land and
dwell upon it forever.

Psalm 37:29 ESV

PROLOGUE

The boy settled cross-legged beneath a mammoth live oak. The tree reminded him of happier times when he and his best friend had practiced their Tarzan yells while swinging from a thick rope on a similar tree into a pond. Then his parents had decided to move, and he'd had no vote. Not that two against one would have made a difference, but at least he'd have had a say.

He'd turned sixteen a few months ago. Getting his driver's license was exciting, but the feeling eventually passed.

Yesterday his English teacher had pulled him aside and asked how he was fitting in at school—if he was making friends. Her questions and concern touched him, then rolled off his shoulders like water off a waxed car hood.

"You're moody," his mom had said as he left the house after supper. "Adjust and find something to be happy about," his dad had added.

He leaned against the oak. "I'm following orders, Dad," he said, pulling happiness from his pocket.

Within minutes, vapor danced above heat waves. He filled the syringe and slid the needle in like he'd been shown, and, oh yeah, happiness arrived in a rush.

He looked at the rising moon and enjoyed the show.

CHAPTER ONE

WE DON'T WANT YOUR KIND HERE.

Darcy Cooper felt the deputy's gaze slide over her, seeming to repeat the statement spray-painted in bright, accusing red on her foyer wall.

The porch swing squeaked as she shifted to look through her open front door. Inside, a second Tell County sheriff's deputy—a blonde that could pass for Dolly Parton's granddaughter—raised a camera and photographed the graffiti.

We don't want your kind here.

Darcy sat back. She was moving in today. The vandal had no idea who or what kind she was. Since the population of the Texas Hill Country town of Lost Creek barely topped 6000, the citizens would find out soon.

September heat sent a trickle of sweat down her spine. Sighing, she flipped her braid over her shoulder.

Her inheritance of the ranch house and a hundred acres came as a surprise. She'd known Alex Anderson only nine months, and he had family here. All she knew was what his lawyer told her—Alex changed his will to include her three weeks before his death.

The male deputy rounded the corner of the limestone porch that surrounded the ground floor. Darcy stood. "Did you find anything else?"

"No, ma'am," he drawled, making her feel older than her twenty-seven years. "The message in your entry appears to be all."

"That's a relief."

"Yes, ma'am." He glanced over her shoulder.

Darcy turned. The female deputy walked out of the house, shaking her head. "My guess is kids. This house sat empty for months, and kids like to explore." She pointed at the door. "Think about replacing your locks. A screwdriver or credit card can open these."

Kids, Darcy thought. She could handle kids. She tugged a notepad and pen from her pocket and flipped to a blank page. "I'll add locks to my list."

"We'll file a report. You can pick up a copy for your insurance claim."

Darcy shook her head. "Thanks, but I'll repaint the wall."

As the deputies drove off, she searched the paint buckets stacked on the porch. If she worked fast, she could get a coat of primer over the graffiti before the moving van arrived. No prank would diminish her joy in Alex's bequest. She was counting her blessings, not regretting a gift.

Thursday, Darcy stood in the living room and collapsed a cardboard box. Four rooms finished if you counted the foyer. The house was looking like a home.

After catering for a local bank's grand opening celebration on Tuesday, she'd hoped for a referral or two. So far, her phone hadn't rung, and her supply of freshly printed business cards wasn't getting much smaller. Starting a new life in Lost Creek was proving more challenging than the eleven moves she'd made while her father was on active duty in the military.

She carried the flattened box to the porch and added it to the growing stack.

The phone rang—a rare enough occurrence lately that she almost missed telemarketers. She entered the kitchen and answered the landline. "Hello?"

"Darcy, it's Maggie."

"My favorite client from my former life!"

"I bet you say that to everyone who booked three parties a year at the hotel."

"No. Just the ones that knew Alex and once lived in Lost Creek."

"Well, now I do feel special. Your replacement tries hard, but she's not you."

"Give her a chance. And I told her to call me if she has questions."

"Good to know. Listen, I received the email with your new contact information. If you've already moved in, your remodel is going smoother than any I've endured in my seventy-plus years."

Darcy laughed. "I arrived Saturday, but the crews have worked three weeks. The downstairs is finished, but my contractor's wife fell ill, so I'm looking for someone to start on the upstairs guest rooms and bathrooms."

"I've had contractors quit on me. Don't worry; you'll find another."

"I suppose so, but all the Lost Creek contractors are busy."

"All of them?"

"If they're in the phone book, I've called them. I'm looking in San Antonio now."

Her normally talkative friend seemed at a loss for words.

"Do you know something I don't?" Darcy asked.

"I thought things would have changed since I left." Maggie sighed. "You know how every town has something it's famous for locally? Like the sweet potato capital of Texas, or the largest ball of string? Alex and Cindy's love was legendary in Lost Creek."

"You mentioned that once when Alex took us to dinner."

"I mean really legendary. Elizabeth Bennett and Mr. Darcy legendary. I'd rather clean my 8000 square-foot house than have anyone in Lost Creek think I'd replaced Cindy in Alex's heart."

Darcy sat at the table. "You think the locals think Alex left me the house because we were dating or something?"

"I'd bet money on the 'or something.' The Lost Creek contractors can't be so busy that you couldn't get on someone's waitlist."

"But even if I had dated Alex, that attitude seems outdated."

"You ran the demographics for Lost Creek?" Maggie asked.

"Yes. Sixty percent of the residents are sixty or older."

"And country people don't feel obligated to keep up with

modern trends."

Darcy leaned her forehead on her hand. "I need to start explaining that even if I don't know why Alex left me his property, it wasn't because we were romantically involved. Any suggestions?"

"Start with Alex and Cindy's contemporaries at the independent living community. My mother lived there several years—Looking Forward Living—that's the name. Make some of your delicious treats, pay a visit, and explain your friendship with Alex to the residents."

Darcy wrote notes as Maggie continued. "If you find out there is a rumor going around about you and Alex, I have a favor to ask."

"Sure."

"I don't visit Lost Creek often, but I still have friends there that remember I dated Alex for a few months before he met Cindy. While he was here in Dallas, Alex asked me not to mention him to anyone in Lost Creek. I thought he didn't want to spread the news of his dialysis, but maybe he was protecting his and Cindy's legacy. Please don't mention me."

"I won't name drop."

"Thank you. And before I forget, how many rooms are you renting? I'm starting a list of friends to refer to your bed and breakfast."

"Two rooms. And referrals would be greatly appreciated." Darcy aligned the salt and pepper shakers in the center of the table. "You could make referrals better if you visited first. I'll comp your stay."

"I'll pick dates in October, and I'm paying—I know how expensive a remodel is. Let me know how your visit goes with the residents. Now, I've got to run. Stay out of trouble."

"Yes, ma'am."

Eli Whitepath squinted against the Monday morning sun as he negotiated the loose limestone rocks littering the slope that spilled to the blue-green shallows of the Guadalupe River.

Last night's full-color vision—and the woman in it—had jolted him awake hours earlier than usual. She'd first visited his dreams last week and watched him as if judging his response to her presence. This time, as she watched him, her dress color changed from white to red.

Uncle John would tell him to look for a deeper meaning after dreaming of her twice, but he was a sheriff, not a shaman. She hadn't stayed long or spoken, so he'd pulled a pillow over his head and slept until the dispatcher called about this morning's grim discovery.

His slick-soled cowboy boots had him surfing on the rocky soil. He put a hand down, checked his descent, and straightened to scan the crime scene.

Like a mantis looming over its prey, the lanky coroner crouched over the body of a teenaged male. A deputy walked away from the body, occasionally pausing to stab a yellow evidence flag into the ground. Footprints, Eli guessed, given their linear trajectory.

Near the river's edge, his department's sole detective interviewed a man outfitted like a model for a fly-fishing catalog. Eli joined the coroner.

"Doc."

"Sobering way to start the morning," the coroner said without glancing up.

Eli lifted the brim of his Stetson and squatted. "What can you tell me?"

"It's what I can show you."

Doc pushed up the teen's left sleeve and exposed needle tracks.

Eli's mouth tightened. "Heroin?"

"A tox screen will tell for sure. I found two punctures." Doc pointed. "Judging by the lack of bruising here, I'm guessing the seller set up the first taste about a week ago. The boy probably injected himself last night." He indicated another site. "Which explains this bruising. If it is heroin, and the boy mixed it himself, this could be an accidental overdose."

Seeing the needle marks added years to the thirty-eight Eli had already accumulated. He pulled examination gloves from the open medical kit and snapped them on. "Wallet?"

Doc pointed.

Eli reached inside an evidence bag. In his nearly four years as sheriff, he'd made other notifications—though not as many as he'd made as a San Antonio homicide detective. It wasn't something you got used to. He studied the driver's license; the boy lived nearby. He replaced the wallet as Doc shook out a body bag.

"I'll call when I finish the autopsy. And I'll rush the tox screen," Doc said.

"I appreciate it."

The coroner unzipped the bag. "How's your reelection campaign coming?"

"As well as can be expected after the first overdose, now a second, and no suspects yet."

Approaching footsteps dislodged rocks worn smooth by the river. Eli glanced over his shoulder and stood.

The September morning had started near eighty degrees and would rise from there. He tugged off the gloves and stuffed them into his vest pocket before facing his detective. Bruce Wainright had arrived two years ago from Galveston with an impressive résumé and more forensics training than the sixteen deputies on the force combined. Men of his caliber didn't just show up in a rural county like Tell—they arrived for a reason.

Two months ago, Eli had learned Wainright's reason. He could handle competition, he reminded himself.

The detective held a fistful of paper bags. "One used hypodermic, one shoestring, one spoon, one lighter. Looks like the kid shot up under this tree to enjoy his high."

"Alone?"

"That's my impression." He waved a hand. "All footprints match the kid's athletic shoe treads or the fisherman's wading shoes. I'll trace the kid's movements last night. Maybe a friend saw him with someone."

"And the fisherman?"

"A newly-retired import upset about finding the kid."

Wainright looked at the body bag. "Second O.D. in a month and still no solid leads. The Lost Creek Weekly will have a field day with this."

Eli nodded. "I'll inform the parents."

Darcy braked hard, raising a cloud of dust on the gravel parking lot. Four fifty-eight. Two minutes spared her from arriving late and jeopardizing the only steady catering job she'd landed.

She stepped out and fought the wind to open her Ford Explorer's back door. T-shirt and shorts weren't professional attire, but she'd dozed away her opportunity to change. Baskets in hand, she let the strong wind slam the door shut. Head lowered, she aimed for the industrial-green cinderblock building that stood alone outside the city limits.

Darn the exhaustion that had encouraged her unplanned nap and the unexpected dream of an unsettling man who'd stared into her eyes until a pleasurable shiver shook her awake.

It wasn't the first time he'd invaded her dreams. She'd dreamt of him after the graffiti incident. In that dream, she'd walked into the foyer and found him scowling at the words on her wall. He'd turned his green eyes on her, and she'd immediately woken.

She shoulder-butted the gray metal door and blew into Border's Roadhouse. Across the room, a knot of men aligned mismatched tables and chairs. A few glanced her way. Conversation suspended then resumed, punctuated with laughter. She crossed the scuffed pine floor and settled the baskets on the bar, four feet from the only client seated on a stool. The man wore a black cowboy hat that shadowed his profile as he focused on a half-full glass of what looked like cola.

"Appetizers for the retirement party as ordered, Carl," Darcy called out.

"Hey, young 'un." A giant emerged from the back room. A bottle of Jack Daniels dangled from each fist. His smile broadened. "I hear supermodels pay big money for that hairdo."

"The wind's picked up." She glanced at the mirrored backsplash and released a disgusted breath. "I look like I stuck my head in a cotton candy machine."

She attempted to finger-comb her hair and winced when her fingers caught a tangle. "This explains the local oak trees' prevalent southeast lean."

Carl Border's smile crinkled the corners of his gray eyes. The lower half of his face sported a shaggy brown beard and walrus mustache grizzled with gray; the top half reflected as much light as the pyramids of polished beer mugs stacked on the back counter.

He set the whiskey on the counter. "Something smells good."

She lifted the cloth covering the baskets. "Jalapeno-beef empanadas with homemade salsa, peeled shrimp and cocktail sauce, and fresh vegetables with ranch dressing."

"Looks great. You want a soda before you head home?"

She slid onto a stool. "Forget soda. Let's talk wine."

"Grape juice in a roadhouse?"

"It's called catering to tourists."

The black-hatted loner motioned Carl over. They exchanged a few words, and Carl walked back to Darcy.

"The Sheriff thinks you're underage, Darcy. That's a nice compliment. Why don't you show him your ID and set his mind at ease."

"Carl—" The sheriff stood and placed cash on the bar.

"She'll show you," Carl said. "I carded her myself when she walked in the first time."

Although the afternoon temperatures exceeded ninety, the approaching man wore a light-weight vest partially buttoned up.

Darcy looked up and met his eyes. "No way," she blurted out.

Shock scrambled her brain. He was literally the man of her dreams.

Thick black hair teased his collar. His firm mouth and frown complemented his erect posture. He must have interpreted her denial as a refusal to show him her ID because his eyebrows rose. He probably wasn't used to his requests being denied. But he hadn't made a request—Carl had.

Flustered, she looked at Carl. "Are you serious?"

The bartender winked and tossed a bar towel over his shoulder. "Show the man, young 'un. I'll take care of the meat pies." He gathered her baskets and headed for the men rearranging his tables.

She turned back and felt her face flush. The sheriff was studying her intently.

"My purse is in my car, and Carl vouched for me," she said.

"I'll walk you out then."

"First, I want to see your ID."

He held up a black leather wallet displaying a badge and photo card identifying him as Elias Whitepath, Tell County Sheriff. That explained the vest; he probably carried a gun.

She slid off the stool and stepped back, needing to put distance between his reality and her dreams. He bested her five-foot-four by a good eight inches.

She walked to Carl and scooped her empty baskets from the table. "Any requests for Friday?"

He grinned. "Surprise me. Whatever you make sells as fast as I put it out."

"Okay." She walked to the door where the Sheriff waited.

"Hey, young 'un," Carl called. "I haven't written your check."

She turned, and bumped shoulders with the sheriff.

"Sorry," she said. She'd stumbled into concrete posts with more give, but none had smelled like a pine forest, and none had made her tingle.

Carl's grin widened into a smile. She sighed. What warped sense of humor had inspired him to pit her against the sheriff? If this was Carl's idea of an introduction, she needed to loan him her copy of Miss Manners. "Pay me

Friday night."

Carl waved his towel in acknowledgment.

Darcy stepped through the door the sheriff held open. The cloudless western sky harbored the sun, its heat made bearable by the stiff breeze. Their footsteps crunched across the gravel to her white SUV.

She set the baskets on the ground and wiggled the keys from her pocket. Beside her, the sheriff surveyed her car's interior.

"You're inviting a break-in, leaving your purse on the front seat," he said.

Judging by the set of his mouth, his first impression of her was worsening. "I don't normally stay inside long." She unlocked the car and opened the door.

"Then why ask Carl for wine?" the sheriff said.

She faced him.

"I'm twenty-seven. And when I drink, I drink wine. So do others, so adding a small selection of wine to the beverage menu might expand Carl's clientele and his profits. I think Lost Creek has hospitality-market potential." Curiosity overrode caution. "Do people usually tell law officers more than necessary?"

He studied her. "It signifies anxiety. Or a guilty conscience."

"Do you think I'm lying?" Her fists settled on her hips. When he didn't answer, she exhaled and stretched across the seat to pull her wallet from her purse. She extracted her license. "My ID."

He took the card and glanced from her to the photo.

"You live in Dallas?"

"I lived in Dallas. Now, I live outside Lost Creek." She waited while he gave the card more attention than the end-of-the-workday photo deserved.

"When did you move?" He paused a moment too long. "Ms. Cooper."

He'd said her name with recognition. Maybe Maggie was right: someone had started a rumor about her and Alex. Or perhaps she was sensitive to the suggestion of a scandal.

"Ten days ago."

"You have thirty days to change your address at the DMV. After that, you can be ticketed. What's your current address?"

"Do you keep a calendar of people to ticket?"

"Your current address?"

"I live in the old Anderson house east of town."

Darcy Cooper, Eli thought.

He'd walked her outside because she'd visited his dreams. He wouldn't approach her again. He'd heard the rumors and he had enough problems with the heroin overdoses and his struggling reelection campaign. He squared his shoulders.

"My deputies answered a vandalism call at your home."

Despite the heat, she shivered. Eli's protective instinct surged, along with images of the crime scene photos: WE DON'T WANT YOUR KIND HERE, sprayed in crimson enamel across her wall—formerly Alex and Cindy's wall. Was she the kind to con a sick man out of his property and tarnish a sterling reputation? Not if his instincts were right—and they usually were.

"The graffiti was there the morning I arrived. The last time I spoke with your deputies, there were no leads. Have you learned anything new?"

"No. Have you had difficulty since?"

"No."

"Then change your address on your license if you intend to remain in Tell County."

Her chin lifted. "I'm staying. I'm opening a bed and breakfast next month." She extended her hand.

He was surprised to see he still held her license. He handed it back. Their fingertips grazed, and electricity arced like they'd shuffled their feet across carpet. She jerked her hand away, then sat in her car and clicked the seatbelt.

Eli stepped back. "Living outside the city limits puts you in my jurisdiction. I'll have a cruiser include your place in a regular patrol."

"Thank you."

Her smile conveyed relief. Was she worried about another break-in? When the engine caught, Eli shut the door.

Refusing to glance back, Darcy rubbed still-tingling fingertips along her thigh. Her nerve endings were taking their sweet time recovering from his touch.

Twelve minutes later, she turned into her long driveway. She parked beside the kitchen door, reached into the back seat, and felt nothing. Her heart stampeded as she twisted to look. She'd left Gramma's baskets in Border's parking lot.

She dialed Carl on her cell phone and waited while he searched. Five long minutes later, his voice returned.

"Sorry young 'un. The wind must have blown your baskets out of the lot."

She swallowed hard to dislodge the knot in her throat. "Thanks for checking, Carl. I'll see you on Friday."

She blinked away tears and exited the car. Farming was a labor of love that had put Gramma and Grampa at the mercy of rain, hail, drought, and market prices. One year comfortable, the next depleting their savings to cover losses.

She was in college when they died. When the bank auctioned the farm and their belongings, all she could afford to bid on were Gramma's handmade, everyday baskets.

She scuffed up the steps and sat on the porch swing. Gramma's encouraging words filtered through her sorrow. Think of something good.

A tough one. Darcy pushed against the porch, swinging until the thought came.

If trouble arrived in threes, she could breathe easy. Between the vandalism, the rumors about her and Alex, and losing Gramma's baskets, she'd met her quota for trouble.

High clouds parted, exposing a half-moon that cast a glow across the rocky field. Squinting, the smuggler deleted a set of coordinates from his GPS. Tonight's exhumation reduced the total of buried heroin-filled containers to forty-three. The small, watertight ammo boxes suited his needs. A whisper away, a laborer lifted another box from a hole while a second man tamped rocks and dirt into the cavity.

"La ultima, Jefe," he said.

Jefe. One corner of the man's mouth lifted. Boss was a title he intended to keep.

Switching off and pocketing the GPS, he dodged ambushing prickly pear cactus.

CHAPTER TWO

Tuesday morning, Darcy left the painters at work upstairs and, armed with cookies, drove to the Looking Forward Independent Living community. It was time to mend Alex's reputation and hers. She'd always respected and valued her elders for their life knowledge. She could make friends here—if the residents listened.

She walked through the front doors. She'd called ahead to clear her visit and cookies with the chatty director who hadn't reacted to her name. Now, the woman escorted her to a recreation room teeming with residents playing cards, dominoes, board games, or working jigsaw puzzles. The director paused inside the doorway.

"Everyone, this is Darcy Cooper. She baked cookies for a snack. Why don't you introduce yourselves as she passes them out?"

The director smiled then left, missing the reactions her announcement prompted. Three-quarters of the facial expressions changed from curious to surprise and shock. The murmured conversations went silent.

Darcy began serving at a table of four women playing bridge. "Hi! Ginger snap and chocolate chip?"

Three women nodded. The fourth stared at her cards.

Darcy laid out napkins and placed cookies on each before moving on and receiving similar responses.

As she distributed cookies, she said, "I'm sure you've all heard about Alex Anderson leaving me his house."

Wop! Something smacked her in the back. She looked down. Ginger snap crumbs littered the floor. Surprised gasps mingled with nervous laughs.

A woman wearing red-framed glasses lifted a cookie and sniffed. "Ginger is an aphrodisiac," she said. "With Alex gone, are you hoping to stimulate another man's appetites?"

"May I explain my side of the story?" Darcy asked.

The woman wearing red glasses walked out of the room. Seconds later, others followed.

Darcy set the remaining cookies on an empty table then shook out a napkin and cleaned the crumbs from the floor. She possessed evidence her friendship with Alex had been platonic, she hadn't figured out how to present that information as demonstrable proof. And she couldn't bring up Maggie for corroboration.

"I want to know why Alex left you his place," a woman said.

"I wish I knew," Darcy said. "But he didn't tell his attorney or me. I didn't know I was in his will until after his funeral."

"That sounds convenient," a man said.

"I understand, but it's the truth," Darcy said.

"How did you meet Alex?"

Darcy stood where everyone could make eye contact.

Plenty of arms were crossed, and more than one face showed doubt.

"You may know that Alex came to Dallas for medical treatment?"

Several people nodded.

"He stayed at the hotel where I worked. I walked into the hotel restaurant one afternoon and found it filled with convention members. As I looked for an empty seat, Alex offered to share his table. He was a gentleman."

After ten minutes of questions, Darcy picked up her food carriers. "I'll come back next week," she said.

"We'll be here," a man said. "I'm partial to muffins."

"I'll remember that."

Darcy walked outside to her car, cranked up the air-conditioning, pulled out her cell phone, and dialed Maggie.

"I'm not available to take your call because I'm living life to the fullest. Tell me how to reach you, and I'll call you back if you're not a solicitor."

Darcy waited for the beep.

"Hi, Maggie. I'm filling you in on the independent living community. You were right about why I'm being snubbed. Most of the residents listened to my explanation. They'd all heard a rumor from someone who'd heard it from someone else, so I don't yet know where it started. I'm going back next week to reinforce my case. Let me know if you've chosen dates for a visit. My calendar is wide open. Bye."

She had one more stop, and if she hurried, she'd be back before the painters left for lunch. A few minutes later, she pulled up to the convenience store and parked beside a beer delivery truck. She looked at the storefront. Sheriff Whitepath stared grimly back from a window poster asking voters to re-elect him November sixth. She stared back. Had she seen this poster on one of her early visits to Lost Creek and subconsciously recreated him in her dreams?

Unlikely. No way would she forget seeing his face.

He should have smiled, she thought, tilting her head. Did he ever smile? Smiling or not, the man was photogenic. If she were sixteen, she'd pin his poster to her bedroom wall.

She hurried inside, tossed a hello to the clerk, and cut toward the coolers. With one hip propped against the open dairy door, she checked the expiration date on a milk carton. As the glass fogged, male voices carried from inside the cooler.

"Then my wife said, 'Of course he was sleepin' with her. He cast off his family and left her everything he owned.' Doesn't bother me, but the wife's gonna have to go back on blood-pressure medicine if she doesn't get over Alex 'betrayin' Cindy', as she puts it."

Cindy? Alex? Darcy leaned in.

"Granted, Cindy Anderson was a mighty good woman, but it's a year since she passed. I say, 'way to go, Alex.' But I don't say it at home because I like to eat regularly."

"Have you seen this Darcy Cooper?" a second voice asked.

"No, but Chris has, and he says Alex definitely died a happy man."

Laughter billowed out with the refrigerated air.

Darcy let the dairy door slam shut as she yanked open the beer door.

"Excuse me."

"Ma'am?" Two startled pairs of eyes framed by sun-induced wrinkles looked at her from between six-packs.

"I couldn't help hearing your conversation. I'm Darcy Cooper, and Alex Anderson and I were not lovers."

Four eyebrows elevated. "Then why'd Alex leave you his place?" the owner of blue eyes asked.

Faced with the question she still asked herself, Darcy lowered her chin. "He never said, but we weren't lovers—just friends." She shifted her feet. Shorts and short-sleeves weren't the best of outfits for a refrigerated discussion.

"No offense, miss, but Bob here's my friend." Brown eyes looked left to indicate blue eyes. "And I wouldn't cut my family out of my will for him."

Blue eyes broke in. "Alex and Cindy were inseparable. True love. Forever and ever and all that. The standard for all local relationships. My mother, when I told her I'd asked my Lanie to marry me, asked, 'is it an Alex and Cindy kind of love?'"

Her stomach somersaulted. "You think I tarnished a Lost Creek icon?"

"That's pretty much it." Blue eyes blinked. "We're running up the electric bill."

Cheeks hot, she opened her mouth then shut the door. She paid for the milk and returned to her SUV. Her fingers tapped the steering wheel. How was she going to clear her name and Alex's reputation?

She looked at the store window. The sheriff's poster offered no advice.

At one o'clock, Eli pulled up to Darcy Cooper's house and parked beside her Ford Explorer. He stepped out and buttoned his suit jacket. Reaching back inside, he gripped the baskets he'd found in Border's parking lot.

Non-stop meetings with the Mayor and various other county officials had consumed his morning. Discussions centered on the latest overdose victim—with a mix of oblique hints and direct pronouncements of his doomed reelection chances coming in a close second. The heroin suppliers and dealers were cautious. Without a significant lead, the seven weeks until the election might be his last in Tell County. He hadn't thought about where he'd go from here—or how his family would take his departure.

He shut the cruiser's door. He'd needed an official task to clear his head and calm his stress-soured stomach. He should have left the baskets at Border's with Carl for Darcy to pick up Friday night, but his visions of her had stimulated an interest he had no official business pursuing.

She puzzled him. Her wide brown eyes and expressive face made her easy to read. She was attractive in a girl-next-door way, although, given the rumors, wholesome was not a word some might use. She'd confirmed the inheritance, but his profession had taught him to avoid assumptions.

He shook his head as he climbed the front steps. Why couldn't he receive a vision of the persons responsible for the heroin in Tell County instead of dreaming of Lost Creek's notorious newcomer?

A booming bass beat, muffled by wood and stone, pulsed from inside the house. His abuse of the doorbell went unanswered, so he tested the knob. It turned in his hand. Had the break-in taught her nothing? He leaned inside. "Ms. Cooper!"

His bellow lost a decibel competition with guitar-dominated heavy metal. He closed the door and followed the wraparound porch. The kitchen door was open, the screen door unlocked, and every screened window was wide open. Why did some city dwellers equate living in the country with everyone being friendly and everything being safe? He wasn't Andy Griffith, and Tell County wasn't Mayberry.

A paint-spattered tarp protected the back porch from the drips trailing down the outside of sealed buckets. Glass crunched underfoot. On the other side of the broken window, more glass lay in a neat pile on the living room floor. Thieves didn't usually tidy up. So why hadn't Darcy responded to the doorbell or his shout?

He opened the French doors and walked into the living room.

"Ms. Cooper!"

No answer.

He glanced at the Southwest-patterned armchairs and leather couch then turned right, past a dining table surrounded by eight chairs. Following the kraft-paper path protecting the refinished wood floors, he pushed through swinging doors into the kitchen. The baked cookie smell reminded him he'd missed lunch.

Sunlight glinted off stainless steel appliances and counters. Eli set the baskets on the kitchen table beside a rolled and rubber-banded newspaper. Nothing in the sink. She'd left no signs of lunch. Maybe she had two cars?

He walked through the foyer into a sitting room where her keys and purse shared the desktop. That could be good or bad. Her bedroom came next. Braided throw rugs, cherry furniture, and a bed topped with a patchwork quilt of forest-floor colors. For a modern woman, she exhibited old-fashioned tastes.

Eli followed the music upstairs. Two rooms opened onto a narrow landing, the first empty but freshly painted. In the second, also freshly painted, a boom box with the repeat button engaged played to two swollen trash bags and a ladder. He checked the bathroom then turned too quickly and stumbled into a full trash bag. He caught the ladder, nearly knocking it over. Rubbing his shin, he looked out the open balcony doors. No sign of a struggle. Where was she?

So much for a soothing drive to the country. Eli pulled the plug on the boom box and walked out.

Darcy unplugged the box fan and the music below abruptly ceased. She looked up. It couldn't be a thrown breaker—the attic bulb still burned.

She rolled her shoulders, rocked the kinks out of her neck, and admired her work. The attic, if not her life, was in order.

Two boxes of Anderson family memorabilia were now neatly packed. Alex's nephew practiced veterinary medicine in Lost Creek; he'd been easily found with an internet search. Delivering the boxes offered a valid excuse for meeting him and learning if he knew why Alex had chosen her to inherit the house and land.

She gulped water from a bottle then used the final half-inch to clean her hands. She'd used the last paper towel minutes before, so she shook off droplets then wiped her hands down the sides of her formerly pink shorts, and now, literally, dusty rose I-don't-suffer-from-stress-I'm-a-carrier emblazoned T-shirt.

She lifted the door on the floor and dropped the last trash bag to the floor below. She turned off the light, sat, and balanced on the edge of the attic opening. She swung one leg in a circle, searching for the ladder.

Not connecting with anything, she leaned and spotted an aluminum leg to her left. Gripping the sides of the opening, she lowered her body. Even with a ladder, the ten-foot ceiling made getting in and out of the attic a gymnastic event.

"Note to self, buy an attic door with a folding ladder."

Her to-buy list lengthened while her bank balance shrank. The stair that only creaked when stepped on groaned.

Had the vandal returned?

Below her sat a trash bag filled with items with sharp corners. She tried to swing away from it.

Strong hands gripped her waist from behind. "Let go."

She nearly screamed, but since when did vandals wear suit jackets? She released her grip. When her feet hit the floor, she turned and recognized narrowed slits of green. Relief beat out fear.

"This answers the question, 'Where's a cop when you need one?' The painters knew I was up there. I don't know why they moved the ladder." She tried to slow her breathing.

"They didn't. I bumped into it a few minutes ago." His scrutiny didn't falter as he read her T-shirt and nodded.

"Why are you in my house?"

"A downstairs window is broken, and your doors are unlocked." He looked from the boom box to the attic opening. "I rang the bell and shouted."

She tugged her T-shirt straight. "The painters turned up the music before they left so I could listen while I cleaned the attic. Since the windows are open to disperse the paint fumes, I didn't see the point in locking the doors. The broken window was an accident."

"You have dirt on your nose," he said.

Despite the sweat and dust she wore, and a sudden urge to tidy her braid, she surrendered to the absurdity of vanity at this moment. "I'm guessing that you don't personally patrol this area," she said, using her shirt sleeve to rub her nose.

"I brought the baskets you left in Border's lot."

Happiness filled her. "You found my baskets?"

"They're on the kitchen table."

She raced past him, downstairs to the kitchen. She reached for the basket handles, noticed the grime on her hands, and turned to rinse her hands, arms, and face at the sink. She dried them and tossed the kitchen towel aside. Her hand caught the counter's lip. "Ouch!"

The sheriff entered and folded his arms. "What happened?"

"I'm okay." She stepped past him to touch the woven willow baskets. "Thank you. These belonged to my grandparents. Carl checked outside, but you'd already rescued them."

"I serve and protect. And I haven't driven out this way in a while," he said, exploring the counter lip. "You should have this repaired. If you caught the edge right, it would slice deep."

"I'll add it to the contractor's punch list," she said, though getting her former contractor back out was unlikely. "You deserve a reward. Milk and cookies?"

He looked up. His growling stomach answered before he nodded. Darcy poured two glasses of milk while the sheriff prowled her kitchen.

"Who is this?" He tapped a finger against a framed photo on the windowsill above the sink. A woman with short dark hair protected her formal dress by stiff-arming a T-shirt and jeans-clad Darcy.

"My best friend, Beth. She'd rather wear white shoes in winter than get her clothes dirty. We met in college. Later, she convinced Thompson's Hotels to hire me. It wasn't difficult since her husband is the owner."

When he turned to look at her, she defended herself.

"It wasn't cronyism. I'm good at organizing meetings, parties, receptions, and other events."

She spiraled chocolate chip cookies on a plate then picked up her milk. She looked at his jacket. "You must be sweltering. Let's sit outside; there's usually a breeze on the porch."

He picked up his milk and opened the screen door for her. She used an elbow to toggle the porch ceiling fan switch then led him out. She set the cookies on a low wrought-iron and limestone table between two mesquite rocking chairs. The sheriff removed his jacket and hung it on the back of one rocker. Darcy glanced at his shoulder holster as she sat down.

He selected a cookie and leaned back. Legs spread, he used his heels to set the rocker in motion.

She glanced sideways at him. The sheriff possessed the lean, muscular build of a distance runner. Using visual ads was a good campaign strategy for him.

He picked up another cookie. "These are good. What's the brand?"

"I made them. It's my grandmother's recipe." She nudged the plate closer. He stopped rocking and studied her.

"Why do I get the feeling you want to say, 'You're kidding'?" she asked.

"Occupational hazard. I categorize everyone I meet, and you keep punching your way out of your alleged profile."

She froze. The sheriff had heard the rumors.

He resumed rocking. His gaze tracked the tan sedan passing on the road. The people in the car must live nearby, she thought. She'd seen the car several times now—once or twice in her rearview mirror.

Lost Creek was a small town; she was bound to see the same vehicles. The vandalism still spooked her, although new exterior door locks helped her feel secure. No matter how rocky the soil, she was putting down roots.

"I walked through your house while searching for you. Since you'll have strangers in your bed and breakfast, you should put a lock on the door that leads to your private rooms," he said as if tuned in to her thoughts. "What made you think you'd like living in Lost Creek?"

"I like small towns. I lived with my grandparents on their South Dakota farm while I was in high school and loved it."

He reached for another cookie and nodded at the construction materials stacked in the yard. "The remodel must keep you busy. I saw Hal Strong's business card on your fridge. Did he sub-contract Jim Rose as your painter?"

Darcy set her glass down. "Hal quit last week when his wife became ill, and Jim is busy until next month. My crew is from San Antonio." She interpreted his silence as criticism for not using local labor. Well, she'd tried.

"What's the name of your bed-and-breakfast?" he finally asked.

"I considered Alexander's Retreat, but that sounded like an ancient battle maneuver." She'd almost made him smile, but he stopped with a minuscule lift of mouth corners. "For internet search purposes, I chose Lost Creek Bed-and-Breakfast."

He finished his milk in one long pull. His face had lost its earlier strain.

"More milk?" she asked.

He shook his head no and picked up the last cookie as he stood. "I have to get back to work. I appreciate your hospitality."

Not nearly as much as she'd enjoyed his company—even if duty motivated the visit. She missed casual conversations. Rising, she followed the sheriff to the porch steps. "Thanks again for returning the baskets."

He nodded then walked down the steps to his cruiser. "Keep your doors locked when you're alone."

"Yes, sir."

Knowing someone cared, even if that someone was paid to care, lifted her spirits.

CHAPTER THREE

Darcy parked near the worn but tidy barn extension at the back of Keith Anderson's veterinary clinic. Judging by the packed parking lot, business boomed.

She rolled down her windows. Raised voices carried from a corral where a heavy-set man jabbed a finger into the barrel chest of a younger, taller man.

Hefting a box from the Explorer, she crossed the asphalt to the clinic. The occupancy-challenged waiting room overflowed with dogs, cats, rabbits and a squatty, but cute, pig. Was Lost Creek battling an epidemic? Darcy set her box on the floor beside the reception counter. When she returned to the car to retrieve the second box, the men in the corral were gone.

Back inside, she rested the second box on the counter and sneezed at the combination of pets and perfume. A petite blonde was attempting to wheedle an unscheduled appointment for a Yorkshire terrier.

"Since it's not an emergency, Dr. Anderson can't see Missy until Tuesday." The receptionist's voice rose to compete with the bluetick hound challenging a newly arrived border collie.

The blonde's voice turned as sharp as her stiletto heels.

"What time Tuesday?"

Darcy glanced over her shoulder and witnessed a sea of smirks. She raised her eyebrows. No epidemic packed this waiting room with attractive females. Dr. Anderson must be considered a catch in Lost Creek.

Did any of these animals require attention? Or were their owners hoping to catch the vet's attention? Given his workload, she'd probably have to schedule an appointment to meet him. At least she could leave the boxes.

"Can I help you?" The receptionist eyed the box Darcy had set on the counter.

"I'd like to leave two boxes for Dr. Anderson. When can I come back and speak to him?"

"Your name?" The woman's pen hovered over a cube of purple sticky notes.

"Darcy Cooper."

The receptionist's eyes widened and the room fell silent. Darcy forced a smile.

"Just a moment." The receptionist scurried off and returned in under a minute, her eyes cold. "Dr. Anderson will see you."

Darcy lifted the box on the counter and followed the receptionist to an office that smelled faintly of wet dog. The door snicked closed, leaving her alone.

Diplomas hung on a beige wall. A battered oak desk faced two upholstered chairs bearing unidentifiable stains. Darcy set the box on the more questionable of the two chairs as the door opened.

A handsome, thickly-mustached man entered, drying his hands on a paper towel, and kicking the door shut with a dirt-caked boot heel. His blue jeans and brown shirt sported bits of hay and a comfortingly familiar barnyard odor reminiscent of her grandparents' farm. Darcy recognized his muscled frame and the red ball cap he tossed onto the desk. He was one of the men who'd argued outside.

She stepped forward. "Dr. Anderson, I'm Darcy Cooper."

As they shook hands, his smile stretched his closed lips and expanded his dark blonde mustache like an accordion. Darcy estimated his age as mid-thirties. Hazel eyes flashed a combination of suspicion and curiosity.

"So you're the woman who has Aunt Cindy spinning in her grave."

She had expected his question. "Only if you believe rumors."

"Rumors, huh? Ms. Cooper, there's no way to find out but to ask. Exactly how friendly were you and Uncle Alex?"

Anger colored her answer. "I considered Alex a good friend, Dr. Anderson."

A long pause later, he nodded. "Have a seat. What's in the box?"

Darcy brushed her fingertips across the remaining chair seat before she sat. "Anderson family photos and papers. I left a second box by your receptionist's desk."

"Are you interested in selling the property?"

She decided to be equally blunt. "No, I'm here to stay."

"My dad leases your south pasture for his goats."

"Alex's lawyer told me the goats keep the agricultural exemption current."

"So you'll continue to honor the lease agreement?"

"For the duration of the lease. By December, I'll know if I want to use the land for something else. If you give me your father's number, I'll call and let him know."

Keith shook his head. "Not a good idea. You're not one of his favorite people."

"Your family probably expected to inherit the place."

"Alex sold most of the land before he moved to Dallas to be closer to the medical center. When he excluded the house and surrounding hundred acres, we thought he'd keep them in the family." Keith dropped into his chair. "But rumor has it, he loved you more than us. Understandable."

Under his sweeping scrutiny, Darcy stifled an urge to rearrange her blue sundress' skirt.

Keith propped his feet on his desk.

"Years ago, Dad and Alex had a falling out over the ranch that resulted in my parents moving to town. Dad and Alex never spoke again, but Alex did leave Mom his bank accounts."

"I didn't know."

"We figured you'd read the entire will." His eyes narrowed. "Do you plan to contest it now?"

Darcy frowned. "Of course not."

Keith picked up a pencil and bounced the eraser end against the desk. "Then I'd appreciate your keeping the part about the bank accounts to yourself. If Dad or my brother-in-law find out, they'll nickel and dime Mom penniless."

Curiosity overcame good manners. "Your dad doesn't know about the money?"

"Nope." Keith grinned. "Dad installs fencing. Mom figures working keeps him out of trouble."

"Was your dad outside with you earlier?"

His grin slipped. "Heard us did you?"

"Not the words, only the tone of your—conversation."

He relaxed. "Yep, that was Dad. He wants help with a project. We disagreed on how to proceed. About the house—"

"Would you have moved in if you'd inherited Alex's house and property?"

"I'd have moved my business there. It would lower my overhead significantly." He laced blunt-tipped fingers behind his head. "I hear you're opening a bed-and-breakfast. How about a partnership? I'll lease the pasture, build a clinic and kennel, and you can advertise as pet-friendly." He waggled his eyebrows.

"Thanks, but no." Darcy smiled to soften her refusal. His abrupt switches from caution to friendliness were perplexing, but his grin was contagious and distracting. "You mentioned a brother-in-law. Did your sister want the property too?"

"No. Angela has kids and a job cutting hair. She'd rather live in town."

He dropped his feet to the floor and used his forearm to sweep bits of debris off the desk before glancing at his watch. Darcy hooked her purse strap over her shoulder and stood. "I appreciate your time, Dr. Anderson."

She walked to the door. Their meeting had gone better than she'd expected. Alex's nephew didn't seem overly concerned that she'd inherited the house and property, or malicious enough to start rumors, or possessed of enough free time to spray paint graffiti on her walls.

He stood and opened the door for her. As she walked out, his voice carried down the hall.

"Call me Keith. See you around, Miss Darcy."

Friday evening, Darcy drove at a leisurely pace down the two-lane highway. Food setup at Border's took all of fifteen minutes, but she'd spent nearly an hour choosing an outfit, applying makeup, and French-braiding her hair.

The sleeveless, antique-yellow and white-checked dress clung in all the right places and buttoned down the front to her knees where the flared skirt ended. She glanced at her sandals and cringed, picturing her vulnerable toes exposed to a multitude of cowboy boots.

The sheriff probably wouldn't even be there, and she shouldn't care. He was compelling in a tall, dark, and unsmiling way, but her life held complications enough with the rumors and remodel.

She lowered the visor. Despite wearing sunglasses, she had to narrow her eyes against the setting sun. A dark blue pickup and a tan sedan approached in the opposing lane. As the vehicles closed, she sent a casual two-fingered wave and tried to get a look at the sedan driver. She glimpsed dark hair. Was he her neighbor? For some reason, the thought sent a shiver down her spine.

The truck driver tightened his grip on the steering wheel as Darcy Cooper passed. Instead of packing up and selling out, she had waved at him.

Since she'd moved into Alex's house, he'd had trouble retrieving his buried heroin. Twice, deputy patrols and her comings and goings had forced him to postpone accessing his inventory. His smooth operation had developed rough spots as rescheduled deliveries cost him time, money, and contacts.

The frequent Federales raids in Mexico last July had prompted his suppliers to move their existing product north. He'd been forced to take everything they'd sent to avoid losing a known and trusted supplier. He couldn't risk his buyers locating alternate sources of heroin.

No more sizeable shipments would cross the border until new routes were established. The buried boxes represented early retirement. By December, he'd be looking at palm trees, white-sand beaches, and the Pacific Ocean. His partner's plans did not concern him.

He pulled a cigar from his chest pocket. So far, Darcy Cooper hadn't changed the lock on the south pasture gate or removed the goats, but unless she sold out, he'd be working months longer than planned—in a business where extra time on the job site was not an advantage.

The fire needed stoking, and since he was turning up the heat, why not generate an inferno?

Border's vibrated with country music and energy as the evening crowd joined the after-work crowd. A boisterous group formed neat rows on an expanse of polished wood, anticipating a line dance tune from the band.

Clutching her cardboard box close, Darcy edged toward the cypress bar occupying one long wall. A six-point star topped the center arch. According to Carl, the mirror had been replaced at least a dozen times in the last 50 years—an inherent danger in a successful roadhouse. Now, chrome barstools—bolted to the floor—replaced the free-ranging stools that had saddled more than a few belligerent patrons with seven years of bad luck that started with a night in jail. A decade of denim-cased derrieres had buffed the stool's red leather seats to a dull sheen.

She absorbed the energy of the roadhouse as she walked. The aroma of her pork dumplings turned heads. Carl would be pleased. He let her prepare whatever finger foods she liked, so long as they complimented the beer and weren't so fancy his patrons couldn't identify or pronounce them.

"Hi, Carl!" she called, hip-bumping through the swinging bar door.

Carl pulled a rectangle of paper from beneath a bottle of beer. "Strange, seeing you without your Gramma's baskets."

Her smile widened. "I forgot to tell you, the sheriff found them and brought them by the house. I don't want to lose them again. Hence, the box."

"The sheriff, huh?" Carl grinned, swiped a dumpling, dropped the check into her hand, and went back to filling drink orders.

Darcy shook her head, checked the chafing dishes for water, and lit the fuel canisters. She eased on a pair of food-service gloves and transferred a batch of dumplings to the first chafer as the band ended their song.

Two women squeezed past the crowded bar. One darted curious glances at her; the other stared straight ahead. Neither lowered her voice.

"She looks friendly," the glancer said.

Her companion snorted. "Friendly enough to seduce a true man with a broken heart out of the house and money his family should have got. She must have inherited plenty the way she's fixing up that place."

Humiliation and anger churned Darcy's stomach, but she held her tongue. She was working for Carl. Arguing with his customers would endanger her job.

A waitress with white-blonde curls pinned atop her head and "Shirley" embroidered above the generous swell of her red tank top released a disapproving sigh after the pair. She set her tray on the bar and rolled her eyes.

"Ignore them, sweetie."

"I will." Darcy was sharing the truth every chance she got. She'd talk to Carl and Shirley tonight—if they had time to listen. Revealing Keith's mother's new bank account might change a few minds, but it would create problems for Keith's mom.

Head down, she filled the second chafer and settled the lid. Removing the gloves, she slipped Carl's check into her purse.

"I see you're carrying your purse tonight, Ms. Cooper."

She met the sheriff's green eyes in the mirror and glanced toward the women entering the restroom. Had he heard them talking?

CHAPTER FOUR

Darcy stacked small cups of scallion-soy sauce and hot mustard sauce beside the chafers while she searched for her voice. The sheriff looked handsome in his lightweight black blazer that topped his white cotton shirt.

"Carl seems to appreciate your catering," he said.

"So should you. Having something besides alcohol in Carl's customers' stomachs keeps some of them sober longer."

She placed a plump appetizer on a napkin. "Here, try a dumpling." She set it before him with a container of each sauce.

He reached for his wallet.

"This one's on me. It's not a bribe, just smart marketing. Maybe your department can occasionally use a caterer. And don't worry about cheating Carl; I operate on the baker's dozen theory. For every dozen he orders, I make thirteen."

Finally feeling composed, she rested her forearms on the bar and watched him dip the dumpling in mustard sauce. White teeth closed on half. He chewed. Unable to stop herself, she swallowed with him. She hadn't been this mesmerized since she'd seen her first eight-burner Thermador range.

"Delicious," he said.

Darcy licked suddenly dry lips. "Try the other sauce." She turned and rearranged the napkins she'd just arranged. His compliment had taken her mind off the snarky woman.

"You didn't bring your grandmother's baskets," he said.

"They're sentimentally priceless, and safer at home." She looked at him in the mirror. "At the risk of sounding cliché, do you come to Border's often? It's the second time I've seen you here," she explained.

His reflection focused on her. "I'm here with one of my officers and his wife. Why don't you join us?"

Eli watched Darcy freeze. She appeared caught off guard by receiving his invitation—as he was about offering it.

Darcy's chin rose. She was deciding how to say no. He quieted his internal prejudgment and exhaled relief. He'd had no business issuing the invitation.

"I believe I will," she said, picking up her purse.

He swung the bar gate open for her. "My dispatcher reported a call from a retirement home resident yesterday. A disturbance and your name were mentioned."

"I was making friends," Darcy said, blushing.

He smiled before he thought better of it.

Darcy's eyes widened. "You should do toothpaste commercials," she said, her expression serious.

The couple sitting at the table he'd stopped beside erupted in laughter. Eli pulled out a chair for Darcy. "Lisa and Dan Lantz, meet Darcy Cooper."

"Hi." The very pregnant Lisa extended one hand then tilted her head toward Dan as he stood to greet Darcy. "Dan is Eli's lieutenant, but they go back fifteen years at least."

"Sixteen," Eli and Dan said simultaneously.

Darcy visibly relaxed as she shook hands. She was nervous, Eli realized, as he seated her then sat beside her.

"When are you due, Lisa?" Darcy asked.

"Mid-October. This is our first, and I'm positive it's a boxer or gymnast." She smoothed her red and black dress over her swollen belly. "I hear you need to update your driver's license."

Dan choked on his drink. Lisa reached out and patted his back.

"I plan to visit the DMV next week," Darcy said.

Eli glanced at Dan, duplicating the narrow-eyed stare Darcy turned on him. He'd only mentioned her in passing today when he'd invited Dan and Lisa to Border's tonight.

The waitress, Shirley, stopped at the table. "Another round of cola and water?"

"I'll have water, too," Darcy said.

"And a dozen dumplings," Eli added as the lights dimmed and the band switched rhythms. The opening strains of a slow dance floated across the floor.

"Dan, that's our song." Lisa fought to scoot her chair back.

"It is?" Dan automatically rose to assist her. Lisa tugged him onto the dance floor.

"Aren't you going to do something?" Darcy said. "We just witnessed a hijacking."

She almost made him smile again. "I never argue with pregnant women."

Darcy straightened. "Sounds like you speak from experience. Are there little future sheriff's running around?"

Eli sipped his cola. Contrary to the rumors he'd heard about her, she possessed moral standards if thinking she'd accepted a married man's invitation disturbed her. "No wife, no kids. I don't do permanent relationships." Not after witnessing firsthand the temporary duration of happiness and the lingering duration of grief. "My sister has a son. I learned from her that life is easier if you accommodate pregnant women."

As the dancers circled the floor, Dan enforced a no-bumping zone around Lisa by scowling at anyone who encroached. Eli glanced around the room and caught curious patrons staring at him. Their eyes quickly averted. No doubt tongues were wagging about him keeping company with Darcy Cooper.

"How old is your nephew?"

"Six. He started school this fall. What about you?"

"I graduated years ago."

His focus returned to Darcy's face. She smiled. "That was a joke, Sheriff."

He smiled. Tomorrow, seldom-used facial muscles would ache from the smiles she instigated.

"I've noticed your reelection posters," she said. "I'll update my voter's registration card when I change my address on my driver's license, so tell me why I should vote for you."

He leaned in and delivered the spiel he'd worked on in front of his bathroom mirror. "I have a criminal justice degree from the University of Texas. I spent six years in the Army and another six with the San Antonio Police Department. I'm a graduate of the FBI Academy, and I have training in narcotics interdiction, advanced search and seizure, and forensic and technical services."

She smiled. "Your résumé is impressive, but your presentation is impersonal. Tell me how you feel about your job and your constituents."

"Law enforcement isn't about feelings. It's about facts and, occasionally, intuition. Feelings can get you wounded or killed."

"Okay, that makes sense. But I still don't know why you became a cop."

"Because bad things happen to good people. If I can stop some of those bad things from happening, I'm doing my job correctly. And given Tell County's current problems, I'm the best man for this job."

Her expression softened. "I read about the teenager who died by the river."

He scrutinized the room before looking back at her. Citizens seldom acknowledged the work he or his deputies performed. "I'll find the drug dealers."

Shirley appeared with drinks and food. Eli pulled out his wallet as she distributed glasses, gathered empties, and held up a finger to acknowledge a cowboy, arm raised, dangling an empty beer bottle between two fingers.

"Darcy, your dumplings are selling like hotcakes," she said. "Do you share recipes? I'd like to surprise Jack during a football game."

"Dumplings are a challenge if you've never made them before. If you come by, I'll show you. Carl has my number; call me when you want to cook."

"Thanks, I will."

"Keep the change," Eli said. He caught himself adding a note to his mental file on Darcy. "It was nice of you to offer cooking lessons."

"Initiative should be rewarded."

She tilted her head. "So you were Army. I'm guessing you were a Ranger. You have a quiet confidence and a tendency to take charge of situations. And you're hyper-aware. My Dad was Army. Fort Hood was his last post before he retired."

He nodded and picked up his water. Darcy's frequent smiles disguised a sharp mind. He'd helped her save face tonight, but finding drug dealers and suppliers, and his reelection responsibilities took priority. He wouldn't return to Border's just to see her again.

Darcy scooted to make room for Dan and Lisa returning to the table.

"I love that song." Lisa's angelic expression melted to delight. "O-o-o, food!" She ate a dumpling.

"Hey, Miss Darcy, I didn't know you were acquainted with the local law." Keith Anderson rested both hands on Darcy's chair back and leaned in. "Sheriff, I'll be in next month to give the four-legged members of your K-9 Unit their shots."

Eli nodded coolly. "We'll expect you."

Keith touched a finger to the brim of his hat and winked at Darcy. "Hope you're considering my proposition."

Darcy's face heated as Keith sauntered off. His statement smacked of innuendo.

Lisa leaned in. "How did you meet Keith?"

"I found some Anderson family items in the attic and dropped them off at his office." Darcy sipped her water and hoped the questions would end.

"And his proposition?" Eli asked, his voice disapproving.

"A business merger. I declined." She glanced around. She shouldn't have accepted Eli's invitation. Keith wasn't the only one wondering why she was sitting at the sheriff's table. Battling one rumor was enough for her.

The keyboard player pounded the distinctive opening riff of Bob Seger's "Old Time Rock and Roll." When Lisa and Eli leaned in, Darcy reached for her purse. Dan's ebony hand intercepted hers and pulled her to her feet. "Let's dance."

Her surprise at being propelled toward the dance floor gave way to laughter. "Thanks for the rescue."

"I owed you one for Lisa's driver's license dig. Believe it or not, she usually doesn't repeat our private conversations. I guess she's as happy as I am to see Eli dating."

Darcy's pulse pounded even faster. "The sheriff and I aren't dating. We just seem to keep running into each other." Dan whirled her and her denial across the floor. She changed the conversation when she'd caught her breath. "He gave me his re-election spiel."

Dan grimaced. "It needs work, right? Lisa and I are doing what we can. Eli's expertise is in law enforcement, not politics."

She relaxed and followed his lead. "He must have some skills since he won the last election."

"The former sheriff backed and campaigned for him before he retired to Arizona."

They used the rest of their oxygen to finish the song. Breathless and laughing, they returned to the table. Darcy fanned her face with a coaster. Eli silently pushed her water glass forward. He could take a hint. She liked that in a man.

"Try this, Dan. Darcy made them." Lisa stuffed a dumpling in his mouth. "If I cooked like this, I wouldn't have had to get pregnant to convince you I was useful."

"Honey," Dan said, "If you cooked like this, we'd both look pregnant."

An insistent beeping interrupted their laughter. Eli and Dan checked their cell phones. Dan punched a button. "Lantz." He covered his other ear with his free hand; his eyes narrowed as he listened. "I'll be there in ten minutes." He slipped the phone into his pocket and stood. "We have an auto accident with fatalities."

"I'll follow you." Eli stood and lifted his black hat from the middle of the table.

Dan turned to Darcy. "I know we just met, but would you drive Lisa home? With only three weeks to go, I'd rather she not wait around for the town's only taxi."

"Of course," Darcy agreed. Dan squeezed her hand in thanks; Eli nodded. As the men shouldered their way through the crowd, she blinked. "That was fast. Are you used to sudden departures?"

"Not entirely." Lisa stroked her belly as she watched Dan's exit. "It's harder at night. But as sad as this call will turn out for some poor family, I'm relieved to know they're not going after an armed suspect who robbed a gas station."

Darcy nodded as she watched the door close behind Eli. She raised an eyebrow and looked at Lisa. "Do you want me to take you home now?"

Lisa patted her belly. "After he or she arrives, there won't be many nights out. I think I have another half hour in me if that's okay with you. This baby likes to be in bed by nine, a trend I sincerely hope continues after the grand entrance."

And by nine, Dan would probably have called, ensuring Lisa could sleep, Darcy thought.

"Darcy, we're going to be great friends. Tell me what you think of Eli."

She shook her head. "He seems like a very conscientious sheriff. Now, let's talk about my bed-and-breakfast."

Twenty-five minutes later, Lisa reached for her purse. "I'm done in. These days, my energy levels spike and crater quickly."

"That's understandable." Darcy led her through the crowd to the exit. "I'm parked in the fifth row."

Ancient security lights did little to dispel the gloom outside the roadhouse. The blue and yellow fluorescent tubes that spelled out "Border's," hummed, and cast a dim glow over the packed lot. Warm, night air cleared the combination of beer, perfume, cologne, and perspiration that had filled the roadhouse.

They threaded past cars and pickups to her SUV. She unlocked the passenger door and tossed her purse onto the back seat then helped Lisa negotiate the elevated step. Nearby, boot soles crunched across gravel. Darcy jerked around—her city-honed internal alarm triggered. A man stood in front of her car.

"What's your hurry, ladies? The party's just gettin' started."

CHAPTER FIVE

Don't freeze, don't freeze, don't freeze. Darcy dropped her keys in Lisa's lap, slapped the lock, and slammed the door, racing through the steps that hotel security had outlined during an employee-safety seminar. She'd already blown vigilance.

The wiry male lounging against her Explorer's hood straightened. The fluorescent lights lent a ghoulish aspect to his white-blonde hair and pale flesh. His intimidating smirk caused sweat to dampen her palms. Could she avoid conflict?

Behind her, Lisa's muffled voice rose urgently. Thank heaven for cell phones and personal law enforcement connections. Picturing deputies on their way helped Darcy's brain to reengage. It was time for a strategic retreat.

She kept her tone polite and firm. "My friend is expecting a baby. We're leaving."

The ghoul removed his denim jacket and laid it on the car hood. "Pregnant women can have fun too," he said.

"We're not interested." She turned toward the rear of the vehicle, intending to circle to the driver's door. A Hispanic man stepped from behind the car, trapping her between him and the ghoul.

Recognition struck her. Her heart hit overdrive. Taller, heavier, and older than the ghoul, the tan sedan's driver wore his black hair pulled into a low ponytail. A wispy goatee trailed down his chin. Faint light glinted off dark, emotionless eyes. Shark eyes. She glanced between the men. The roadhouse, though close, wasn't close enough. Even if she got past the men, she couldn't get help and return before they got to Lisa.

Her attempt to swallow failed. She could kick and scream with the best of them, but fight?

"My friend's having contractions," she lied, hoping decency would sway them. "I'm taking her to the hospital."

Lisa leaned on the horn, causing them all to jump. The ghoul removed a length of iron pipe from his waistband and shattered her passenger window.

"Hey!" Darcy lunged toward him as he reached inside and groped for the lock release. Lisa beat at his head and hands. Darcy pictured the gearshift and elevated console between the bucket seats that prevented Lisa's escape to the driver's seat. She shoved the ghoul, knocking him off balance.

He dropped the pipe, caught her arm, and connected with a backhand. She bounced off another car but stayed on her feet.

Stay calm and stay alive. The instruction penetrated Darcy's pain.

Determination surged. She glanced left. Shark-eyes seemed content to continue letting the ghoul take the lead.

The ghoul pulled a knife from his back pocket and sprang the four-inch blade erect. Her racing pulse accelerated.

Fear merged with the metallic taste in her mouth. She clenched the skirt of her dress to dry her palms.

Shark eyes spoke, his words slightly slurred. "He said discourage, not disfigure."

"Shut up, Raul," the ghoul said. "This is more effective."

One at a time. Darcy gauged her distance from the ghoul and visualized her next move as his wiggling fingers beckoned her closer. "Play or get cut," the ghoul warned.

She rushed him, grabbed his knife arm, and drove it up.

He grabbed her arm with his free hand.

She let him pull her in and drove her knee into his groin.

He screamed and dropped the knife. He grabbed his groin with one hand and the neckline of Darcy's dress with the other.

He collapsed, dragging her with him onto the gravel.

Raul shambled forward, laughing. "Yeah, that was effective."

Darcy slapped the ghoul's hand away and rose to her knees.

Surprise entered Raul's eyes. She reached up and pinched his inner thigh. Hard.

Raul's leg buckled.

The ghoul grabbed his knife. Darcy scrambled to her feet as he slashed.

Her car's headlights pierced the darkness.

The ghoul cursed and shielded his eyes. Another horn

blast drowned out Raul's groans.

Darcy grabbed the ghoul's jacket from the hood as she ran to the driver's door. Lisa released the lock.

Darcy jumped in, engaged the door with her elbow, and dropped the jacket on her lap. She floored the clutch and twisted the key Lisa had inserted in the ignition. She shifted into reverse.

They roared out of the lot, gravel flying.

Tepid night air rushed through the shattered window. Darcy watched the rear-view mirror. "Are you hurt, Lisa?"

"N-no. I was scared for my baby and us."

"Me too." Darcy glanced at Lisa.

Chunks of safety glass glinted on Lisa's lap and the console. Lisa's mahogany hands protected her stomach; her breaths came shallow and fast. Fearing shock and hyperventilation, Darcy switched the heater on full blast. "You need to fasten your seat belt, Lisa." She repeated the statement firmly until Lisa complied. "Do you and Dan attend Lamaze classes?" she asked, her voice as calm as she could manage.

Lisa's upper body rocked forward and back in answer.

"Let's do the slow, deep breaths, okay? Here we go." Darcy inhaled and exhaled slowly, and loudly, the way she'd learned during her friend Beth's classes. When Lisa's breathing didn't change, Darcy sharpened her voice. "Come on, Lisa, follow me."

Gradually, Lisa's breaths slowed. Darcy touched her hand. It felt cooler than the outside air. "You're doing well.

Did you call for help?"

"I called the—department."

"That's good." Darcy dug a packet of tissues from her console and handed them to Lisa. Lisa blotted her eyes and nose then crumpled the tissue.

Seconds later, oscillating red and white lights approached. Two cruisers raced past. Darcy watched the rear-view mirror. Let Raul and the ghoul still be in the lot, she prayed. Her gaze swept Lisa and caught a dull reflection in her grip. "Is that your cell phone?"

Lisa nodded. Darcy tugged the phone from Lisa's stranglehold and activated the speaker function. A woman's voice calmly repeated Lisa's name.

"Hello, this is Darcy Cooper."

"This is Deputy Carlisle, is Mrs. Lantz with you?"

"Yes, we're driving towards Lost Creek on Highway 21. We passed two cruisers." She lowered her voice. "I think Lisa is suffering from mild shock. I'm taking her to the emergency room."

"Stay on the line until you arrive at the hospital. Tell Mrs. Lantz her husband has been notified. He'll meet you there. Can you describe the men the deputies are looking for?"

Darcy complied then said, "I'm setting the phone down until we arrive." She propped the phone in the console cup holder. "Did you hear that, Lisa? Dan's going to meet us at the hospital."

Fat tears rolled down Lisa's cheeks. Darcy took her hand and gently squeezed; Lisa's skin felt warmer. "You and the baby are all right," she repeated until Lisa's tears dried.

Blue-uniformed orderlies waited at the emergency entrance. They eased Lisa from the car, brushed away a shower of safety glass, sat her in a wheelchair, and hurried inside.

Darcy picked up Lisa's cell phone as the trio disappeared through sliding doors. "Deputy Carlisle? Lisa's inside. I'm going in to wait."

Hearing the deputy's affirmative, Darcy disconnected and put the phone in Lisa's purse. She pulled out of the ambulance lane and parked in the lot next to a Sheriff's Department cruiser. Two tries later, she managed to shut off her car. Her adrenaline drained, sapping strength from her muscles.

The ghoul's grip had torn two buttons from her dress. She put on his jacket, hoisted Lisa's purse, and retrieved her own from the back seat. She walked quickly to the glass doors while buttoning the denim coat to her throat and rolling the cuffs. Inside the emergency room, she headed for the admitting desk.

A hand caught her shoulder.

Darcy whirled and swept one arm across her body to dislodge the hand. The other cocked to deliver a punch.

"Whoa!" The sheriff stepped back, his hands raised. His eyes narrowed. "You need to see a doctor."

Relief flooded her. Eli represented safety.

"I'm fine. Let's check on Lisa. And then I want to sit down. Do you mind holding these?" The purses suddenly seemed to have doubled in weight.

He took the purses and guided her through the off-white waiting area toward empty blue chairs, away from the knot of people being tended by a deputy.

Gentle hands gripped her upper arms and eased her down. "I'll find a doctor."

She sat back with a sigh. "I really am fine. I want to make sure Lisa's all right then I'm going home to drink hot chocolate."

"Nothing stronger?" he asked. He glanced at his fingertips. His expression turned hard. "You're not fine; you're bleeding."

"I thought it stopped." She touched a finger to her lip then examined the tip. "See," she showed him, "no blood."

He pulled her to her feet and hustled her to the reception desk. "Ms. Cooper needs to see a doctor."

The receptionist extracted a pen from lacquered red hair and selected a clipboard from a precisely arranged stack. "Fill out these forms."

A tall brunette in a lavender uniform entered and walked swiftly toward another door. "Nurse Ellison!" Eli snapped.

The woman froze mid-stride, then pivoted towards them. "Eli?"

She'd used the sheriff's first name Darcy noticed.

"She's bleeding. Where do I take her?"

"She hasn't filled out her forms!"

The nurse's head swiveled between Eli and the receptionist.

"Where do I take her?" Eli repeated.

Despite the fatigue setting in, Darcy recognized his authority voice.

The nurse crooked a finger and pointed. Darcy followed Elis's abrupt change of direction, controlled by his hold on her arm. They entered an examination cubicle.

"Being towed like a trailer is making me cranky," she said to Eli.

The red-faced receptionist followed them. "She can't be treated until she fills out these forms. We don't have her insurance card—if she has one."

Eli's glacial green stare froze any remaining comments the receptionist might have voiced. Darcy felt her feet leave the ground as Eli lifted her to sit on the examination table. His fingers went to work on the jacket buttons.

Nurse Ellison, her eyes on Eli, laid the clipboard next to Darcy. "Could you fill out these forms while I see if a doctor is available?" Darcy nodded, and the nurse herded the receptionist outside.

Eli eased the jacket off her shoulders and let it drop onto the table. She shivered in the cold room and drew the edges of her torn collar together with her right hand as Eli lifted her left arm. Dried and fresh blood trailed to her elbow from a cut across her upper arm.

"I didn't even feel the knife," she said. The room began to spin. "Why does knowing you're hurt make it worse?"

He pushed her head toward her knees. "Why faint now?"

"I'm not fainting. I'm resting."

"Don't fall off the table."

She lifted her head to glare at him then lowered her uninjured cheek to her knee. He set the clipboard down within her view and wrote out her name, address, height, and date of birth.

Her eyebrows rose. "You remember all that from my driver's license?"

"I need your phone number and the name of your insurance provider."

She reeled off her number and the name. "Do you remember every license you've ever seen?"

"Is your insurance card in your wallet?"

Either he didn't like being sidetracked or he was angry—maybe both.

"Yes, in the back pocket."

He found the card and secured it to the clipboard.

The curtained enclosure swung open, and Darcy sat up.

The physician's rumpled green scrubs and finger-combed hair reminded her that the emergency room was busy tonight. The people in the waiting room were probably relatives of the crash victims. "How are the people who were in the car wreck?" she asked.

"The sober couple didn't make it," Eli said. "The drunk driver survived. I'd spoken to the families when dispatch called about Lisa."

How many times had Eli told people a loved one would never come home again?

"I'm sorry," Darcy said, including both men in her sympathy.

The doctor looked up from examining her arm and gave her a tired smile. "When was your last tetanus shot?"

Darcy counted in her head. "Nine years ago."

Nurse Ellison reentered the cubicle. Darcy looked for Eli's reaction, but the doctor blinded her with a penlight.

"Pupils are normal. I need a tetanus booster and a suture tray. Sheriff, do you want to use your camera or mine?

"Camera?" Darcy frowned.

"This is an assault case." Eli pulled out his iPhone. "The photos will become part of the case file. When we catch the men, we'll use the photos at their trials."

She was a case she thought as the camera flashed. And he'd said when. "They weren't in the parking lot when your deputies arrived?"

"No." His eyes revealed an inner fury that contradicted his outer calm. Heaven help the muggers stupid enough to attack his best friend's wife.

Eli put his phone away.

"Lie back." The nurse's gaze shifted from Eli long enough to clean Darcy's lip and the scratches on her chest. "I'll scrape your fingernails for DNA evidence," she said.

The doctor scrubbed her arm. Darcy grit her teeth against the burning pain.

"You're fortunate," he said. "The cut's not deep, no muscles involved." When he picked up the anesthetic hypodermic, she turned her head and concentrated on the sheriff. He stood with his arms crossed and his back against the wall. His presence comforted her.

The doctor made a series of quick injections and her upper arm numbed. He picked up the threaded needle. Darcy searched for a distraction from the needle's pressure and the stretching feeling of the stitches going in. Tomorrow, she'd call Beth, she decided. She needed a friend-fix.

The doctor trimmed the sutures. "Change the dressing twice a day and, to minimize scarring, don't use the arm any more than necessary until the stitches come out." He patted her shoulder, then walked out.

Darcy smiled at Eli. His eyes lost some of their gravity.

As he pushed away from the wall, Nurse Ellison slipped a blue examination gown over her dress. "It's not much of a fashion statement, but it will cover you. Let's get this sling on." She adjusted the strap and handed Darcy two slips of paper.

"The doctor prescribed antibiotics and pain medication. When the local wears off, your arm will hurt like mad. I'll fill an ice pack for your face and bring it to the waiting room."

The nurse shot Eli one last meaningful glance before she left with the clipboard. Darcy followed her out of the room. She sank onto the waiting room couch.

"Where were you attacked?" Eli asked, handing her purse to her.

"Outside Border's when we were getting in my car."

"Did either of the men touch your car?"

Fingerprints. Darcy nodded. "I'm pretty sure both men touched the exterior. And one tried to get the lock open after he broke my passenger window. He may have left prints inside the door, but the orderlies also opened that door on the outside to get Lisa out."

"Where are you parked now?" he asked, his cop face in place.

She waved a hand toward the doors. "Outside. Next to one of your cruisers."

He reached for her purse and retrieved the keys he must have seen while getting her wallet. With a nod, he stood and brought out his cell phone.

CHAPTER SIX

Holding the phone between his shoulder and ear, Eli removed the ignition key from Darcy's key chain.

"What are you doing?" she asked.

Instead of answering, he spoke to a deputy and arranged for her car to be towed to the station impound. "Check the exterior and inside the passenger door for fingerprints. The key will be at the hospital admitting desk. Get prints from the orderlies who took Mrs. Lantz out of the car." He ended the call.

"How long will you have my car? I use it for deliveries." She sounded worried.

"You'll have it back soon. In the meantime, your arm needs to heal, and driving a standard won't help. I'll be right back."

He returned a few minutes later with her insurance card, an ice pack, and two cups of coffee. He saw Darcy fighting a yawn.

"They're out of hot chocolate," he said, sitting and offering her a cup.

"Thanks, but I don't drink coffee. I figured if I didn't start drinking it in college, I probably didn't need to start drinking it later." She eased the cold pack onto her cheek.

"Any word on Lisa and the baby?"

"It won't be long. Dan asked if you'd stay until they come down."

"I'll stay," she said.

He sipped his coffee, remembering the strain on Dan's face and imagining the fear in his friend's gut. Tonight's events reinforced his own belief that the fewer permanent relationships you had in life, the less emotional upheaval you experienced. If Dan had lost Lisa, or the baby, or both, overwhelming and enduring pain would have crippled his lieutenant.

The cut on Darcy's arm reminded him of his dream when her dress changed from white to red. What if the guy swinging the knife had connected with an artery instead of her arm? He still hadn't made time to call Uncle John and ask him to interpret the dreams.

"This seems like a good hospital," Darcy said, sounding tired.

He glanced around the room then looked at her. "It opened about five years ago. The original building was close to 50 years old. But they did a good job of setting my arm there when I broke it in middle school."

Her brown eyes widened.

He nodded. "I grew up here. When Dad went to fight in Iraq, Mom and my sister and I moved to Lost Creek. Dad was a Ranger, too. He was killed eight months into his third tour."

She touched his arm, then rested her hand on her thigh.

"His death must have been difficult for all of you."

He nodded. She had no idea.

"I'll bet your mother loves having you here."

"She died two years ago."

"I'm sorry."

"Thanks."

He tossed the second coffee into the trashcan beside his chair. He'd exceeded his daily quota two cups ago. He smoothed back his hair and kneaded his neck muscles—they always tightened when he spoke of his parents.

"You must be worn out." Darcy rested the uninjured side of her face against the chair.

"It's been a long day, but I want to get your statement tonight. I'll drive you to the station then take you home. Tomorrow morning, you and Lisa need to view mug shots and meet with the forensic artist."

"Okay." Darcy's eyes closed.

He frowned. Only exhaustion would allow her to give in so easily.

He realized he was reading her like he'd known her for years instead of four days. And he was sharing parts of his personal life. He'd have to watch himself around her. The going-nowhere drug investigation and his struggling campaign left him vulnerable to her gift for listening.

The ice pack slid from her fingers as her head lolled against his shoulder. Palming the pack, he held it to her lip. This went above and beyond his duties as sheriff, but he needed her to give him a statement tonight.

The admitting clerk, who'd failed to stare him down, now stared again. Another vote lost?

He looked away. Darcy wasn't to blame for his struggling reelection bid. The unknown supplier and the mole feeding details to the local press were his biggest adversaries. He needed to make time for target practice. When he was a kid, Uncle John had frequently sent him outside with a homemade bow and arrow to work out his aggressions after his mother died. He still used the technique but shot a gun instead.

The elevator doors opened, and Dan wheeled Lisa out into the waiting room. Eli withdrew his arm from Darcy's shoulders and stood, waking her. Dan knelt to hug her.

"Thank you for protecting them."

Darcy hugged back with her right arm. "Lisa protected me too." She took Lisa's hand. "Thanks for using the horn and headlights. Are you okay?"

"The baby and I are fine." Lisa's voice caught. "What happened to you?"

"It's a scratch," Darcy said.

"Scratches don't require stitches," Eli said.

"Do you fight often?" Dan asked. "I could place a few wagers and get the baby's college fund off to a healthy start."

"This was my debut unless you were counting the first day of kindergarten when I knocked down Willie Kane for making fun of my pink and orange playsuit."

Lisa smiled. "In some cultures, if you save a person's life, you own them forever. Instead, we'd like you to be the baby's godmother."

Eli stiffened.

Darcy raised her hand. "Lisa, you wouldn't be here if you hadn't met me tonight. The sheriff would have taken you home. I'm flattered, but you and Dan should rethink this."

"We're sure," Dan said.

Eli saw tears shimmer in Darcy's eyes.

"Then I'd be honored," she said.

"Good." Dan fist-bumped Eli's shoulder. "We'll see you two tomorrow."

Dan made it sound like they were planning a double date. Stifling a growl, Eli waited until the doors swung shut behind the Lantzes before turning to Darcy. "Wait here while I pull the car around."

"I'd rather walk with you." She scooted to the edge of her chair. "My muscles are feeling stiff."

He supported her as she stood, silently cursing the men who'd put fear in her laughing eyes.

They walked through the emergency exit and into the parking lot. He stopped at the patrol car next to her Explorer.

"You drove a patrol car to Border's?" she asked.

"I traded vehicles with one of my officers at the accident scene. I prefer to drive a cruiser when I inform the next of kin. Watch your head," he said automatically, helping her into the front seat as the emergency room doors slid open behind them.

"Eli!"

Nurse Cathy Ellison hurried toward him. "Ms. Cooper left this in the examination room." Cathy's expression was calculating as she looked at Darcy. She must have connected Darcy with the rumors about Alex.

He took the denim jacket.

"Thanks for your help tonight, Cathy."

"Anytime, Eli. You know that, right?" She turned and walked back to the hospital.

He watched as Cathy shot him an over the shoulder invitation he wouldn't be accepting. He'd managed to discourage her interest once before without alienating her.

He closed Darcy's door then walked to the driver's door, slid inside, and laid the jacket across Darcy's lap. Her gaze moved from Cathy to the coat.

"Um, Sheriff?"

"Yes?"

"This isn't my jacket. It belongs to one of the men who attacked us. The one who looks like a ghoul."

Darcy's words sank in. Eli opened his door, walked to the trunk, and returned with an evidence kit. Setting it between them on the bench seat, he put on gloves, removed a paper bag, and placed the coat inside.

He switched on the dome light, illuminating their shoulders, and then folded the bag away from the jacket. "Did you put your hands in any of the pockets?"

"No."

The right-side pocket held a plastic bag filled with a dark, viscous substance. His pulse jumped. He checked the left pocket. Bingo. Another bag. He turned to study Darcy's bruised face and swollen lip. She'd provided his department's first break in the heroin case.

"What is that?" She edged closer.

"I won't know for sure until the lab tests it." Nerve cells ricocheted as he sealed the wads into paper bags, wrote on each, and sealed the one holding the jacket.

"You must have some idea." She touched her sling. "Is it a drug?"

He stayed silent. The less she knew, the better.

She sighed. "I get it. You can't tell me because it's official business. That's okay. When I get home, I'll do an internet search for an illegal drug that resembles something I'd scrape off my shoe."

He returned the evidence kit to the trunk then sat beside her. If curiosity could kill a cat, she had no chance at all. "It might be heroin."

Her brow contracted. "I thought heroin was a white powder."

"That's pure heroin. This variety has impurities and is cheaper to buy."

She shivered. "How can people put that stuff in their bodies?"

He started the car. "I haven't figured it out either."

His brain raced. The men carrying this much product must be suppliers or dealers. But why would they attack Lisa and Darcy with this much product on them? Dan wasn't in charge of the drug case, Wainright was. Had the men recognized them as law officers and decided to go after Lisa and Darcy as soft targets? Or were they at Border's to make a sale?

Whatever the answers, Lisa and Darcy had seen their faces and could identify them. Would the men move on, lay low, or try to recover the heroin? He picked up his phone and dialed Dan's cell number.

"Lantz."

"It's Eli. Ms. Cooper picked up an attacker's jacket containing what looks like two pounds of black tar heroin."

"No kidding."

Eli trusted Dan to keep his side of the conversation casual to avoid alarming Lisa. He checked his rear-view mirror. "We're headed for the station. Take your time driving and watch your six. I'll have a patrol check your house. And lower your scanner volume."

"Great idea. We'll see you in the morning."

Eli called the station then replaced the transmitter.

Darcy looked sideways at him. "They won't like that I took their drugs."

Eli rubbed his bristled chin. "The street value of that quantity of heroin is close to two-hundred thousand dollars. They may come looking for you."

She swallowed hard. "And then you'll catch them."

"You and Lisa are not bait. We'll be watching you both. Besides, you couldn't pull off being bait. Your face is too expressive."

"You say that like being a poor liar is a bad thing."

She hugged her injured arm closer and flashed a faint version of her bright smile.

He pulled into the late-night pharmacy.

Eli glanced at the prescription she handed him. "Where's the other one? The one for the pain pills?"

She held it up. "I'm not filling it."

"Those stitches are going to hurt soon, and you'll be no good to me tomorrow when you're looking at mug shots if you're exhausted from the pain and lack of sleep."

"I'd rather sleep with the pain than be painlessly oblivious while alone. Would you take medication that would knock you out if you were home alone and your attackers were at large and wanting their jacket back?"

Eli frowned. The department didn't have the overtime budget for a deputy to sit outside of Darcy's house. "I see your point."

"Good."

He snatched the other prescription from her hand and passed everything to the waiting pharmacy assistant.

"Wait!" Darcy cried, but the pharmacy window closed.

He ignored her glare as he dialed his cell phone and waited for an answer.

"Brooke, it's Eli—nothing's wrong, and yes, I know what time it is. I'm bringing a woman over. She needs to use your guest room tonight. We'll be there in an hour or so." He hung up after Brooke's response.

Darcy shook her head. "Call this Brooke person back and tell her you made a mistake."

"Ms. Cooper, your body needs rest to heal. You're uncomfortable being alone tonight, and you have a long morning ahead of you. You're spending the night with my sister. Think of it as protective custody."

She seemed to perk up. "Your sister? Are you sure? I can check into a hotel and not disturb or impose on her family."

"It's Brooke and her son. Her husband died from an aneurysm four years ago."

"How horrible for them!"

"Yes." He looked inside the pharmacy. The assistant was bagging the amber pill containers.

Darcy gave him her credit card. "Can we stop by my house to pick up a change of clothes and a toothbrush?"

"Brooke's about your size. She'll loan you clothes and a toothbrush."

CHAPTER SEVEN

Darcy glanced around the second waiting room she'd entered tonight. Friday night at the Tell County Sheriff's Department resembled Friday night at the roadhouse—busy. She wondered if their clientele overlapped.

She blinked at the bright lights, unable to ignore the curious stares tracking their progress across the room. Her bruised body protested her lengthened stride as she hurried to keep up with the sheriff. Two cowboys, their faces in worse condition than hers, sat handcuffed in neighboring chairs. One cowboy wolf-whistled.

"Hey, Sheriff, you can put her in my cell!"

The cowboys hooted and bumped shoulders—partners in crime. "What'd he bust you for, blondie? Indecent exposure?"

Darcy tightened her hold on the hospital gown as a second wave of laughter ensued.

"Wait here," Eli said.

She cupped her elbow, replacing the warmth of his hand with her own. He retained his grip on the evidence bags as he strode over to the men.

"Apologize then shut up." His voice emanated a quiet force.

"Jus' tryin' to conserve jail space," the whistler slurred. "Papers are always sayin' how jails are overcrowded."

The whistler received a rough nudge from his partner, who followed up with, "Stuff it." The second man leaned around Eli to look at her. "Ma'am, we've been celebratin' tonight. No disrespect intended."

The mouthy drunk leaned, caught himself before he fell from his chair, and wiggled his fingers at her. Eli reclaimed her elbow and propelled her toward a solid door. He tapped a swift series of numbers on the adjacent keypad.

"Do you cause mayhem wherever you go?" the sheriff asked.

The door opened. He followed her through as she counted to ten. The sheriff's night had been no picnic either. She'd give him a reprieve—this once.

"Since moving here, I've experienced an excessive amount of trouble. But I haven't instigated any of it."

He looked unconvinced. They stopped in front of a battered counter as the heavy door thudded shut behind them. He addressed the deputy behind the counter. "Has Wainright arrived?"

"He's on his way in, Sheriff."

"I need a tape recorder and coffee in my office." He plucked the mostly melted pack from Darcy's hand and tossed it across the counter. "See if you can round up some ice."

"Do you have hot chocolate?" Darcy asked.

"Coffee, hot chocolate, ice, and a tape recorder. I'll bring them up. And Sheriff, your truck keys are on your desk."

"Thanks. I also need you to scan Ms. Cooper's prints."

"My prints?" The sheriff's reprieve ended. "What for?"

"So we can rule out whose prints belong on your car and whose don't. We'll take Lisa's tomorrow."

"Oh," she said as he walked away.

"This way, Ms. Cooper." The substantial deputy stood.

"I've never been fingerprinted before," she said, feeling like a criminal instead of a victim.

"Nothing to it."

The deputy was right. The process took only a few minutes. Afterward, Darcy plucked an antibacterial wipe from an open container and wiped her hands free of dirt. She frowned at the grimy wipe.

"Where's the restroom?" she asked.

The deputy pointed past her. "First door on the right. The sheriff's office is on the second floor to your left."

She entered the restroom and groaned at her reflection. Why on earth had the cowboys hooted and not screamed?

Twisting the hot water knob, she stuck her hands under the stream. As the water warmed, she gingerly rinsed her face then ripped a paper towel from the dispenser and glanced in the mirror.

Her braid resembled a cat's tail repeatedly stroked the wrong way. And though ice had reduced the swelling, her cheek sported an unbecoming reddish hue.

She poked at her braid. For every stray lock she tucked into place, another escaped. Her only achievement was an aching left arm. She pulled the cloth band from the end of her braid and unraveled her hair before she remembered her brush lay in the console of her impounded car. She'd have to finger-comb the snarls.

The door opened.

"Ms. Cooper?" a voice asked. A familiar petite woman with short platinum curls and Dolly Parton's figure entered.

"You're the deputy who came to my house after the vandalism."

"That's right. I'm Deputy Carlisle. We spoke on the phone earlier tonight. The sheriff thought you might like to borrow these." She held out a set of dark brown sweats with Sheriff's Department in bright yellow letters across the top. "No hurry returning them. I have another pair."

Darcy smiled. "Thank you; I appreciate this. And thanks for talking us into the hospital."

She would never understand the sheriff. He lectured her one moment, and the next he was thoughtful enough to realize she'd want to change clothes.

The sweat bottoms went on smoothly. She struggled with the top until Deputy Carlisle offered help. Working together, they eased her injured arm through the sleeve and secured the sling on the outside. Her ruined dress went into a paper bag.

"With the bloodstains and missing buttons, it's a graphic piece of evidence to present to a jury when the case goes to trial," the deputy explained.

Darcy looked up from adjusting the sling. "The sheriff mentioned a trial." And he wanted to preserve evidence. Maybe the act she'd considered thoughtful was simply practical. Suddenly disappointed, she leaned a hip against the sink and raked her fingers through her hair.

Deputy Carlisle stepped forward. "My daughter has long hair, so I'm pretty good at working out snarls." She set the evidence bag on the sink and pulled out a pocket comb.

Five minutes later, Darcy fidgeted in the upstairs hallway. The splash of running water filtered from the not quite closed men's lavatory down the hall. She turned right and tapped on the doorframe next to a bronze plaque engraved: Sheriff Elias Whitepath. When he didn't answer, she stepped into his office and looked around.

His black jacket hung from a coat rack beside the door. His desk, parallel to the room's back wall, faced the door. A tape recorder and tray occupied a desk corner. Messages and folders formed neat stacks in the center. Drawn by the bracing aroma of the coffee, Darcy found her hot chocolate mug, and pressed the newly filled ice pack to her cheek, silently thanking the deputy.

Twin filing cabinets flanked a credenza. Venetian blinds covered two windows, shutting out the night. Still no sheriff. She switched on the museum lamp attached to a framed painting on the wall.

The painting sprang to life. Young braves on horseback raced a summer storm across the plains. She could almost smell the dust stirred up by galloping hooves and the tang of ozone preceding the rain.

The skin between her shoulder blades tingled. The sheriff could sneak up on his own shadow. She continued to face the painting. "Who's the artist?"

"She's local." He walked to the desk, picked up his coffee, and joined her.

Darcy glanced sideways. His collar and the ends of his hair were damp. She felt his gaze slide over her.

"Thanks for thinking of the sweats," she said. Even if Eli hadn't suggested them for her comfort, she appreciated wearing clean clothes.

Knuckles rapped the doorframe.

"Come in." Eli moved away.

A man with light brown hair approached with the lazy grace of the exceptionally coordinated. "Sheriff," he said, then offered Darcy his hand. "And you must be the new lead. I'm Detective Wainright."

Was that how the sheriff had described her?

"Hello." She transferred the ice bag to her immobilized hand and shook the detective's hand.

"Cold hands, warm heart."

"Cold hands, ice pack." She smiled.

The sheriff set his coffee on the desk, and tersely completed introductions. He briefed Wainright on the jacket. "Have a seat, Ms. Cooper, Detective."

Darcy faced the desk and abandoned the ice. If she numbed her lip further, they wouldn't understand her words. She watched the sheriff shrug his holster from his shoulder. He placed it in a desk drawer before situating the tape recorder between them like a barrier, his lawman façade firmly in place. Wainright pulled up a chair, hit the record button, and stated their names and the date.

Twenty-five minutes later, after her fourth or fifth painful yawn, Wainright repeated earlier questions. "Why do you think you and Mrs. Lantz were targeted?"

Darcy shrugged then recalled the sheriff's earlier reprimand that the recorder couldn't hear her shoulders move.

"At first I thought they'd seen me put Carl's check in my purse, but they never asked for money." She stroked her arm through the sling.

"Tell me about Raul."

"That's what the ghoul called him. I passed a tan sedan when I left home tonight. I got a look at the driver—it was Raul, and he was driving in the opposite direction. If he'd turned and followed me, I'd have noticed. Then, in the parking lot, Raul said, he, whoever he is, said to discourage, not disfigure. It sounded like they were sent to scare one of us."

She turned towards the sheriff. Her left arm contacted the chairback, making her flinch. She repositioned. "I didn't notice them inside Border's, did you?"

"No."

Wainright leaned in. "Who might send thugs after you?"

Darcy shook her head. "I can't think of anyone. Lisa seems the more obvious target because of Dan's job."

"Have you made any enemies in Lost Creek?" he asked.

She opened her mouth to say no then recalled the spray paint on her wall and the rumors. Whoever had done those things might harbor a grudge.

"My home was vandalized not long ago, but I don't know the specific motive of the person or persons responsible."

"Besides Carl and me, who else did you recognize at Border's?" Eli asked.

"Shirley, the waitress. And Keith Anderson."

"He might not appreciate Alex leaving you the house and land," Eli said.

"Keith? When I spoke to him Wednesday, he expressed disappointment I'd inherited the property but not anger."

"Greed is a strong motive. Keith saw you at Border's. He could have set you up or mentioned your presence to another family member who could have set you up," Wainright said.

"I haven't met the rest of the Andersons." But it wasn't the first time she'd wondered how they would react if she ever did meet them.

The sheriff turned to Wainright. "Do you have further questions?"

"One. Ms. Cooper, besides Raul and the tan sedan, have you noticed anyone else following you, staring at you, or looking suspiciously at you?"

Heat swept up her neck. Plenty of people had stared since she'd moved to Lost Creek, but no one stood out in her memory.

"The only one I specifically noticed was Raul."

Once again, Wainright stated the time. He turned off the recorder. "I'll review the transcript and probably have a few more questions for you tomorrow, Ms. Cooper. Goodnight."

When the detective left the room, Darcy rubbed her forehead. Classifying Alex's family as potential enemies made sense, even if it felt disrespectful to Alex.

"We'll need to photograph you over the next few days as your bruising becomes more vivid," Eli said.

"It's going to get worse?" The thought made her jaw drop painfully. His solemn expression eased.

"Let's say more colorful. Take your antibiotic and pain pills, and I'll drive you to Brooke's."

As she took the pills, he retrieved his gun from the drawer and shrugged the holster into place as naturally as another man would slide a wallet into a pocket.

"Where did you learn self-defense?" he asked, walking past her to the coat rack.

Darcy stood and fiddled with the borrowed sweatshirt's hem. Her kindergarten story hadn't satisfied him. "I attended workshops in Dallas given by the hotel's chief of security, and I work out with a kickboxing exercise class."

"You're kidding," he said, voice flat. "You took on two men because you thought you'd learned some kickboxing moves from a workout guru?"

"No," she bristled back, "I took them on because the alternative was to submit. Raul being drunk out of his coordination helped. If the ghoul had been taller or heavier, Lisa and I might both be in the hospital—or worse."

The faint lines around his eyes and mouth deepened.

A wave of guilt diluted her defiance. Tonight would not make his list of favorite evenings, not after the dead couple, notifying their families, and an attack on his lieutenant's wife.

"Are you ready to go?" she asked.

He nodded and held the door open.

She was curious to meet Eli's sister now that she knew she wasn't being pawned off on an old girlfriend like Nurse Ellison, whose lingering glances revealed a lingering desire.

CHAPTER EIGHT

Darcy took a mental inventory of her body during the drive to Eli's sister's house. The pain in her left arm had increased. She raised her right hand a few inches off the armrest and held it steady. She'd finally quit shaking. Her lip no longer stung—unless she smiled.

She took a deep breath. Lisa and the baby were alive and so was she.

She fiddled with her seatbelt then leaned back against the beige interior of Eli's cherry-red truck—a provocative "notice-me" color for a man adept at concealing his emotions.

They entered a middle-class neighborhood. What a night, she thought. Terror aside, she'd enjoyed meeting Lisa and Dan. Though why Eli had invited her to join them still puzzled her.

Maybe he'd felt sorry for her after the women at Border's snubbed her. Or—

She suppressed a groan. He'd said earlier tonight that he didn't do permanent relationships. If he believed the rumors about her and Alex, did he think she might agree to an affair?

She opened her mouth to deny the rumor as Eli pulled into

the driveway of a limestone, two-story house. Light filtered from several windows. By the time she released her seat belt and opened her door, he'd arrived to help her step down. A good thing because her muscles were tightening up. He led her to the house and knocked softly.

"Brooke, it's Eli."

The door opened, revealing a tall, slender woman with enviable golden skin, long black hair, and hazel eyes. Her flowing turquoise robe shimmered in the light as Eli made introductions.

"Thank you for letting me stay," Darcy said.

"You are welcome."

Darcy noted Brooke's musical voice and the faint scent of mineral oil.

"You're upstairs in the guest room," Brooke said. "If Eli hears or sees anything suspicious, he can come running."

She faced Eli. "You're not sleeping in your truck!"

She cringed, hearing the distress in her voice. She vaguely registered Brooke's smile.

"No," Eli said. "I live next door. And I sleep lightly, no matter how tired I am. Open your window a few inches. I'll hear you if you call."

She wanted to believe him, but next door seemed a hundred miles away, and he had to be exhausted. Was she putting his family in danger by staying here? What if he slept through her screams?

"I can sleep on Brooke's couch," he said, sounding resigned.

Do my thoughts scroll across my forehead like an electronic billboard? Darcy thought the sheriff looked tired enough to sleep on the floor, but he'd rest better in his bed.

"Thank you, but that won't be necessary."

He kissed Brooke's cheek and relayed something in a language she didn't recognize. Brooke answered in English, "Go and sleep, brother."

Eli walked outside. The sound of the closing door emphasized the reality of his leaving. Darcy felt a moment of panic. She should have asked if he had a guest room or couch. Her shoulders slumped. A dozen stitches and she'd become a wimp.

She faced Brooke.

"It's kind of you to take in a stranger in the middle of the night. Do you do this often?"

"No, you're the first." Brooke scanned Darcy's face with interest. "I'll be right back."

She returned with clothes draped over her arm. "Follow me."

Darcy trailed upstairs after Brooke to a room with whitewashed plaster walls. The peach shade on the lamp cast a soothing blush of color. The painting above the headboard caught Darcy's attention. Covering a yawn, she moved closer. "Is this painted by the artist who did the storm scene in your brother's office?"

Brooke stood beside her. "Yes. Do you like it?"

The painting depicted a group of dancing warriors circling a bonfire. Seated tribal members encircled the dancers. Some beat drums, some played flutes, others sang.

"Very much. You can almost smell the smoke and feel the rhythm of the dance." Darcy turned. "Do you know the artist? When I can afford to, I'd like to buy some paintings."

"I know her very well." Brooke handed her an oversized T-shirt then crossed to the closet to hang a skirt and blouse. Another whiff of mineral oil enlightened Darcy's dimming brain.

"You're the artist."

"Yes." Brooke opened another door and switched on a light. "The bathroom is through here. I'm downstairs if you need anything. Sleep well." The door closed softly behind her.

Alone, Darcy worked her way out of the borrowed sweats. She rinsed her underwear and hung them to dry on the shower rod. Given the increasing frequency of her yawns, and lack of dry dressings, she passed on a shower and washed what body parts she could with a washcloth.

Back in the bedroom, she picked up the faded blue T-shirt, washed to softness and read: S.A.P.D. San Antonio Police Department. She sniffed. No pine scent, only lavender fabric softener.

Brooke wouldn't give her one of Eli's unwashed T-shirts. But Darcy wouldn't have minded. Leaning against him tonight, she'd found the sheriff's scent reassuring. She folded Deputy Carlisle's sweats and stacked them neatly on a chair.

The bed and pillows beguiled. Turning back the spread,

she switched off the lamp and parted the drapes. Moonlight entered, creating a silvery path on the carpet. Outside, a half-moon and stars claimed the night sky. She raised the window two inches.

A few yards away, Eli's red truck occupied a carport beside a metal-roofed cottage. Light shone from a window. As if she'd conjured substance from thought, he appeared, silhouetted against the lamplight, a towel slung low around lean hips. Wet hair reflected moonlight as he faced Brooke's house.

She watched him rake his hands through his hair. For a moment, his straight shoulders lost their perfect posture. She felt like a voyeur—like a witness to a snapshot hidden in the bottom of a drawer.

Eli glimpsed movement at Brooke's guest window. He glanced at the clock on his nightstand. His mother and sister had never protested his protection. Ms. Cooper, however, had planned to face her pain and fears alone.

He raised his window a few inches. A sultry east wind drifted through his window. He switched off the lamp and removed the towel from his hips to vigorously rub his hair. He sat on the bedspread.

Had Darcy realized recognizing Raul implied she could be the target? What link did she share with the men selling drugs?

He tossed the towel across a chairback. Answers would come; he hoped they arrived while he was sheriff and able to address them.

An image of Darcy's bruised face surfaced. First, the gold-digger rumor, and then the assault—adding injury to insult. Tonight, she'd offered cooking lessons to a waitress and refused to abandon Lisa. Neither were traits he'd associate with a mercenary or self-absorbed personality. Still, caring about people didn't disprove greed—and he hadn't heard her deny an affair with Alex.

It was tough luck for her to be the one to disillusion the locals' Alex and Cindy true-love legend. He'd seen too much evidence of the downside of loving and losing to put faith in happily ever after. Why strive for an ideal that could cripple you emotionally and physically?

One thing was certain. Ms. Cooper hadn't loved Alex Anderson romantically. Via his mother and Brooke, he knew deep love inflicted deep pain. He knew what a woman who'd lost the man she loved looked like, and Darcy didn't wear that look. He couldn't picture her seducing Alex, but he could understand her friendly nature attracting pretty much anyone. If she'd engaged in a relationship that hadn't involved her heart, that was her business.

He punched his pillows into shape and lay back, closing his eyes.

He'd speak to Wainright tomorrow. The detective was supposed to put Darcy at ease about the interview, but he shouldn't have made a personal remark. The woman might have cold hands, but everything else about her promised warmth.

CHAPTER NINE

The mattress dipped.

Darcy knew she wasn't alone.

She forced her eyes open. Sunlight backlit the black-haired, unmasked, miniature Batman sitting cross-legged at the foot of her bed.

"How," he said solemnly.

"How—what?" she asked the brown-eyed superhero as she eyeballed the vaguely familiar room. She rolled onto her back, and the attack rushed painfully into focus. Every muscle in her body protested, and a dull throb in her arm signaled she'd gone too long between pain pills.

"Just how," the boy said. "It's a traditional Native American greeting to a paleface."

"I think you've watched too many old westerns," she mumbled. The boy, Brooke's son she guessed, frowned.

She tried again. "Okay, how about, what tribe am I dealing with?"

Her question prompted a smile. She was getting the hang of this. Her attempt to return his smile felt more like a grimace.

"We're Comanche."

"Comanche?" Gramma was right—God did have a sense of humor. "Who's we?"

"Me, Mom, and Uncle Eli."

She pushed her unruly hair off her face—a one-handed braid had exceeded her abilities last night. As her fingers snagged a tangle, she winced. Maybe Deputy Carlisle and her comb lived nearby.

"Hey!" He sat up straight, eyes wide. "What happened to you?"

"I was in a fight last night." She probed her still tender cheek and lip. The swelling had subsided. "What colors am I?"

The boy leaned in. "Purple, blue—and red." His eyes met hers, curious, and a touch awed. "Mom says people shouldn't fight."

"Your mom is right. Unfortunately, I couldn't avoid this one. What's your name?"

"I'm Jeremy; I'm six. My Uncle Eli is a sheriff. He can help you."

"My name is Darcy. And your uncle brought me here last night; he's already helping."

She struggled upright, hampered by the pillow pile she'd constructed to keep from rolling onto her injured arm. She'd slept deeply, her dreams haunted by green eyes that questioned, challenged, and comforted. She narrowed her eyes. The room wasn't precisely spinning, but neither was it perfectly still.

Moving slowly, she lifted her left arm from beneath the covers to examine the bandage.

"Holy smokes, you're bleeding! I'll get Mom!"

"Jeremy, I'm all right!" she called. But he was already off the bed and out the door.

After checking to make sure she hadn't bled on the sheets, Darcy staggered into the bathroom and cranked on the shower. Maybe hair-conditioner would remove her tangles.

Eli caught Jeremy as the boy raced into the kitchen. He swung his nephew into the air and over a shoulder.

"Uncle Eli!" Jeremy shrieked. "Are you here for breakfast? It's waffles morning!"

"I know, and I'm famished. Can I eat yours too?" He ruffled Jeremy's hair and straddled the giggling boy on his hip. "What are you doing today?"

"We're weeding the vegetable garden, right, son?" Brooke said.

Jeremy slumped against Eli's shoulder. "Yes, ma'am."

"Tell me about Darcy," Brooke said, closing the waffle iron lid.

Aware of Jeremy's saucer-eyed stare, Eli related a censored version of the previous night. "So I called you," he finished.

"Wow, Uncle Eli," Jeremy said, "She's a real warrior. No wonder she's bleeding."

"She's bleeding?" Eli's head snapped toward the boy.

"Yes, sir. I saw her come in last night, so I visited her this morning. She's pretty, even with her face and arm messed up. Oh, that's what's bleeding, her arm."

Eli deposited a startled Jeremy on the kitchen table and

grabbed the first aid kit he'd brought from his bathroom cabinet. He took the stairs two at a time and stormed the bedroom.

A blow dryer whined behind the closed bathroom door.

She couldn't be bleeding badly if she'd taken a shower. Relieved, Eli walked to the bed, picked up his old T-shirt, and brought it to his nose. Honeysuckle. She had slept in his shirt. His stomach tightened.

He still held the shirt, loosely bunched in his hand, when the bathroom door opened. Seeing him, she hesitated. How could she be nervous about the man she had trusted to watch over her last night?

He dropped the T-shirt on the bed. "Jeremy said you were bleeding. Did the stitches hold?" he asked.

"The stitches are fine; the wound seeped a bit."

Her eyes and smile held self-consciousness. She wore a sleeveless black polo shirt tucked into a flirty, rust-colored skirt that fell below her knees. Except for the length, Brooke's clothes fit like her own. She walked forward, feathering the fingers of her right hand through her semi-dry hair.

"I'm almost ready to go. Can we stop on the way to the station so I can pick up some dressings?" She plucked at the bandage. "I used the blow dryer on this, but it's still damp and needs changing."

"I brought supplies." He stepped to the window and fully opened the curtains. Morning sunlight poured into the room, dispelling intimacy. He pointed to the bed. "Have a seat."

When she settled on the edge of the bed, he sat beside her. One scissor snip and the bandage fell away. She shivered.

"Are you cold?" he asked.

"No. Not cold. I was—remembering."

He noticed she watched his hands and avoided his eyes. He examined the neat pattern of stitches that puckered her skin. She handed him materials while he doctored her wound.

"That should hold you until tonight," he said, releasing her arm. He remained seated, watching her.

"Thanks for the first aid." She smiled crookedly, blinking back tears. He frowned.

"Did I hurt you?"

"No," she whispered, looking down as drops fell to her lap.

A smart man would hand her a Kleenex and call Brooke. Instead, he eased her against his chest.

"You're safe." He rocked her, feeling her ragged attempts to regain control.

"I know. I'm sorry; I don't know why I'm crying. My arm isn't that painful."

"You're having a delayed reaction to last night."

She deserved the flood. She'd hung tough when it counted. Tucking her head under his chin, he held her until her tears subsided. Gradually, she relaxed against him. Contact with her felt good.

He needed distance.

He loosened his embrace to pull a Kleenex from the box

on the nightstand. A fist pounded on the door. He shot to his feet.

"Uncle Eli? Miss Darcy?" Jeremy called. "Breakfast is ready!"

"Tell your mother we're coming, Jeremy," he said.

Light footsteps retreated down the stairs.

He should have heard the boy's approach.

"Let's go down," he said brusquely.

Eli shut his truck door and answered his ringing cell phone. Calls had occupied his drive to the station, but he wasn't too occupied to notice Darcy's death grip on her purse. She was keeping her fear to herself.

Knowing she'd slept in his old T-shirt gave him an unprofessional pleasure. She's a witness, he reminded himself, pulling into his parking space. Stepping from the truck, he shrugged into his suit jacket as he walked around to open her door.

A copper-haired woman approached.

"Sheriff, I'm Cheryl Greer, the crime reporter for the Lost Creek Weekly. "What can you tell me about last night's wreck?"

"I'll issue a statement within the hour." He brushed past the khaki-clad reporter, opened the passenger door, and offered Darcy a hand.

The woman caught sight of Darcy's bruised face and bandaged arm. "Were you involved in last night's wreck?" she asked.

"No." Darcy shook her head and faced away.

Eli hurried Darcy inside and through the security door. "Don't talk to anyone but Detective Wainright about the jacket or heroin." He stopped in front of a desk.

"Sergeant Tyler, Ms. Cooper is here to look at mug shots."

"I found the ghoul!" Darcy called out.

Several deputies looked up from doing paperwork. Sergeant Tyler rose from his desk and approached to look over her shoulder.

"Good work. Any luck with Raul?"

"Not so far." But if she'd found one, surely, she could find the other.

After another hour spent scrolling through page after page of faces that made her two attackers look like Boy Scouts, she stretched her uninjured arm overhead. The popping along her spine went so well she tried rolling her neck. "Is there another file?"

"That was the last." The sergeant glanced at his watch. "It's nearly lunchtime. Are you hungry?"

"No, I had a late breakfast."

After Eli's gentle doctoring, she hadn't done justice to Brooke's waffles. Her appetite had waned as she wondered why finding the sheriff in her room had scrambled her brain cells. She knew better than to take his gentle doctoring and compassion personally since he'd admitted he didn't do permanent and permanent was what she sought in a place to live and eventually a man to share her life. She must not have hidden her feelings well because Brooke had watched them with interest from across the table this morning. Darcy noticed the sergeant's concerned expression.

"I'm sorry, what did you say?"

"I said it's lucky for Mrs. Lantz and the baby that you were their ride last night. Things could've turned out a lot different." He walked over and closed the computer program. "Are you all right, Ms. Cooper?"

"I feel better than I look. And thanks for the chair." She stood and rolled it to his desk—it was the only chair in the room with a cushioned back and seat.

"You're welcome. I'll see if Wainright's ready for you."

"Is there a soda machine nearby?" She dug in her purse for change.

"Out the door and to your right."

Coins jingling in her loose fist, she found the machine and selected a Dr. Pepper. With luck, caffeine and sugar would reinvigorate her brain and banish all those faces she'd studied.

She walked down the hall to Dan's office. She'd seen him when she'd walked in earlier. He waved her over.

"How's the warrior-godmother this morning?"

"Colorful. This crime-fighting business is tough on the body, not to mention the wardrobe. You heroes must spend a fortune on capes."

"Yep," he agreed with a manly hitch of his pants. "The cape budget needs addressing."

They laughed.

"How's Lisa?" Darcy asked.

"Fine. She's confirmed your identification of Randy Hall, the man you called 'the ghoul.' Since neither of you found Raul, we'll call in a forensic artist from Austin and let you know when to come back in."

Sergeant Tyler looked in and crooked a finger at Darcy. "Ms. Cooper, Detective Wainright is ready for you."

"Come back when you finish and say hi to Lisa," Dan said as she stood.

The sergeant guided her to another beige-walled room, and then through a warren of grey metal desks. Wainright stood behind one in the corner. "How are you feeling this morning, Ms. Cooper?"

"Better than last night." She returned his smile.

"Have a seat," he said, taking his own. "I've read the transcript of your statement, and I'd like to go over the events again. Let's start with your arrival at the roadhouse."

She concentrated on details and specifics. Wainright scribbled notes while a small digital recorder ran between them. When she finished, he glanced at his jottings.

"How long have you known the sheriff?" he asked.

"We met on Tuesday."

He laughed. "You must have made an impression for him to ask you to join him. He's not known for socializing."

"He didn't invite me to Border's. He invited me to meet the Lantzes when I was delivering food there." She shifted uneasily. "What does the sheriff have to do with this?

He wasn't there when Lisa and I were attacked."

"You never know what might prove relevant."

Darcy leaned back. An undercurrent she didn't understand was at work here. She scooped up her purse and stood.

Wainright switched off the recorder. "Remember, Ms. Cooper, don't discuss any aspect of this case with anyone, and be careful. The men may attempt to recover their heroin. Failing that, they may do worse so you can't testify against them in court." He plucked a card from a holder on his desk. "Call if you think of anything else."

"I will." She took his card and was headed for Dan's office when the sound of Lisa's voice caught her attention.

Lisa sat in the break room, entertaining the deputies with her account of last night's events. Terror no longer shadowed her face. One hand repeatedly returned to the mound of her belly where it smoothed a green and gold plaid maternity dress as she retold Friday night's events.

"She grabbed his knife hand—the girl is fast. The next thing I knew, the second man was on the ground. I'm telling you, it was like watching Wonder Woman."

Darcy rolled her eyes. "Hello, Lisa."

"Darcy, my hero," Lisa said.

"I'm no hero," Darcy said. "I was as scared as you were."

"You're still my hero. You didn't run and leave me. Too bad I couldn't get my behind or my belly over that console so I could run them over as you knocked them down. But in retrospect, I was so scared I might have hit you and I'd probably have smashed your car."

When the deputies stared at her, Darcy sat in a chair to lower her exposure. She should have walked on past and let Lisa's audience disperse. Helping Lisa might earn her the department's gratitude, but that didn't mean she'd earned their respect.

Dan walked in.

"Backrub!" Lisa said. She rested her arms on the table, and her head on her arms. Dan started kneading the small of her back.

"O-o-o-o, right there, baby." Lisa arched her back.

Darcy looked at Dan. "When I can have my car back?"

He smiled at Lisa's purr of pleasure. "It's ready to go. I have your key. We matched Randy Hall's prints to some on your car." He stopped massaging long enough to dig in his pocket and hold out her key.

As she reached for the key, Dan's fist closed around it.

"We want to pay for the new window," he said.

"That is so sweet." Her hand remained palm up. "But I haven't paid all those insurance premiums for nothing. That reminds me, I haven't called my agent yet. May I use a phone?"

Dan reluctantly dropped the key into her hand. "Use my desk. There's a phone book in the top right drawer."

Lisa sat up with a groan. "Massage time is over?"

"Afraid so, babe." He pulled out two business cards. "Darcy, I'm officially on paternity leave. I wrote our home number on this card. Write yours on the back of the other for us."

She complied. Dan hadn't said, but she guessed he was taking off because he didn't trust anyone else to watch Lisa. He pocketed the card she returned.

"I'm taking Lisa home. Keep in touch."

"I will."

She watched them walk away, Dan's arm around Lisa's waist. Oh, to be so loved and cherished. Sighing, she walked to his office, sat at his desk, and found his phone book.

The insurance company agreed to fax a claim form to her house. Next, she arranged for a replacement window to be delivered to a local garage.

Gritting her teeth as she flexed her arm muscles, she worked the car key onto her key ring. Eli hadn't reappeared. Last night's fatal traffic accident and the attack on Lisa and her had probably buried him in meetings and phone calls.

Sergeant Tyler gave her directions to the vehicle impound, then added, "Deputy Carlisle is organizing a baby shower for Dan and Lisa, September twenty-fourth. You're invited."

"Thank you. I'd love to come!" The silver lining of last night's events was that she was making headway in meeting people and letting them get to know the real her, not the rumored her. "Where and what time?"

"Here at two. The sheriff's secretary, Janet, has copies of their registry."

"Thanks!"

Darcy picked up a gift list for the shower and Janet's

assurance that nothing else was needed for the party. The last line on the harried woman's phone lit up, joining the insistent blinking of four others. Darcy walked away from the muffled voices behind the sheriff's closed door.

She found the impound and her car. The manual transmission was no real problem after she removed her arm from the sling. Keeping an eye on the rearview mirror, she drove into town and pulled into a crowded parking lot. She needed a real weapon.

Returning home, Darcy filled a glass of water at her kitchen faucet and swallowed two ibuprofens to quiet the dull throbbing in her arm. Hefting her new self-defense weapon, she grinned, recalling the cashier at the sporting goods store when she'd laid the model of her choice on the counter. The gum-chewing, middle-aged woman had blown and popped a tight bubble while looking from Darcy's bruised face to the bat in her hands, then said, "Honey, I hope I'm on the jury after you get him."

Darcy set her glass in the sink and walked outside. She settled in one rocking chair and propped her feet on the other. As the fiery sun sank toward the horizon, a ladybug landed on her knee and wandered in a ticklish circle.

Her stomach growled a reminder that she'd skipped lunch in favor of sleep. Eyes closed, she performed a mental inventory of the refrigerator's contents. She needed to grocery shop tomorrow. Nudging the ladybug into flight, she stood.

A horn blared in the distance. Shading her eyes against the setting sun, she made out a blue and white patrol car, a waving arm, and the platinum blonde curls of Deputy Carlisle. Darcy waved back, her heart lighter.

CHAPTER TEN

Sunday morning, Darcy scrutinized her alarm clock. She'd sat outside on her porch last night until dark. The sheriff kept his word—his department's cruisers passed frequently. Once inside, she'd slept soundly. No tossing, turning or jerking awake. She shivered. If someone had entered the house, would she have woken?

The remodeling crew wouldn't return until tomorrow, and the doctor had told her to take it easy with the stitches. The day stretched endlessly.

She rolled out of bed and hobbled to the bathroom to fill a water glass and swallow another ibuprofen. After a quick shower, she changed into cutoffs and a fuchsia T-shirt. Changing the bandage on her arm produced ugly, but serviceable results.

She combed her rope of wet hair to the front of her left shoulder and managed a passable braid. Picking up a map of Texas back roads, she left the house, buckled up, and drove west at a leisurely speed. Since her guests would ask about nearby touring options, she'd explore a few.

The wind poured through the broken window, reminding her of Friday night. She deliberately pushed the attack from her mind to concentrate on the winding two-lane road and rolling hills. Deer browsed beneath live oaks, and she spotted a red-tailed hawk perched on a power line, scanning for prey.

After winding through the high hills and canyons for over an hour, Darcy stopped at a convenience store in Leakey to fill her gas tank and buy a sandwich, chips, and water. A few more miles down the road, she paid admission to Garner State Park where the Frio River's flowing calmness invited her to tug off her tennis shoes and socks.

Carrying her lunch, she waded into the clear, cool water, over the slabs of limestone rock, and settled on the dry half of a semi-submerged tree. Iridescent minnows immediately swarmed her feet.

With the warm afternoon, the park filled with people. She waved back at an armada of college students floating past in inner tubes with umbilical ropes attached to smaller tubes that buoyed coolers of snacks and beverages. Their laughter lingered as they bobbed around the bend.

She lifted her face as the sun emerged from behind a sheltering cypress tree. College, for her, hadn't been carefree. She'd lost her grandparents, but she'd also cemented her closest friendship. From that first aborted semester, until her graduation walk, Beth had called with class news, encouragement and, eventually, a job offer in Dallas. She owed Beth a call, but how would she explain the last few days without causing worry? Her stomach growled a welcome distraction from her thoughts.

The minnows darted for crumbs as she ate her sandwich.

She refused to accept a victim label. Once the sheriff's department figured out the reason for last night's attack, she'd know how to approach the problem. One of the Andersons might resent her enough to vandalize the house, but premeditating an attack suggested vengeance.

She opened the chips; no sense in borrowing trouble. Since the sheriff's department was working on a motive for the attack, she would focus her efforts on the rumor mill.

Results in supplementing her income by catering were sporadic, and her savings account was dwindling. In business, reputation was everything. Unless she salvaged hers, she wouldn't have a business to worry about.

Crumpling the remains of her lunch, she walked to her car, tossing the wrappers into a trashcan on the way.

She drove south, stopping in Concan for tourist brochures and a bottle of water, continued to Uvalde then turned east to cruise through Sabinal. Then north to Utopia and on to Vanderpool and a stop to hike an easy trail at Lost Maples State Natural Area. In the late afternoon, she headed for Lost Creek.

Close to home, but no closer to answers, the graffiti that recommended she leave, replayed in her mind. Who benefited if she left Lost Creek? Keith Anderson had seen her Friday night—along with a roomful of others. But those others hadn't lost a chance to live in the house and own a hundred acres. Keith hadn't seemed resentful, but what about the rest of his family?

And what about the attack? Randy, the ghoul, and Raul,

his sidekick, weren't an experience she'd care to repeat. She adjusted her seatbelt.

If Raul had driven the tan car each time she'd seen it that suggested she was the target last night. But why would drug dealers be interested in her?

The sun hung low in the west when she caught sight of her house. Her house. She stopped to get her mail and the weekly newspaper from the mailbox. Her Dallas doctor had forwarded a postcard reminder that her annual exam was coming due. She tossed it all onto the passenger seat and turned into the driveway. She slowed to stare at the black pickup truck parked by the front steps.

A man rose from one of her rocking chairs.

Keith Anderson. She parked beside his truck and left her car running. She called out of the busted-out window. "Doctor Anderson, what brings you here?"

"Call me Keith." He sauntered down the steps and leaned crossed forearms on the open window. "I heard about your trouble and came to check on you." His hazel eyes narrowed as he scanned her face. "They better hope the law finds them first. Taking a knife to a woman doesn't go over well in Lost Creek."

Darcy's heart rate jumped. She should have driven away the minute she recognized him. Her knife wound was the one piece of information Dan had said would not be released to the press. She put her hand on the gearshift, ready to shift into reverse.

"I appreciate your concern, but you barely know me."

"You're living in the Anderson homestead. That practically makes us family." He shook his head. "Wish I'd stuck around a little longer Friday night. I could have escorted you ladies to your car."

"Who told you I was hurt?" Darcy checked her door locks.

Keith pointed at the newspaper on her passenger seat.

She snatched up the rolled newspaper and flattened it against the steering wheel. The lead story covered the DUI deaths. Below, a smaller headline read "Expectant Mother Rescued by Newcomer." The by-line was Cheryl Greer's.

"You've got to be kidding," Darcy groaned. She anchored the paper with her elbows and read the first few paragraphs. Sure enough, Cheryl mentioned her knife wound. She turned off the car and massaged her temples. Inside the house, the phone rang.

Keith checked his watch. "It's rung every ten minutes since I got here a half-hour ago. Cheryl probably wants an exclusive." He grinned at her glare. "You know, you're cute when you're mad, but I prefer your smile."

A scathing reply eluded her as she collapsed against the seat. "Ouch!" She yelped her arm's protest. His expression turned serious.

"Let me take a look." He tried to open the locked door.

She hesitated.

"I'm a doctor, remember?"

"You're a veterinarian. I'm not a pet."

"Well you're as stubborn as a goat with its head caught in the fence, so I'm qualified to look at your injury."

Eli's warning about the Andersons flashed through her mind. Still, if Keith had wanted to add to her injuries, he'd spent a lot of time talking instead of coming through her broken window. She stepped out and lifted her sleeve. Keith peered beneath the dressing.

"Do you have clean gauze?" he asked. "Your bandage needs to be changed."

Since no one else was likely to show up and help her change it, she scooped up her mail. "Come on in."

They entered through the kitchen door. Darcy tossed the newspaper on the table then faced Keith. "Wait here."

She retrieved the bag of medical supplies from her room and spread them out on the kitchen table. Keith sat beside her, cut the bandage away, and started cleaning.

"I like what you've done with the place," he said.

The doorbell rang. He put a hand on her shoulder and stood.

"I'll get it," he said. "It could be that our friendly reporter Cheryl decided to make a house call and maybe get a scoop."

His words silenced her protest. Her arm ached, and she didn't feel like taking on Cheryl the persistent reporter—today.

She closed her eyes and listened as Keith's steps moved from the kitchen tile to the foyer wood floor. She heard the door open, and the deep timbre of masculine voices. Moments later, Keith reentered the kitchen followed by a grim-faced Sheriff Whitepath.

"Why didn't you let the department know where you'd be?" he snapped at her.

"Excuse me?" She hadn't heard from him since yesterday morning. If he thought he could barge in and accuse her of negligence, he wasn't thinking straight. She stood and put her hands on her hips. She flinched then ignored the twinge in her arm, and Keith's raised eyebrows.

"You're in trouble now, Sheriff." Keith smoothed the grin below his dark blonde mustache with a thumb and forefinger before continuing to bandage her arm.

"The newspaper story came out, and we couldn't contact you." Eli nodded to the paper on the table. "You've read it?"

Concern or duty? Either way, his explanation, and now-reasonable tone made her continued indignation feel childish.

"Just the headline, and the first column," she said.

"The paper gave out your name, and, in a roundabout way, your address."

She stared at him. "Can they do that?" Her arms fell to her sides.

Keith re-propped her left arm on her hip, and muttered, "Stay."

Eli's attention snapped to Keith then back to her.

"Legally, yes. Although mentioning your house is ethically questionable."

As the implications sank in, she wobbled. Keith placed steadying hands on her hips. "Easy girl. If you faint, I'll have to administer mouth-to-mouth."

She pushed his hands away. "You don't give mouth-to-mouth to people who faint."

He grinned. "Shoot. Caught again." He gathered the medical supplies and placed them in the bag. Mischief lit his eyes. "Want me to take these back to your room?"

The sheriff's jaw tightened. Darcy curled her hands into fists. The inner calm she'd found earlier in the day at the river was long gone. The dull throb in her head intensified to a sharp pound as testosterone levels in the kitchen reached smothering proportions.

"No. But thanks for changing the bandage. I'll walk you out." She turned, leaving Keith no option but to follow her to the front door.

He stopped on the porch and caught her wrist. "Umhmm, your pulse is racing. Could be the newspaper story or me—or the sheriff."

She tugged free. "I think it's the headache I've developed since arriving home."

He stepped closer and smiled. "You know the best remedy for a headache?"

She looked up, then back at the vet. "Goodbye, Keith."

He touched his hat brim then looked beyond her and gave a casual salute. "Whitepath."

Not ready to deal with Eli, she slow-counted to thirty while watching Keith enter his truck and drive toward the county road. When she turned, her home phone's ring carried through the empty doorway.

Eli left Darcy and Keith on the porch and returned to the kitchen. He could guess where Keith's interests lay—that headache remedy had to be the most overused innuendo in male existence.

He took a deep breath. He'd jumped her verbally when he knew accusatory questions provoked defensive answers. Still, the woman gave as good as she got.

He rubbed both palms over his face. He'd arrived at ten last night and slept in his truck beneath a stand of trees— the closest concealment to her house that her property offered. He'd left at daybreak to change for work. At his cottage, he'd stepped out of the shower to answer the phone and learned from Dan about the newspaper article. When Darcy didn't answer his call, he'd worried that someone else had also watched—and waited for him to leave.

He had dispatched a deputy who had reported her car gone and no answer at the house, with no signs of forced entry or a struggle. He'd left work early to check her. Seeing the unknown truck suppressed his relief at seeing her car. Keith answering her door pulled the pin on his temper, and he'd exploded like a three-count grenade.

He shrugged out of his jacket, tossed it over a chairback, and tugged his tie free. His eyes and stomach burned, thanks to an uncomfortable night and a day spent fielding calls from local politicians and citizens demanding to know why drug and DUI deaths had increased during his tenure as sheriff. He suspected his campaign opponent's political allies had staged some of the complaints.

He crossed his arms and settled back against the sink. In less than a week, Darcy Cooper had provided a break in the drug case and revived his second-term chances.

The phone rang. Once. Twice. He knew from his calls today that her machine picked up on the fourth ring.

Darcy stalked into the kitchen, forced her gaze to slide past the sheriff, and picked up the receiver.

"Hello."

She listened.

"Not interested. Tell me, Cheryl. If you were attacked, would you want your name and location printed in the paper for the bad guys to read?" She rolled her eyes and slammed the receiver down. "The right of the public to know my Uncle Sam—"

She desperately needed to reacquire her composure.

"Would you like something to drink, Sheriff? I have tea or water."

"Tea would be great. Nice bat." He nodded at the weapon propped by the door.

"Thanks."

She poured two glasses, cut a lemon into wedges, then pulled a bowl of watermelon chunks from the refrigerator. Finally, she shook two ibuprofens into her palm.

"Let's sit on the porch," she said.

Eli picked up the tea glasses. His conservative charcoal-gray slacks and starched white shirt emphasized his lean build.

114

She led him outside to the rocking chairs and a welcome breeze. Tossing the ibuprofens into her mouth, she chased them with tea.

Eli ate a watermelon chunk then asked, "Why was Keith here?"

She drew a deep breath. "He read the story in the paper and wanted to see if I was all right." She pulled her legs up to sit cross-legged in the rocker. "I'd like to meet the rest of his family—in bright daylight—and see how they react to me."

"No," Eli said, voice and eyes hard. "This is an ongoing criminal investigation. My people will ask any questions that need answers. Your job is to avoid the Andersons until we've interviewed them and to call my deputies anytime you leave the house."

Darcy sighed. "Sheriff, we need to address your authoritarian tendencies."

Eli leaned forward. "Randy Hall is a drifter with a hot temper and a history of drug infractions. The fact that you've seen his partner Raul several times could indicate that you hold interest for them, not Lisa." His eyes pinned her. "We're questioning all of the Andersons. And we don't yet know who hired Randy and Raul. You shouldn't be alone with any of the Andersons until my investigators finish interviews and corroborations."

His hands closed on the rocker's arms. "At seven this morning, Dan called me about the newspaper story. I called your house. When you didn't answer, I sent a deputy out and learned you weren't here. When I arrived, I found you alone with a suspect." He plowed his fingers through his hair. "It would make my job and life easier if you followed my orders."

"Orders? I was following and agreeing with your logic. And now I learn you're giving me orders?"

"I need you to do what I say. I—we can't keep you safe if you won't listen." He realized he'd raised his voice.

Her voice rose. "Why don't you ask nicely?"

"Because I feel like shouting will make you understand the gravity of what I'm trying to get across to you."

She couldn't help it. She laughed. His expression was so severe, and his words rang so true, she had to laugh.

The band of tension squeezing her ribs, relaxed.

Looking worried, he dropped to one knee in front of her. His hands cupped her shoulders. "Post-traumatic stress is a normal reaction after an attack." His voice took on the soothing tone he'd used on her in the emergency room. She liked that voice.

His warm hand closed around her nape, repeating instructions to breathe deeply and sending her heart racing as his touch replaced laughter with the sobriety of awareness.

"You took all the fun out of our argument," she said, touching her mouth. "Thank goodness I didn't split my lip open again. And my headache is gone. It must have been stress."

"How do you do that?" Eli's fingers relaxed against her neck. She lost the conversation thread.

"Do what?"

"Go from irritated to happy so fast."

"I learned as a teenager." She smiled. He had the most attractive green eyes. "Gramma was a big believer in perspective. No matter what happened, I had to find the humor or good in the situation. The practice became a habit."

He stared. "You're unusual."

"I get the impression you've yet to decide if that's a good thing."

"I'll let you know." His hand slipped away, taking comfort and heat with it. "Where were you today?"

He sat back in his rocker.

"Sheriff, I appreciate your hard work and concern. And I'm sorry I added to your tension level. I'll give you my cell phone number if that will help."

"It will. So where were you?"

"I went for a drive and visited some of the surrounding towns."

He looked at her. "If Randy and Raul have seen the paper, they'll figure out where you live—if they don't already know."

"They satisfied their employer's instructions to discourage me or us, and surely they'll assume I turned in the drugs."

"The street value of the heroin is motive enough to attempt to retrieve the drugs. The paper reported the incident as an assault. Somehow, Cheryl missed hearing you'd recovered drugs. We have to assume they'll return and that this is the first place they'll look."

He sipped his tea, then added, "Brooke called me. She's invited you to stay as long as necessary."

Darcy leaned back. His offer was tempting. Having him right next door—within shouting distance—would be a comfort. But if she didn't open her bed and breakfast on schedule, her finances wouldn't allow her to keep Alex's inheritance.

"That's kind of her. But I'm in the final stages of the remodel. I have workmen coming every day for the next two weeks. I'll need to be here from sunup to sundown.

"And if you're right about Randy and Raul finding me, what will stop them from following me to Brooke's house and endangering her and Jeremy? I appreciate the offer, but I won't risk your sister and nephew too.

"I'll keep the outdoor and indoor lights on all night. My locks are all new. And your deputy patrols are regular. That might help discourage Randy and Raul."

"If you stay and are hurt again, your opening could be delayed."

"Since I was twelve, I've dreamed of living in a small town. This house represents the realization of that dream. If I move out, I might as well pack up and return to Dallas."

His brows drew together. "My department's patrols can only watch your house from the county road." He waved a hand. "Is this worth another encounter with those two?"

"No," she admitted.

"Then it's settled."

"I'm not staying with Brooke, but I have a suggestion."

He leaned forward. "Let's hear it."

"Detective Wainright said I was the 'new lead' in the drug case."

When Eli stared, she continued.

"Doesn't law enforcement protect their leads?"

His eyes narrowed. "You want to stay at the jail?"

"No! Can't a deputy stay here at night?"

He opened his mouth and then closed it, apparently considering her question.

Her request held merit, Eli thought. But assigning a deputy would further restrict his already tight budget. He mentally ran a deputy's salary times eight or ten hours. And then he considered the alternative.

"All right. If you won't leave, someone will keep watch from your property at night."

She nodded. "They're welcome to stay in the house."

He gave a slow nod. "That will make protecting you easier."

"And I'll be careful during the day," she promised. "The plumber and electrician are coming this week. I have to be here to tell them what I want done and to answer questions as they come up."

"Do you know them by sight?"

"Yes."

"Do you have outdoor security lights?"

"I have the pole light outside the kitchen. And sconces

beside the doors."

He glanced around. "Be sure to leave them all on at night. I've increased the drive-bys out here, and I hope you don't tend to speed. Until this is over, you'll see a patrol car in your rearview mirror more often. Do you have more watermelon?" he asked.

She nodded. "Yes, but you can't live on watermelon. I was about to fix dinner. I'll share." She stood as he rose.

"How can I help?"

"Follow me."

They walked inside.

"Who's staying tonight and what time will they arrive?" she asked.

"I'm staying."

Darcy's ears hummed as trepidation and exhilaration vied. Exhilaration won.

"It's too late to schedule a deputy," he said.

"Oh."

She hid disappointment with a cooking frenzy. Fifteen minutes later, a salad chilled in the refrigerator, ground beef bubbled in a savory tomato sauce, and a pot of salted water simmered on a back burner. She popped a loaf of homemade sourdough bread into the preheated oven before facing the sheriff.

"I'm taking a quick shower while the sauce simmers."

"I'll watch it."

She walked to her bedroom, feeling safer than she had

in weeks.

Eli locked Darcy's doors—refreshing his memory of her home's layout. Noticing her CD player, he pushed the play button to hear what she'd listened to last. The soothing Native American flutes and drums surprised him. He studied the warm neutrals of her wood and leather furniture. The reds and blues in her rugs and wall hangings added vibrancy. Like her, the room was hospitable—alive.

Lighted shelves held rock collections, pinecones, Native American baskets, and pottery. The baskets and pottery looked authentic, although, he didn't recognize the tribe. He picked up a bowl and raised an eyebrow at the artist's name. Signed pieces were usually expensive. Were they a gift from Alex?

He paused before the fireplace mantle and a black and white photo of Alex. He hooked his thumbs in his belt loops and studied Anderson's weather-beaten face. What had this man meant to Darcy?

He heard her in the kitchen and turned. She stood at the stove in a calf-length denim skirt and sleeveless white shirt. She'd bathed carefully—her bandage was dry. His kitchen talents were limited, so he leaned against a counter and watched her efficient movements as she tested a strand of pasta then slid the bread into the oven.

Her hair flowed in waves to the small of her back. In a sudden vision, she leaned over him, and that curtain of gold surrounded them. The buzzing timer brought him back to reality. As she reached to lift the pasta pot, he commandeered the potholders.

"No lifting until the stitches come out," he said, noticing the rapid pulse beating in her throat as she stepped back.

Darcy pulled salads from the refrigerator and lingered a moment in the chilled air to cool her overheated face and senses. She drew a fortifying breath then turned to take the bread out of the oven. She dished up two helpings of pasta, ladled sauce, and added slices of hot bread. "If you'll carry these, I'll bring the salads." She headed for the dining room. "This is the first time I've used the formal table."

"We'll eat here in the kitchen," Eli said.

She stopped, halfway through the swinging doors. "Why?"

"You don't have curtains."

She glanced at the naked expanse of windows, about-faced, and set the salads on the small kitchen table. Eli settled the pasta plates, placing the most substantial helping at the seat that gave him a view of her kitchen door and the foyer and dining room entries. When she sat, he scooted her chair to the table. She looked from his holstered gun to his green eyes.

CHAPTER ELEVEN

"Do you always wear your gun at meals?" Darcy asked.

The sheriff sat on the other side of the table. "I never thought about it. Usually. Does it bother you?"

"No. I grew up around guns." She picked up her fork. "And given that Randy and Raul are loose, it's comforting."

After that, their dinner conversation followed a mutual avoidance of drug-related subjects. She appreciated the reprieve. Maybe he did too.

"Thank you," Darcy said when the meal ended.

"For what?"

She reached to stack his plate atop hers. "For caring whether or not I'd disappeared this morning. It's reassuring to know someone would be looking for me."

"You're a key witness. I'll do my best to keep you safe, but you have to help." He took the plates from her and scooted his chair back. "If you'll make coffee, I'll clear."

She walked into the kitchen, smiling. Key witness sounded like a step up from new lead. She brewed coffee, poured a glass of milk, and arranged six chocolate chip cookies on a plate. The county would benefit if she could help him catch the men selling heroin; the overdoses would stop, and she'd make some new friends along the way.

She turned to watch Eli rinse the plates and load the dishwasher. Had Brooke or bachelorhood taught him his domestic skills?

"Let's sit outside," he said, taking the hot mug from her.

He crossed to the door and released the deadbolt. Stepping out, he looked around then reached past her and turned off the exterior lights. He held the door as she carried the cookies and her milk.

He nodded her toward the porch swing where an overgrown pyracantha, in desperate need of pruning, screened her from the road. Setting the cookie plate on the small table, she kicked off her shoes, tucked her legs up, and arranged her skirt over her bare feet.

Eli pulled up a rocker and stretched out his legs. He picked up a cookie and set the chair in motion while scrutinizing the shadowed landscape. To the west, ambient light from Lost Creek blushed the horizon like a fading sunset.

Darcy reached for a cookie. "Where do you think Cheryl Greer got her information?" she asked.

"At the department yesterday. Either Cheryl overheard someone talking, or she has a source feeding her details. It's my fault your safety is compromised."

"How is it your fault?" She shut her eyes. The aromatic coffee he drank teased her nostrils. How could a beverage that smelled that fragrant taste so bitter?

"I'm the sheriff. What happens in my department is my

responsibility."

Darcy opened her eyes. "I agree it's your responsibility, but it isn't your fault. The station was packed with people. Did you notice that Cheryl dressed to blend in with your khaki uniforms? And like you said, at least she didn't hear about the heroin."

"Looking at the bright side?" he asked, sounding cynical.

The rocker creaked as he leaned forward to watch a vehicle on the county road. When it passed her driveway, he relaxed. "What do you expect to find here?" he asked, tossing her thoughts in a new direction.

"A chance to establish a permanent home and a successful business."

"A business that will fill your permanent home with temporary faces?"

She frowned. "That's not how it. Some guests will pass through, but others will return and become friends. My hotel management degree didn't cover B&Bs, but I know the aspects of life that I enjoyed while living with my grandparents on their farm. Those, I can share."

"Like getting up before dawn to tend to animals or plow a field or repair a fence?"

"No." She extended a foot to nudge his rocker. "Like sitting on the porch listening to crickets, eating home-cooked meals, and ignoring television, cell phones, and social media." She leaned her head back. "And seeing stars undimmed by city lights.

"I admit farm life wasn't all idyllic. But I asked to live

with my grandparents. At fifteen, I realized my parents would be traveling in their retirement if my birth hadn't surprised them so late in their lives. Don't get me wrong; they love me. But I loved the summers spent with my grandparents. I loved them and living on the farm—so I asked to stay year-round."

She rested an elbow on the swing. "Where do you see yourself in four years?"

He reached for a third cookie. "Exactly where I am today, as sheriff of Tell County." He resumed rocking, a solitary figure in a solitary pursuit.

"With no one but Jeremy tagging along after you?" She regretted her question the moment his shoulders tensed.

"Ms. Cooper, any given day, I deal with people from whom you could expect the worst and seldom be wrong. Why would I want to bring children into that?"

"Because you know the difference. Because the world needs more good people. Because a law enforcement career enables you to make a difference in people's lives. Tell County is a better place because you're looking out for those of us who don't know how to deal with the kinds of people and events you come across in your work as sheriff."

Headlights illuminated the county road. The vehicle slowed and turned up her drive. Eli pulled her to her feet and hurried her to the kitchen.

"Stay inside," he said.

Heart thundering, she watched him walk back out.

Eli stopped at the corner of the house. Recognizing the unmarked department car and its occupant, he stepped out of the shadows. "Wainright."

"Sheriff."

The detective's eyes darted around the porch. Eli interpreted his assessment: The sheriff wore no jacket and no tie. A cup and a glass sat atop the wood table, Darcy's sandals rested under the porch swing. Wainright's brows lifted. He leaned to pick up the last two cookies.

"Looks like you've discussed the situation with Ms. Cooper. What's been decided?" He chewed and swallowed. "Man, these are good."

Eli stifled a surge of irritation. He'd had plans for at least one more cookie.

"Ms. Cooper wants to remain in her house."

"She's vulnerable at night." Wainright bit into the second cookie.

"Not if I'm on the couch."

Silence ensued.

Wainright finally spoke. "Given current hearsay, you know what you're risking if county residents learn you're staying here nights."

Eli nodded. "But it shouldn't be long before we know if the suspects plan to contact Ms. Cooper."

Eli noted the man's small smile. Wainright thought his boss was committing political suicide. Unfortunately, he might be right.

"I'll be back in about thirty minutes," Eli said. He

walked inside for his jacket.

"Why is Detective Wainright here? Does he have news?" Darcy asked.

He realized that she hadn't hidden. She'd been watching from a window. And she was holding her bat. Backing him up, he thought.

"No, he'll stay with you while I pick up a change of clothes."

Wainright walked inside. "Do you have any more cookies? I missed dinner."

Darcy turned and opened a container. "Would you like milk or coffee with them?"

"Coffee," he said.

Eli opened the door. "Ms. Cooper, stay inside. Detective, I'll be back soon."

Wainright finished another cookie. "No hurry."

Eli managed not to slam the door as he left.

Darcy poured coffee and set a cup in front of the detective, along with her last four cookies. He sat in the seat Eli had used, and ate while she washed her glass and Eli's cup.

"I appreciate your staying while the Sheriff gets his things for tomorrow."

"The Sheriff called the department and asked dispatch to send someone over. I was leaving Border's so I took the call."

"I guess you didn't see Randy or Raul there?"

"No, but I left a photo and sketch for Carl."

She sat across from him.

"He's taken an interest in you," Wainright said.

"Carl's a good man. He's offered to keep an eye on me when I make deliveries."

"I wasn't talking about Carl. I was talking about the Sheriff."

Darcy sat up straight. "As you said, I'm 'the new lead.' It would be strange if he didn't take an interest in my safety."

"True. This seemed like something more."

"More than what?"

"Professional interest. I mean, you're a pretty woman."

"What I am, is a citizen of Tell County who's been assaulted and who found heroin when the sheriff's men haven't."

Wainright's face tightened. And then he smiled. "That's true. Sorry if my comment seemed out of line. I was making conversation."

Darcy stood. "If you'll excuse me, I need to find linens for the couch."

"Of course." He picked up another cookie.

She wrinkled her nose. She'd take Eli's stoicism over Wainright's speculative scrutiny, any time.

Relieved that Wainright hadn't drawn babysitting duty, she made up the couch. The detective re-checked her door and window locks. She told him about Keith Anderson's visit.

Thank You, God.

Eli's headlights were a welcome sight. "Detective, thank you for your company," she said politely.

"I appreciate the cookies and coffee," Wainright said as he

unlocked her kitchen door. "See you tomorrow," he added as he passed the sheriff.

Eli held a suit bag and overnight kit on a hangar with one hand while he locked the door with his free hand.

"My guestroom furniture doesn't arrive until next week," Darcy said. "So I made up the couch for you. You can hang your suit here." She led him into the foyer and opened the empty entry closet.

He removed his kit handle from the hangar, then reached past her and hung his bag.

"I put a clean towel in my bathroom. The upstairs baths aren't functional but there's a half bath off the living room. I hope you'll be comfortable." She walked into the living room, pleased with how attractive the couch looked with new sheets, a pillow, and a light blanket.

"I showered at home; and the sheet is enough," he said, pulling the blanket loose and folding it into a neat square. As he handed it to her, their hands touched.

Zap! "Static electricity," she said quickly.

"We aren't barefoot or standing on a rug," Eli pointed out.

Darcy looked down at the sandals she'd put back on. The sheriff was staying in her house, and he was all business. She needed to get herself under control.

Rising early came naturally to Darcy.

She'd expected to lay awake with the sheriff in her house, but she'd slept soundly—a condition she'd best not get used to until Raul and the ghoul were caught.

She dressed in khaki shorts and a blue polo shirt then used makeup to disguise the yellowish-green bruise on her cheek. She tiptoed down the hall, into the foyer, and heard water running in the half-bath.

She entered the kitchen and rummaged through the pantry for a clean plastic bag. Folding Deputy Carlisle's laundered sweats, she put them inside the bag for the sheriff to return for her.

She opened the refrigerator and sniffed a carton of milk before pouring some over cereal. She'd have to shop today. Law officers probably required more for breakfast than cereal. Since one would be keeping an eye on her at night, the least she could do was feed them. Better yet, she could try out the breakfast menus she'd put together.

Yesterday's Lost Creek Weekly lay on the table. Flattening the rumpled paper, she started reading. "Two local women escaped without serious harm after an attack by two armed assailants Friday night in the Border's Roadhouse parking lot. Lisa Lantz and Darcy Cooper left the popular bar around nine PM and were accosted as they entered Ms. Cooper's vehicle."

An account of the attack followed. She lowered her spoon and continued reading. "Lisa Lantz, wife of Sergeant Dan Lantz of the Tell County Sheriff's Department, is expecting a baby in late October. Darcy Cooper, friend of former long-time resident Alexander Anderson, recently inherited Anderson's estate including a house and property east of town."

She pushed the paper away. The words "Anderson's estate" made it sound like Darcy had received everything—house, land, and money. Weren't reporters supposed to verify details? Elbows propped on the table, she lowered her face to her palms.

"Do you have more coffee?" Eli's morning-rough voice interrupted her wallow.

She peeked through her fingers. "I put coffee beans by the grinder."

"Can you stop by the department today and work with the sketch artist?"

"What time?"

"Around ten. He's making a house call to see Lisa first." Beans rattled into the grinder's metal bowl.

"I don't rate a house call?" Darcy grumbled.

The motor pulsed then stopped.

"What happened, Pollyanna? Someone steal your prism?"

"I am feeling prism-deprived. And how do you know about Pollyanna?"

"Brooke has watched that movie every year for as long as I can remember." Eli looked over his shoulder. His eyes moved from her to the paper in front of her. "You read the rest of the article."

"I did."

"Well, here's your bright side—Dan is home with Lisa, and you have the department protecting you nights."

"I guess that's more practical than buying and training

a German shepherd."

He added water to the coffee maker. "Grumpy and sarcastic. This is a new side of you. Do you have any trips planned today?"

"Grocery shopping and a stop by Carl's to discuss Friday's menu."

"Come by the department first then I'll have a patrol follow you to the roadhouse and wait outside while you're there."

She stood and carried her bowl to the sink. "I was hoping you'd say that."

"Finally, you're showing maturity."

She resisted the urge to stick out her tongue.

"Is that breakfast?" He pointed at the cereal box with a rabbit on the front.

"For me, it's comfort food. For you, it's breakfast."

He opened the box, eyeballed the contents, and closed the flaps.

"Do you have any more cookies?"

"Detective Wainright finished them off last night."

She could have sworn that the sheriff growled.

The visit with the sketch artist hadn't taken long because Lisa did a good job of getting Raul's features right. Darcy added a few details. Eli's door remained closed. He must have left instructions because when she walked out, the duty sergeant told her to wait while he called a deputy to follow her to Border's.

"I won't be long!" Darcy called to the deputy, who'd rolled down his windows. He sent her an acknowledging wave.

She walked inside and sat on a barstool. At eleven in the morning, she and Carl pretty much had the roadhouse to themselves.

"How you doing, young'un?" he asked, studying her face carefully and looking pointedly at the slight bulge under her sleeve where the bandage circled her arm.

"Not bad. Someone from the sheriff's department is staying nights, so I'm not as scared as I was. A deputy is waiting outside for me."

"It grills my gizzard that they chose my place to attack you and Mrs. Lantz."

"It's not your fault. They could have been waiting for anyone," she said, leaving the details vague until the sheriff and his department finished their investigation. "And there is a bright side. My so-called heroics have atoned for my alleged greed and shocking behavior in some eyes."

Carl flipped a bar towel over a shoulder. "I was beginning to wonder if you'd heard the rumors. You never said anything."

"Neither did you." She placed her forearms on the bar and leaned forward. "But since you mentioned it, Alex and I were friends. We were never romantically involved."

Carl braced both hands on the bar. "You should be hollerin' it from the courthouse steps."

"That particular option hadn't occurred to me."

Carl smiled. "Okay, that explains that. Now talk to me about Friday's food."

"I was thinking of meat empanadas with pico de gallo on the side."

"That'll work. Now get on home and rest."

She started to stand then eased back onto the barstool. "Carl, how well did you know Alex and his brother?"

"We didn't run around together, but I knew them. Alex was older than me, and Dale was almost a decade behind me in school." His smile turned grim. "After I graduated high school, I worked here for my dad. Dale and some kid visiting for the summer used to come around the back and try to talk me into sneaking them beer. I chased them away."

"I'm trying to figure out why Alex left the property to me instead of his brother, especially since Dale had a family to pass it on to."

"Young'un, I don't know why Alex left it to you, but I think I know why he didn't leave it to Dale." Carl came around the bar and sat beside her. "Dale was in his twenties and Alex was in his forties when their parents retired and left them the ranch in equal halves." Carl reached for his towel and absently polished the counter. "That ranch was Alex's life. To Dale, the ranch was a rope tying him down."

"He said that?"

"Didn't have to. After his kids were born, he spent a lot of time here at Border's—called it his 'bolt hole.'"

A couple entered and sat at the far end of the bar. Carl left to fill their orders then returned.

"Dale got involved in a floating poker game that a fellow from San Antonio ran out of the back of a panel truck. Alex didn't know about Dale's gambling until a man showed up at the ranch with an IOU for Dale's half."

"No!" Darcy slapped a hand over her mouth, wincing as she hit her bruised lip.

Carl nodded. "Dale was in here drinking when Alex found him. Alex called Dale weak, said he'd gambled away his birthright, told Dale he'd bought the IOU and Dale had two days to clear his things off the ranch."

"Did Dale leave?"

"Yep. His wife must have set some money aside because they rented a house in town." Carl shrugged. "Alex and Dale pretty much ignored each other after that."

"Is Dale vindictive?"

"He can fly off the handle, but I've never had to throw him out." Carl crossed his arms over his chest. "Dale might want your place, but I doubt he expected Alex to leave it to him. I can see him thinking that one or both of his kids would inherit it."

Carl glanced at the couple then turned back to Darcy. "Keith's well-liked around the county, but he's big on self-gratification. Tread carefully there, girl."

"You don't have to tell me twice," Darcy said. "I haven't met his sister."

"Angela's a sweet kid, but she chose a poor husband. Greg bought an auto garage after they married. Too bad he never learned to balance books. He sold out a year ago to avoid bankruptcy."

Three cowboys entered, and Carl stood.

"Time for me to go to work. You be careful. And if you need to be met this Friday when you deliver, let me know."

"Thanks, Carl."

Darcy walked outside, pondering what she had learned about the Anderson family. She waved goodbye to the deputy and drove to the grocery store.

She raced up and down the store aisles then headed for a check-out counter and dropped two giant bags of chocolate chips onto the conveyor. The clerk scanned the bar codes and moved on to the two steaks that followed. Darcy didn't know what time tonight's deputy would arrive, but if they showed up around dinnertime, she'd share.

"Do you need carry out?" the clerk asked, eying her sling.

"I do, thanks."

The store's automatic doors opened at her approach.

"What?" She backpedaled to stare at the poster taped beside the door and barely avoided being run down by the teenager pushing her cart. Vote November 6th for Gavin Wainright for Sheriff. The detective was running for sheriff?

"Ma'am?" The bag boy shot her a puzzled look.

"Sorry."

She walked outside. Wainright's questioning her about the sheriff suddenly took on a new meaning.

Could he use her against Eli? Would he? She smiled grimly. If she requested that Wainright stay tonight, would that even the playing field?

Eli stared at the numbers he'd written. After running

every financial scenario he could think of, he still hadn't discovered an alternative.

Dan had his home security under control because he was on paternity leave. Adding another deputy to the night shift would take Eli off Darcy-guarding duty, but it would also delay purchasing computers for the department cruisers.

He dropped the pencil onto the desk. He'd curtail any negative political talk that might circulate about him spending nights at Darcy's, but with a drug element working in Tell County, his deputies needed the advantages computers offered.

So he'd do his duty, keep Darcy safe nights, and deal with the political fallout.

The necessity didn't bother him as much as it should have. He needed to work on professional distance. He'd barely concealed his reaction to the electric jolt he'd felt when they'd touched hands last night.

Eli tossed his calculations in the trash and reached for the phone. His uncle answered after the third ring.

"Uncle John, it's Eli."

"How are you, nephew."

"In need of some dream analysis."

He explained while Uncle John listened.

"The dreams are serious, and they would be easier to interpret if I knew Darcy."

Eli thought for a moment.

"I'm due for a vision quest," he said.

It was Uncle John's turn to think. Finally, he answered. "Bring her with you."

"Do you want your old job back?"

Darcy tucked the phone between her shoulder and ear then carefully poured a package of chocolate chips into a huge mixing bowl full of cookie dough. She began stirring. "No, Beth. That's not why I called."

"But I miss you. We all miss you," her best friend urged.

"I miss you all too. But I like living here. I already know my banker and postman by name. And Tell County has a small airport. Stan can fly you down." Darcy wiggled her eyebrows and toes. "Before I left Dallas, I encouraged Annie to beg to visit."

"I know." Beth sounded annoyed. "Shame on you for fueling the badgering capabilities of a five-year-old." Papers rustled. "Speaking of persistence, that downtown realtor sent you another letter care of the hotel. Should I forward the envelope?"

"No. Open it."

Beth's mumble accompanied the sound of tearing paper. "It's another offer on your new place." She gave a low whistle. "They upped the amount."

"Throw it away. I'm not interested," Darcy said, lining up sheet pans.

"Decline the offer of a lifetime? Darcy, you could sell, and buy something that already has modern plumbing and wiring."

139

Darcy rolled her eyes. "I like this house, Beth. It has history and character and will soon have modern plumbing and wiring. Does this offer list a buyer's name?"

"No, the letter states that the client wishes to remain anonymous. You know, I've read that movie stars buy property in the Texas Hill Country. They wouldn't want the public knowing their business."

"No, but you'd also think they'd want more than a hundred acres." Darcy scooped dough and spaced it evenly on the cookie sheets.

"Maybe they've made offers on surrounding properties."

"Excellent point, but I'm staying. Toss the offer."

"Why don't I keep this for you—for a month or two. I know you don't plan to change your mind, but consider this an insurance policy. If the place is more trouble than it's worth, sell, and buy something manageable."

If Beth were a dog, Darcy thought, she'd be a highly bred and immaculately groomed terrier with the instinct to sink her teeth in and hold on until she shook you into agreement. The preheating oven light blinked out.

"You can keep the offer if you fill me in on Annie and Stan," Darcy said, sliding pans into the oven.

Twenty minutes later, she hung up without having told Beth about the attack. She saw no point in alarming her friend. She pulled two more sheets of perfectly browned cookies from the convection oven. She'd baked enough to feed her next five bodyguards—unless they shared the sheriff's and detective's appetites. Stretching her uninjured arm overhead, she walked out to the backyard.

The waning September day had subsided to seventy-eight degrees, complete with powder blue skies and billowy white clouds. Picking up an oak branch, she stepped on the large end and pulled the small end toward her. The wood snapped. She tossed the pieces toward the grill. Beth's call had delayed dinner preparations, but the sun hadn't set.

She picked up another branch, stepped on one end, and pulled. As it broke, she stumbled.

Hands caught and righted her.

"What are you doing outside alone?" The sheriff's touch and voice slammed her already adrenaline-accelerated pulse further into overdrive.

"I'm the only one living here, so I'm alone whenever I go outside." She tossed the wood towards the grill. "I'm grilling tonight, and the store clerk recommended oak. Unfortunately, she forgot to suggest I buy an ax or a chainsaw." She paused. "Thanks for saving me from bruising yet another part of my anatomy."

"You're welcome." He released her waist, which allowed her brain to reengage.

"Why are you here? Did you find the bad guys?"

"No." He pointed to his suit bag hanging on the porch. "I'm here for the night."

"Oh."

The implications of the rumors about her and his running for reelection flashed through her thoughts. "I thought you'd assign a deputy. Do you plan to stay every night until you catch the men?"

"Or until I think you're no longer in danger." He scavenged around, adding wood chunks to her meager pile.

"I figured you for a man who knew how to delegate."

Green eyes snared hers. "Anxious to get rid of me?"

With no idea how to answer his question truthfully, she blinked.

He picked up a branch, used her technique, and pulled until it snapped.

Darcy stacked wood as Eli broke enough for several barbecues.

"Have you eaten?" she asked.

"You don't have to feed me. I bought a burger; it's on the porch." He brushed his palms against his slacks as they walked to the house. He picked up his suit. Curious, she opened his fast food bag and sniffed.

"Do you want to eat this, or would you prefer an inch-and-a-half-thick bone-in rib-eye?"

"You're not responsible for feeding me."

"I'm grilling anyway." She handed him the bag. "Did you read that article in the Wall Street Journal about fast-food chains and how cops sometimes got more than they ordered on their food?"

He followed her into the kitchen and dropped his burger into the trashcan.

"I'll take the steak. But I'm doing the grilling."

CHAPTER TWELVE

Tuesday morning, Darcy stood at the stove, dropping thick slices of battered bread onto a hot griddle. Last night, Eli had again helped with the dishes. Then he'd watched Monday night football while she'd prepped food for Carl. He'd walked around her house during commercials and half time and come into the kitchen to check on her and sneak bites of food.

She smiled. She hadn't been scared since he'd shown up at her house yesterday.

The phone rang. Still smiling, she picked up the kitchen extension with one hand and shook batter from the other. "Hello?"

"I hope I'm not calling too early, but I wanted to give you enough time in case you said yes."

Darcy struggled to identify the frantic voice—Eli's sister? "Brooke?"

"Yes? Oh! Sorry, I didn't tell you who was calling."

"Is that Brooke?" Eli entered the kitchen and headed for the coffee maker, his brown trousers belted and brown uniform shirt partially buttoned.

Darcy nodded as her throat constricted. "Brooke, is everything all right?" she managed to ask.

"No, I have an emergency."

"What kind of emergency?" Darcy barely finished the words before Eli plucked the phone from her hand.

"What's wrong?" Eli asked. As he listened, his shoulders relaxed. He returned the phone to Darcy. "This is your department." Green eyes stared. "Where's your sling?"

"I'll put it on when I finish cooking." She breathed a sigh of relief as he left the kitchen. She put the receiver to her ear.

"What can I help you with, Brooke?"

As she talked, she transferred golden slices of French toast onto a plate and added two pieces of medium-crisp bacon before sliding it under a warming lamp.

"I have a showing at the Lost Creek Gallery at five tonight, and my caterer canceled because her son broke his arm badly and is being medevaced to San Antonio for surgery. The only other caterer in town isn't answering her phone. I was about to pull my hair out when I remembered Eli said you catered for Border's. Could you possibly help me out?"

Darcy scooped up pen and paper. "How many people are you expecting, what's your budget, and what style of food do you want?"

"Peter, the gallery owner, has received forty-three positive RSVPs, and we should have some walk-ins. I don't know the budget because the cost comes out of Peter's commission. The caterer was going to do an appetizer buffet. Peter is handling beer, wine, and margaritas."

"Was she providing tables, tablecloths, napkins, or chafing dishes?"

"I don't know," Brooke wailed.

"Okay," Darcy said. "Here's the plan. First, give me Peter's phone numbers." She wrote down the numbers Brooke recited and repeated them back. "I'm going to call Peter, work out a menu, look at the gallery, and figure out what needs doing. I want you to make a cup of your favorite warm beverage and listen to relaxing music. I'll call you in two hours with an update."

"Darcy, you're a lifesaver."

"I'm happy to help. Tell Jeremy I said, how."

She sat and made notes.

The sheriff entered, knotting his tie. His pistol rode his hip. Handcuffs, cell phone, mace, and a flashlight occupied his wide leather belt. All thoughts of catering fled.

"You look very law officer-ish this morning," she said. His raised eyebrow only added to the impression.

He walked to the coffeepot. "Sounds like you have Brooke's emergency under control."

"This kind of trouble I know how to handle. Are you ready for breakfast? I made French toast and bacon. And, yes, I know I don't have to feed you. I'm testing menus. If it helps, think of yourself as a guinea pig."

He set his cup on the table. "I've eaten enough of your food not to feel threatened." He picked up a second mug. "What are you drinking?"

"Milk." She set their plates on the table while he poured

her milk and set the mug by her plate.

He took her notepad and scanned her list. "Will your arm hinder your cooking?"

She drizzled warm maple syrup over her toast. "No. The mixer does the heavy work."

"Looks like you'll need help." He sat.

She passed the syrup and watched as he poured until his toast swam in an amber sea. The man must have the metabolism of a four-year-old.

"Not with the cooking. I'll use the empanadas I made and froze for Border's and prepare something else tomorrow for Carl. I've outlined a menu. Oh!"

She tugged the pad back to scribble "microwave" then tapped the pen against her chin. "Brooke's show opens at five. I need to set up at the gallery between four and four-thirty depending on who's available to help."

"Peter must have employees."

"I'm counting on it." She set the pen aside and picked up her fork. "What are you doing today?"

"The usual—after I deliver an anti-drug speech to the middle school kids over in Dickins.

"That's why you're wearing your uniform?"

He nodded. "Kids pay more attention to uniforms than suits."

She chewed and swallowed a sliced strawberry. "I know. It always worked on me."

"Maybe I should wear it more often."

Darcy smiled and popped a last corner of toast into her

mouth before collecting and carrying their dishes to the sink. "I need to hurry."

He followed with their cups. "Give me your schedule; I'll call it in." He pulled the cell phone from his belt.

"Tell whoever's babysitting, that after I contact Peter, I'll view the gallery layout, shop for food, and start cooking." She followed him out on the porch and squelched a sudden urge to straighten his tie and kiss him goodbye. "Will you be at the gallery tonight?"

"Yes." He stopped on the top step and turned to face her, one finger ready to push his phone's call button. "Despite the RSVPs, Brooke has this crazy idea that no one will come and she'll be the only person there. I know better. In thirty minutes, she'll be too busy to acknowledge my presence."

"You're right. But she will cherish the fact that you cared enough to offer support."

She backed away. "You'd better get going; you don't want to be late for school."

Eli arrived at his cottage at three PM. He removed his uniform, showered, then dressed in pressed jeans and a denim shirt. His talk at the school had gone well. The remainder of his workday hadn't.

He entered the living room and paused. He hadn't realized how much Brooke's paintings had diverted attention from the monotone of the now bare beige walls, old brown couch, and scuffed coffee table. The cottage held none of the welcome and comfort of Darcy's house. He relaxed in her home and company.

He sat to tug on black ostrich boots. After two days of changing Darcy's bandage, he'd translated her nervous reactions as attraction to him.

The discovery had stunned and alarmed him. But, having expressed his attitude toward permanence, he knew that unless he made the first move, she would maintain her distance. He never got involved with someone that was involved in one of his investigations. Her witness status would keep him from making that move.

Spending nights at her place was the closest he'd come to living with a woman other than his mother and sister. Darcy's teasing and appreciation of pretty much everything diluted the stress of his job. She made him forget death, campaigning, and doubts—his own and his constituents. He was sleeping better. And eating her cooking had cut his antacid consumption.

Shrugging into a black sports coat, he tugged down on the lapels and sleeves. Darcy hadn't yet realized the fragile lifespan of relationships. Better to live without strings. Picking up a suit bag with clothes for tomorrow, he walked happily from the dim bareness of the cottage to the sunlight outside.

Eli glanced at the bins stacked outside Darcy's screen door. He paused for a moment to inhale the mix of sweet and savory scents. His stomach growled. She stood at a counter, stacking containers and singing along with an oldies station.

Her khaki skirt flirted with her knees; her white shirt possessed enough sleeve to cover her bandage. A fitted pink vest topped the shirt and emphasized her trim waist. His knock brought her head up with enough momentum to swing her long blonde braid forward. A smile replaced the fear that flickered across her face.

"Hi." She turned down the radio, wiped her hands on a towel, and then crossed to unlock the screen door. "You look nice. How did your talk go?"

How was your day, dear? The notion made his answer brusque. "Fine."

Her eyes widened. "Okay. Did you forget something?"

"No." He laid his suit bag across a chair. "I came to help you get everything to the gallery."

"That's great! I was about to load the car." She snapped a plastic lid over a large glass bowl loaded with pink, jumbo shrimp. "Everything outside the kitchen door goes. The rest of the food is in the refrigerator."

He walked outside and opened the back of her Explorer. She'd already cleared space and collapsed the back seat. He slid two folding tables inside then added chafers and utensils. When Darcy shouldered the door open, he sprang to the porch and relieved her of stacked containers.

"You're not supposed to lift."

"I'm not an invalid."

"No, you're not. Bring the napkins. I'll load the rest, and

I'll drive."

He hid a smile as she picked up a paper sack, made a show of locking the door, and followed him to the car, muttering under her breath.

"Brooke, if you move it one more time, Peter will pull out what's left of his hair."

Eli laid an arm across his sister's shoulders to restrict her reach toward another painting's frame. Brooke clasped her hands tightly behind her back. "Can you tell I'm nervous?"

"Loud and clear." He steered her toward the back of the gallery. "Come see what Darcy's done. If you haven't eaten, I'm sure she'll let you poach."

"So it's Darcy now?"

Her satisfied glance made him hesitate mid-stride. Calling Darcy by her first name was unprofessional. When had he stopped thinking of her as Ms. Cooper?

"Protection duty breeds first names."

"Then maybe you should suggest she call you Eli, instead of sheriff."

As the buffet came into view, Brooke's hands flew to her mouth. Darcy stood to one side, eyeing the arrangement.

"Darcy, you're amazing," Brooke said, walking forward. "I was prepared for Vienna sausages and baby carrots. How did you manage this?"

"Trade secret." Darcy smiled and expertly fanned a stack of cocktail napkins. "I could tell you, but then I'd have to hire you, and I think you're better off painting. By the way, you look great! Turquoise is definitely your color."

Brooke walked closer. "What did you make?"

"Beef empanadas, ranch biscuits with ham, tequila shrimp, roasted red pepper dip with vegetable sticks and crackers, assorted fresh berries, and miniature bread puddings for those with a sweet tooth."

She filled a plate and handed it to Brooke along with a travel-sized toothbrush and toothpaste. "Eat something before the show opens. It's difficult to market your work when your stomach speaks louder than your sales pitch."

"You thought of everything." Smiling, Brooke accepted the plate and headed for the kitchenette in the back room.

Eli stopped beside Darcy. "You're very attuned to others' needs."

She shrugged. "I guess it stems from moving so often as a kid. I made friends by figuring out other's likes and dislikes. And the hotel industry is a service business. The better the service, the happier the guests."

"What makes you happy?" Eli leaned against an antiqued plaster wall.

Her smile, when it came, illuminated the room. Slow, brilliant, childlike joy. How long had it been since he had last smiled with such genuine pleasure?

"That's easy," she laughed. "Belonging, being useful, seeing Brooke's face light up when she saw the buffet." She faced him. "What makes you happy, Sheriff?"

"You calling me Eli would make me happy."

Her face flushed before she turned away to move a platter two centimeters. "You're easy to please, Eli."

"Ms. Cooper, I understan' you're responsible for this delicious spread."

Darcy looked up. The white Stetson on the tall man's head made him appear even taller. He'd been the bar's best customer for the last hour. His slightly unfocused eyes fixated on her chest. She refused to be offended. Tonight, she'd passed out seven business cards to potential clients.

"Thank you. Yes, I prepared the food. Are you enjoying the artwork?"

"Yes, ma'am. I've bought four pictures for my ranch house." He leaned in and blasted her with beer fumes. "This is the breast bed pudding I ever tasted."

She bit her lip to keep from laughing at his misspeak then looked up as a familiar hand cupped the back of her neck. Eli's mouth formed a thin line.

"Darcy, the shrimp need restocking. I'll see that Mr. Grant gets a ride home."

"First make sure he's written a check for his four purchases," she whispered. Then louder, "Mr. Grant, I'm sure you'll receive many years of pleasure from Brooke's paintings."

Eli released her neck. She scanned the buffet and turned toward the kitchenette as Grant swerved towards Eli.

"She's a looker. And I hear she's not opposed to older men. I picked up her card off the counter." He held it up.

"Think I'll hire her for a private party."

Eli jerked Darcy's business card from Grant's hand and quick-walked the man to the gallery entrance. "Have you paid for your paintings?" he snapped.

"Yep. Got my receipt right here." Grant fumbled in his pocket and came up with a set of keys and a folded piece of paper. Eli took both, glanced at the paper, and then stuffed it in Grant's shirt pocket. He kept the keys. Outside, he hailed one of the off-duty deputies Peter had hired. Grant tried to push him away.

"Hey, I came in my truck, and I'm leavin' in my truck."

"Not tonight, Mr. Grant." A quick twist of Grant's arm staggered the man enough to fold him into the sedan's back seat. Eli tossed the keys to his deputy. "He doesn't get those back until you get him home."

"Yes sir, Sheriff."

Eli took a deep breath before returning inside. No one looked at him oddly, so he presumed his neutralization of Grant had gone unnoticed. Peter wouldn't approve of his removal method, so, to be safe, he'd tell Peter to deposit that check first thing in the morning. He scanned the room. Darcy had restocked the buffet, but he couldn't see her.

He checked the kitchenette then opened the back door and almost knocked her over. Her eyes were suspiciously moist. Her ghost of a smile tore at him.

"You heard that idiot mouth off," he said.

"So did everyone in that part of the gallery." She looked at her watch and set her shoulders like she faced a firing squad. "I should go back in and check the table."

"The food is fine. Take a break."

He led her down the narrow alley to the front of the gallery and steered her to the right. They passed a clothing boutique and a Texas-themed shop. The sun hid behind the buildings, but the streetlights hadn't blinked on yet. Eli pushed her gently onto a wrought iron bench then sat beside her.

"You're strong. Don't let a drunk break your spirit," he said. He silently applauded the hint of anger that showed in her eyes.

"It's my fault. People believe what they've heard from people they do know, and don't believe people they don't know. I have no proof, so I have no credibility. I'm still the woman who stole the Anderson's inheritance and ruined Alex and Cindy's true love legacy." She looked at him.

"Even if the rumor were true, Alex was one man. To deserve this degree of criticism in Dallas, I'd require a long and well-publicized history of seducing men for their money." She blew out a long breath. "Sorry, I'm venting."

He inhaled like he'd been body slammed. She'd denied a physical relationship with Alex. He tried not to acknowledge interest in her denial. Her personal life was none of his business except as it related to the case or actions taken against her. He shifted on the bench, not wanting to be curious but curiously wanting to comfort her.

"Alex was a homeboy, and Cindy was his woman. People can't figure out why he'd leave you anything if he weren't repaying a—favor."

She crossed her arms. "Well, he wasn't. We became good friends the minute we met, but we were never romantic, never intimate. Only I can't figure out how to prove that to people. I didn't know he'd chosen me to inherit his property until his lawyer contacted me after the funeral."

He lifted his hat and ran a hand through his hair. Given her actions and his intuition, Darcy's story rang true. She was what she appeared to be—a nice woman.

He shifted to face her.

"The first rule of fighting—never let them see they've hurt you. Eventually, they'll stop thinking of you as Alex's lover and accept you. It'll take time."

"Is that how you deal with your political opponents?"

He nodded. "And don't count on changing everyone's minds. Some people are only willing to believe what makes them comfortable."

She pulled a napkin from her pocket and wiped her nose. "I've only faced the rumors for a month. I'm a wimp."

"Impulsive, optimistic, an occasional pain—I've thought you all of those, but never a wimp. All actions—real or perceived—have consequences, some foreseeable, some not. You deal with consequences as they arise. The next time someone says something hurtful, think one of your happy thoughts."

"Good advice. Thanks."

Her hug caught him by surprise. His arms tightened, and he breathed in her honeysuckle scent. Aggravated with his response, he loosened his hold. Darcy continued to grip tight, her breath warm against his ear, her voice a whisper.

"Eli, I see Raul."

CHAPTER THIRTEEN

"Has Raul seen you?"

Eli cupped the back of Darcy's exposed head. The plate-glass window in his view reflected nothing useful. His free hand eased between them to release the snap on his holster.

"I don't think so. He's in a light-colored car up and across from the gallery. I think that's where he's looking. If he hadn't lit a cigarette, I wouldn't have noticed him."

Eli turned her face into his shoulder, shielding her from Raul's view and exposing his back. He hadn't felt this vulnerable since his last mission in Afghanistan.

"Two people are leaving the gallery and walking toward us." Darcy's quiet words brushed across his ear.

"Stand up and stay between me and the building. Walk casually."

He glanced toward the sedan and its occupant. Mud obscured the license plate. Keeping his arm around her shoulders, he extracted his cell phone as they walked.

"This is Whitepath. Ask Lost Creek P. D. to block Main at Creekside and Drury. The suspect known as Raul is in a tan four-door sedan across from the Lost Creek Art Gallery. Assume he's armed. Let me know—"

The sedan roared into the street and sprang toward them.

Eli shoved Darcy toward the alley and drew his Glock.

One tire climbed the curb then descended. The couple froze in his field of view. He aimed his pistol upwards as Raul disappeared around the corner. Eli holstered his .45, picked up his phone, and gripped Darcy's hand. "Inside!"

They sprinted to the gallery's back door. "Suspect is eastbound on Creekside from Main. Keep me advised." He pocketed the phone. Darcy held her elbows in a self-hug.

"Are you all right?"

She nodded, her eyes huge. Reluctantly, he spread his arms. "Come here."

Without hesitation, she walked into his embrace. Her arms wrapped around his waist, her face burrowed against his chest. He held her and smoothed her hair, trying to calm her fear with comfort.

He lifted her sleeve to check her stitches. They had held.

"Is this the first time you've almost been run down?" he asked.

Her short laugh encouraged him.

"Yes. You?"

"The cars are oh-for-four."

She looked up, brown eyes wide, pupils dilated.

"Occupational hazard," he said.

She laughed.

"Feel better?"

"No."

He gently brushed loose hair from her cheek.

"Oh!" Brooke spun a one-eighty then completed a three-sixty and looked at them closely.

Eli muted a curse and held Darcy in place. How had he not heard Brooke approach?

"What happened?"

"Darcy spotted one of the attackers outside."

"Is he still out there?" Brooke glanced toward the door leading into the gallery.

"He took off. The city police are looking for him."

Brooke touched Darcy's arm. "I came to tell you that the show is closing. Peter said cleanup can wait until tomorrow morning. I'll put the leftovers in the fridge. You two should leave."

Darcy pushed gently against his chest. Eli let her go.

"Raul was following me, right?" Darcy asked.

Eli glanced at her. "It looks that way."

The sun was setting behind her house when they entered the driveway. Darcy leaned forward.

"I could have sworn I turned on the porch and security lights."

Eli veered left, making her thankful she hadn't unbuckled her seatbelt. He parked under a stand of live oaks.

"Stay in the car." He took her keys, walked to her house, climbed the steps, and vanished around the corner. Leaning forward, she held her breath until his familiar length glided along the porch. He used her key to enter through the door.

Ten agonizing minutes later, he returned to the porch and holstered his pistol. He examined the porch sconces with the flashlight function on his cell phone then walked to the breaker box attached to the floodlight's pole and flipped a breaker. Light flooded the yard. He walked back to the car.

"The house?" she asked, her throat tight.

"All clear." He started the engine and drove to the graveled parking area. "Your doors and windows are locked. The porch bulbs are loose, and someone shut off the floodlight breaker. I'm calling in a deputy with a fingerprint kit. Do you have a padlock you can put on the breaker box after they finish?"

"No, but I'll buy one tomorrow."

Darcy climbed the porch steps. Beside the door, a grapefruit-sized rock anchored a stack of mail. She gathered the letters into her sling then gripped a corner of the box. "I must have missed the postman this afternoon. He usually rings the doorbell when he comes to the house."

Eli hauled her backward. Her fingers curled, tipping the package. Her surprised cry turned to fright as a pair of snakes slithered from beneath the box.

Eli's arm circled her waist as her back attempted to merge with his chest. One snake slid to the steps and continued into the grass. The second coiled and began to rattle its tail.

Darcy held her breath as Eli reached for a long-handled paint roller leaning against the house. One moment the snake menaced. The next, Eli pinned its head to the porch. "Hold the roller," he said.

She did. Eli pinched the rattlesnake behind its head and gripped its body behind the roller. "Lift," he said.

He carried the snake to the yard, knelt on its length, pulled out a knife, and cut off its head.

"What about the other one?"

Eli rose. "It probably headed for the pasture."

She nudged the upturned box with her foot. "No bottom on the box."

"Get inside."

Eli lifted the box with his knuckles.

She let him pass, then switched on the foyer light and twisted the deadbolt closed.

"I need a paper bag," he said.

Grateful for a task, she led him to the pantry and shook a bag open.

He secured the box and folded the top of the bag closed. Setting it on the counter, he dialed his cell phone.

"Talk to me," he said, then listened. "Let me know if anything changes, and send a deputy with a fingerprint kit to Ms. Cooper's." He hung up.

"Raul got away?" she guessed.

"Yes." He cupped her elbow and led her into the living room, bypassing the couch stacked with pillows and linens to seat her in an armchair. "I'll be right back."

He returned minutes later and handed her a steaming mug of hot chocolate. "Drink this."

"Thanks."

She sipped. Raul's attempted hit and run, and the snake

threat had emptied her comfort reserves. "So either Raul came here first, or someone else paid my house a visit."

"I don't know yet." Eli sat on the coffee table, facing her.

The mug warmed her hands, and the chocolate warmed her stomach. "Any suggestions?"

She waited as he went into one of his contemplative silences. Whatever he said, or didn't say, next, must be important to require that much thought. Finally, he spoke.

"A month ago, I wrote myself in for a few days off. I want you to come with me."

Mr. I-don't-do-permanent was asking her to go on vacation with him? Say yes, her brain screamed.

"Why?"

"You need protection, and I need to process threats, evidence, and possible connections. I'll be performing a vision quest while you stay at my uncle's ranch."

"A vision quest?"

"My uncle started me on them when I was six. At first, he disguised them as camping trips. At ten, I had my first revelation—that the time alone was mind-clearing and allowed me to focus on and resolve my problems. I usually come away with answers, so I make it an annual trip."

Darcy smiled. "It sounds like a version of prayer. I've been doing a lot of that lately. Are you sure your relatives won't mind me coming?"

"Don't worry. Aunt Mary will put you to work. You won't even know I'm gone."

"Will your deputies watch my house?" She was looking

forward to the trip, but she didn't want to appear too eager.

"They will."

She stood. "Unless you need a statement from me tonight, I'm taking a shower and going to sleep. I need to think about the remodel schedule before I give you an answer."

Eli studied her. "I'll give a statement to the deputy when he arrives. We'll be busy for a while."

A thought made her smile fade. "What about your campaign? Should you leave town now?"

"Politically, no. But I never come back from a vision quest without answers of some kind."

She was careful not to brush his knees as she edged from the chair. "Goodnight, Eli."

A moment of silence. Did he already regret suggesting they use first names?

"Goodnight, Darcy."

The weight of his gaze followed her from the room.

He was strong, steady, and honorable. He made her feel safe—and he made her want more. Precisely what he didn't want.

Wednesday morning, Darcy woke later than usual. Faint noises from Eli and the deputy, and questions and what-ifs, had kept her awake long after she'd gone to bed.

When she walked into the kitchen, she noticed that Eli's truck was gone and that Detective Wainright was walking around outside her house, looking at the ground. Having dressed, she carried a cup of coffee out to him.

"Have you found anything?"

"There are a lot of footprints out here."

"I still have a remodeling crew working." She handed him the cup.

"Thanks." He sipped, watching her. "I hear your couch is comfortable."

Darcy felt her jaw tighten. "Good to hear. I want comfy furniture for my guests. If you hear of anyone needing a bed and breakfast, you can recommend me."

"The sheriff asked me to follow you into town after I got a list of your errands."

"Give me fifteen minutes?"

He nodded and continued his circle.

Wainright waved and accelerated away as Darcy parked at the hardware store. She bought a padlock then drove to the gallery to load her dishes and utensils. At the grocery store, she shopped for empanada ingredients.

She drove home and carried her groceries inside, then walked to the breaker box. The new padlock fastened with a secure snap.

Friday afternoon the phone rang as Darcy set two pans of empanadas on potholders to cool.

"Hello?" she answered.

"Hey, young 'un. Can you swing by early tonight?" Carl asked.

A Texas tornado whirled in her stomach. Was she about

to lose her favorite catering account?

"Of course. Is there a problem?"

"Nah. I want to talk to you before things get busy. See you when you get here."

She baked the last batches while packing her new picnic basket. Had she been optimistic about buying the basket?

She entered the roadhouse at four.

"Hey, Carl," she called past the boulder in her throat. "Do you want to talk now, or after I set up?"

"Shirley!" He bellowed the waitress over. "Take care of the food, would you?" He pushed the picnic basket in the blonde's direction then motioned Darcy behind the bar. "Let's talk in the office where we won't be disturbed."

"Use the reheat setting on the microwave," Darcy called over her shoulder to Shirley. "The heat lamps will hold them from there." She slipped behind the bar and through the door that opened into Carl's cubbyhole office. The room barely held a tiny metal desk, two metal-framed chairs, and random piles of paper. He used empty liquor boxes as filing cabinets.

"Have a seat." Carl removed a stack of invoices from the second chair and transferred them to his desk. "Young'un, I thought long and hard before asking you to come in early, but things always came down to what's best for the community."

Darcy's stomach turned over. Carl had supported her from the moment she'd shown up and sold him on serving snacks.

"Word's getting around that the sheriff's spending his

nights at your house."

She nodded. "The word is true. The sheriff believes that the men who attacked Lisa Lantz and me might try again. He's been staying on my couch to keep me safe."

He frowned. "Why would those guys come after you again?"

"You'd have to ask the sheriff," Darcy hedged. "But one of them tried to run me down last night, and then someone left rattlesnakes on my porch. I was glad to have the sheriff there both times."

Carl patted her shoulder. "I like the sheriff. I voted for him four years ago, and I'll vote for him again in November. When I tend bar, I hear a lot of talk. So I'm not saying this to hurt you; I'm saying this so you'll know what's going on." He folded his arms. "Some folks are suggesting that the sheriff's taken up where they think Alex left off."

Darcy stiffened. "What have you heard?"

"Folks are saying—well, they're saying it's time for a change. That maybe that son-of-a-gun Wainright would be a better choice because the sheriff's too caught up with you to catch the men selling the drugs that are killing our kids."

She jumped to her feet. "That's ridiculous! The sheriff is working hard to catch them."

"Now don't go getting all flustered. Folks have to blame somebody, and you're the newcomer. They'll eat your food and give you credit for saving Lisa Lantz, but you're still a convenient scapegoat. And you're not the only hitch. The sheriff runs a tight ship, but he's got a leak. The newspaper coverage is slanted. Someone's talking, and I have my suspicions."

"Wainright." Darcy clenched her fists. "I've ruined Eli's career."

"Maybe not." Carl stroked his beard. "Could someone else stay with you nights? A female officer?"

"Don't worry; I'll take care of this rumor." She straightened her shoulders. "Are you canceling your Friday orders?"

Carl stood. "Shoot, no! Friday night sales revenues are up ten percent. I'd be a fool to fire you and a bigger fool to kick a friend when she's down." He rounded the desk. "Think about what I said. When you take away the fuel, the fire goes out. If I can help, you let me know. Now I'll walk you out."

"No need, a deputy is waiting for me. Thanks for the heads up, Carl." She hugged him.

Outside, she crossed the parking lot, her mind raced. Helping her was harming Eli. Today was September twenty-first—was there enough time to salvage his reelection bid?

When she beeped her car open, she realized a deputy no longer parked beside her car. A hand clamped her shoulder. She recoiled violently.

"Of all the places to walk with your head in the clouds, this is the worst," Eli said.

She released a shaky breath as she opened her car and set the picnic basket on the backseat. He opened her driver's door while scanning the lot. She sat inside.

He filled the open door. "I'll follow you to your place."

"No!" She lowered her voice. "We need to talk. Here. Now."

"Make it quick."

"I'm worried about your reputation."

His eyebrows rose. "That's a first."

"I'm serious. You know people talk about me. They've learned you're staying nights at my place—they're calling you my new Alex."

"And your point is?"

"You knew?" She crossed her arms. "Protecting me shouldn't cost you your job."

He looked toward the open field with an unreadable expression on his face. "My job is to serve and protect. The only people who should know I'm staying at your place are in my department. If one or more has chosen to cause me trouble, the damage is done. If I don't do my job, I don't deserve to keep it."

"Wainright," Darcy said bitterly.

"Maybe."

"Can you assign a deputy to stay with me?"

"Full-time surveillance requires extra shifts and extra expense. My deputies need computers more than overtime."

"They need you too."

He glanced around. "We'll talk about it at your house."

She looked out her windshield at a couple staring from a few rows away. More gossip in the making? "We'll talk about it now."

Eli followed her glance. "Let me close your door. I'll follow you home."

She braced her hand on the door. "I don't want you coming to my house again."

"Darcy, you know you're in danger."

"I mean it, Sheriff. You can't stay if I don't let you."

She didn't relish being alone nights, but she wouldn't let her fear cost Eli his job and Lost Creek a good sheriff.

"You saw Raul last night. He won't have gone far," he said, his voice hard.

She glanced around the lot. Raul and Randy, aka the ghoul, lurked somewhere, waiting for an opportunity to retrieve their heroin or a pound of flesh.

She dredged up anger—anger with herself for being unable to exonerate herself, Alex, and Eli—and anger at Wainright for using her to compromise Eli.

"I'm not changing my mind. I'm refusing your protection, and I won't be going to Colorado with you."

"Because of the rumors?" He reached for her arm.

His touch would undo her. Panicked, she said what she was trying to avoid saying. The thing she'd realized the first night he'd stayed at her house.

"No, Sheriff. Not just because of the rumors. My Gramma would turn over in her grave if she knew a Comanche was sleeping in my house."

His aggravated but concerned gaze changed to confused, then froze to green ice.

She'd drawn blood.

Darcy blinked away tears as the taillights of Eli's truck

receded down the county road.

He had followed her home despite her directive. But instead of driving to the house, he'd parked outside the entrance to her property. She'd wondered if he'd planned to spend the night until a patrol car arrived and took his place.

He wasn't leaving her unprotected.

Her fear eased, but pain and guilt continued to erode her composure. He was wrecking his budget to keep her safe. She sank to a seat on the porch swing.

If only she'd had more time to think of how to convince him he shouldn't stay.

She scrubbed her cheeks with her palms. He'd left her no choice. That the rumors affected her was one thing. She wouldn't let them hurt him too.

Two sharp reports, a pause, and two more reports produced a tight group centered on the silhouette target's chest. An identical pattern perforated the silhouette's head.

When the slide locked back, Eli ejected the empty magazine and laid the .45- caliber semiautomatic on the counter. With the flip of a switch, the target whirred forward. He scrawled the distance, date, and his name across the bottom.

A speed loader facilitated the refilling of three magazines. He slapped one in his pistol, then closed the action and holstered his gun. He secured the spare magazines in his belt sheath. Over two hundred brass shell casings littered the battleship-gray, concrete floor.

Leaving ear protectors, safety glasses, and targets on the counter, he signed out. At a quarter to midnight, he was the only shooter on the range. His steps echoed—as the gunshots had—in the long room. Darcy's declaration that her grandmother wouldn't like her having an Indian in her house replayed in a mental surround sound.

She took the rumors about her and Alex in stride, but when people associated her with him, she threw his heritage in his face. He hadn't thought she'd had it in her.

He shoved the glass doors with more force than necessary, rattling the doorframe.

Long ago he'd restricted his emotional life to Brooke and Jeremy. Darcy, with her ready laugh and her gift for listening, had breached his defenses. He knew better than to become personally involved with a witness. Guilty of violating his own rule, he now paid the price. He wouldn't forget again.

CHAPTER FOURTEEN

Darcy reached from under the covers to grope the nightstand surface until she encountered the persistently ringing landline.

"Hello?"

"You have something of mine."

The distinctive reverberation of a rattlesnake tail echoed through the phone's receiver, clearing Darcy's sleep-fogged brain. She shot up among the covers.

"You should know by now that I've turned your heroin over to law enforcement. Why don't you call them?"

"Next time, golden girl."

A buzzing dial tone replaced the buzz of the snake and the masculine whisper.

Next time?

Slamming the receiver down, she wrestled her bat from between the bed and nightstand and rested the reassuring weight atop the covers. She looked at the clock. Five AM.

The caller ID blinked number unavailable. She switched the answering machine to automatic pickup.

She jumped out of bed and ran to the window. The cruiser remained by her gate. She could have invited the deputy in last night, but she hadn't wanted a witness to her pain or, if the deputy was a man, to start more rumors.

She carried the bat down the hall and rechecked the door and window locks she'd checked last night. Someone wanted her scared. Her shoulders straightened in defiance, but her hands shook as she set the bat aside, turned on the kitchen light, and picked up a broom.

Today Eli left for his vision quest. The selfish part of her didn't want him to go. And despite what she'd said to him, she knew he'd come if she called—and they'd both suffer for his sense of duty. The man needed a break. He'd come back with answers, feeling more relaxed, and perhaps feeling some forgiveness?

She started sweeping. If she told the deputy outside about the call, he'd radio it in, and Eli might find out before he left. She could tell Detective Wainright, but that felt like conspiring with Eli's enemy. Or—she could call Lisa and have her promise not to tell Dan until tonight when Eli would be in Colorado.

She set the broom aside to flex her injured arm, then reached for the mop.

Even if she explained her hurtful statement and apologized to Eli, a second chance with him wouldn't come easily. She hadn't burned that bridge; she'd done a demolition job. She rinsed the mop. If an alternative to driving him away existed, she still hadn't thought of it.

Someone knocked on the kitchen door. Darcy looked outside before opening it. "Good morning."

"Yes, ma'am." The Deputy looked doubtful. "It's early,

and I saw your lights come on."

"Thanks for checking on me. I'm doing housework. If you're hungry, I can bring a mug of coffee and some banana nut muffins to the table on the porch. You'll have a good view of the driveway and sunrise from there."

He perked up. "Yes, ma'am. And if you don't mind, I've heard about your chocolate chip cookies."

Eli drank his coffee at the kitchen sink. The small kitchen didn't tolerate disorder—neither did he. His military training, he supposed. He looked out the window and saw Brooke approaching. Without Darcy around to distract him, his situational awareness skills had reasserted themselves. Swallowing the last of the coffee, he rinsed the cup. Not as good as Darcy's coffee.

He shoved the thought aside.

"I suppose that was your breakfast." Brooke pushed the screen door open and nearly tripped over his duffle bag. "And I see you're leaving for Colorado."

"Yes. And yes." He plucked a denim jacket from the back of a chair and walked to the door.

"You said Darcy was going with you."

He didn't break stride.

"Change of plans. She doesn't travel with Indians."

When the sun came up, the deputy left Darcy's with a list of her plans for the day. She had finished mopping the kitchen floor and moved on to the living room where the furniture now shone and smelled like lemons.

She sat at the kitchen table and made notes. When she got to, who wants me to leave town, she snagged the phone book and scanned beauty shop listings. Carl had told her that Keith's sister, Angela, cut hair. But he hadn't mentioned her married name.

She started dialing. The search didn't take long once she mentioned Keith Anderson recommended his sister. The receptionist at the first salon she called gave her the number. She booked an appointment for Monday and hung up without leaving her name.

At nine AM, she called Lisa.

"What's this I hear about you and Eli almost being run over?" Lisa asked.

"True. Unfortunately, Raul got away."

"Don't worry, they'll be caught. Now, why are you calling? Dan is making breakfast, and I'm eating when he says it's ready because I'm encouraging him to continue the habit after the baby comes. I'm going to be worn out by the feedings, changings and all of the cuddling."

"I need to tell you something to tell Dan, but you can't tell him until tonight before you go to bed."

"This sounds serious or kinky."

"Promise me you won't tell him until tonight?"

"If you insist, I promise."

Darcy related the early morning phone call.

"I think I should tell Dan now. I also wonder why you haven't called Eli yet."

"Who do you want to win the sheriff's election?"

"Eli, of course."

"Have you heard the rumors?"

"About you and Alex or you and Eli?"

Darcy winced. "Me and Eli. He left for his annual vision quest today. I want him to clear his head."

"Dan told me about that tradition. He's amazed how refreshed and focused Eli is when he returns from those. It would be a shame if he missed it with all he's dealing with."

"Tell me some good news," Darcy said.

"The good news is the doctor says my pregnancy is going fine. The bad news is I haven't seen my feet in a month."

Darcy laughed for the first time since insulting Eli. "Come on, admit you love every aspect of your pregnancy."

"Not every aspect." Lisa snorted. "Would you like to see your gynecologist ten times in one year, or not be able to roll onto your stomach when it's your favorite sleeping position?"

"Good points," Darcy conceded. A seed of a plan came to her. "Who's your doctor? I'm due for an annual exam, and I need a recommendation." She wrote down the information as Lisa recited it.

"Oh! Breakfast is ready. Gotta go!" Lisa said.

"Thanks!"

"I'm going pay for keeping this secret until tonight, but making up is always fun. See you!"

Saturday evening, Mr. Owens called from the auto garage.

Her window had arrived and could be installed Monday morning if she dropped her car off at nine AM. Darcy agreed.

Sunday, Dan called and scolded for withholding information after she'd received the threatening phone call. He told her to call Wainright and report the call. She did.

Monday morning, Darcy checked in with the independent living home attendant.

"Are you sure you want to do this? I heard about what happened last time." The woman sent her a look that seemed to question Darcy's sanity.

"Absolutely. As long as I'm not over-exciting anyone."

"The last time you came, they were more energized than I've seen them in a long time. They talked all day and into the night. The administrator thinks your visits are good for them—in moderation. What did you bring today?"

"Mini loaves of banana bread and zucchini bread. I thought they'd make a nice morning snack. I brought enough for the staff too."

The woman's eyes brightened. "Thanks. Several of us tried your cookies last time; they were delicious. Once word gets out about the bread, there won't be leftovers. We turn right, here."

Darcy nodded. "I remember."

They walked into the recreation room.

"Who wants banana or zucchini bread?" the attendant asked in her perky voice. Everyone turned to look. Most of the men raised their hands. Other hands rose to switch off or remove hearing aids. Darcy kept smiling; she'd come prepared.

She slipped on serving gloves, picked up two boxes, and started at the nearest table. "Does anyone have a preference?"

Some of the residents answered; some ignored her. She dispensed the loaves as directed—or with her best guess— adding a slip of paper with each serving.

"What's this?" One man adjusted his glasses and read aloud: "Coming soon breaking news."

Darcy smiled. She'd finally figured out a way to get her message across.

"Keep your ears and minds open. The next rumor you hear might be the truth," she said.

Three-quarters of the way through serving, WOP! A loaf of bread hit her squarely in the back. Darcy kept smiling. More of the residents were talking to her and asking questions. She was making progress.

Half an hour later, Darcy left her car at Owens' Garage and walked three blocks to the Coif & Curl. Inside, a brunette with familiar hazel eyes greeted her. "Hi, I'm Angela. Are you my eleven o'clock?"

"I am. Thanks for taking me on such short notice."

"I know you want a trim. Do you want a shampoo?"

Darcy nodded. "Yes. I think I have some of my morning snacks in my hair."

She followed Angela to a shampoo station. She placed

them at about the same age. Angela's brown hair and slim build contrasted with Keith's blondeness and stockiness. She relaxed under the combined influence of warm water and Angela's scalp massage.

"Whatever is in your hair smells like bananas," Angela said. "Were you at a party?"

"Something like that."

"Well, it's out now. What's your name?" Angela continued to massage.

Darcy took a deep breath. "I'm Darcy Cooper. And I know you're Keith's sister; you have the same eyes."

Those eyes went flat, and Angela's massage became more like bread-kneading. She rinsed Darcy's hair and wrapped a towel around the wet mass. Darcy followed Angela's stiff shoulders to a styling station.

"People from the sheriff's department came by last night." Angela's face mirrored the wary set of her body language. She picked up a comb then set it down.

Darcy met her eyes. "I was told they'd question your entire family. I'm sorry if it was upsetting."

Angela shrugged. "The detective was nice. And my kids were already in bed."

"I'm glad. I apologize for not giving my name, but I wanted to meet you, and I was afraid you wouldn't talk to me if you knew who I was. And I do need my bangs and ends trimmed."

Angela chewed a thumbnail. "I shouldn't. Not after Uncle Alex and all. I drew strength from his and Aunt

Cindy's marital commitment. I hoped that their luck ran in the family. I might not believe in happily ever after anymore, but Keith says you're okay. I called him after the detective left."

Angela went to work combing out and pinning up sections of Darcy's hair.

"Don't give up on happily ever after, "Darcy said. "My grandparents overcame a lot before they found theirs. Alex and Cindy probably did too." Darcy took a deep breath and continued. "The rumors about Alex and me are just that—rumors. He didn't betray Cindy."

"Only his family?"

Angela made her first cut. Darcy glanced at the floor and breathed a sigh of relief. It looked like she would get the trim she'd asked for instead of a scalping.

"Did you know that Lost Creek has one of the lowest divorce rates in the country?" Angela continued. "People come here to be married because they believe happiness is something they can take away with them. And if believing can make it so, maybe they're lowering the divorce rates where they live. I guess I haven't entirely given up believing, but I've sure modified my expectations."

"It must have been wonderful having Alex and Cindy as an uncle and aunt."

"They got along much better than my parents did. I should have realized a long time ago that their love was the result of dedication to one another."

Darcy stretched to pick up a business card, glanced at it,

then slipped it into her pocket. Angela's last name was Ryan.

"Keith says you've done a nice job remodeling the old house. I was pretty young when we lived there. Everything seemed too big—the furniture, the rooms, Uncle Alex. I was glad to move."

"Did you hear about the vandalism at the house last month?"

Was it her imagination, or had Angela tensed?

"I read about it in the paper."

"Does that kind of thing often happen in Lost Creek?"

"You'd have to ask the police. Why ask me?"

"I thought that since you've lived here all your life, you might have heard something a newcomer like me might not have."

Angela shook her head. "No one's told me anything."

Darcy released a breath that lifted her newly trimmed bangs. All she'd learned from her inept questioning was that Angela's marriage hadn't lived up to her dreams, she hadn't liked living in the house, and she didn't seem to hold a grudge.

She shifted the two plastic bags she toted. The salon was close to the garage and grocery, so she was accomplishing her errands on foot. The bank's LED display relayed a temperature approaching ninety. She kept to the shade of the Monterrey oaks lining the sidewalk as she approached Owen's Garage. Mr. Owens had kept his word. Her car, parked beneath a massive elm, held a new window.

Leaving the groceries in the car, she headed inside to sign paperwork. From the second of three garage bays, a mechanic with overlong black hair watched her approach. She hadn't noticed him when she'd dropped off the car. A grease-stained uniform covered his lanky frame. Hostility filled his dark eyes and narrow face. He held a lug wrench in one hand and slapped it against his empty palm.

Yet another fan. Darcy crossed the seemingly infinite distance to the office. The empty room echoed her, "Hello?" Mr. Owens had said he'd be in all day. She could wait inside, away from the mechanic with an attitude, but she had fresh chicken thighs in the car.

Maybe the wrench slapping wasn't personal. Maybe his girlfriend had run away this morning with someone who didn't enjoy intimidating women.

When she stepped back outside, he hadn't moved.

"I'm looking for the owner; do you know when he'll be back?"

His hostile stare intensified.

No, Darcy thought. Fate couldn't be this twisted. She glanced at his embroidered name patch—Greg.

"Mr. Ryan, I presume."

"Keith said you were smart." Obsidian eyes appraised her.

She'd wanted to meet Angela's husband, but meeting Greg was like encountering a pit bull that needed one-on-one time with a dog whisperer. "Can you tell me when Mr. Owens will return?"

Greg leaned towards her. "So you're the woman Alex

took up with and left everything to."

Her uneasiness grew as Greg's wrench slapping continued. He circled her, and she turned with him, unwilling to expose her back to him.

"When do you expect Mr. Owens?"

"I heard you got beat up at Border's. You bite off more then you could chew?" He ended the statement in her face as a white sedan entered the lot with Mr. Owens behind the wheel.

"How do you like livin' in that old house? Lots of varmints around?"

"Varmints?"

"You know, spiders, scorpions, snakes. You're not scared of varmints are you?"

Before she could answer, Mr. Owens approached.

"Ms. Cooper, I hope you haven't waited long. The paperwork for your insurance claim is ready for you to sign."

"I'll be right in," she said.

Mr. Owens went inside. When the door closed, Greg spoke.

"The thing about varmints is that you never know when or where they'll turn up."

"Snakes can be trapped, Mr. Ryan. And then you can cut their heads off."

She escaped into the office before her knocking knees betrayed her.

That afternoon, Darcy stood barefoot on the upstairs balcony applying varnish to the door's exterior. Painting it herself helped her budget, and the varnish should dry to touch by dark.

She backed away and squinted from several angles. Finding no drips, she walked to the rail and raised her face to the cool breeze.

Soon, the balcony would hold a wicker loveseat and table—a perfect place for guests to read, watch sunrises, and share romantic interludes. As she dismissed the last image, a capricious wind blew the door shut with a bang.

She reached for the doorknob and encountered two cutouts with the internal workings of the knobs. The door had latched. For ten minutes, she poked and prodded with her fingers and the paintbrush handle.

She frowned through the glass at the roll of paper towels lying on the floor inside. Resigned, she wiped her hands on her happy face T-shirt then settled the varnish lid into place with a few taps.

Stranded on the eight-by-six-foot balcony, she surveyed her predicament. What would she do if Randy or the ghoul chose this afternoon to appear? Dump varnish on his head?

The ground was further than she cared to drop. She leaned over the railing and ran her fingertips along one of the rough-cut cedar posts. If she shimmied down one, she'd spend weeks picking splinters from her arms and legs.

She scooted over the balcony railing onto the porch roof and tugged on a window. An engine rumbled from the road. Spooked, she crouched on the roof until the vehicle came into view. Brooke's van! Darcy pulled off her T-shirt and waved wildly.

Brooke turned in and disappeared until she walked around the side of the house, her neck craned back.

"Do you often flag down cars with your shirt?"

"Only when I've locked myself out." Darcy finished tugging her shirt into place. "Could you unlock a window? I keep a spare key under the flat rock beneath the bird feeder near the kitchen door."

In minutes, Brooke appeared and opened a window. Once inside, Darcy used a screwdriver to reopen the balcony door. She looked it over.

"At least I won't have to re-varnish it." She propped a tennis shoe in the doorframe. "I'm glad you stopped."

"I thought Eli had deputies patrolling this road."

"He does. If you hadn't come along, I'd have flagged the next one down. Join me for iced tea?"

"Sure."

They walked to the kitchen. "Your show seemed to go well," Darcy said.

"Better than I expected. I sold most of my paintings and accepted commissions for several more." Brooke leaned a hip against the kitchen counter. "Did you notice the painting of the two braves holding knives and circling each other?"

"Of course. You captured their concentration—each watching the other for an opening to strike without being struck. It is compelling."

"Anger is a powerful emotion," Brooke mused. "The problem with fighting—physical or verbal—is that it can inflict deep wounds, and if not treated quickly, those wounds fester and don't heal well or at all."

Darcy tensed. Had Eli talked to Brooke? Before she could ask, Brooke smiled.

"I didn't show one painting. It's a favorite of mine, and I wouldn't sell it. But I thought you'd like to see it. I'll be right back."

Darcy had two glasses of tea poured when Brooke returned and propped a cloth-covered canvas on a counter against the upper cabinets. She removed the cloth.

Darcy's breath caught. She stared.

Eli stared back, arms crossed over his chest, legs splayed, hips clad in a dark blue breechcloth, his lean body burnished copper. Long, wind-whipped hair framed a defiant face.

"How old was he?" she asked softly.

"Twenty-six."

A tormented pain shadowed his extraordinary green eyes.

"What had happened to him?"

"Death. Tours of duty in undisclosed locations while serving in a Ranger reconnaissance group. He was a sniper; Dan was his spotter. Eli's never formed a lasting friendship—except for Dan. I don't know what brought them together, but I'm grateful for Dan's presence in Eli's life."

Brooke shook her head. "Sixteen years rolled back when Eli smiled at you during breakfast last week."

Darcy hugged her elbows. There was a lot she didn't know, would probably never know, about what Eli had seen or done or survived. She knew him as an honorable man who performed his job because of the need that existed, not because of the political gain it offered. And she'd dealt him more pain. She stepped back.

"Thank you for showing me." She covered the canvas; her hand lingered on the cloth. "Has Eli talked to you?"

"No." Brooke shifted in her chair. "But before he left for Colorado, when I asked if you were going with him, he said you didn't travel with Indians."

Darcy closed her eyes. "I didn't want to hurt him, but he wouldn't listen when I told him he couldn't stay here nights."

"Why did you change your mind about him staying?"

Darcy sat across from Brooke. She repeated Friday's scene, starting with Carl's warning that people were talking about Eli staying at her house, and ending with how she convinced Eli to not stay at her home.

"Did you mean what you said about your grandmother not liking your seeing a Native American?" Brooke asked.

"I said a Comanche, not a Native American."

"Is there a difference?"

"There is if you're Sioux."

Brooke's eyes widened. "Your grandmother was Sioux?"

"Yes. And as a child, Gramma grew up hearing how her great-aunt was kidnapped in a Comanche raid. The family never found her, never knew what became of her."

Brooke nodded. "Well, that's good."

Darcy blinked.

Brooke quickly added, "It's good because you didn't lie to Eli." She paused to drink her tea. "You were clever but truthful. He'll appreciate the subtlety of your statement—eventually. If he hadn't taken it personally, he'd have already questioned your word choice."

"He won't spare me any kind of thought any time soon."

"Eli likes you."

"Not anymore."

"I've seen how he looks at you, how he reacts to you. He's protective of women. But because Mother fell apart and leaned on him after father died when Eli was a boy, and I fell apart and leaned on him after Jeremy's father died when Eli was a man; he views women as care-requirers, not caregivers."

Brooke grinned. "Your rejection of his protection must have thrown him. When his anger and pain subside, and you've explained, he'll realize that you put him first."

Darcy pushed away from the table. "Eli told me early on that he doesn't do permanent."

"Before he met you, I would have agreed. But now—"

Brooke tilted her head. "Do you love him?"

"He doesn't want my love."

"You hurt him to save him. That's love."

"You forget the part where I ruin his career when he loses November's election."

"This will require some thought. People are angry about your inheriting Alex's property—and angry because they perceive you as his weakness. Many women cherish the idea of one true love. Alex and Cindy shared an exceptional marriage because they never forgot why they fell in love in the first place and they worked hard to keep their marriage strong."

"That's what Alex told me." Darcy smiled. "You're passionate about them."

"Cindy visited me after my husband died. We talked. A lot. She kept me sane. Kept me from taking my mother's path of withdrawal. Kept me focused on the future. On Jeremy."

"Since you knew Cindy so well, I'm surprised you didn't barricade your door when Eli brought me over."

"I might have had I known it was you Eli was bringing. But now that I know you, I like you. I think you possess a kind heart that would attract and soothe a lonely man. Alex was such a man. I can understand why he'd seek your company."

"We were friends, nothing more."

Brooke blinked. "Why didn't you tell me before?"

"You believe me just like that?"

"Of course."

"Thanks. But since Eli's retaining his job means retaining the popular vote, if he stays at my house, he won't be popular. If he's not reelected, will he stay in Lost Creek?"

Brooke frowned. "Probably not." She stood. "I have to pick up Jeremy from school." She nodded toward the covered painting. "I'll leave Eli here for now; maybe he'll inspire an idea."

Tuesday morning, Darcy sipped hot chocolate. Her brain had switched on at six and refused to switch off. She needed to clear her name. Otherwise, she'd lose her chance to make peace with Eli, and she might lose the house. If she couldn't work here, she couldn't live here.

She stared at her cell phone. She should call Beth and catch up but she couldn't explain the past few week's events without mentioning the heroin.

Without thinking, she answered the ringing phone. "Hello?"

"Did I wake you?" a familiar voice asked.

"Hi, Maggie. No, I'm not asleep. I'm waiting on electricians and plumbers. How are you?"

"That's what I called to ask you. How's life in Podunk?"

It felt good to laugh. "You sound like Beth. I like Lost Creek and the house. I've hit a few snags, but they won't hold me up long."

"You'll be ready to open October twelfth?"

"That's still my target date."

"Wonderful. Hold both rooms for Friday, Saturday, and Sunday night. I'll bring some friends. Oh! I have to go; my son's dropped in. I'll talk to you soon, honey. Bye."

The call cheered her up, but she needed something to fill her morning while the crews worked.

Gramma always said, "When in doubt, work it out." Cleaning the concrete storm cellar—the size of a walk-in closet with an arched ceiling—was a perfect chore for thinking.

Eli had helped her haul the heavy door open last week. She'd made it halfway down the steps before retreating from a silver-dollar sized, hairy-legged spider. She'd sprayed the hinges with WD-40, then tossed a bug bomb inside and shut the door. By now, it should be safe to enter.

After telling the plumbers and electricians what she wanted done upstairs, Darcy slipped on old jeans and a long-sleeved T-shirt. She covered her braid with a bright blue bandana. Slapping leather gloves against her thigh, she headed for the backyard. The cellar door opened easily.

The first layer of accumulated dust and haphazard storage gave way to a more organized accumulation of undated home-canned goods. Lids on many of the jars had popped up. A canvas tarp held nests that had served as homes to mice that had vacated with the spiders.

By nine, she'd thrown four bulging trash bags into the construction dumpster. She headed out the kitchen door with a broom and dustpan when the phone rang. Shirley, the waitress at Border's, was ready to try her hand at making dumplings.

CHAPTER FIFTEEN

Four oiled baking sheets lined the countertop, each filled with plump dumplings waiting their turn in the steamers.

"Be careful of the lower lip of the counter," Darcy warned Shirley. "It wasn't finished properly, so it's sharp."

Shirley tapped the jagged edge of stainless steel. "I see what you mean." She turned away from the sink and plucked a paper towel. "You were right about the dumplings. I would have messed up the recipe if you hadn't shown me how to make them first." She dried her hands and inspected her hot pink nail polish that matched her Capri pants and halter-top. "Why'd you offer?"

"Because you were interested."

The aroma of steamed beef and spices made Darcy wistful. The last time she'd made them, she'd watched Eli enjoy eating them at Border's.

"If I can ever do anything to help you, let me know," Shirley said.

"Thanks, I will."

Darcy carried a mixing bowl to the sink. "Do you remember when you first heard rumors about me?"

"Not the exact day, but it was before you started catering at the roadhouse. I heard rumors at Border's one night, and the post office and drug store the next day." Shirley rolled her eyes. "It's part of living in a small town. Even if you don't know what you're doing, you can bet someone else does."

Darcy nodded. "So, after I inherited this place, but before I moved to Lost Creek." At that time, the Anderson's were probably the only people in town who knew she'd inherited. The timer buzzed. Using tongs, they plucked dumplings from the steamer baskets. "I was hoping to be judged by my actions, not by rumors."

"Carl said you told him the stories aren't true." Shirley's blonde ringlets bounced in unison as her head jerked up. "I mean, I wondered. You don't seem the type, and in Lost Creek, rumors spread faster than your dumplings disappear at Border's." She sampled one.

Darcy followed suit, stopping mid-bite as a plan fell into place. Part of the answer she'd been looking for to put the rumors to rest stood in the kitchen licking her fingers.

"Shirley, I've thought of a way you can help me."

"Name it."

Darcy explained.

"Are you sure?" Shirley asked, her expression doubtful.

"Positive."

She fed Shirley lunch then waved her out the door.

When the kitchen was clean, she upended her purse onto her sitting room desk and started sorting the contents.

Lipstick and brush went back in, keys and wallet followed. She tossed gum wrappers and tissues, thumbed through receipts, and paused to study paperwork from Owens' Garage. She'd been so anxious to get away from Greg Ryan that she hadn't looked at her copy of the work ticket.

The hand-printed block letters on the itemization looked familiar. She opened her cell phone and scrolled through her photos, stopping at the ones of the graffiti on her foyer wall. She placed the phone and work order side by side. She was no expert, but the block letters looked similar.

She reached for the phone to call the sheriff's department, hesitated, then found Angela's business card and dialed.

Darcy sat in a red vinyl booth and inhaled a combination of sautéed onions and garlic. According to the sign outside, the Mexican restaurant had occupied the same location for thirty-five years. The spicy scents and eye-appeal of cheese-slathered dishes explained the restaurant's longevity.

Angela Ryan stepped inside; her anxious expression and reluctant entry reflected her reaction to Darcy's invitation. Darcy waved. Angela approached and scooted onto the seat across from her.

"Thanks for coming, Angela. I'll be brief."

"I have to pick up my kids in thirty minutes."

They declined menus, ordered drinks, and made small talk until the iced tea arrived. When the waitress moved on, Darcy laid the graffiti photo she'd printed and a copy of the work order from Owen's Garage on the table and nudged them toward Angela.

Angela's expression changed from confusion to dismay.

"They're both Greg's writing, aren't they?" Darcy asked.

Hazel eyes darted up then back to the papers. "Are you going to the police?" Angela asked, her voice flat.

"That depends. Did you know Greg broke into the house?"

A long pause ensued. When Angela spoke, Darcy had to lean in to hear her.

"Greg's talked crazy ever since Uncle Alex left the property and money to you. After the paper reported the break-in at the house, I got a feeling. I checked the trash and found empty spray paint cans in a bag at the bottom." Angela's hands lifted, fluttered, settled in her lap. "Greg wanted a piece of Alex's inheritance. After the mess we made of the garage business, I never expected anything, but Greg did. When the house and money went to you, he was furious."

"Who told you I got the house and the money?"

"Dad. The lawyer called Mom, and she told Dad that Alex hadn't left anything to the family."

Semantics, Darcy thought. Alex hadn't left anything to his immediate family, but he had left money to his sister-in-law.

"I didn't know what to do when I found the cans. I lied to the detective." Angela buried her face in her hands.

The door opened. Darcy watched as Greg spotted her. He stiffened when he recognized his wife and stalked to the table. "What's she sayin'?" Greg asked Angela.

"We were discussing similarities," Darcy said.

Greg eased onto the seat beside Angela. He glanced at

the paper and photo Darcy pushed before him.

"What do you think that proves?" He crumpled the photo and paper and stuffed them into his shirt pocket.

"Hello, Ms. Cooper. Everything all right?" Deputy Carlisle stood at the end of the booth.

"Hi, Deputy." Darcy smiled, happy to have backup, though Carlisle's appearance smacked of a tail. "Everything's fine, thanks for checking."

"No problem." Carlisle took a facing seat at an open table.

Darcy turned to Greg. "The sheriff's department has a copy of that photo, and can find examples of your handwriting at your home and work."

"What are you doing about it?" Greg's eyes narrowed.

"That depends on where you were Tuesday night."

"The night you and the sheriff almost got run down? Yeah, I read about it in the paper. You've sure ticked off a bunch of people." He smiled. "I wasn't anywhere near you that night."

He might not have been at the gallery, but he could have delivered a box of snakes. "Where were you?" Darcy pressed.

"None of your business."

Greg's raised voice turned heads. Darcy sent a reassuring smile to Deputy Carlisle. She hated what she was about to do. Any threat she made to Greg would also impact Angela and their kids. But backing down would invite Greg to have another go at her.

"Then I'll inform the deputy of my suspicions.

She'll take you in, and you'll spend time with the detective while Angela explains to your children why Daddy is late coming home tonight." She shifted toward the booth opening.

"Wait." Angela held out a supplicating hand. "Tell her."

He glared at them both.

"If you don't, I will," Angela said, her mouth a determined line.

To Darcy's surprise, Angela won the staring match.

Greg leaned back and shrugged. "I was in Junction at my parents."

"What time did you leave for Junction?"

"After work."

"What time was that?"

"Five-forty-five." He looked at Angela.

"He's telling the truth. I called at six-thirty to see if he'd made it. His mom answered, then I spoke to Greg."

Darcy did the math. Junction was an hour's drive from Lost Creek. She lived east of town, outside the city limits and Owens's Garage was in downtown Lost Creek. Greg couldn't have driven from work to her place, left snakes, and arrived at his parents by six-thirty. "When did you return to Lost Creek?"

"Wednesday morning."

Angela nodded.

"Why did you ask me about varmints?"

He smirked. "Women are afraid of critters."

"What would frightening me accomplish? You still

wouldn't own the house."

Greg's face closed with anger. "You don't belong there. The house should be ours!"

Darcy approached the counter at the Department of Public Safety. She wondered if Eli would eventually show up at her door if she didn't change her address on her driver's license.

Probably not, she decided. He'd send a deputy to deliver a ticket.

Finally, she stood before a woman whose brown hair defied gravity.

"Hi, I need to change the address on my driver's license."

"Sure thing. Let me see your old license." The woman glanced down at the card then back up. "Darcy Cooper?"

"Yes."

"We've been waiting for you! Bella!" the woman hollered over her shoulder, "Darcy Cooper's here to change her address."

A beaming black woman hurried from the back and circled the counter.

"Honey, let me hug you!" She smothered Darcy in her ample bosom. "Lisa said you'd come. The hug is for helping her and the baby!" Bella squeezed again. "Let's get you updated!"

Darcy's doctor appointment didn't involve hugs. She signed in with the receptionist, glad for once that her name elicited raised brows. An hour later, she strolled happily to her car.

At two, Darcy sat on the edge of Deputy Carlisle's desk and watched Dan contemplate a nursing bra while Lisa laughed.

"It's too big," he said.

"It won't be," chorused half the people in the room.

Dan handed Lisa the bra, loosened his tie, and bestowed a kiss on his wife before wading through the growing pile of wrapping paper, to swipe a bit of icing from the pink, blue, and yellow cake. "You're almost good as new," he said to Darcy.

"I am." She touched her cheek where a faint bruise hid beneath a thin layer of foundation. "What's the latest?"

"DNA results from your fingernails match Randy Hall; no surprise there. And the investigators finished interviewing the Anderson family. I understand you've met most of them."

She ignored his disapproving look. "What do your people think? Am I in any danger from Alex's family?"

"Everyone has an alibi. That doesn't mean you're not in danger."

She lowered her voice. "The packages in the jacket were confirmed as heroin?"

"Yep. Wainright's research shows that several Texas cities are experiencing an increase in heroin availability. They're faxing analysis reports so we can compare the chemical signatures with the batch you found." Dan settled beside her. "It's a good thing Eli's taking time off. He won't get much rest after he returns on Friday."

Friday? Eli had cut his vacation short. He'd be back sooner than she'd expected—or deserved. She gripped the edge of the desk. "I want to talk about the patrol car spending nights outside my place. It's not a speed trap, so I'm assuming Eli ordered it there."

"He's concerned about your safety. Raul tried to take you out last week, not to mention the snakes."

"I don't want to be responsible for patrol cars not having computers."

"While you're alone at night, you'll be watched. You could always move in with us."

"Then where would your mother-in-law stay?"

"Oh yeah, I forgot," Dan said unconvincingly. From behind the colorful array of opened gifts burying Dan's desk, Lisa mimed dying of thirst. Dan stood. "Take care of yourself."

She watched him walk to the punch bowl. He took good care of Lisa. Their love was different from but as strong as, the love her grandparents had shared—as strong as Alex and Cindy's must have been.

How did one member of such a pair carry on after the loss of the other? Her grandmother had followed her grandfather as if her life force was tied to his. Alex had continued after losing Cindy. Likewise, Maggie hadn't seriously dated anyone after her husband's death.

"Hey darlin', has anyone ever told you you're beautiful when you're pensive?"

The familiar drawl drew a reluctant smile.

"You haven't returned my calls," Keith complained.

Darcy looked up. "I've felt unsociable lately."

"Is that the real reason? I thought since detectives were talking to everyone in my family, you might have been warned not to contact me."

"Well, there is that," she said. "Are you here for the shower?"

"No, I vaccinated the K-9 dogs." Keith crossed his arms, spread his legs, and planted his scuffed boots. "It's amazing how the sight of me can turn a well-trained animal into a quivering mass of nerves. Kind of like the effect I have on women."

"In your dreams, cowboy." She smiled for real.

Across the room, Dan hand-signaled Deputy Carlisle. Half amused and half irritated, Darcy watched her saunter over to the cake and meticulously measure each slice she cut.

"How's the arm?" Keith asked.

Darcy looked back at him. "The stitches come out this afternoon."

"That calls for a celebration. How about dinner afterward?"

"I don't think that's a good idea."

"Come on, you have about as much color as a lab rat. I'm prescribing a hot meal, eaten outdoors. I know a place in Merritt that fills the prescription. Who's removing the stitches and what time is your appointment?"

"Keith, no."

Arms still folded across his chest, he sat beside her. "I

planned to surprise you, but I'll pull out the big guns." He paused dramatically. "I know why Alex left you the house."

Her pulse skipped like a smooth stone across a calm pond. As Keith's grin widened, her eyes narrowed. Keith could be full of the substance that sometimes flaked off the soles of his boots. "How do you suddenly know why Alex left me the house?"

"Alex told someone and that someone told me."

"I see Dr. Jeffers at four."

"I'll pick you up and take you to the Pecan Grill in Merritt," Keith announced the restaurant name in a loud voice.

Deputy Carlisle continued placing cake slices on plates and filling punch cups as if she didn't hear every word of their conversation. Darcy appreciated Dan's concern, but she couldn't pass up this opportunity.

"I'll meet you at the restaurant at six. And you'd better not be lying."

"Scout's honor." A satisfied smile stretched his mustache as he stood and walked out.

Deputy Carlisle handed her a cup of punch, shot her an I-hope-you-know-what-you're-doing look, and then crossed to Dan, passing Lisa on the way.

Darcy hoped she knew what she was doing too.

Lisa settled into Deputy Carlisle's chair. Exhaling, she slipped off the purple flats that matched her maternity dress. "It's more trouble every day to cross a room, and my shoes feel a half-size too small. What did Keith say?"

"You and Dan make a great tag-team."

When Lisa kept staring, Darcy shrugged. "I'm having dinner with him tonight. He says he knows why Alex left me the house."

"I don't think Eli would like you having dinner with Keith."

"I can assure you the sheriff is not concerned with my social life."

"Dan said Eli was in a bear of a mood before he left. Did you two fight?"

"Drop it, Lisa," Darcy said kindly. "By the way, you will call me when you go to the hospital to have the baby, right?"

Lisa pushed herself to her feet with an effort. "If you're that big a glutton for punishment, I'll call."

Stitches came out faster and less painfully than they went in. Darcy flexed her arm. The five-minute procedure had seemed anticlimactic. She drove home to dress for dinner, then got back in her car. Glancing up, she headed east beneath a threatening sky to meet Keith at the Pecan Grill.

At Border's, Shirley delivered longnecks to the two women who had snubbed Darcy two weeks earlier.

"Hey, have you heard the latest?" She bent over the table and whispered, gratified when the women's jaws dropped. "She'd probably prefer it stays a secret."

The women nodded furiously.

Grinning, Shirley returned to the bar and called out a drink order. Carl pulled the beers and placed them on her tray.

"Setting wildfires?" With a twitch of his mustache, he

indicated the two women canvassing the room like politicians.

Shirley stared into the mirror behind the bar and fluffed her curls. "They owe Darcy an apology. They don't know it, but they're saying they're sorry."

Keith waited at a table sheltered by an umbrella and a tall stone wall covered with fragrant jasmine. The outdoor patio overlooked a limestone creek bordered by ancient pecan trees. He rose to greet her, handsome in olive twill pants and a crisp white shirt. Gathering her stone-colored broomstick skirt, she sat.

"Let's see your scar."

He slid the lightweight, sage jacket down her shoulder, revealing a silk tank several shades lighter than her skirt. His index finger ran lightly over the pink scar.

She shrugged. "I can't feel much, although the doctor says it will probably start itching soon."

Keith dropped his hand and returned to his seat. "I ordered for you. I hope you don't mind."

She did, but, anxious to learn what he knew, she even tolerated the polite small talk that accompanied their meal. She picked at venison medallions, green salad, sunburst squash, and wild rice while listening to Keith's amusing animal stories. He was attentive, charming, and handsome. And he was treating this meeting as a date.

"Darlin', I can tell when a woman's mind is somewhere else, and yours drifted the moment that patrol car drove by." He sipped his wine.

Had he realized it was the cruiser's third pass?

"You could at least fake enjoyment in the meal if not in my company."

"The food and the company are good. I'm distracted because I'm waiting to hear why I inherited Alex's property."

A denim-shirted waiter cleared their plates and served the house dessert, a decadent pecan pie with fresh whipped cream.

She tasted her pie. "Heaven. I wonder if the chef shares his recipes."

Keith finished his pie then pulled the remainder of hers toward him. He leaned forward and beat a two-fingered drum roll on the tabletop.

"Here's your story. Alex kept in touch with a neighboring rancher. The same rancher bought most of his land. Like Alex and Cindy, this fellow and his wife are old-timers; they keep to themselves. But I'm his vet, Alex's nephew, and easy to talk to."

Darcy looked up at the stars then back at Keith. He snapped his napkin at her wrist.

"I am," he insisted. "Personable and curious guy that I am, I asked the rancher if Alex ever said why he chose to leave the property to you. He said Alex wanted you to have the property because you and the house would be good for each other. And maybe you'd find what you were really looking for."

Darcy set her napkin on the table. She had shared her plan for a rural bed and breakfast with Alex, but she'd never imagined that he'd make her dream a reality.

By giving her the house, Alex had given her a fixed base and the opportunity to fill her own home with happy memories. Was that what he'd meant about discovering what she really sought?

"One more thing." Keith brought her back to the present. "The rancher's wife said Alex was seeing a woman named Margaret who grew up around here."

Darcy's pulse jumped. "Have you told anyone else about Maggie?"

"No." Keith leaned back and crossed his arms. "Why'd you let yourself be labeled an opportunist? Why haven't you told anyone Alex was dating Maggie?"

"They weren't dating. They were old friends who'd each lost a spouse. I promised Maggie I wouldn't mention her because she knew some of Lost Creek's citizens would misconstrue their friendship—as they have with Alex and me—and I'm not breaking that promise."

"Okay. I'll let it slip to Cheryl Greer, and it'll show up on the front page, along with her apology to you."

Darcy exhaled. "Keith, I appreciate what you're trying to do, but you can't tell anyone. I've kept my word to you and let people think I inherited Alex's money so Greg won't badger your mother. I'll only continue my silence if you promise not to expose Maggie."

He sat quietly. The approaching darkness triggered landscape lights. "If it were anyone but my mother—" He extended a hand. "Deal."

That night, Darcy paced the living room with a cup of hot chocolate. Turning toward the fireplace mantle, she confronted Eli's painting.

"I think I've fixed the rumor problems, so I hope you'll listen when I apologize and that you'll forgive me."

She sipped. "I wouldn't blame you for wishing I'd never moved to Tell County. If I weren't here, your department would be getting computers sooner."

She straightened. If she weren't here! She stared into Eli's painted eyes.

Uneasiness and excitement vied. She'd be leaving the bed and breakfast when she should be preparing for her grand opening. But losing a few days was nothing compared to Eli putting his job on the line for her.

And she missed him.

She'd tried not to dwell on loving a man who wouldn't return her love. And easing the pain she'd inflicted on him wouldn't decrease her own. But she owed him.

She turned and picked up the ringing phone.

"Hello?"

"Golden girl..." The rattling began.

"Grow up!" she yelled, then slammed down the receiver.

He rubbed his ear as he stuffed the rattle into his pocket and walked from the payphone to the café. What had riled her? She'd sounded scared the other morning, and scared was good, defiant was not.

Raul and Randy's warnings had failed, and their faces now stared at him from posters on every storefront and telephone pole in the county. His best setup team was compromised while his deliveries fell further behind schedule.

Selecting a corner booth, he turned the plastic-coated menu from the breakfast selections to the lunch and dinner selections. A waitress approached.

"You want the usual?" She pulled a pencil from behind her ear and started writing on her order pad, anticipating his answer.

That shook him. He didn't remember this girl, but because she remembered him, he wouldn't eat here again.

The Cooper woman had made them all careless. Irritated, he ordered a cheeseburger, making the waitress rewrite his ticket. He ate quickly, declining coffee refills. Finished, he tossed his napkin over his plate, stood, and walked to the register. He glanced at the opening door then away from the entering deputy, resisting the urge to tug down the bill of his ball cap. He would have enjoyed another look; she sure filled out her uniform.

The platinum blonde surveyed the café before strolling to the counter and placing money on the laminated surface. He handed over his ticket as the cashier greeted the deputy.

"Coffee to go," the cashier called over her shoulder. "That'll be six seventy-five," she told him.

He pulled a wallet from his jacket and fumbled after the plastic baby rattle that hung on the leather. The deputy caught the rattle before it hit the floor and handed it back.

"Grandkids' toys are everywhere," he muttered. He passed the cashier a twenty and left with his change.

CHAPTER SIXTEEN

Tuesday night, after hanging up on the rattler, Darcy called Brooke.

"I hope I'm not calling too late, but I need to find Eli."

"He's in Colorado until Friday. What's wrong?"

"I'm ready to apologize. Before I made my comment about Gramma, he invited me to go to Colorado with him. He said I would stay with your aunt and uncle." She rushed on. "Brooke, I want to apologize to him in person and as soon as possible. I want to fly up there tomorrow."

"Vision quests can be demanding. He might not be ready for you."

Indecision tossed Darcy like a paper boat in a whirlpool. An apology might not change anything, but with her reputation in the process of being cleared—along with Alex's—Eli could stay at her house again and save the department's computer budget.

"Brooke, if I don't go, he might never speak to me again. If I do go, he still might not speak to me, but I'll have attempted to set things right. He'll see that I think him important enough to make an effort."

"Let me make a call. I'll call you back."

"Thank you."

Darcy wiped down already clean counters until the phone rang.

"Yes?"

"Here's the deal," Brooke said. "Uncle John wants you to fly to Alamosa tomorrow morning. He'll meet your plane. John is our father's older brother and a second father to Eli and me. He owns a ranch near Alamosa where he breeds and sells Paint horses. Uncle John also has great puha and always awaits the return of the family men when they seek visions."

"Puha?"

"Spiritual powers. Listen, there's a catch. Uncle John may tell you to get back on the plane. If he tells you to leave, you must, even if you haven't seen Eli. On the other hand, if you stay, he'll mediate your talk with Eli and keep you both focused. Do you have a backpack and a sleeping bag?"

"Yes."

"Take them. Oh, can you ride a horse?"

"It's been a few years."

"It's not a skill you forget." Brooke hesitated. "I want to ask you about something I heard."

Darcy smiled. "Give me a ride to the airport, and I'll tell you all about it. You can pick up Eli's portrait."

From twenty-thousand feet, southern Colorado resembled a crazy quilt of green velvet patches stitched to brown and beige corduroy.

With Alamosa in sight, Darcy took a deep breath. What would Eli do when he saw her? She deserved whatever she got, but a good part of her counted on his forgiveness.

She started to scratch her scar then remembered not to irritate the skin. The adhesive gel-strip covering the tender skin was supposed to minimize scarring. Too bad the material didn't work on emotional scars. She could wrap a massive sheet around Eli and dissolve the words she'd used to send him away.

The pilot compensated for a rough approach over a mountain pass with a smooth landing.

Inside the terminal, she claimed her luggage then walked outside and scanned faces until she met impenetrable dark eyes in a smooth face. Brooke had shown her a picture of Uncle John. The man's long, graying hair was parted down the middle and tied on the sides. He wore a faded scarlet shirt and broken-in jeans.

"Mr. Whitepath?" she asked. At his nod, she solemnly said, "How."

His eyes twinkled. "How is Jeremy?"

"Still channeling Batman." She smiled. "Thank you for agreeing to meet me."

"Call me Uncle John. Is that all of your luggage?"

She patted her backpack. "Yes."

"Then let's get started."

"That's it?" She followed him to a white pickup truck hooked to a horse trailer.

He looked back at her. "Beg your pardon?"

"I thought you'd have more questions for me."

"The important questions are answered."

When he didn't elaborate, she set her pack in the bed of the truck then paused to scratch the ears of the Paint sticking its head out of the trailer. Uncle John put his hand on the shoulder of a tall youth.

"This is my grandson, Joseph. He will drive us to the base of the trail."

They made a fuel stop in Antonito, where Darcy bought a fishing license. On a whim, she'd brought her grampa's four-piece fly rod and a small box of trout flies. Driving on, sage and scrub oak gave way to towering conifers and pines as they entered the Rio Grande National Forest. Joseph pulled off at the Elk Creek Campground, and Darcy breathed deeply of air that echoed Eli's scent. The well-mannered Paints accepted saddles; the long-eared mule carried tents and packs.

"Eli hiked in," John explained. "We'll lead a third horse for him to ride out on Thursday. Joseph will return for us then."

The pack trail ascended wooded switchbacks and bisected open meadows to the campsite Uncle John selected. When he dismounted, Darcy followed his lead and watered her horse and Eli's using a collapsible vinyl bucket. They groomed the horses then picketed them on long lines. At nine thousand feet, the air was crisp and a little thin. She welcomed the late afternoon sun's warm caress.

John cut an apple in two and tossed her half.

"Thank you," she said as he fit feedbags over the horses' noses.

He ate his half of the apple and fed the core to the mule. "You sit a horse well," he said.

"My grandparents had horses. I learned to ride, although I haven't had an opportunity lately." She smiled. "I've rediscovered some forgotten muscles."

"These were your Sioux grandparents that Brook told me about?"

"Gramma was Sioux; Grampa was Scandinavian." She bit her apple and chewed.

"What do you know about the Comanche?" John asked.

"Nothing flattering. Only the stories Gramma told me."

John shrugged. "We fought most of the plains tribes, including the Sioux. Our ancestors' raids were legendary."

To Darcy's left, a marmot scrambled atop a nearby boulder and viewed them from its lichen-covered perch. Deciding they posed no threat, the short-tailed rodent stretched out to nap in the sun.

"Eli is half Anglo, but his dominant half is Comanche," John said. "You cannot suppress what is in your blood. The military trained him as a warrior. He continues to follow a warrior's path in life."

"His path suits him." Darcy took a deep breath and plunged in. "When I was a child, I saw people snub Gramma and talk down to her. She'd laugh about it, but I know the words hurt." Darcy looked John in the eye. "I'm ashamed to have caused Eli the same pain."

"Your chance to apologize is coming."

"If Eli is willing to listen."

Uncle John nodded.

"Brooke said you've been a second father to them."

He smiled sadly. "As children, Eli and Brooke spent a great deal of time on the ranch with their mother. It takes a strong woman to be a warrior's wife. Their mother was a good woman, but not a strong woman. My brother's death was hard for us all—but hardest on her."

Darcy stared at the mountains. Between the loss of his father, and witnessing his mother's pain and death, Eli must have a shell as thick as her storm cellar's walls. She'd almost broken through once, would he let her in again?

"Let's set up tents before we lose the light," John said.

They pitched the tents on level ground, unrolled sleeping pads and bags, and arranged packs. Darcy gathered and stacked wood while John organized dinner.

Brooke had said he would provide the food, but Darcy was surprised when he unpacked pre-marinated steaks from a collapsible cooler. He tossed her four foil-wrapped cylinders.

"Bury these in the coals. My wife baked the potatoes and boiled the corn. We only need to reheat them."

"The food looks wonderful, Uncle John. I expected beans and wieners, not rib-eyes."

"I wanted to make a good first impression."

She grinned. "I'm impressed."

He erected a small grill and set the steaks to sizzle above the ash-covered coals. When he handed her a plate, she sat on the edge of a tarp, using a fallen tree for a backrest. John sat on the log beside her.

"Eli requires a woman who understands the demands of his work. Brooke thinks you are that woman. I think so too. Although you look Anglo, your spirit is of the People."

Darcy rested her plate on her knees. "Uncle John, Eli isn't looking for a permanent relationship. I won't appeal to his heart when I see him. I came to apologize."

John continued eating. "It is good you made this journey. Remember that when Eli ignores you."

She shook her head. "I don't expect him to be happy to see me."

"He won't be, but Brooke says you are honest. Eli responds to honesty, but it may not be enough. I wish you luck, little one."

"Thank you. I have a feeling I'll need it."

As the darkening sky filled with stars, the temperatures dropped dramatically. The fire sent sparks into the air and warmth into their bodies.

Darcy finished her steak then rolled over and grabbed her daypack. "How about dessert?"

"I have dried fruit—" John smiled off as she pulled chocolate bars, marshmallows, and graham crackers from her pack. "S'mores?"

Darcy waggled her eyebrows and passed him an extending fork. She suspended her securely skewered marshmallows over the coals.

"Eli's been alone since Monday. Do you worry about him?"

John unwrapped his chocolate bar, placed it on a graham cracker, and slid two seared marshmallows on top.

"He has a satellite phone, and we each have one of these." He pulled a bright yellow walkie-talkie from his coat pocket. "Mine is always on. He will use his if necessary. I have been checking Eli's messages on his cell phone in case there was an emergency. There are several from Eli's friend, Dan saying you received threatening phone calls."

"Two, so far. And I now keep a whistle beside the phone—in case he calls back."

Uncle John grinned.

His third night on the mountain, Eli faced south, draped a blanket over his head, and tucked the ends beneath his crossed legs. The covering would form his shroud until dawn.

Perhaps tonight he'd succeed. So far, instead of solutions or visions, his mind continuously replayed Darcy's rejection of him. Eyes closed, he cleared his mind of distractions by chanting a song given to him by his spirit guide during a previous vision quest.

He must have chanted himself to sleep because when he opened his eyes, a weak morning sun beat down on the rocky granite ledge. A white hawk perched on a nearby scrubby shrub. Large, unblinking brown eyes watched him.

An albino should have pink eyes, he thought. She—somehow he knew the hawk was female—studied him.

Slowly, he stretched out a hand. She let him stroke her. He thought he'd won her trust, but, without warning, she stabbed him with her beak and flew away.

He clenched his hand into a fist to staunch the trickle of blood and concentrated on the circling hawk. She spiraled lower, closer, until she hovered before him. Suddenly, she jerked. Red blossomed across her breast.

Enraged, he lunged to his feet and reached for her. She fluttered past his fingers. As her spreading blood stained the rocks at his feet, her eyes fixed on him—confused and then empty. Her wings stilled.

His clenched fists challenged the empty sky as he howled in pain and fury.

Darcy rose to her elbows and met the cougar's brilliant green eyes. As the staring cat settled into a watchful crouch, her fingers curled, aching to caress his golden coat. The cat's muscles bunched. He sprang! She cried out and flung her arms up to ward off the attack.

She jerked awake as Uncle John unzipped her tent.

"What happened, little one?"

Exhaling erratic breaths, Darcy scanned the darkness outside. "It was a dream. I'm in my tent, and it was a dream," she repeated like a mantra.

"You must tell me, little one."

Haltingly, she related the dream. Still searching the shadows, she sipped from her water bottle.

"You woke too soon. You must finish the dream.

The cat must spring, and you must watch what happens. It is important."

"I'll try," she promised. Gramma had taught her from childhood that dreams were powerful. She settled uneasily into her sleeping bag.

The cold, clear night sharpened the stars overhead. She didn't remember leaving her tent, but she sat outside. The green-eyed cougar settled nearby.

Evil drenched the air but did not flow from her silent companion.

The cat crouched; its muscles bunched beneath its pelt. Tail twitching, the cougar focused on her—or did he look beyond? He sprang—she steeled for slashing claws and ripping teeth, but he bounded past.

A furious fight ensued. Darcy twisted to glimpse the cat's opponent, but darkness cloaked the threat. A sense of peace stole over her as if she drifted with the stars. Sounds subsided. She wondered what had stained her shirt red.

Uncle John knelt beside her. She spoke, and he listened without expression until she related how her shirt changed color. He stroked her brow.

"Rest, little one; there will be no more dreams tonight."

Eli waited impatiently to feel the sun's first rays. He'd received his vision and was anxious to get off the mountain—to get back to Lost Creek. But Uncle John would scalp him if he didn't finish the ritual and show thankfulness to ensure future visions.

When warm light crested the mountain, he flung off the blanket and stood to face the sun and absorb its power. He planned to reach camp as quickly as the rising sun and rough terrain allowed. He'd call Dan on Uncle John's satellite phone when he reached camp. Darcy needed to be in protective custody while he arranged to get his truck back to Lost Creek and bought a plane ticket to San Antonio. His deputies were good, but few had combat experience.

He hastily rolled the pipe and tobacco Uncle John had provided for enlightenment inside his blanket then checked the contents of his medicine pouch—searching specifically for the cougar fang he'd found as a youth. Pouch secured, he tied the laces of his trail-running shoes and started downhill.

The vision of the brown-eyed hawk haunted him down the mountainside. He didn't need Uncle John's interpretation to know he'd focused so intently on Darcy that he'd missed the danger threatening her. Could he change the outcome, or was he already too late?

CHAPTER SEVENTEEN

Thursday morning, Darcy splashed icy creek water on her face until her skin tingled. She used her blue bandana as a towel then tied it around her neck. Despite her black anorak, thermal T-shirt, and fleece-lined leggings, she shivered as she brushed her hair into a high ponytail. She looked toward the mountain peaks. Eli was at an even higher altitude. How was he faring this chilly morning? Had he received his vision? She'd certainly experienced wild dreams last night.

She stood and glanced at the horizon. The sun rose in an orange and pink ball. A new day, when anything could happen. Jogging back to camp, she saw Uncle John had a fire crackling, water boiling, and was now feeding the horses. Darcy tossed her toothbrush and soap into her tent then walked to the fire.

Placing a coffee bag in one mug, she emptied a packet of hot chocolate into a second. Using her long sleeves as potholders, she filled the cups with boiling water. Oatmeal, brown sugar, and raisins went into the remaining water.

A tawny figure caught her eye, making her start. Rising into a half-crouch, she pivoted towards the movement as remnants of her dreams merged into unsettling reality.

Eli ran into camp wearing only a breechclout and a sheen of sweat despite the forty-two-degree temperature. Her heart stuttered. His body had changed since Brooke had painted him. Hard planes and defined muscles had replaced sharp angles and combat-lean limbs.

He dropped his bedroll beside the fire. His green eyes filled with a mixture of anger and—what? Surely not relief.

"Why are you here?" he asked.

Scratch relief. She swallowed, abandoned by her voice.

"Darcy has come to make peace with you," Uncle John said, joining them at the fire. "But first we will eat."

Grateful for the reprieve, Darcy carried her oatmeal to a log near her tent. The apology she'd practiced fled her mind as Eli's nonchalance about his body and attire overloaded her senses. She stole another look as Eli and Uncle John conversed in what she presumed was Comanche.

Based on the way Eli froze suddenly, Uncle John must be telling him why she'd come. The sheriff shot her a piercing glance then looked back at Uncle John. Neither man's sharp hand movements encouraged optimism.

Unable to taste her food, Darcy gathered the dishes for washing. When she returned from the small lake, the men sat cross-legged on saddle blankets beneath an aspen tree. Eli had changed into jeans, a red flannel shirt, and a black fleece vest. Dried grass rustled as she walked, heralding her approach, but Eli continued staring into the fire that burned between the three saddle blankets. Uncle John motioned her to sit.

She crossed her ankles and sank to the ground. A long-stemmed pipe lay on the grass between Uncle John and Eli. When Uncle John closed his eyes, Eli followed suit.

Darcy shut her eyes. The brisk morning air carried bird songs, a light breeze, and the fire's crackle. Her breathing slowed.

"It begins."

Hearing Uncle John's words, Darcy opened her eyes and watched him pack the pipe with aromatic tobacco and touch a match to the bowl. First lifting the pipe skyward, he puffed then passed it to her.

She inhaled a shallow breath and struggled not to choke as she handed Eli the pipe. He inhaled evenly. Smoke streamed out of his nostrils. He completed the circle, returning the pipe to Uncle John. Thankfully, three cycles consumed the tobacco.

"Darcy will speak," Uncle John said.

She glanced down at the fingers she was twisting. If a peace talk protocol existed, surely Uncle John would have told her. She flattened her hands against her thighs and focused on Eli's green eyes as he focused on the mountains behind her.

"Eli, I've come to apologize. I didn't want the rumors about me to impact your reelection and cost you votes. So I let you think I turned you away because of your heritage."

"Then you lied about your grandmother being prejudiced against Indians?"

"No, I didn't lie. And I didn't say Indians, I said

Comanche. Gramma didn't care for the Comanche."

A flicker of confusion crossed Eli's face.

"So it doesn't matter that I'm half Indian, only that I'm half Comanche?"

"In Gramma's eyes, yes. She was Sioux. Her family lost a relative during a Comanche raid. She wasn't favorably disposed toward your nation."

"So you're here to tell me you're part Indian and not prejudiced?" He wouldn't make eye contact.

"I came to apologize for hurting you. I only vocalized Gramma's feelings because I couldn't let you continue to stay at my house, and you were too bullheaded to take no for an answer." Realizing her voice had risen, she paused for a breath of composure. "People were talking. I was desperate. I'm sorry.

"Before I left, I told Dan I'd be away several days, so the deputies could go back to drive-bys. I figure my trip here has saved you at least one computer."

"You haven't saved me a dime. Dan knows better than to call off the night surveillance. We're not just protecting you; we're looking for Randy and Raul. That doesn't stop because you left town."

"Oh." Darcy's shoulders fell. "Then I apologize for that too."

"Are you finished?" he asked, his voice flat.

"Almost." He viewed her presence as an invasion, but his stubborn indifference demanded she invade one more area. "I fell in love with you that night at the gallery while we sat on the bench."

He controlled flickers of emotions too quickly for her to interpret them. She swallowed. Had she broken through or marched too far?

"Then you read a lot into my doing my job that night."

Her heart fell and landed in her stomach. She turned to Uncle John. "I'm finished."

Eli closed his eyes. How could she tell him she loved him then say she was finished? And what made her think she felt love and not gratitude?

When he'd entered the camp, he'd seen hunger on her face and reacted with a desire he'd disguised as contempt for her inconsistency and his confounding attraction to her.

Indian vs. Comanche. He should have registered her specificity to begin with, but her words had hurt more than they should have, and his brain had jumped to reinforce the prejudice he'd assumed.

Eli opened his eyes and raised an eyebrow at his uncle. Unperturbed, Uncle John refilled, relit, and passed the pipe. Eli savored the tobacco's harsh tang until the bowl emptied. As Uncle John nodded, Eli turned to Darcy. A light breeze fanned the campfire, sending a sheet of red flames as high as her chest—across her throat.

"Darcy, I accept your apology and offer my own for behaving unprofessionally. You're a witness in an ongoing investigation. I shouldn't have touched you at the gallery and given you the impression that I was interested in you."

He frowned as she pressed a hand to her stomach. She

sat straighter and seemed to be concentrating. Beads of sweat formed on her upper lip.

"Are you all right?" he asked.

Hand to her mouth, Darcy sprang to her feet and rushed from the circle. She rounded a boulder before retching breakfast and tobacco smoke from her system. Scraping a hole to bury the evidence, she wished she could regurgitate the cold ball of rejection occupying her stomach.

She trudged to her tent for her water bottle. Tempted to soak her entire head, she settled for wetting her bandana and used the cloth as a compress. Given her sudden departure, the men would understand if she remained in her tent—but she hadn't come eight hundred miles to take the easy way out. She returned to the fire, face clammy, stomach settled, and sat.

"I shouldn't have inhaled. Tobacco and I don't get along."

Eli frowned. "You knew you'd get sick? Why didn't you say something? The pipe was for effect."

His exasperation hit hard. She pressed the bandana to her forehead with both hands. "I didn't know the pipe was optional. I thought I was participating in a traditional Comanche ritual."

Uncle John touched her arm. "Should I put out the fire?"

Darcy shook her head. "I'm okay now." She swallowed weakness and misery. She'd come to explain her words and actions, and she had. She'd known that might be all she accomplished on this trip. Known, but hadn't believed.

"Well, I'm glad we had this chance to talk," she managed, desperately searching for a sliver of humor to disperse the pain. The only slivers she found, pierced her heart.

Eli stood. "I need to make some satellite phone calls." He walked to his uncle's tent.

Darcy started to stand. Uncle John's touch stopped her.

"I thought the pipe would add to the serious nature of the talks. I apologize for not explaining that participation was optional."

Darcy settled back onto her saddle blanket. "That's okay. I'm a sucker for tradition, real or imagined."

"Are you allergic to smoke?"

"No, my aversion stems from Gramma's efforts to get me to adulthood as safely as possible."

Uncle John tilted his head. "Tell me."

She smiled at his attempt to soothe her. "You're a horse whisperer, aren't you?"

His grin answered. She leaned back on her elbows and stretched her boots toward the fire.

"The fall I moved in with my grandparents, I decided that smoking would help me fit in at the new high school. Gramma caught me practicing in the barn. She marched me to the porch, and instead of saying smoking was bad for me, she pointed out the risk of fire with the drought and the danger to the animals if a fire got out of hand. I was fifteen, and my juvenile response was, 'And your point is?'"

Uncle John smiled.

"Gramma didn't think I was funny. She gave me a

cigarette and told me to smoke it. I'd learned to inhale before I'd left the Army base, so I managed okay. Despite the coughing and eye-watering, I finished the cigarette thinking, 'That wasn't so bad.' Then Gramma handed me another. By the fourth, I was green. After six, I headed for the side of the house. I've never touched a cigarette since, and I always sit upwind at a barbecue."

Uncle John belly-laughed. "Your grandmother was a wise woman."

"I miss her and Grampa."

"Did your friend, Alex, remind you of your grandfather?"

She met his wise, dark eyes. "Yes. Both were strong, quiet men with an underlying sense of humor. I seem drawn to the type." She offered a small smile then sat up and kissed his cheek. "I'm going to tempt the trout."

"Want company?"

She stood. "No, thanks. I need sorting-out time. Call me when it's time to pack."

She retrieved her rod and flies. Eli stood on a rise, satellite phone to his ear. A determined sun warmed her shoulders as she followed a trail downhill to the lake a quarter-mile away. Her grampa's fly fishing lessons returned after a few casts.

Relationships were fluid, she thought. When one bond stretched or broke, another formed to enhance or replace. Eli's childhood had forged a bond between him and Uncle John stronger than most uncle-nephew bonds. And Eli was attentive to Jeremy, another Whitepath growing up fatherless.

Eli's self-imposed limits on love kept him emotionally safe, expressively aloof, seemingly untouchable—but he'd let her in—briefly. The connection they'd shared had promised a beginning—until she'd destroyed its potential.

His vision of the white hawk dying haunted Eli. Finishing his calls to Dan and Wainright, Eli set the phone inside John's tent and joined his Uncle by the dying fire.

"She is good." John passed the binoculars.

Eli focused them on Darcy as she cast a tight loop with her fly line. She must be using dry flies because her presentation didn't create ripples on the lake.

"She hurt you badly for you to come here so close to the election," John said. "But I have enjoyed seeing you, and it is an honor to meet the woman who put your reputation before her own."

His words flowed like a river with hidden undercurrents that threatened firm footing.

Eli frowned. "Uncle, I came because I needed to clear my head and find a fresh perspective on the drug case." He explained his vision and continued. "Darcy was the white hawk, which means I can only offer her protection if I remain emotionally distanced from her."

John nodded. "I agree. But are you emotionally distanced from her?"

"Not as much as I'd like since she continues to distract me."

"When this is over, you should examine that distraction more deeply."

"Uncle, that is not—"

John interrupted him. "Let me tell you what Darcy dreamed last night," Uncle John elaborated and finished with, "She dreamed of your cougar spirit guide beside her— and still she was injured, though I don't know how badly."

Eli's stomach clenched. A double vision with both ending similarly. "I will find a way to keep her alive."

"This will not be easy. She has strong feelings for you." John passed the binoculars.

Eli raised the binoculars again. Darcy's leggings molded her hips. She drew the anorak over her head and tossed it aside, revealing an equally form-fitting tank top. He abruptly passed the binoculars. "She's resilient. She'll get over what she thinks is love."

"Are you sure that is what you want? You dreamed her face before you met her. You have seen her spirit guide. You have shared a vision. She may be your spirit mate."

"Even spirit mates die and leave behind pain for the survivor."

John raised the binoculars. "Some things in life are worth eventual loss. But if you are not willing to accept her love, you are right to back away." He shrugged. "She wounded your pride. That is hard to forgive."

"I accept her explanation and apology, but I'm keeping my distance. I didn't want her protection," Eli said, loathing his abrupt tone.

John nodded. "I wonder how she feels about you protecting her. She is strong. And accepting protection means giving up control and depending on your protector. Trust is required." John shook his head. "It is complicated."

"Leave it, Uncle. She did what she thought best when she sent me away. Now I'll do what I think best to keep her alive."

Eli picked up a stick and drew circles in the ashes around the fire.

John shrugged. "It is gallant of you to save her. Some other man will appreciate your efforts someday."

Eli tossed the stick into the coals.

"When will you tell her about your vision and your plans?" John asked.

"Her safety comes first; explanations come later."

"She is a proven warrior. She can help take care of herself."

John passed the binoculars.

Eli shook his head. "She knows the men are at large. She'll be careful enough without explaining our visions."

He lifted the glasses to his eyes. A breeze played the surface of the lake and rippled dried reeds along the empty edge.

"Where did she go?"

"The wind is changing," John observed calmly.

Eli scooped up a water bottle. Minutes later he closed on the area where he'd last seen Darcy. He found her asleep, curled atop a granite boulder. He jumped a small spring that fed the lake, relieved she'd put her anorak back on.

She loved him.

A peculiar warmth defeated his halfhearted attempt to

stifle its spread. He'd swiftly adjusted to her presence here—like a vital element he'd lost had returned.

He'd missed her. Sharing her life, even briefly, had raised unwanted comparisons to his self-imposed isolation. He shoved the admissions away. Her life was more important than his weakness.

Crossing to the boulder, he sat beside her, arms loosely draped around bent knees. Sunlight crept across the lake's still surface. Somewhere up the forested hill, a woodpecker fed. He closed his eyes and concentrated on the monotonous tapping.

Having her close to him endangered her. So he'd develop a plan to protect her from a distance. Their attraction would pass. He'd emotionally distanced himself from people and events since childhood. This would be no different.

Eli was near.

Darcy blinked away the remnants of sleep and smiled until reality recalled his rejection. She sat up. Crushed pine needles—caught between her body and the granite—emphasized the scent she associated with Eli. The morning's uncertain shadows, now dissipated by sunlight, left her vulnerable.

She brushed her clothes clean. "Is it time to pack?"

"Almost, but first we need to talk about protecting you in Lost Creek. Since you don't want me staying at your house, will you install an alarm system that my department can monitor?"

She pushed away sorrow. Eli had finally agreed to not stay at her house. That was good, she thought. Because seeing him daily—knowing he didn't love her—would slowly destroy her.

"Those are good alternatives given the awkwardness now between us."

"It's only awkward if we let it be. If you think of me as a friend, it could work."

"I'm feeling a lot of emotions concerning you, Sheriff—embarrassment, pain, attraction—but not friendship."

"Look deeper; it's there."

His eyes swept her. Regret flashed so fast that she must have imagined it.

She looked away to watch ripples created by feeding trout then created her own by tossing pine needles onto the water.

Eli scooped up some loose rocks, examined them, and chose one. He cocked and released his arm and sent the stone skipping across the lake's surface. He dropped the remaining rocks and slid from the boulder to his feet. "Rain is coming. We need to help Uncle John pack."

Thinking, Darcy slid off the rock and gathered her rod and flies. Friends came when you needed them. Friends shared their time. Friends could guess what the other was thinking.

Eli had done all those things for her. What had she done for him other than feed him, disparage his tribe, and decide she was the one who could change his mind about permanent relationships because she wanted more?

The storm gathered in the northwest. The clouds' bruised coloring matched Darcy's thoughts as she stuffed her sleeping bag into her backpack.

She'd come to Colorado and cleared the air between her and Eli. She could return home and not feel guilty when she saw him in town. The happy thought evaporated.

No, she wouldn't feel guilty—but desire was another story.

Lifting her pack, she carried it over to rest on the ground beside the camping gear. Eli moved among the horses speaking softly, adjusting loads, and tightening girths. His green eyes locked with hers. She refused to be embarrassed because he'd caught her staring. He knew she loved him.

She tied her rain jacket behind her saddle's cantle. The curious horse shifted, and the saddle connected with her tender scar.

"Ouch!" She grabbed her arm. Eli vaulted the gear pile.

"Are you okay?" Voice curt, he pushed her sleeve up to examine the angry red scar. She stiffened. His hands lowered abruptly.

"I'm fine." She adjusted the gel covering.

"When did the stitches come out?"

"Tuesday."

His small talk threatened her composure. As if sensing her discomfort, he turned away.

CHAPTER EIGHTEEN

Darcy bounced awake as the truck pulled up to a large barn. Muscles stiff, she climbed awkwardly from the backseat she'd shared with Joseph.

"Head inside the house, little one," Uncle John said. "We will unload the horses and gear."

"I'd like to help."

"We are familiar with the horses and the barn, we will not be long," Uncle John promised.

Eli's frown stifled any further protest. Lifting her pack, she ran through the rain and leaped to the wide porch fronting the adobe-walled house. She shook off her raincoat and hung it on one of several wooden pegs anchored in the adobe and removed and upended her wet boots. Gripping her pack, she knocked. A short, plump woman with a long, silver-laced braid answered the door.

"Come in. I'm Mary Whitepath. I saw John return." She showed Darcy to a shower and handed her a lavender-scented towel. "Would you like something hot to drink?"

"I'd love a cup of hot chocolate or tea," Darcy said.

Fifteen minutes later, she entered the kitchen. Mary poured steaming water over a teabag. "Are you warm now?"

"I am. Thank you for your hospitality."

Darcy sipped tea, liking the clean look of the pine cabinets, and the contrast of the red curtains and countertops. A beef roast simmered on the cook top. "How can I help?"

"You can chop vegetables."

They were discussing Brooke's art show when Uncle John entered.

"Eli is sleeping until we eat. The drive to Texas is a long one."

And she wouldn't be joining him. She hoped that they'd blame her watering eyes on the onion she chopped. She needed to call the airlines and see if she could get a flight today.

John tugged Mary's braid. "Do I smell roast?"

Mary threatened him with a wooden spoon. "It's for supper."

John took Darcy's arm. "I'm taking the Anglo hostage. You can ransom her with food."

He led her to his study. Trophies and ribbons filled an entire wall; photos of horses at shows or in training lined another wall. Darcy picked out a young, gangly Eli in some of the images. Finally, she looked at Uncle John.

"Thank you for helping me clear the air with Eli."

"Little Anglo-Sioux girl, consider yourself adopted by this band of Comanche. You will always be welcome here. I hope you will come again."

"I appreciate your offer, your counsel, and your trust." She straightened her shoulders. "May I use your phone? I need to check returning flights for tonight."

"Stay. We have plenty of room, and there is a morning flight."

"Thank you, but I've finished what I came for, and I have a bed-and-breakfast to open."

Uncle John sighed, handed her a phone book, and left the room.

Darcy called the airport. Due to storm delays, the flights were overbooked. Hanging up, she crossed the room to stand inside a bay window. A rain-blurred view of Mount Blanca shimmered in the distance. As barley fields turned into a green marsh, she reviewed her options.

Like a breeze, Darcy wafted through his dreams.

Eli woke and growled. He was supposed to protect her, not wonder how close his imagination came to physical reality. He crossed the hall to the shower.

The initial icy blast reminded him of their earlier ride down the mountain. Rain mixed with sleet had transformed the trail into a treacherous slough. The horses had slid and stumbled, but Darcy hadn't complained. Not even when they reached the campground and her hands had proved too numb to unsaddle her horse. She'd silently moved aside at his command. He'd dismissed the desire to tuck her hands inside his coat and share the warmth of his body.

He dried, dressed, and followed two of his favorite scents—beef and freshly baked yeast rolls—to the kitchen.

"Smells good, Aunt Mary." He kissed her cheek.

"Your uncle is in the dining room," she said curtly, her back to him.

He paused. "Have I done something to upset you?"

She didn't look at him. "Your uncle is in the dining room."

Eli tickled her ear with the end of her braid then joined Uncle John at the dining room's picture window. Outside, the storm had settled into a fuchsia and tangerine sunset that bathed the long valley. Eli looked over his shoulder at the table set for three.

"Is Darcy sleeping through dinner?"

"She is gone."

"Where?" Eli's hands fisted.

"Joseph dropped her off on his way home, but not at the airport. He called and said she told him the storm delayed her flight until tomorrow, so she made other arrangements. He took her to the bus station on Stockton Street."

Mary entered and thumped the roast onto the table. Eli stared after her as she stalked back to the kitchen. "When did she leave?"

"The bus to Santa Fe left forty-five minutes ago. From there, she can connect through San Antonio to Lost Creek. It is a two-day trip."

Eli stared out the window. "Maybe it's best. I'll get back ahead of her and set my plan in motion."

Mary returned to slap a basket of rolls on the table. "What are you going to do about that young woman riding alone on a bus for two days?"

"Aunt Mary, I didn't know she was going to take a bus. If I'd known, I'd have offered her a ride."

"The woman flies from Lost Creek to apologize to you, and you don't even ask how she's getting home!"

"Why didn't you wake me?"

"It's a long drive." Mary picked up the third place-setting. "Now you've rested, you can get started."

Eli narrowed his eyes. "Started where?"

"Santa Fe. The bus stops in Taos and Española and has an hour layover in Santa Fe before it continues to Albuquerque. Your red truck travels faster than the bus." Her fierce scowl eased slightly. "I'll make sandwiches while you pack so you won't need to stop to eat."

Muttering under his breath, Eli snagged a yeast roll then turned his back on the hot meal. In his room, he crammed his shaving kit into his pack. Why hadn't Darcy told him she needed a ride home?

The answer slunk up like a guilty dog. She hadn't said anything because he'd made it clear the only relationship they could share was that of a sheriff aiding a citizen. She was trying to give him space. He tossed his clothes into the bag and went to claim his sandwiches.

Three hours later, he parked at the Santa Fe bus terminal. Remnants of the storm crawling off to the east had kept him from breaking the speed limit. He walked inside and immediately spotted Darcy.

She looked like a teenager in her white T-shirt, faded

jeans, and hiking boots. She'd pulled her golden hair into a high ponytail that emphasized her delicate neck. A daypack hung from one shoulder as she fed change to a vending machine.

Darcy studied the machine's options. No significant decisions here—she'd made all those earlier.

Accepting Uncle John's hospitality would have meant sitting across the table from Eli and forcing down what would otherwise be a delicious meal. Sleeping under the same roof was unthinkable, as was asking for a ride. She'd gotten herself here; she'd get herself home. She pushed a button. A bottle of water dropped to the opening.

Fifteen minutes until the bus left. Judging by the sparse group in the station, she could claim a row of seats and get some sleep—if she could continue to avoid the persistent Romeo who'd pestered her since she'd boarded in Alamosa.

A hand clamped her shoulder.

She suppressed a groan.

"For the third time, I'm not interested in having your children." She rolled her shoulder. The hand didn't release as she turned.

Surprise replaced frustration. "Eli?"

"Who's bothering you?" His eyes hardened to green ice.

She shook her head. "No one I can't handle. Why are you here?"

"I came to give you a ride."

"A ride?" she repeated, dumbfounded that he stood six

inches from her. "How did you know where to find me?"

"Joseph called Uncle John."

Comprehension dawned on her. "John and Mary made you come."

His nod reminded her that she'd have to get over the urge to wag her tail like an ecstatic puppy every time he showed up.

"I'm sorry you drove all this way for nothing, but I bought a ticket and the bus leaves shortly. You asked; I said no. Don't delay your trip any longer."

He was tempted to leave her, but she couldn't spend the rest of the trip fighting advances from some guy with paternity ambitions. He scrutinized every male in the bus station. "I'll be in Lost Creek tomorrow afternoon. The bus won't arrive until late tomorrow night."

"A few more hours won't make a difference." She opened her water.

"Don't be bull-headed. Your greeting indicated someone is harassing you. You'll be safe with me, so get your bag."

"She doesn't want to go with you," a male voice interrupted.

A sense of calm descended on Eli. Finally. A situation he could sink his teeth or fists into. He turned. "You must be the volunteer sperm donor."

Eli held a four-inch height advantage, yet the younger man bristled back at him. Brave but stupid.

"Let's take this outside," the man challenged.

Eli turned for the door.

"No!" Darcy cried. "I'll get my pack off the bus, Eli."

"You want me to call the cops?" the man asked.

Eli gave him credit for bravado. Darcy's sigh caught his ear.

"He is the cops," she said.

Eli followed her outside and retrieved her backpack from the luggage compartment. He tossed it onto the back seat of his truck. It was going to be a long, tense drive.

The succession of CDs that he fed into the player saved them from an otherwise silent night. Occasional small towns and rural homes winked in then out of sight, illuminated by security pole lights and the occasional colored patch of a glow through curtained windows that indicated a night owl. Fortified by his afternoon nap, he planned to drive straight through to Lost Creek.

Toward midnight, Darcy drifted off on the verge of consciousness. After her third sudden head jerk, Eli raised the console separating them. He pulled a jacket from behind the seat and laid it on his thigh.

"Lie down."

"I'm fine,"

Two minutes later, her head jerked again.

He gentled his voice. "Loosen your seat belt and lie down."

Headlights from an approaching eighteen-wheeler briefly illuminated the truck's interior before the semi roared west. She yawned and gave in. Sliding out of the shoulder strap, she loosened the lap belt, curled onto her side, and pillowed her head on his coat-cushioned thigh. His inevitable reaction irritated him.

Physically close but emotionally distant. Darcy battled tension and fatigue as the Eagles harmonized about the damage a woman could inflict on a man's soul.

Brooke's optimistic opinion that Darcy had broken through Eli's emotional reserve had not proven correct. He'd let her through once, but she'd spoiled that. She wanted to repair the damage, but he'd rebuilt and reinforced his barriers. He'd accepted her apology but wasn't allowing anything more.

"I'm sorry," she murmured, eyes closed.

He didn't answer. Had he heard the words meant to convey regret for her unkind—if kindly meant—Indian remark, sorrow for the pain in his past, an apology that Mary and John had asked him to come after her, and sorrow for the gap widening between them?

The Eagles' harmony and Eli's scent on the jacket lulled her closer to sleep. So close, she almost missed his reply.

"Don't beat yourself up about it. You did what you thought was right. We'll leave it at that."

A blade flashed. She twisted, but the heavy weight pinning her denied escape.

"Darcy, you're with me. You're safe."

Eli's voice penetrated her disorientation. She scanned the truck cab's ceiling, the dash, his face. According to the speedometer, they'd slowed to forty-five. The number began to climb. Conscious of the pressure of his hand splayed protectively across her hip, her breath caught. She sat up and broke contact. "Where are we?"

"We've been in Texas for the last forty minutes." He shifted in his seat then continued, "A billboard promised a motel ahead. We'll both travel better after a few hours' sleep."

She adjusted her seatbelt shoulder strap and looked at him. Dash glow produced enough light for her to notice the additional tightness in his jeans. She raised her hands to straighten her ponytail and hide her heated cheeks. He was the sheriff who would treat her like any other citizen of Tell County, whether she wanted him to or not. Or was he?

Minutes later, they pulled into a U-shaped, vinyl-sided motel with a flashing red VACANCY sign. Darcy walked inside with Eli. Décor-wise, the cramped office had achieved permanent stasis in the Sixties, where dirt-concealing, gray Formica covered the reception counter and linoleum floor.

The night clerk, engrossed by a television movie, ignored them until Eli rang the bell. "Be with ya in a minute," she called without looking away from the program.

When a commercial interrupted, she rose from the recliner and plodded toward them, her black hair tightly curled and secured with bobby-pin pinwheels. She had enough metal on her head to function as an antenna. Darcy watched to see if the fuzzy television image deteriorated the further away the woman moved. It did not.

The woman set a registration form and pen on the counter.

"We need two rooms," Eli said. He snapped a credit card onto the counter. Darcy dug in her purse and laid her VISA next to his. She calculated interest on the cost of a room. After the airline and bus tickets, she might not be paying next month's bill in full.

The woman picked up another form and pen. She swiped their cards then squinted at the wall clock, recording their check-in time: twelve twenty-eight AM.

"Check out is noon." The woman looked toward the television as the movie resumed. She reached under the desk, retrieved two keys, and dropped them on the counter. "Rooms seven and eight." She shuffled back to the recliner.

"I'll take seven." Darcy scooped up her key and walked outside toward the rooms. Moments later, the truck's engine started. Eli parked between their doors, then pulled their packs from the back seat and thrust hers toward her. She gripped the pack's straps.

"I'll wake you at seven." He unlocked his door and disappeared inside.

Darcy addressed his closed door. "Goodnight to you too, Sheriff."

She opened her door and leaned her pack against the wall. Irritation vied with relief.

The bedside lamp barely illuminated the room. The clattering air-conditioner drowned the highway noise so she switched it from high-cool rattle to low-heat rattle.

She removed her shoes, then started on her shirt.

Light pierced the dimness behind her.

"Querida! This is what I call room service!"

CHAPTER NINETEEN

A dark-haired man possum-grinned from the bathroom doorway. Water droplets glistened on well-defined shoulders and pecs. A diplomatically positioned towel exposed his muscular flanks.

"Oh my gosh!" Darcy leaned toward the wall separating her from Eli and pounded wildly. Her arm hit the lamp and sent it crashing to the floor.

"I'm willing to share if you are," the backlit, smiling man said.

"I'm sorry!" She edged toward the door and fumbled with the lock behind her back. "The clerk gave me a key. She said this room was available, but obviously, it isn't. I'll get my things and go."

The man advanced a step.

"Stop!" she cried.

The knob turned. She jumped aside, barely avoiding the door as it slammed inward. Eli crouched in the opening. The outside light bronzed his bare back and glinted off the pistol trained on the stranger.

The man dropped his towel and shot his hands high. Darcy spun to face the wall.

"I'm okay." She edged toward Eli as he stood and eased

into the room. "This room is already occupied." She pointed unnecessarily over her shoulder. "He, uh, startled me."

"I offered to share," the man said.

"That won't be necessary," Eli said, his words clipped. He slipped the pistol into his waistband, shouldered her backpack, then gripped her elbow. "Let's go."

He quick-walked her outside.

"Excuse me, querida. You left these."

Darcy's wannabe roommate now wore the towel. The man extended one hand—offering her tennis shoes. Eli grabbed them and slammed the door in the man's face.

"Give me your key," he snapped, opening his door.

She tugged her shirt down, then pulled the key from her pocket.

"Stay inside and lock the door," Eli said. "Don't open it until you hear my voice." He grabbed his shirt off the bed and slipped it on.

He slammed his door too.

Eli left the tail of his shirt out to conceal the gun in his waistband then waited to hear the lock click. The fresh night air helped counteract the adrenaline surge of finding the stranger in Darcy's room. He'd get her another room and get some sleep—if he could block the image of her toned midriff from his mind.

The night clerk was still engrossed in her movie. He tossed the key onto the counter. "One of the rooms you gave us is occupied. We need another."

"Not any," she said, her eyes never leaving the flickering screen. "We're full. We have eight rooms, and I let six during the storm. Earl must have let another while I ate. He never tells me anything." The show's credits rolled. She switched off the TV and shuffled to the desk.

"Your room is a double, so you can share. It costs more with two to a room, but not as much as two rooms. I'll give you the difference."

"Keep it," Eli said. "A lamp broke in room seven. We'll call it even."

She grunted and flipped a switch that lit up the NO above VACANCY.

"Full?"

Darcy sank onto one maroon bedspread. Eli's room was a carbon copy of hers except for the two double beds and avocado green carpet. She glanced at the far wall. Would the man next door trade places?

"Not an option," Eli said. "And you're on my bed. You take the one farthest from the door." He dropped his wallet beside her and released two shirt buttons.

She shot to her feet and stalked to the second bed.

He shrugged out of his shirt. Seeming indifferent to her presence, he walked past as if she were a piece of furniture. She'd left Alamosa because she didn't want to stay in the same house with him. How would she handle him sleeping four feet away?

"I'm taking a shower. You're in charge while I'm gone."

"In charge of what? The remote control?"

He closed the door before she'd finished speaking.

"Okay, the remote control it is."

A search of the nightstand and dresser failed to produce a remote. The television looked slightly newer than the carpet. She found the power button and manually scrolled channels, stopping on the least snowy choice—a local talk show with a panel of four guests.

"Have any of you high school principals confiscated any of the heroin or other drugs at school?" The host asked.

All four guests nodded. One woman spoke.

"We find drugs or evidence of drugs at least twice a month and sometimes more frequently. This is not acceptable. We, our teachers, and our school counselors are talking with the students. And we encourage parents to talk with their children. Parents should know and verify where their kids are spending their time after school, and who they are spending it with."

The rest of the panel murmured agreement.

"Well," the host said. "The good news is that Sheriff Connor has a suspected dealer in custody. We'll have more details on that fellow as the Sheriff's Department releases them. And that's all for tonight on What's Happening in Our Region," he finished.

Darcy turned off the TV and leaned against the veneered headboard. The discussion implied recent activity.

The sound of running water continued behind the

bathroom door. Darcy jiggled the nightstand drawer open to retrieve a thin phone book. Flipping to the back, she found a lone listing under "Television Stations & Broadcasting Companies." She dialed. The phone stretched into its sixth ring.

"Channel Twelve," a breathless voice rushed.

"Hi, I'm calling about the segment you aired on drug use in high schools," she said.

"Yes, ma'am." The man's voice altered from surprised to enthusiastic. "I'm Mike Sage, producer and host of What's Happening in Our Region, how can I help you?"

"I missed the first part of your program. I'm from out of town, but our county is having similar heroin issues. I was wondering when the heroin first showed up here, and what type is it?"

"Sure. The overdoses started in March. It's Mexican heroin—the kind that looks like tar. We're averaging one death a month, and the sheriff has a suspected dealer in custody."

She noticed she could hear better. Eli had shut off the shower.

"Thank you; and good luck." She hung up as Eli emerged from the steamy bathroom. A white towel hugged his hips. Turning away, she focused on the blank TV screen.

CHAPTER TWENTY

"Who did you call?" Eli asked.

"Don't worry, the call was local." Darcy watched as he folded his arms across his chest and planted himself in front of her. She ducked her head and covertly inhaled his pine scent.

"Darcy," he warned.

"I caught the end of a program on drug use among local students. They mentioned heroin, and I got curious." She explained her questions and the answers she received. "Do you think there's a connection?"

She looked up to judge his reaction. Big mistake. His stance reminded her of Brooke's painting. Her eyes drifted down. He looked good in skirt-like attire. Breechcloths, towels—

"Darcy."

"Yes?" Her eyes snapped to his face. Her cheeks heated.

"It's your turn to shower."

She scurried to the bathroom and pinned her hair on top of her head. The day's travel washed away, but the questions circling inside her brain clung like a stain. Did Eli honestly prefer solitude? When he'd calmed her in the truck after her nightmare, he'd instigated the contact. His physical reaction to her implied interest, but if physical attraction was all he felt, she was fighting a losing battle.

The water heater abruptly emptied. She fumbled to shut off the faucets then reached for a towel. Her mind continued to work on untangling the snarl that was Eli as she smoothed on honeysuckle-scented body lotion.

He'd opened up to her before. She wanted to break through and make him smile again. The mortar of his current walls was fresh. If she could create a chink, they might crumble.

Switching off the light, she opened the bathroom door. Muted light filtered through the shade of the table lamp on the nightstand separating the beds. Eli lay on his side, facing the door, one bare shoulder and arm exposed.

She gave one last downward tug to the hem of her oversized T-shirt before entering the room. Frigid air raised goosebumps. She briskly rubbed her arms. What was it with men and air conditioners? The room was colder than a Sub-Zero freezer. She sat on the edge of her bed and revved up her courage.

"Are you going to turn out the light?" he asked.

"Before we met at Border's, I saw you in my dreams," she said.

She held her breath as he rose to an elbow and twisted to face her. The sheet slipped to his chest. He squinted into the light.

"You saw me in a dream before we met?"

"It sounds crazy, but yes. Several times. Your eyes, your

face, your body. You."

He leaned and switched off the light. She heard him drop back onto his bed.

Great. Now he thought she was certifiable. He'd worry about her credibility as a witness. It was time for a less mystical approach.

"I don't believe you're opposed to lasting relationships," she said.

"Believe it."

"I believe you reject the idea of permanent relationships because of what happened to your parents and Brooke's husband."

"You're right."

His admission didn't feel like a victory.

"But what about Brooke and Jeremy? And Dan and Lisa and Uncle John and Aunt Mary? You'd walk through fire for any of them. You're more emotionally involved than you realize."

"Drop it, Darcy."

A warning tinged his words. She dug her fingers into the bedspread.

"Eli, you frequently face the ugliness that I've only recently experienced, and I understand that you have to insulate yourself to perform your job effectively. Good and evil harbor risks, but you don't shy away from the evil in your life, so why shy away from the potential good?"

Instead of answering, he flipped the covers back. A shadowy form, he pulled on jeans and a shirt. "I'm sleeping in the truck. Lock up behind me."

Gathering keys, wallet, and gun, he walked out the door.

Friday morning, a slamming door brought Eli instantly awake. He rose from his truck's back seat and scowled at the well-rested man exiting room seven. The man stopped at Eli's window and grinned.

"Looked like she was worth it to me," he said, unlocking the cab of an adjacent pickup.

Eli wasn't about to confess he'd run away from Darcy when he'd never run from an argument or situation in his life.

Her announcement last night had kept him awake for hours. They'd seen one another in visions—twice. Uncle John would say that made her his woman—made him her man. But he'd ordered his life to avoid emotional entanglement.

Or so he'd thought. Her observations had struck a nerve. Of course, he cared about Brooke, Jeremy, Uncle John, and Aunt Mary. They were his family, and Dan was his best friend.

Engaging with Darcy distracted him mentally and her proximity added a further distraction. He couldn't risk an unbalancing act that might cost her life.

He waited for the man to leave before starting his truck.

At seven, Darcy answered Eli's knock on the door and stuck her head out. She swept her wet hair onto her back. "Hi," she said, relieved that his truck had reappeared in the parking lot. "I'm using the hairdryer, then I'll be ready ."

"I filled the gas tank. Hand your pack out and meet me next door in the café when you're ready."

Darcy ducked back inside to dry her hair.

She turned in the room key and walked to the café. Semis, trucks, and cars packed the parking lot. She pushed open the swinging glass door with its clanking cowbell and stepped inside to the stomach-rumble-inducing smells of bacon and coffee.

She spotted Eli in a back booth that allowed him to face the room and entrance. An attractive, thirty-ish waitress smiled with intent as she refilled his coffee cup.

Eli smiled back.

Darcy straightened her shoulders. He knew she was here; he never missed a thing.

As she moved towards him, a trucker invited her to join him. She smiled and declined his offer. When she looked up, she had Eli's attention.

She closed the distance between them and slid onto the seat across from him. The waitress offered to return in a few minutes for their order.

Eli's gaze traveled from her face to the swell of her breasts.

Her black tank top fit snugly, and the neckline scooped low enough to display cleavage. "It's the last clean shirt I have," she said.

She picked up a menu to block his view. "Funds are tight. I'm not buying a souvenir T-shirt."

"What about your inheritance from Alex?" he asked.

"That's what's eaten up most of my savings. Remodeling

is not for the faint of heart or the short of cash."

"Not the house, the money he left you."

"Alex didn't—" She clamped her mouth shut before she revealed anything else.

"Didn't what? Leave you any money?" His eyes narrowed. "If Alex didn't leave you his money, who got it?"

"I can't tell you."

Any moment now, she expected his stare to sear a hole in her menu.

"But you know who got the money."

She laid the menu on the corner of the table and glanced around. Where was that flirty waitress?

"You realize that whoever got the money might have expected to get the house. They could be behind the vandalism," Eli said.

"I doubt it."

"Based on what evidence?"

"I can't say."

Keith had vouched for his mother, but she'd never met the woman. For all she knew, Mrs. Anderson harbored a grudge the size of Texas.

"Will someone be physically hurt if you reveal this information?"

Good question. The worst thing she'd heard about Dale Anderson was his former gambling problem—nothing about wife-beating. "I don't think so."

"Then why keep quiet?"

She imagined Keith's mother doling out her inheritance

to Greg and the faceless Dale. "There are other ways to be hurt."

"If the secret you're keeping were made public, would the people involved know you divulged it?"

"Yes."

His fingers drummed the tabletop then came to an abrupt halt. "Then I'll get a copy of Alex's probated will from the courthouse to see who inherited the money."

Her eyes widened. "You can do that?"

"Once a will is probated, it becomes part of the public record."

Darcy smiled. "I'm sorry to cause you extra work, but I appreciate your not pressuring me to break a confidence."

The waitress returned. When she sashayed off with their orders, Darcy leaned forward.

"Are you going to tell me where you went this morning? I woke when your truck started, and you were gone longer than it took to get fuel." She pointed out the café window at the gas station on the opposite side of the highway.

Eli's gaze dropped to her breasts.

"No distraction tactics." She yanked a napkin from the dispenser, tucked the rough paper across the tops of her breasts, and secured the ends under her tank top. She crossed her forearms on the table and leaned toward him again, pleased that his eyes now met hers, and even more pleased that a hint of humor lit their green depths.

"I checked out the map in the phone book," she said. "You had enough time to drive to the county seat and have a discussion with the sheriff about what I found out last night. Did you speak with the dealer in custody?"

He sipped coffee and continued to watch her.

"Are the incidents related?"

"Ms. Cooper." He slid his cup to the edge of the table. "I won't comment on an ongoing investigation." His hand darted forward and stripped the napkin from her shirt. "Enjoy your breakfast," he said, tucking the napkin into his collar.

"This isn't finished." She leaned back, giving the waitress room to deliver their food.

"Pass the ketchup."

She passed the ketchup and picked up the saltshaker.

"What did you do while I was gone, Darcy?"

He chewed and swallowed scrambled eggs while watching her face. She tried to look innocent.

"I taught Shirley how to make dumplings, and I renewed my driver's license."

"And."

"I got my hair trimmed, and my car window replaced."

He drank some coffee and set the cup down. "I told you to leave the Andersons to my investigators."

She hesitated. Deputy Carlisle had seen her with the Ryans. That fact was probably in a text on his phone in bold uppercase letters. Trying a diversion, she crossed her arms beneath her breasts. His eyes dipped, then returned to hers.

She restrained a childish "made you look" and settled for

juvenile: she took a deep breath and watched his focus flicker.

"Is it my fault that Angela Ryan cuts hair and I needed a trim? And how was I to know that Greg Ryan is a mechanic at the garage that replaced my car window?"

His tightening jaw made it clear he didn't believe her. Darcy rolled her eyes. "Eli, I admit I wanted to meet them, but I'm not stupid. I made an anonymous appointment with Angela."

"What happened?" Eli leaned back and extended one arm along the top of the booth.

"When I told Angela who I was, she became reserved. But by the time she finished my trim, she was warming up. She said she didn't care about Alex's house. I believe her."

"And the husband?"

"Greg was a surprise. I wouldn't have chosen to meet him alone."

She picked up her fork and pushed hash browns around on her plate. "He must have seen my name on the work order because he knew who I was before I figured out who he was." She dropped her fork to rub goosebumps from her arms. "Greg was verbally hostile and physically intimidating."

Eli's lips thinned. "Did anyone else see or hear what happened?"

"No, he was the only one there when I returned for the car. He commented on how remote my house is and asked if I liked 'varmints.' That made me wonder about the snakes, but Greg's alibi checked out. He couldn't have left the snakes. I didn't find out the rest until Tuesday."

"What happened on Tuesday?"

She explained the similarities in handwriting and her subsequent meeting with Angela and Greg Ryan.

"Has Greg been arrested?" he asked.

"No, he and Angela have two children. I told them I wouldn't press vandalism charges."

"You're putting yourself in danger by snooping," Eli said, voice tight.

"I was all right. Deputy Carlisle arrived while I was talking to the Ryans. She stayed until they left then followed me home. And whether you like it or not, if people attack me, leave snakes on my porch, and make threatening phone calls, I'm asking questions."

"Tell me about the phone calls."

She sighed.

"A man called and whispered to me twice after you left. My answering machine is fielding calls, but he hasn't left messages. He calls me 'golden girl' and shakes a rattlesnake tail while he talks. The first call, he said, 'You have something of mine.' The second call, I hung up on him. The only thing I acquired lately that belonged to someone else—"

"Is the heroin or the house." Eli released his grip on the booth back to rearrange the condiment bottles and salt and pepper shakers like chess pieces. "Dan got a warrant for a tap on your line after you reported the calls."

"Yes, he mentioned that."

"Do you have caller ID?"

"Yes. But his number is blocked."

"Tell me the rest of it."

Her blushes started at her chest, Eli noted. Seven hours alone with her in that tank top wasn't a good idea. Maybe he'd loan her one of his shirts. He sat quietly, watching, waiting.

"Well, maybe one more thing," she said. "I had dinner with Keith after he bribed me to meet him."

"He bribed you?" His anger mounted as she nodded her head.

"He said he knew why Alex left me the house, but he wouldn't tell me unless I had dinner with him. I noticed that one of your patrol cars made several passes by the Pecan Grill that night. Keith was a perfect gentleman."

Eli wasn't interested in hearing about the veterinarian's perfection or his choice of the priciest restaurant in Tell County. "What did Keith tell you?"

"That a client of his who'd bought most of Alex's land had told him that Alex believed the house and I would be good for each other." Her eyes watered.

With a quick tug, he pulled the napkin from his throat and handed it to her. He ran all ten fingers across his scalp and locked them behind his neck. She stood up to armed assailants, socialized with suspects, and got sentimental over a house that caused her nothing but trouble? What would he to do with this woman?

"Did the information make any difference to you?" he asked.

Her eyes widened. "Of course. I've wondered for months why Alex would leave the house to me, and not his family."

"Because you weren't Alex's lover."

"That's right."

They sat in silence for several moments. She wondered if Alex had told Maggie he was giving her the house. Maggie hadn't seemed surprised that the rumors were based on Darcy knowing Alex intimately. She'd suspected that might happen. Had she discussed that possibility with Alex? She'd have to ask Maggie the next time they talked.

"You've thought of someone," he said.

She was getting used to him guessing her thoughts. "I've thought of someone who might have known Alex was giving me the house. He might have told her something he didn't tell me."

"You're keeping her identity a secret?"

She pushed her plate to the side of the table. "Yes. But I'll call her when I get home and let you know if Alex discussed my inheritance with her."

Eli signaled for the check.

Four hours later, with the sun directly overhead, Darcy watched Eli offer a two-finger wave to a passing driver.

She clasped her hands in her lap. Despite her attempts at conversation, he'd barely said two sentences since they'd left the café.

The Tell County road sign felt like a line of demarcation—like words on an ancient sailing map: There be monsters here.

Eli's voluntary and involuntary actions indicated he felt something for her. She wasn't sure how much more frustrated Eli could get with her, but she was about to find out.

"Do you feel the attraction, too?" she asked.

"You already know the answer."

"I can wait to act on it until after the men are caught. Can you?"

"Sure. Then we'll enjoy each other until one of us walks away."

Pain crowded her already teeming insides. They both knew who was most likely to do the walking. "I don't want an affair," she said. "I don't want to picture the end at the beginning."

"An affair is all I'd offer." His grip tightened on the steering wheel.

Emptiness flooded her, drowning hope. "Then nothing has changed. I thought—I'm sorry I didn't take you at your word. I won't make that mistake again."

Three of the longest hours of her life later, Darcy checked the clock in Eli's truck while Eli checked her house—2 PM. She stirred the ashes of her heart for the warm coals of homecoming. This was the sanctuary where she could nurse her pain, sort her thoughts, and mourn her mistakes. Alex's prediction that the house would be good for her could still come true.

She checked her watch. Eli had been inside for almost ten minutes. What was taking so long? She'd only been gone three days. He'd had enough time to peek under her bed and inside the closets. She jumped down, lifted her pack from the back seat, and walked to the house. As she reached for the knob, the door opened.

"I told you to stay in the truck." Eli grabbed her arm. Her pack hindered his attempt to turn her around.

"You've never taken this long to—" She glimpsed chaos over his shoulder. "No!" Dropping her pack, she struggled to twist free of his hold and push past him.

"Darcy, stop. You can't go in."

"It's my house!" As she pulled away, her voice broke. "It's my house."

Eli stood between her and the front door. Compassion softened his eyes. "I've called a crime scene team."

Her voice caught. "How bad is it?"

He hesitated. "Whoever did it was angry. I'll call Brooke; you need someplace to stay tonight."

She swallowed. "Fine, but I'm staying here until the team finishes. I need to know what I'm dealing with." She hugged her arms and walked away to sit on the porch swing.

Over the next two hours, Darcy transitioned from panicked shock to drained acceptance. When Eli came to get her, he looked as exhausted as she felt.

"You can come in now." He looked at her long and hard. "Brace yourself."

She took a deep breath and followed him inside. The narrow foyer table lay toppled; everything displayed on it now lay on the floor—some items whole, some shattered. She walked into the living room and wrapped a protective hand around her scar. Someone had taken a knife to her leather couch and love seat.

"How did they get in?"

"One of the panes in your kitchen door is broken."

She tried to compartmentalize the damage. If she let it overwhelm her, she'd sink to the floor and weep—or get in her car and drive as far away as she could as fast as she could.

"I should check my car."

"It's fine. You were smart to leave it parked under the security light. They would have been too easily seen while outside, and my deputies would have noticed the damage before now."

She bent and picked up a photo of Gramma and Grampa. The glass was unbroken. I am grateful for small favors, she thought. She imagined Gramma saying, Count your blessings, don't dwell on hardships.

Faith, family, friends, home. She could do this.

She stood in the kitchen doorway. Canisters, their contents emptied, and unboxed food littered the floor. Dishes and glasses, pots and pans, were randomly scattered on countertops and the floor.

"I need a change of clothes," she said, turning for her bedroom. Eli followed.

Once again, her chest tightened. All her clothing and linens—emptied from drawers and closets—lay strewn across the room. Most looked salvageable. All seemed tainted.

Back on the front porch, she pulled her dirty clothes and sleeping bag out of her backpack and tossed them inside. She gave the clothes from her bedroom a good shake, then rolled them up and settled them in her backpack.

"I'll be at Brooke's by dark," she said.

"I'll stay and help you clean," he offered.

"Thanks, but I'd rather you didn't." Having him here would combine her two crises and threaten her self-control. "I need to see some progress before I leave or I won't sleep tonight."

He nodded. "I understand."

Darcy listened to him drive away.

She started the washing machine and returned to the kitchen to unload the dishes the vandals had missed in the dishwasher. Once she swept and mopped the floor, the damage looked like less than she'd first thought.

Using the internet on her phone, she ordered two video cameras and an install-it-yourself alarm system that would arrive the next day and could be monitored by the Sheriff's Department.

She gulped from a bottle of water then held the plastic's barely-there coolness against her burning eyelids before lobbing the empty bottle towards the trashcan.

She heard a vehicle approaching. She reached for her bat, then breathed a relieved sigh when she recognized Brooke's van. She unlocked the screen door.

"Come in, Brooke. Did Eli send you?"

Brooke entered, and Darcy relocked the door.

"He mentioned you could use some help." Brooke crossed to the table and ran a finger through the gray fingerprint dust that seemed to cover every surface. "Is the rest of the house like this?"

"Pretty much. They put holes in the walls upstairs since there wasn't any furniture to destroy. Thank goodness I delayed the delivery until Monday."

"How did Colorado go?"

"Colorado?" Darcy stifled a hysterical laugh. "I'd almost forgotten." She paused to patch her fraying composure. "I enjoyed meeting John and Mary. I apologized to Eli. He accepted my apology. He prefers we keep our relationship professional. End of Colorado story."

"I'm sorry."

"Me too. But I'll respect his decision." She raised her head. "I'd offer you coffee, but the machine is in the trash."

"I had plenty before I came." Brooke glanced around. "Which room do you want me to work on?"

An invisible dam broke, and relief rushed over Darcy. She wasn't alone.

"The kitchen is my priority. If the health inspector makes a surprise visit and sees this, he'll shut down my catering business. I can't afford that."

When they finished the kitchen, Brooke tackled the living room while Darcy worked on her bedroom. They cleaned steadily until dusk.

"Time to get going," Brooke said. "What would you like

to do with these?"

Darcy turned from scrubbing her bathroom. Her throat closed. Strips of willow held together by their handles were all that remained of Gramma's baskets.

CHAPTER TWENTY-ONE

Saturday morning, Eli leaned back in his office chair. He'd felt relief last night when he'd arrived home and seen Darcy's car in Brooke's driveway. She hadn't gotten stubborn and decided to clean all night.

The ransackers had presumably hit her house during the daytime, in between deputy patrols. If she hadn't followed him to Colorado, she might have been home when the vandals arrived.

Eli slammed a wadded phone message into the trash. Greg Ryan's alibi had been confirmed this morning. And since the seizure of two pounds of black tar heroin hadn't been publicized, Raul and Randy might have gone looking for their stash.

To keep Darcy safe, he could request extra funds from the county commissioners for protective duty, but he doubted they would authorize a budget increase. He'd have to use the money he had and try to locate additional grants to pay for the cruiser computers. Or he could sleep outside her house in his car. It wasn't comfortable, but—

Voices in the hallway carried.

"It's all over town." He heard Deputy Carlisle say. "Darcy Cooper sure put the rumors about her and Alex Anderson to rest. You can't fake virginity in a gynecologist's exam."

Before Eli could recover his stunned thoughts, the deputies passed.

He glanced at the hall clock. The department shift-change briefing was about to begin. He walked into the hall, stopped at the water fountain, and pressed the button.

Darcy was a virgin? Ten seconds later, he remembered to release the fountain's button. Where had that story originated? He entered the briefing room and sat in the back of the room. The sergeant had already started talking.

"None of the prints collected matched those lifted from the bags of heroin found in the jacket Ms. Cooper recovered. But the vandals could have worn gloves. We're waiting to hear from Ms. Cooper if anything is missing. Since Greg Ryan's alibi checked out, our working theory is that the break-in is linked to a search for the heroin.

"Yesterday, the sheriff questioned a suspected heroin dealer in custody in Raven County. A photo and sketch of the men who attacked Mrs. Lantz and Ms. Cooper were faxed to Raven County. Their prisoner identified the suspect known as Randy Hall, as his supplier. He provided little other useful information."

Eli shifted in his seat. Darcy had guessed right. He had followed up on her lead at the motel and visited the local sheriff. He made a mental note to speak to Dan about the virginity rumor. Lisa heard everything. By now, she'd have told Dan.

The sergeant shuffled papers. "Ms. Cooper has reported

receiving threatening phone calls from someone shaking a rattling device—presumably imitating a rattlesnake. The first call came Saturday, September twenty-second, at approximately five AM, the second Tuesday, September twenty-fifth, at approximately ten-forty PM. The caller may be the individual who left snakes on her porch."

"Sergeant?" Deputy Carlisle said, thumbing through the pages of her notebook. "Tuesday, September twenty-fifth, at approximately eleven PM, I stopped for coffee at Sally's Café. When I entered, a man at the counter removed a wallet from his pocket. A baby's rattle came out with the wallet. He mentioned a grandchild, paid his bill, and left. The man seemed flustered."

"In what way?" Eli cut in.

The deputy hugged the back of her chair to look over her shoulder. "He didn't make eye contact, sir, and he was in a hurry to leave. I heard the waitress complain that he didn't leave her a tip. He'd been in several times before, always paid cash, and always tipped her."

"Description."

Her brow furrowed in concentration.

"Mid-fifties, stocky, five-ten, 200 pounds, tanned. Brown hair graying at the temples—what I saw of it. He wore a dark blue ball cap, navy windbreaker, khaki pants. I only saw him in profile, but he was clean-shaven. Sally and Cathy were working; they might know something about him."

"Did you see his vehicle?"

"Dark blue crew-cab pickup, fairly new, American made with Texas plates. I didn't get the number."

"Why not? You said he was flustered."

"Yes, sir," she agreed. "But I sometimes have that effect on men. I mistook his reaction."

Eli stifled the laughter in the room with a glance. "Deputy Carlisle, visit the café and see if the man returned. Make arrangements for Sally and Cathy to come in. I want the three of you to work with a sketch artist."

He returned to his office and called Dan.

"What's up, boss?" Dan answered.

"I need to ask you about something I heard today."

"About Darcy?"

"Yes."

"Lisa's network is good. It's true. I think that Lisa is going through the phone book, making sure that everyone in the county knows."

"Thanks." Eli hung up.

Uncle John's words echoed in his head: It is gallant of you to want to save her. Someday, another man will appreciate your efforts to protect her.

Darcy let the insurance adjustor in early Saturday morning. He took pictures and copious notes and mentioned that she could offset some of her next premium increase since she was installing alarm and video systems. He offered condolences and left her with a promise to call her on Monday.

She tossed the sixth load of laundry into the washer. She felt amazingly rested. Brooke had brewed a cup of herbal tea that let Darcy sleep through the night. Unable to stop herself, she'd looked out the bedroom window before she went to bed and when she'd woken. Eli's truck hadn't been at the cottage either time.

She passed the living room where blankets swaddled the couch, love seat, and armchairs, hiding eviscerated upholstery. Entering the kitchen, she picked up a pen and paper and added to her list. Replace: food processor, mixer, blender, toaster, coffee maker. Things to do: call sheet rocker and painters, call the printer and postpone B&B opening mailer, check bank balance.

A calendar from the local electric co-op lay on the table, open to October. The twelfth, her opening date, was circled in red. She crossed it out. Even if insurance replaced the appliances and furniture this week, she couldn't rent rooms while she and the house were targets.

She called Maggie, got her voice mail, and told her there'd been a glitch and asked her to reschedule her booking. At least she didn't have to cancel other clients yet—and that was as close as she could come to a happy thought.

An hour later, Darcy pushed through the heavy glass doors of the Sheriff's Office and approached the front desk. Sergeant Tyler greeted her.

"Afternoon, Ms. Cooper."

He buzzed her through the security door. "Go on back.

Detective Wainright is expecting you."

She walked down the hall. The vandalism had driven the chill that had numbed her emotions after Eli's rejection, into her bones. Nothing could penetrate any deeper.

Wainright stood at her approach. "Ms. Cooper." She met his extended hand with hers. "If you don't mind," he said, "we'll use the interview room. It's quieter."

She nodded and followed him. He held the door for her.

"Have a seat." He sat across from her. "How's the cleanup coming?"

"Slowly. I have a lot to do. Where do you want me to start?"

He switched on a recorder and stated their names, the date and time. "When did you leave your house, Ms. Cooper?"

"I left about six forty-five AM, Wednesday, September twenty-sixth and returned Friday the twenty-eighth."

She continued to answer questions. This time, none were related to her and the sheriff. Wainright must have given up on casting doubt on Eli's morality now that her gynecologist visit had defused the rumors.

When Wainright switched off the recorder, she picked up her purse. The door opened, and Eli filled the doorway.

Irritated by the eagerness she instantly felt upon seeing Eli, she looked at Wainright. "Is that all?"

Wainright's eyes darted between her and his boss. "Yes. Thanks for coming in so promptly, Ms. Cooper. If you think of anything else, give me a call."

She approached the door, willing Eli to step aside. He didn't.

Darcy stopped in front of him. Eli waited for her to look at him but her eyes remained fixed on his shirt. Her shoulders tensed.

"Sheriff," she said.

"Ms. Cooper." He knew she wanted to pass. He continued to block her exit—continued to want a response.

"Is there a secret password?"

He stepped aside, and she passed. He took the stairs to his office and pulled the door shut. He had heard she was here, but hadn't planned to block her exit. Her withdrawal haunted him as her observations during the drive from Colorado still haunted him.

She'd pointed out the fallacy of his alleged isolation. He would walk through fire for Brooke or Jeremy, Uncle John or Aunt Mary, Dan or Lisa or Darcy. She had penetrated further past his defenses than he'd realized. His attraction to her hadn't ended just because their views on permanent relationships differed. Seeing her stirred pleasure and regret. His life wasn't returning to normal.

He crossed to the window and scanned the parking lot. She exited the building and walked, head down, to her car. Her lips moved in a self-directed lecture as she fumbled for her keys. She exited the lot at a speed that left him frowning.

He'd wanted to say how sorry he was about her house. To ask how the cleanup was coming. But one look at her discouraged face silenced his words. He didn't like seeing her despair. He wanted her to smile again—one of those smiles that warmed him and made him believe that good could prevail.

He slapped the wall hard enough to rattle the windows.

Two hours later, Eli left the courthouse and drove to the east side of Lost Creek. He crept slowly along the street until he found the right address. He parked in front of the frame house. The homes and yards in the older neighborhood were well kept.

He exited his truck—driving a cruiser would have added fuel to an already simmering fire caused by previous visits by Wainright and his deputies. No point in causing the woman additional anxiety or creating adversity.

The fence's gate opened smoothly. Eli walked to the door. Knocked. Waited.

The door opened. Curiosity filled her hazel eyes. "Yes?"

He displayed his badge. "Mrs. Anderson, I'm Sheriff Eli Whitepath. I wonder if I might ask you a few questions."

Resignation replaced friendliness as she opened the screen door.

"Come in, Sheriff. Can I offer you a glass of water?"

"No, thank you. This won't take long."

"Well then, have a seat."

Eli settled in one blue armchair in the living room. She sat in the other and waited.

"You've heard about the trouble out at Alex's old place?" Eli said.

She nodded. "That poor girl must wonder what kind of

town she's moved to."

"You heard about Greg's vandalism?"

"The spray paint?"

"Yes."

Her mouth tightened. "Angela told me what Greg did. I swear I don't know what got into him. We didn't expect to inherit the house, so he shouldn't have either."

"Was it Alex's house he expected your family to inherit, or Alex's money?"

Mrs. Anderson swallowed like she was trying to choke down his words.

"The courthouse has a probated copy of Alex's will on file."

"I see." She clasped her hands tightly.

"Would anyone in your family feel strongly enough about the money to hurt Darcy Cooper because they thought she had it?"

"Only Keith knows that Alex left me the money. Keith wouldn't tell anyone, and he makes plenty of his own money." She stared intently at Eli. "Is it going to become public knowledge that I inherited the money? You see, I haven't told my husband. We didn't have much of a nest egg, and I wanted to be sure that—in case of an emergency—we had something set aside."

"Unless the fact that you inherited the money becomes pertinent to the cases we're working, we won't make your inheritance public." He stood. "Thank you for your time."

"Thank you, Sheriff." She walked him to the door.

Monday morning, Darcy installed the video cameras then set up her new alarm system, armed it, and left to deliver cinnamon rolls and coffee-cake bars to a local bank's open house. Catering orders had picked up. If she'd had a gynecological exam when she'd first moved to Lost Creek, she could have avoided weeks of rumors about her and Alex.

Her steps echoed on the tile floor as she left the bank lobby, paycheck in hand. Think positive, she reminded herself. Her house was clean, and the upstairs wall patches would be painted tomorrow. The insurance check had replaced broken appliances and windows, and she was keeping up with the increase in catering jobs.

She walked outside and jumped when Keith fell into step beside her. Neither of them spoke as he escorted her to her car, helped her in, and then rested tanned, muscled forearms on the open window.

"Are you following me?" Lately, her skin had crawled when she was away from the house—like someone was watching her, but when she turned to look, no one was there.

"Nope. I stopped to make a deposit and saw you coming out. Care to join me for coffee?"

"Thanks, but I have deliveries to make." She swept a hand toward the tray-lined backseat of her car.

"My receptionist tells me you're the main topic of conversation in the waiting room these days."

Darcy sighed. "How long will it take to be accepted as a regular member of the community? I told you Alex and I were just friends."

"Yeah, well there are friends, and there are friends with benefits." He fiddled with his ball cap. "Are you still seeing the sheriff?"

"We never dated. That would have been unprofessional on the Sheriff's part since I'm a witness in an ongoing investigation." Her grip tightened on the steering wheel.

"I heard he was staying at your place."

"He was protecting me. I asked him to stop staying when rumors insinuated I had an ulterior motive for having him there."

"Darlin', you sure put that rumor to rest." His grin faded. "I heard about your place getting trashed. Whoever's pissed at you hasn't got over it. I'm volunteering to watch you at night."

"Thanks, but it's taken care of." She started the engine. Keith leaned closer.

"Come with me on Wednesday."

She looked at him. Curious for the first time in a week. "Where?"

"To Luckenbach, where everybody is somebody. Local bands are playing; it'll be fun. You look like you could use some fun."

Her refusal hung unspoken on the end of her tongue, cut off by a memory of Gramma's voice reminding her that she was responsible for her happiness.

She nodded. "Okay, I could use a night out with a friend. What time do the bands start?"

"Did you have to throw in that friend thing? It's hard on my ego," Keith complained.

"Your ego is fine, and you have a waiting room full of women who would love to prove it to you." Darcy shifted into reverse.

"Yeah," he admitted, tapping the end of her nose with a fingertip. "But you're the one I'm chasing." He straightened. "I'll pick you up at five. The bands play until late so I'll grab food from the deli and we can eat when we get hungry."

"It's a deal. Only I'll bring a picnic. Do you like fried chicken?"

"Does a bull, uh, eat grass in the pasture?" His infectious grin teased a reluctant answering smile. He stepped back. "See you Wednesday."

As Darcy drove north, she checked her rearview mirror often. Keith might withdraw his invitation if he knew where she was headed. She pulled the address from her purse and glanced at the directions.

Yesterday, she'd called Keith's parents' house and inquired about fences. His sweet-voiced mother volunteered that Dale was fencing a yard today. When Darcy suggested she'd like to see his work, Mrs. Anderson had provided an address.

She wanted to see Dale Anderson's face.

The frame house huddled beside another house and a two-story, brick office building. She parked and rubbernecked the house. Chain link fencing lay on the grass, bordering one side of the yard like a metal path. Out of sight, she heard the rhythmic thud and click of a posthole digger chewing earth and rock.

She walked down the narrow alley. Massive air-conditioning units, electric meters, and sealed telephone boxes lined the windowless brick wall. The homeowner had obscured the commercial view by planting a dense hedge. Four-foot metal posts, six feet apart, hugged the outside of the hedge and followed a line of hot pink survey flags.

Halfway down the alley, a low growl froze her in place. Slowly, she turned her head until the menace appeared in her peripheral vision.

"You've got to be kidding," she breathed.

Again, the Chihuahua snarled like a riding lawnmower.

"Don't underestimate Paco. He thinks he's a Rottweiler and I've never told him differently."

Darcy looked up. Dale Anderson's face bore a passing resemblance to Alex's if you looked past the hard expression and the broken blood vessels bracketing his nose. Dale's body bore a hardness gained from years of digging, busting rock, and stretching fence. Gray eyes, so like Alex's, nearly crumbled her resolve. She wondered what color truck Dale drove.

Paco sniffed her ankles. She leaned down and held the back of her hand toward the bat-eared dog.

"Hello, Paco," she said.

Paco snapped.

She jerked her hand away.

Dale smiled humorlessly. "He doesn't take to strangers,

and you're no meter reader, so why are you in a dead-end alley?"

"I came to see you, Mr. Anderson."

"Why?" His eyes narrowed.

"We have business to discuss."

The lines bracketing his eyes eased. "What kind of business? You want a fence put up?"

"I'm Darcy Cooper."

His mouth tightened. The empathetic Paco growled.

"I should let him bite you. Serve you right. We have nothing to do with your problems." He pointed an angry finger. "If you keep sending cops around, you'll have a doozy of a lawsuit on your hands."

"Mr. Anderson, I have no control over who the sheriff's department decides to question. And that's not why I'm here. I came to discuss goats."

"Goats?" Confusion flashed over Dale's face.

"Keith mentioned that your lease runs out at the end of the year. The Tell County Extension Agent recommends I let the land lay fallow a year to recover the grasses. I wanted to let you know, so you'd have plenty of time to locate another pasture for the goats."

His face flushed crimson. "First my family, and now my animals. You're evicting us all."

"My decision isn't a reflection on your family, Mr. Anderson."

He pulled a cigar from his shirt pocket and opened a small knife to trim the end. Lighting the cigar, he exhaled odorous smoke.

She fanned with her hand. "I've met your children, and I like them both."

"You've met Keith?"

His eyes narrowed as he calculated possibilities. She didn't want to offer false hope that the Anderson homestead would again wind up the possession of an Anderson, but if his assumption helped her escape the alley unbitten—

"Keith and I are friends."

Dale nodded then turned and pushed back through the bushes, heeling Paco. Darcy backtracked to her car then drove slowly past the house whose driveway wound annoyingly around back. No vehicles parked in front. She still didn't know what Dale drove. She'd have to find out later. If she attempted to peek, Paco and his sharp little teeth might get lucky.

Luckenbach moseyed into high gear after warming up with armadillo races and the steady sale of long-neck beers. Keith was making short work of her picnic of fried chicken, potato salad, and watermelon.

"You're one beautiful woman, Miss Darcy," Keith said.

She smiled. Her long-sleeved, rose-colored dress flared at the hem that stopped short of her knees. He wore faded jeans and a white cotton shirt with sleeves rolled up to his forearms.

"You're not bad yourself, cowboy," she admitted, tugging her sweater closer. Fall was finally nipping.

Unbidden, the memory of Eli's skin set off against

another white shirt, surfaced. The last thing she needed was the sheriff occupying her thoughts. She reached for her water; it coursed down her windpipe, spurring a coughing fit.

"Serves you right." Keith transferred his cigar to his left hand and leaned in to pound her back. When she held up her hand, he reached for another piece of chicken. Catching a drumstick between his teeth, he gathered their picnic remnants into her basket and carried them to his truck.

Darcy watched him go. Keith was attractive and fun. Why hadn't she clicked with him instead of falling for a man who put no faith in the future or permanence? Had Alex hoped she'd meet his nephew and bridge the distance he and Dale had widened?

Keith returned, a grin on his face. "Ready to show 'em how it's done?"

"You'll have to show me first. The only country dance I know is the Cotton-Eyed Joe."

"Darlin', I'll have you Texas two-stepping before you can say, 'Willie Nelson.'" Capturing her hand, he pulled her to her feet. They crossed the grass toward a dancehall that resembled a barn without stalls. Inside, she claimed a table while Keith bought beer and water. He allowed her one sip.

"Come on, we're burnin' daylight."

Keith brought her along slowly, murmuring the dance cadence. Two songs later, she two-stepped with confidence. When the lights dimmed, the band introduced a waltz. He drew her close, murmuring, "I'll bet you can waltz."

"Sure I can," she said, her voice equally soft. "And I need to warn you about this knee-jerk reaction I sometimes have to unexpected movements on my partner's part."

Keith grimaced. "Shoot, girl. You sure know how to hurt a man."

"So I've been told." She smiled.

A fresh band took over at eleven. Hours of dancing and nights of fitful sleep claimed a toll. Keith caught her second attempt to stifle a yawn behind a hand.

"Time to head for the barn?" he asked.

She nodded.

The half-hour drive to Brooke's house passed in comfortable conversation beneath the star-filled sky.

"There's a deputy following us," Keith said, sounding irritated. "And he just hit his lights. That certainly kills the moment." Keith turned a grin on her. "Guess I'll have to tell Dad the land isn't returning to the Anderson family tonight."

He said it lightly, but she felt like a means to an end. What motivated Keith's attentions?

"Your dad mentioned meeting me?"

Keith pulled over. "He called and asked if I was crazy. I told him that where you were concerned, I was." He laid an arm along the back of the bench seat. As rough fingertips touched her shoulder, she met his probing gaze.

"Right now, I need a friend, Keith."

He withdrew his arm and rolled down his window.

"I enjoyed tonight, Keith. Thanks for teaching me to dance."

He exhaled long and hard. "You're welcome, darlin'."

The deputy appeared at his window.

"Dr. Anderson," he said. He leaned to look at her. "Ms. Cooper, Sergeant Lantz asked me to let you know that his wife is in labor at the hospital."

CHAPTER TWENTY-TWO

Darcy stopped at the maternity ward nurses' station. "Where can I find Lisa Lantz?"

"Darcy!" Dan's voice boomed behind her. She spun.

"She's the godmother," Dan told the nurses.

He took her arm and steered her down the hallway. "Thanks for coming. We were eating Chinese when Lisa dropped her chopsticks and said we had to get to the hospital." His rumpled shirt was open at the throat. "She's dilating, so it could be any minute, or it could be a couple of hours. She talked me into staying in the birthing room. It sounded like a good idea at the time. Now I'm not so sure."

"You'll do fine." Darcy squeezed his arm as he opened a swinging door. She entered the room and stopped short.

Darkly attractive in a black T-shirt, faded jeans and an equally faded jean jacket, Eli stood by the bed talking with Lisa. When he looked up, his smile faded.

Dan drew her forward.

"You made it!" Lisa beamed.

"Thanks for waiting for me."

Eli stepped back and she took his place by the bed. Tense, she reached for a cup of ice chips.

Lisa's tired smile and perspiration-damp gown spoke volumes. "Natural childbirth is overrated. If I weren't sure the baby would pop out before the anesthetic kicked in, I'd break down and order drugs." She paused to chew the ice chips Darcy spoon-fed her. Her eyes widened.

"You look great, did you finally stop turning down dates?" Lisa shifted restlessly. "Dan, did I mention that four different men asked Darcy out this week? Goes to show that some males in Lost Creek aren't fools." She turned back to Darcy. "Who is he, and where did you go?"

Darcy resisted the impulse to shovel a spoonful of ice into Lisa's mouth. A glance to her left revealed Dan's sudden interest in the ceiling. She wasn't risking a look at Eli. She already felt his stare right between her shoulder blades.

"I went to Luckenbach with Keith."

"O-o-o, Dan and I might have seen you there if I hadn't gone into labor. How was the band?"

"Energetic and loud. It's a good thing you didn't go. Dan would have had to throw out half the dancers to keep anyone from bumping into you. It could have turned into a real brawl."

"Crowded, huh?"

"Imagine everyone in the hospital dancing in your room."

"Did Keith bring you here?"

"Kind of. He followed me to Brooke's so I could get my car, then followed me here."

Lisa pressed a hand to her lower back. "Did he take you to dinner?"

"I packed a picnic." The urge to squirm overwhelmed. Why did Eli stare? Keith's alibi had checked out.

She wasn't eager to discuss her evening, but the descriptions seemed to help take Lisa's mind off the birthing business. "I learned to two-step."

A contraction hit Lisa. Darcy sponged her face while Dan gripped his wife's hands and instructed her to breathe, demonstrating until she echoed his breaths. Slowly, Lisa relaxed.

"The doctor doesn't think it'll be long, baby." Dan smoothed his wife's damp hair.

A yellow-uniformed nurse entered. "You've assembled quite an entourage." She fit a blood pressure cuff to Lisa's arm.

"These are the godparents, Darcy Cooper, and Eli Whitepath," Lisa said.

Darcy started. Although it made perfect sense, she hadn't known they'd chosen Eli as godfather.

The cuff on Lisa's arm deflated. "Okay," the nurse said. "Godparents outside, I need to check Mrs. Lantz's dilation."

As Darcy turned, Eli moved past her. "Dan, I'll get coffee if you'll stay with Darcy until I get back."

Dan charged for the door. "Absolutely."

With energy to burn, Eli passed the elevator and took the stairs to the first floor. His thoughts ricocheted between relief at Darcy's presence and annoyance at her date with Keith. He pushed the door open and studied the vending machines.

She hadn't wasted any time. And she could do better than Anderson, a man undoubtedly eager to teach her more than dancing. Keith had dated every unmarried woman in Lost Creek between the ages of twenty-one and thirty-nine. Heck, Darcy could date—

No names came to mind.

She had arrived mere minutes ago and was already distracting him. He should concentrate on the activity around her, not on her date or how her pink dress clung like a memory. He should mention that she'd make his job easier if she didn't date until Raul, Randy and their unidentified cohort were caught.

He scanned the faces of the people seated in the nearly empty cafeteria. A glance at the wall clock told him Dan and Lisa's baby would be born October fourth, not the third.

The coffee machine offered caffeine with every imaginable addition. Eli chose black. As it poured, the bitter scent teased his nostrils. On impulse, he dropped quarters into a second machine.

When he returned, holding two steaming Styrofoam cups and a cold bottle tucked in a jacket pocket, Dan and Darcy were seated in the hall. Darcy slept. A plastic chairback supported her head. She'd lost weight since their return from Colorado. He wished he hadn't noticed.

Dan accepted coffee and returned to Lisa's room. Eli sat in the empty chair beside Darcy. Her nose twitched, and her eyelids lifted halfway. A slow smile parted her lips.

"I dozed off," she began, then sat upright and shifted away.

He sipped coffee and pretended he hadn't noticed her withdrawal. The path and the rules in play were of his choosing; he would not deviate. He drew a deep breath and inhaled honeysuckle. "I brought you water."

He offered the bottle and compared her forced smile to the sincere one she had started with.

"Thanks." She unscrewed the cap. "Have you identified the man in the sketch?"

"Not yet." His eyes tracked a janitor rolling a mop bucket. The man stopped at the end of the hall and wrung water from the mop before launching long, practiced strokes across green-speckled linoleum. Eli adjusted his jacket and transferred the coffee cup to his left hand.

"The tap on your phone line has yielded nothing, and the shoeprints left in your kitchen don't match anything we have on file."

"Which leaves Raul, Randy the ghoul, or the rattler."

"Or anyone else wanting to send a message."

"I hadn't considered the possibility of someone else wanting to hurt me or the house." She pinched the bridge of her nose.

He stood and walked to the other side of the hall and leaned against the wall. He watched her ease her shoes off.

"I looked at some websites and learned that the Drug Enforcement Agency helped Mexico's Federales crackdown on suppliers in Mexico," she said. "The Border Patrol and DEA announced a noticeable decrease in the amount of heroin coming over the border, but there's a pronounced increase in the amount of heroin finding its way into Texas and the southwest."

Irritation and admiration mixed. Curious to hear what else she'd learned, he remained silent and let her talk. The subject animated her face.

"My theory is that the cartels saw the crackdown coming and accumulated a stockpile on this side of the border to see them through the dry spell. Another possibility is that they've found a new way or route to smuggle."

Give her an A for research. He looked away to watch the janitor mop to the next corridor. Lab reports confirmed that the heroin analyzed in the local overdose cases matched the chemical signature of the heroin Darcy had found. But the heroin's source remained well insulated and he still didn't know what had triggered the initial attack at Border's.

Not for the first time, he wondered how Darcy had stirred up this hornet's nest.

A man entered the hallway and started towards them at a jog. Eli set his coffee cup on the floor and slid one hand inside his jacket.

"Hello Dr. Wylie," Darcy said, drawing Eli's attention.

"Hey, Miss Cooper. I'm here to deliver Lisa's baby."

Eli rapped a knuckle on Lisa's door. Dan admitted the doctor.

"Why are you so jumpy?" Darcy asked.

Eli resumed his position against the wall.

"They know Lisa is pregnant. If they're watching the house, they know where she is. And if they're watching you, they know you're here together."

Darcy scanned the hallway as her mind replayed the attack and its aftermath.

"Stop thinking about it," Eli said.

"It's hard to forget when reminders keep popping up."

He sat beside her. Darcy fought the urge to lean toward him, to feel his warm, coffee-scented breath on her face.

"Did you ever run with a rough crowd or date anyone who used drugs?"

"No, and not to my knowledge. Detective Wainright asked me all of this."

"Have you ever testified against anyone in court or gotten into a verbal or physical fight with anyone?" he asked.

"No. I've led a reasonably law-abiding, non-violent life— until the inheritance."

"Did anything unusual occur between the time you inherited the house and property and the time you moved here?"

"Other than Greg's graffiti?"

He nodded.

She shrugged. "I don't know if it qualifies as unusual, but I received unsolicited offers on the house and land after I inherited."

"Who made the offers?"

"The realtor wouldn't say. For a while, I thought Alex's

family wanted to buy the place back, but now I'm sure it wasn't the Andersons. Keith came right out and asked if I'd sell the first time I met him. I can't imagine him being secretive about making an offer. And although he can probably afford the price offered, I don't think Dale or Angela and Greg could."

Eli's face went neutral. Darcy squashed an optimistic flicker of hope. He wasn't jealous of Keith. He'd have to be interested in her before he could be jealous. She dropped her feet to the floor and slipped her shoes on. "I turned down the initial offer, and they countered with an even larger amount."

He pulled a notebook from his pocket.

"Give me Beth's last name and phone number. If she kept the real estate offer, I want her to fax a copy. It won't hurt to find out who wants your property."

"Thompson." Darcy rattled off the phone number she knew by heart.

He pocketed the notebook and pen.

The low murmurs inside Lisa's room became interspersed with cries of pain. Faint but urgent instructions to push, breathe, or pant made their way into the hall followed by a triumphant shout. Minutes later, Dan flung open the door.

"It's a boy!" he shouted, motioning them in. "Eight pounds and fourteen ounces!"

"Congratulations!" Darcy stepped into her shoes. She hugged Dan as she passed through the doorway. The baby lay in Lisa's arms, swaddled in flannel.

"He's perfect," Lisa said with tired wonder.

"Yes, he is," Darcy agreed. A tiny wrinkled face and curled fists peered out from a blue blanket. Dan and Eli shared a manly handshake and shoulder grip on the other side of the bed.

"Hand him to Darcy, honey," Lisa said.

Dan reached for his son then stopped. "What if I drop him?"

"Use both hands, like a receiver carrying a football, remember?"

Dan lifted his son and inched around the bed to hand him to Darcy. She cradled him in her arms.

"So you're what all the fuss is about, huh, big guy?" She stroked one pint-sized cheek. "What's your name?"

"Jared Darcy Lantz," Dan said.

Darcy looked between Dan and Lisa. They nodded their confirmation. "You protected him and Lisa. It's our way of thanking you," Dan said.

Her eyes watered. "I'm honored."

"Told you she'd cry," Lisa said to Dan. "Eli, take Jared before she gets him all wet."

Eli rounded the bed and lifted Jared from her arms. Conscious of his grim gaze, she turned away.

The nurse advanced. "It's time for Lisa and Jared to rest. We're moving them to their room. Dan, your cot is ready."

"I'll follow you," Eli said, expertly returning Jared to Lisa.

"I'll visit you Saturday at home," Darcy promised, backing toward the door.

"Walk with me, Darcy," Eli said.

She stopped, reluctant to depend on him for her safety, but she wasn't the only one involved. Opening the door, he scanned the hall before stepping out and leading the group. He checked the private room then motioned them through.

"I'll see you to your car and follow you to Brooke's," he said.

Darcy matched his stride down the corridor. A door banged open, forcing her into his side.

He pulled her behind him, his hand moving inside his jacket as a mop bucket spiraled into the hall. The janitor appeared in the doorway, muttering an apology and adding a mop to the clean water. Eli kept her moving toward the elevators.

"Lisa's delivery went well." She spoke to calm herself after bumping into Eli's solid strength.

"Given the pain a woman endures during childbirth, I'm amazed we have the population we do," he said.

"Most women are willing to endure temporary pain to achieve a positive result."

The elevator doors opened. They stepped inside.

"Where are you parked?" he asked.

"Second level, next to the stairs."

Eli pushed the appropriate button.

"Do you remember the name of the real estate agent who mailed the offers?"

"No. I threw the first offer away, but my friend Beth kept the last one. She called it my 'insurance policy' in case I decided to sell."

"Have you considered selling?" Green eyes sought hers.

"No. I trust Alex's instincts and my own."

"You're choosing to endure temporary pain to achieve a positive result." Eli braced his hands on the rail behind him.

She shrugged. "Not all endured pain ends positively. But if I left now, I'd never know if I left as things were about to get better. After all, how much worse can they get?"

Eli's expression went blank—like he'd turned his thoughts inward.

The elevator doors opened. Eli took her elbow. Their footsteps echoed on the concrete as she hurried to keep up.

"Are you too worn out from two-stepping to drive?" Eli asked her.

"I'm fine, thank you."

He opened her SUV door.

"I'm parked on the lower level. Follow me down, then I'll follow you to Brooke's."

Or she could burn rubber and leave Eli racing for his truck. She glanced sideways at him. He stared back.

"Don't even think about it unless you want a ticket for disturbing the peace."

Darcy faced the windshield, wishing she could read his thoughts like he seemed to be able to read hers.

She rode the brake and clutch as she paced him to the first level. When his headlights came on, she drove out of the parking garage.

Fifteen minutes later, they pulled into Brooke's driveway.

She cut her engine and stepped out of her car. A night breeze cooled her legs; a cricket chorus sang in surround sound. Fall had finally arrived.

Eli parked then walked her to Brooke's porch. He used his key to unlock the door.

"Thank-you for your escort."

"Just doing my job." He pushed the entry open.

She stepped inside, wishing she could slam the door.

Eli rubbed his eyes. Three cups of coffee hadn't made up for three hours of sleep. At his office desk, he sorted messages and files in order of urgency. He returned calls from the mayor and a county commissioner and then pulled back a shirt cuff and glanced at his watch—fifteen minutes until the morning briefing. He looked at his notepad and dialed Beth Thompson's number. A woman picked up on the third ring.

"Hello?"

"Beth Thompson?" he asked.

"Who's calling?"

"Tell County Sheriff, Eli Whitepath. I'm calling about Darcy Cooper."

"Is she all right? Was she in an accident?"

"Ms. Cooper is fine, Mrs. Thompson. I'm calling on department business. Ms. Cooper said she received two real estate offers before she moved and that you might have one of the offers in your possession."

"I still have it." Beth sounded suspicious.

"I'd appreciate your faxing a copy to my office." Eli recited the fax number and asked her to repeat it back. In the background, a child's voice demanded juice.

"Just a minute, sweetie," he heard her say. "Sheriff Whitepath, I'll have to call Darcy first and make sure it's okay."

"That's fine. Fax it as soon as possible."

He hung up and swiveled his chair to face the window. A quick tap on the door heralded his secretary Janet's entry with a handful of new files.

"Here are the last two month's drug-related death and arrest reports from Houston." She glanced at his empty cup. "Would you like more coffee before the meeting?"

"No, thanks." He stood. Someone, somewhere, knew the thugs' whereabouts and the rattler's identity. Eli set the records aside and walked down the hall.

He sat in the back of the briefing room and waited for the sergeant to take the podium. A late arrival shut the door, quietly but firmly, reminding him of how Darcy had entered Brooke's house this morning.

He regretted throwing indifference in her face, but he'd remembered her holding the baby in the hospital room's dim light and the electric jolt of soft skin when he'd brushed against her during the baby transfer. Again, she'd distracted him, and his distraction could get her killed.

CHAPTER TWENTY-THREE

Darcy picked up her cell phone and squinted at the time. At eight in the morning, she felt like she'd pulled an all-nighter. Oh yeah. She had.

"Hello?" she mumbled.

"The sheriff lied, you're not okay!" Beth's voice raced through Darcy's brain like a bullet train through a tunnel.

"I'm fine. Lisa had her baby last night, a boy. I didn't get home until nearly four this morning. You talked to Eli?"

"You call the sheriff by his first name? If I'd known that, I would have had the nerve to ask why he wanted me to fax him the real estate offer. Why does he? And should I?"

"It depends on how you feel about wearing horizontal stripes daily for the next five years." Darcy grinned. An opportunity to tease Beth was worth waking early.

"What are you involved in now?"

"It's a long story."

"Start with why you're on a first-name basis with the sheriff."

"He's the baby's godfather, and I'm the godmother, so we were both at the hospital—"

"Why did a couple you've only known since September name you their baby's godmother?"

Darcy groaned. Her sleepy tongue had spilled more information than she'd intended to share. She answered slowly. "Probably for the same reason they named the baby Jared Darcy Lantz." She visualized Beth's jaw dropping and relished her friend's sudden silence. Beth quickly recovered.

"You've held out on me."

Darcy skipped the rumors, the heroin, and her trip to Colorado and concentrated on the roadhouse attack and break-in. "So that's my last month, what's happening with you?" She listened to silence. "Beth?"

"I'm here. You're not making this up, are you?"

"Cross my heart."

"A true friend would have called on Lisa's cell phone immediately after the attack."

"Beth!"

"Why does the sheriff want the real estate offer?"

"I mentioned it last night, and he wants to see the papers."

"Annie and I will be there next week."

"What?" Darcy sat up in bed.

"Stan's flying to Houston for a meeting; he can drop us off then pick us up when he returns. I want to see for myself that you're okay. We can stay with you, right?"

"I've been staying with Brooke, the sheriff's sister. Did you forget the part about the break-in?"

"No. But you said the Sheriff's Department is monitoring your alarm system. And we'll bring Hank."

"Hank the security hunk?" Darcy raised her eyebrows.

She'd used the nickname the front desk women had given the handsome chief of security for the Thompson Hotel chain.

"Right—built like a commando—piercing blue eyes—he used to walk you to your car when you worked late."

"Beth, he walked all the female employees to their cars after dark."

"I know. It's company policy. Any chance I'll meet the sheriff?"

"No!"

Saturday morning, bearing a casserole, salad, and rolls, Darcy visited her godson and his exhausted parents and joined Lisa's mother in fussing over little Jared while Lisa and Dan took a nap.

Two hours later, she zipped up her windbreaker, breezed into the independent living community, and started passing out blueberry muffins. Halfway through the tables, a woman asked how her arm was healing.

Darcy smiled. They were warming up to her. "Great, thank you. The stitches came out a little over a week ago. You can barely see the scar now."

Three-quarters of her way through the tables, a muffin hit her shoulder.

The following Monday, Darcy arrived at the local airport in time to watch the twin-engine Beechcraft Baron land smoothly and taxi to the tie-down area. She jogged across the tarmac, waving a welcome.

Beth emerged from the plane, elegant in scarlet pants and a sleeveless, white silk blouse. Annie, a goldenrod-clad dervish, launched her small body into Darcy's waiting arms. Beth's husband, Stan, unfolded his long frame from the pilot seat, looked her over, and took his turn at a hug.

"It's hard to believe you had to leave Dallas and move to the country to get mugged," he said.

"Did I ever thank you for sponsoring that self-defense seminar?" Darcy asked, hugging back.

"What's mugged?" a little voice asked.

"It's what happens to Darcy when she moves away from us," Beth said.

"Oh." Annie's forehead wrinkled.

"Okay, princess," Stan said. "Let's get your bags into Darcy's car." Father and daughter walked to the Explorer.

Hank exited last and hugged her. "Darcy."

"Hank, thanks for coming."

"My pleasure." He shouldered his backpack and walked towards her car.

"Quick, show me your scar," Beth hissed.

"Which one?" Darcy teased.

"You know which one."

Darcy pushed up her left shirt sleeve.

"Yucky." Beth wrinkled her nose. Darcy recognized Annie's favorite adjective.

"You should have seen it a month ago," she said, readjusting the sleeve.

"I would have if you'd told me."

"I've missed you, too." Darcy threw her arms around Beth. "Now, let's get Stan fueled and headed to Houston."

Darcy tiptoed past the sleeping Annie sprawled sideways in her largest guestroom's new king bed. An evening breeze whispered through the partially open balcony door. Beth shifted to make room on the wicker loveseat.

"You've avoided bringing up the sheriff's name all day—must be serious."

"Only in my dreams. To Eli, I'm just a witness."

She settled beside Beth and propped her sock-clad feet on the railing. Heads tilted back, they listened to the cricket symphony. In the pasture, a nervous deer exhaled loudly. Above them, the heavens stretched in dark, glitter-studded splendor.

"Is he married, gay or senile?" Beth asked.

"None of the above."

"Then he needs his vision checked. Here, I brought you something." Beth set a large manila envelope on Darcy's lap.

"The real estate contract? Did you fax Eli a copy?"

"Of course. I'm much too short for horizontal stripes, and I doubt the penal system would change to vertical just to suit me. Since the sheriff didn't ask for the originals, I thought you might give them a second look and reconsider returning to Dallas."

Darcy smoothed her thumbs across the envelope. She didn't want to move back to Dallas, but unless things changed—

"Where's Hank?" she asked.

"He ran a—and I'm quoting here—'perimeter check' after dinner then went to shower and catch some sleep. He pulled the late shift last night and got up early to meet us at the airport."

"I'm glad you brought him along. I wouldn't let you and Annie stay otherwise."

"You've done a great job remodeling and decorating. This place suits you," Beth admitted. "And, if you won't talk about Eli, tell me more about his sister. If she's as good an artist as you say, maybe she'd be interested in a showing at the Dallas hotel."

"That's a great idea! You'll meet Brooke and her son Jeremy tomorrow. We're attending a goat show at the Tell County Fairgrounds."

Beth's nose wrinkled.

"Brooke asked last week if I'd join his cheering section. If you think of it as a social event, I think you'll enjoy it. I'll even make a picnic lunch, so you won't be tempted by the evils of corn dogs and nachos." Smile fading, Darcy stood and leaned against the railing. "Do you see those lights?"

Faint lights blinked on and off in the field.

"Fireflies," Beth said. "Annie's been chasing them all month."

One by one, they flickered out.

Having located the next GPS coordinate, he replaced his night vision goggles. He should be on a beach right now, not taking a chance on being caught in this goat-cropped pasture. He glanced toward the house and froze. Why was she up this late and standing on the balcony?

Judging by the way she stared, she'd spotted the lights. Each man's green-muslin-covered headlamp put out a small amount of light—apparently not small enough. Cursing, he retraced his steps and switched off the digging men's headlamps.

"Fill in your holes then return to the truck. Mend the fence after I drive through."

His fists clenched. He'd put together a lucrative deal and had promised to fill the order tonight. Since Darcy Cooper's arrival, his blazing distribution schedule had banked to a smolder. She wasn't selling, and he couldn't chance her calling the deputy doing drive-bys on her house.

The golden girl had made his life difficult for the last time.

Tuesday dawned in a blaze of peach and gold. It felt good to be home.

Darcy started the coffeemaker then carried her hot chocolate to the porch. She leaned against the railing and inhaled dew-laden air. The shadowy yard slowly brightened into familiar trees and shrubs.

Hank appeared from around the corner of her house. "All clear," he said.

"I didn't hear you go outside."

"You're not supposed to. That's why I asked for your alarm code." He smiled.

There was no denying that he was handsome with his wavy brunette hair and sky-blue eyes. Yet she'd never felt anything but friendship for him. Maybe that was why they had gotten along so well. Neither was hoping the other would ask them out.

"The coffee is brewing," she said.

"Thanks." He took a long look around. "This kind of peace and quiet is a rare commodity. I predict success for your B&B."

The coffeemaker dinged.

"I'll get it." Darcy returned a minute later and handed him a mug.

"What have you not told Beth about the break-ins?" he asked.

She sighed. "I might have left out the extent of the damage. That the vandals took a knife to my couch and love seat. That they put holes in the upstairs walls." She sighed. "They're ticked off."

"Why?"

"I'm not supposed to tell anyone. The Sheriff's department is handling it."

"I noticed cruisers passing by regularly last night. I'll be patrolling for the next two nights if you want to give them a break."

"Thank you, I'll call and let them know."

She glanced at her watch. "My friends, Brooke and Jeremy, are at the fair barn getting a weight card, whatever that is. I'm starting breakfast. And I'm making a delivery before we head to the goat show."

Hank settled on her porch swing. "Let me know if I can help."

She smiled at him. "Enjoy the view and coffee. You're helping by being here."

Darcy parked in front of the independent living community and left her car running. "I'll be back in five minutes."

"Please go with her, Hank," Beth said.

Hank helped her stack containers of oatmeal-raisin cookies and zucchini muffins on her luggage cart and rolled them inside for her. She paused at the door to the recreation room.

"Hank, if anyone throws anything at me, don't overreact," she said.

His eyebrows rose. "Are you serious?"

"It's kind of a ritual."

They walked into a packed room. Enthusiastic greetings came from the crowded tables.

"Good morning, everyone," she said brightly. "I'm headed for the fairgrounds to watch my first goat show, so I can't stay to pass these out today. Come and help yourselves, please." She lifted foil-covered cardboard trays from her containers and arranged them on a table.

Residents lined up. A few offered apologies for their previous behavior. A woman wearing red-framed glasses asked, "Who's the stud-muffin? Your bodyguard?"

Darcy smiled as Hank gave the woman an intense stare—as if sizing her up as a potential threat. "Actually, yes."

"Good choice," the woman said. She picked up a cookie. "You must be feeling secure. A body would feel these more readily than a muffin."

"That's why I made the soft version instead of the crisp."

"We heard the news about your—condition," another woman said.

"So everyone is clear on my friendship with Alex?"

Everyone nodded.

"Great! I'll see you all soon.

She turned and saw Hank flinch. WOP! A muffin, icing and all, struck her between the shoulder blades.

"Good arm!" she called without looking back.

Back at the car, she stowed the carriers. Annie twisted in her car seat. "Your shirt's dirty, Aunt Darcy."

Beth loosened her seatbelt and turned to look. "What is that?"

Darcy unzipped her windbreaker and grinned. "Acceptance." She let down her French twist and shook her hair loose around her shoulders. "Let's go watch goats!"

Darcy led Beth and Annie through the crowd milling around the fairground booths and arena until she recognized a familiar length of silky black hair. She tapped Brooke's shoulder.

"Brooke, meet my friend Beth and her daughter Annie, and my friend Hank. They're visiting from Dallas."

Brooke extended a hand. "Thank you all for coming."

Darcy wondered if she imagined that Hank held Brooke's hand a little longer than necessary when they shook. She knew she didn't imagine Brooke's blush.

"That's a gorgeous outfit, Beth," Brooke said.

If Brooke also thought Beth's coffee-brown silk pantsuit looked perfect for a tea party, she didn't say. "Are you sure you want to wear that?" Darcy had asked Beth before they'd left the house.

"It's the closest I can come to matching the color of manure," Beth had said. Darcy had looked down at her hiking boots, faded jeans, green scoop-neck tank top, and turquoise handkerchief shirt and shrugged. It was her first goat show too, how much of a dress code could there be?

"Come meet Fiddle and Faddle." Brooke pointed at two wild-eyed goats climbing their pen. "And here comes my cousin Sylvia with the boys."

Sylvia herded two boys in front of her with cutting horse precision. "Ready for a different view?" she asked Brooke.

"Definitely. But first let me introduce you to Darcy, Beth, Annie, and Hank."

"Nice looking family," Sylvia said, smiling.

"We're a work family," Beth said. "Hank is chief-of-security for our hotels. He's based out of our Dallas flagship hotel."

Darcy noticed Hank giving Beth the same odd look that she was giving Beth. Too much information. Then she caught Brooke's small smile. Ah-ha! Beth had noticed the

Hank-Brooke handshake also.

"Darcy brought a picnic lunch. Can you and the boys claim a table?" Brooke asked Sylvia.

"On our way!"

Brooke gave them a tour of the barn before they joined Sylvia at a table under a massive live oak. Darcy commandeered the boys to carry food and picnic supplies from her car. Hank set her cooler on the ground, and she knelt to extract salad components while Brooke and Beth set the table.

"Uncle Eli!"

Jeremy's exclamation sent Darcy's head snapping up in time to see Eli lift the boy into the air and spin with him.

"Hey, goat-man, the mayor postponed our meeting, so I came to watch you and your hairballs." His head swung toward Darcy as if she'd spoken his name. She was pretty sure she hadn't managed to squeeze any sound past her closed throat.

Brooke looked from Darcy to Eli. "Eli, I invited Darcy after you said you couldn't make the show."

"So, you're the sheriff." Beth took the salad from Darcy and surveyed Eli, once down and once up. "Funny, you don't look blind."

As his eyebrows rose, Beth balanced the salad on her hip and extended a hand. "Beth Thompson. You received my fax?"

"I did, thanks." He shook her hand.

"Mr. Thompson?" he asked, offering his hand to Hawk.

"Hank Johnson," he corrected. "I work security for Thompson hotels."

Darcy exhaled and stood. The churning in her stomach didn't bode well for digestion. Jeremy's excitement that Eli had come to see him was apparent. She would do the honorable thing.

"Brooke, if you don't mind bringing the cooler to my house later, I'll leave you and your family the picnic. Eli should stay and watch Jeremy."

"Do you have enough food for one more?" Eli asked.

"I do, but—"

Beth pushed the salad into Eli's hands and tugged a jar from the ice chest. "Shake this, pour it over the pasta salad, and toss," she instructed. "Annie, come sit down."

Glad the bright afternoon allowed her to hide behind sunglasses, Darcy sat in the middle of a bench with Beth and Annie on one side and Brooke on the other. Eli, Sylvia, and Hank took the opposite seat with the boys. Darcy's appetite had disappeared with Eli's arrival. His presence threatened her ability to act as if sitting so close to him wasn't affecting her.

The kids ate quickly and started fidgeting.

"Annie, why don't you and the boys check out that tree swing?" Beth suggested, breaking the adult's small talk. She pointed to a tire suspended by a rope from a nearby tree. The three children ran toward the swing and Beth turned to Eli. "Sheriff, is Darcy still in danger?"

"Yes." He scooped more pasta-chicken salad onto his

plate and added a chunk of garlic bread.

Darcy rolled her eyes. She wasn't affecting his appetite.

"Hank should stay until the people threatening you are caught," Beth said to Darcy. "You shouldn't be alone."

"She's not," Eli said abruptly. Darcy joined the other women in staring at Eli. "My patrols keep an eye on her place at night, and my department monitors her alarm system."

"But you're not in the house," Beth pressed him.

"I don't want him in my house," Darcy said.

Everyone looked at her.

Trying to make her outburst sound logical, she continued. "A lot is going on in the county right now, and the election is less than a month away. He needs time to campaign and time to sleep." She looked at Eli. "I called your department this morning and let them know not to station deputies at my gate tonight or tomorrow night. Hank will be watching out for us while he's here."

"My people are handling this. An outsider complicates the situation," Eli said.

Beth glared at him. "This situation happens to be my best friend. Having someone in the house is a better solution than drive-bys watching from outside and depending on an alarm system. Neither is foolproof."

Annie sidled up to Beth and tugged her sleeve. "Mommy," she whispered loudly. "Don't make him mad. Jeremy says he's a sheriff. He might put you in jail."

Darcy laughed and scooped her goddaughter onto her lap. "Don't worry, pumpkin. Only a bad sheriff would put your mommy in jail. Mr. Whitepath is a good sheriff."

Annie's skeptical appraisal of Eli amused Darcy. "Is it your turn on the swing?" she asked. With one last look, Annie jumped down and rejoined the boys. Darcy faced Beth.

"Stan and the hotels need Hank there, not here. And last night you said Hank was headed to Atlanta to help open the new hotel this weekend. With the alarm system, I can take care of myself inside. I trust the sheriff's deputies to patrol outside. Now, time for a new subject."

"Ooo-kay," Beth said as Darcy sipped iced tea. "I ran into Maggie at a party."

Darcy barely managed not to choke. "That's nice."

"She mentioned that some of her friends are coming to stay. She built up the sales job by mentioning that she knew the area and former owner. Does she know you've delayed the opening?"

When Eli's attention fixed on them, Darcy quickly said. "I left her a message to reschedule to November. I'm hoping nothing will interfere with the booking again."

"Maggie is from Lost Creek?" Eli said.

"Yes. She and Alex knew one another as children and young adults, and they renewed their friendship when Alex was in Dallas," Beth said.

"Maggie was seeing Alex?" Sylvia asked.

"Only as a friend. Does everyone here know Maggie?" Beth asked.

"No. But we heard Alex was seeing a woman in Dallas and gossip said that woman was Darcy," Brooke said.

"As in seeing Alex romantically?" Beth looked at Darcy.

Darcy folded her plate around her uneaten food and tossed it into the trash bag at the end of the table. "For a short time, I was fodder for the Lost Creek rumor mill."

"A few weeks before Darcy arrived, rumors began circulating that she had been Alex's—" Brooke paused until sure the children still played on the swing. "Girlfriend is the nicest way I've heard it put. The rumors implied she inherited the house and money because she was nice to Alex."

"What?" Beth shrieked.

Hank's raised eyebrows appeared glued in place.

The kids' heads turned. Beth sent Annie a reassuring smile then leaned toward Darcy. "They think you and Alex were lovers?" she hissed. "And what money? I can't believe you didn't tell me any of this." Beth's foot tapped a rapid you've-got-some-explaining-to-do message against the leg of the picnic table. She stood. "Excuse me. I need to borrow the public-address system and set this town straight."

Darcy caught Beth's arm. "Sit down, please. I didn't tell you because it's no longer an issue. The girlfriend rumor has been retired." She held her friend's angry stare.

"New gossip is circulating about Darcy," Brooke said, gathering up plates.

Darcy dropped her forehead to her hands.

"What could they possibly be saying now?" Beth huffed.

"That she's a virgin."

Hank choked on his tea. Eli crossed his arms.

"How did they find out?" Beth's widened eyes looked from Brooke to Darcy. "You haven't shared that with anyone but me."

"I needed an iron-clad means to disprove the rumor," Darcy said. "And I needed a reliable source to put the word out. I knew the name of Lisa's obstetrician, so I visited him for my annual exam."

"Dr. Wylie's receptionist is a prolific gossip, and a good friend of Lisa's." Brooke touched Darcy's arm. "When Lisa called to tell me the news, she was nearly hoarse from spreading the word."

"That receptionist should lose her job," Beth said.

"Not after I gave her a signed, notarized statement that she was free to share any of the doctor's notes in my file concerning this specific exam," Darcy said.

"How did you manage to stay a virgin this long?" Sylvia joined the inquisition.

Darcy rubbed throbbing temples, aware her face was as red as Annie's jumper. With effort, she tempered the defensive note in her voice. "I moved in with my grandparents when I started ninth grade. Between the new school, new rules, my chores on the farm, and my lack of a car, I didn't date much.

"When I went to football games, my grandparents came too. They had so much fun, I couldn't ask them to stay home. They attended all my school dances as chaperones and loved every minute of it. They gave me the best gift of my life when they let me move in. So I decided to make them proud and ensure they never asked me to leave."

"You didn't go wild when you went off to college?" Sylvia asked.

"No. I was busy." She sighed. Darcy Cooper, this is your life.

"Darcy postponed several semesters of college to help run her grandparents' farm and nurse her grandfather and later her grandmother before their deaths," Beth said.

Sylvia glanced at her watch. "I hate to leave this conversation, but I only negotiated thirty minutes of goat-sitting. Come on, boys," she called. "It's show time!"

Everyone rose and tossed cups into the trash. Darcy began snapping lids on leftovers and packing the cooler.

"Come on, Mom," Annie urged, tugging on Beth's pants leg, "We're gonna miss Jeremy and Allen."

"Go ahead," Darcy told the adults. "I'll throw these in my car and join you."

"I'll help," Eli said.

CHAPTER TWENTY-FOUR

Eli's offer to help sent Darcy's heart racing. How long would it take before she quit reacting to him?

He lobbed trash into an open barrel then hefted her loaded cooler. She carried the tea thermos. "I parked by the fence."

Eli fell into step beside her.

"By the way, Beth brought the original real estate offer. If you need it, I'll drop it by the station."

"I don't need it.

Attorneys signed the contract on behalf of their client. Still, keep the original for now."

Was he suggesting she should move from Lost Creek? She felt like the sun suddenly hid behind a cloud.

"Is that why Beth's here?" Eli asked.

"In a roundabout way. She called to ask if she should send you the fax. I'd only had four hours of sleep; you must have had less than that." She curbed her concern. "She caught me off guard. I'd neglected to fill her in on what's happened since I moved here—"

"She found you out," Eli finished for her.

"Yep." Darcy unlocked the Explorer's lift-gate. He slid the cooler inside and reached for the thermos. Holding it above his head, he opened the spigot and drank wineskin-style.

Unable to look away, Darcy watched the muscles in his throat contract with each long swallow. He drained the last of the tea before locking the lift-gate.

"What's Maggie's last name and phone number?"

She stopped beside an ancient blue pickup. "Why do you want to know?"

"She was friends longer than you were with the man that left his home and property to you. I want Wainright to check her out. Would you rather I get her last name from Beth?"

Cheering and clapping erupted from the barn. Darcy resumed walking; Eli followed. He'd find out with or without her, she decided. And she didn't want to involve Beth. "Williams," she said, walking into the fair barn. "Maggie's last name is Williams."

She found the arena where the first show class was getting underway. Jeremy and Fiddle entered the show ring with fifteen other children and their goats. One by one, the eliminated goats and their handlers moved to the opposite side of the ring. Fiddle placed seventh.

As the children and goats filed out, Eli walked to the holding pens with Jeremy, talking with him. The boy's downcast expression changed to laughter at something Eli said.

Eli would make a great father, she thought. But given his selective personal relationships, that wasn't likely.

Beth's arm linked with hers.

"Rough autumn, huh?"

Darcy nodded. "Losing Grampa and then Gramma taught me how to handle sorrow and grief. Now I've learned to handle extreme embarrassment, hostility, and fear. Okay, maybe I'm still working on fear." She looked at Eli. "And heartache. But God doesn't give us more than we can handle, right? I'm tougher than I thought, and having friends helps." Darcy bumped Beth's shoulder with her own. Beth bumped back.

"I wonder how Maggie would have handled the rumors if she'd inherited Alex's property," Darcy said.

"Maggie's a businesswoman. She would have sold for twice what it's worth."

"You're right."

The announcer called the showmanship class. Annie crowded the fence in front of them as children and goats entered the ring. Jeremy's eyes never left the judge, and a smile never left his face. Faddle was on his best behavior.

"They're perfect. If Jeremy doesn't win, I'll personally kick the judge out of the barn," she muttered.

"If he doesn't win, I'll look the other way while you punt," Eli said.

She hadn't heard him approach. She looked up, but his eyes followed his nephew. She looked back at the ring. The judge winnowed the group down to Jeremy and a young girl with a bright smile, and a bright red ribbon in her long brown ponytail. The judge moved from one side of the pair to the other; the girl's smile followed, but she stood in place. Jeremy quickly shifted sides, placing Faddle between him and the judge.

"Yes!" She pumped one bent arm. This might be her first goat show, but she'd seen enough to know that you never stood between your goat and the judge.

The judge shook Jeremy's hand.

Darcy turned toward Eli, her hand raised in a high five. He slapped her palm then started toward the gate to congratulate Jeremy. She stared after him then at her palm, as if it held an answer.

"I'm confused," Beth said, looking from Darcy to Eli.

"He was excited for Jeremy," Darcy said.

"Of course," Beth drawled. "That's what it looked like to me, too."

Eli cut his truck's headlights and turned into Darcy's drive. About fifty yards from her house, he parked in a grove of live oaks. He turned off the engine and lowered his windows.

Twelve minutes later, he noticed movement behind his truck. He eased his left hand out of the window and dangled his badge.

Hank stepped into sight in the rearview mirror. "Out for a night drive, Sheriff?" He tucked his pistol into the back of his jeans.

Eli relaxed his grip from the butt of his pistol where it lay on the seat beside him. Opening the door, he stepped outside.

"You missed me last night."

"I noticed tire tracks here yesterday when I walked the area between Darcy's entry and house. I was going to offer to clear under these trees, but I decided to see who was coming in."

"Where did you start from?"

"I was coming around the corner from the back porch and saw you pull into the trees. What gave me away?"

"I was looking for you. Which service were you in?"

"The Marines."

"Yeah? Well, Rangers lead the way," Eli said.

Both men stared hard, then smiled.

"All's quiet," Hank reported. "They're asleep. I'll be on duty tonight and tomorrow night. You should take the opportunity to sleep in a bed."

"What makes you think that I do this often?" Eli asked.

Eli was tempted to get two good night's sleep, but in his visions, Darcy's death came at night. He wasn't taking a chance. It was nice to know he'd have backup for the next two nights.

"Thanks, but I'll pull out before daylight."

"This is more than professional interest. What's up with you and Darcy? She tried to give you space this afternoon— like she felt she was intruding."

Eli stiffened. "There is nothing between us. I'm a budget-crunched sheriff pulling a shift to protect a resident."

Hank's eyebrows rose. "Darcy wouldn't tell me either." He pushed away. "I'm running patrols inside and outside every two hours. Want some coffee on my next round?"

"I'd appreciate that," Eli said.

Hank headed back towards the house then turned. "Sheriff, a lot of people appreciate and care for Darcy even if this town doesn't. If you don't plan on appreciating her, make sure someone else can."

Eli frowned. Was Hank one of the men that appreciated Darcy?

"By the way." Hank started walking backward. "I hear Brooke is coming to Dallas to exhibit her work at the hotel—I plan to ask her out." He turned and jogged to the house.

Eli watched him go, relieved that Hank wasn't romantically interested in Darcy, but rattled by his declared interest in Brooke. He smiled. He had two hours to prepare the interview he would conduct when Hank returned.

Wednesday, Darcy and her company kicked back, relaxed, and visited. Thursday, she drove Beth, Annie, and Hank to the Lost Creek airfield. Their brief visit left her feeling relaxed, happy, and loved.

Stan taxied towards them then cut the engines. When the propellers stopped, Hank rolled luggage to the plane. Annie followed, running towards her smiling father.

Beth hugged Darcy. "Promise to call or text me at least every other day?"

"I promise."

Hank walked up and hugged her.

"Thanks for taking care of us for the last few days," she said.

"My pleasure. I like your place. I may come back to book a room and explore Lost Creek more thoroughly."

"Would part of your exploring involve getting to know Brooke?"

He grinned. "I was trying to be obvious. Do you think she noticed?"

"I'm sure she did."

"Good." He shouldered his backpack. "FYI, the food thrower at the retirement home is a lady with shoulder-length brown hair and red-framed glasses."

"Thanks, I've been wondering."

He glanced towards the plane, then back at her. "Darcy you'd be smart to let Eli stay inside nights. I don't know what's going on between you two but think about it."

Darcy frowned. "What do you mean 'inside'?"

"He parks in that grove of live oaks out front and watches from his truck. The man needs a break."

She was stunned.

"I'll think about it," she promised.

And she did—all the way home—pros and cons, emotional pain vs. physical pain, silence vs. confrontation. Silence would have to win, since she knew where Eli stood on relationships. He wasn't budging. And she was still a target.

She parked and went inside to change into a sweatshirt, jeans, and hiking boots. Plucking a plastic bag from the pantry, she walked outside across the lawn and unlatched the metal gate to the pasture.

She refastened the latch and walked the fence-line, picking up the occasional piece of trash that the goats had missed. Her body and soul relaxed as she viewed the lay of her land.

Flat rocks abounded. She'd return later in the week to collect some. She could lay a path to the barbecue and define an outdoor entertainment area with the fieldstones.

Oddly, she visualized a party full of familiar faces— friends and acquaintances—not fleeting, unknown guests. Eli's comment about "filling her permanent home with temporary faces" had made her think.

She hadn't realized how much she would enjoy catering. Calling on familiar faces and recognizing people while shopping for, and delivering food was fun and satisfying. She was beginning to belong.

The first tire tracks appeared at the padlocked gate on the southwest corner. She glanced towards the house. She'd never seen Dale check the animals because a rise bisected the property from north to south. From here, she could only see the second story.

She followed the tire tracks north to the water and feed troughs. The curious creatures fell into line behind her. After seeing kids Annie's size tug goats around an arena, having a quadruped entourage didn't bother her.

The tire tracks circled there, so Dale must come in, feed and water, and drive back out the way he came in.

She kept walking. The goats lost interest and spread out in the field.

Her land had more relief than she'd realized. At the northwest corner, she turned right, and walked a few hundred yards. Tire tracks extended from her field into the neighboring field. But there was no gate.

She looked closely at the fence. Cut wire ends gleamed—they were recent. Dale Anderson fenced for a living; he could have repaired the fence. But why drive across the property line? On her land, the tracks drove a little way into the field then turned around.

She climbed through the fence and followed the tracks uphill. The pasture's grass was high enough to allow her to follow the vehicle's path visually. Twin lines stretched to a dirt road that led to a highway, a mile or so away. Darcy retraced her steps to her land and continued around the fence line. The remaining fence held no cuts, repairs, or tire tracks.

Had someone come in this way the night her house was trashed?

If she told Eli about the fence, he'd tell her to talk to Wainright. Eli was a by-the-book lawman, not a politician. And according to the book, Wainright was the officer in charge of the investigation.

She kicked a rock out of her path. On the other hand, she could flag down the next deputy that drove by.

"Study this sketch of the rattler's likeness and get familiar with his face," Deputy Carlisle said as Darcy closed the gate from the yard to the pasture. They had driven to the repaired fence and back to her house.

Darcy folded the sketch and tucked it in her pocket. "He doesn't look familiar, but I'll watch out for him."

Carlisle stared at the pasture. "That may be how they accessed your house for the vandalism."

"I wondered the same thing. The only place I can even partially see that route from the house is if I stand on the upstairs balcony."

When the deputy drove off, Darcy walked inside and found the phone book.

Dale Anderson answered on the third ring.

"Mr. Anderson, it's Darcy Cooper."

"What do you want?" Dale's gruff voice conveyed suspicion.

"I walked the pasture today and noticed someone had repaired a cut in the fence in the upper back, near the corner. Did you find a break and fix it?"

"No. I put that fence up twenty years ago, and I've maintained it since. There'd better still be twenty-six goats in that field."

"There are. How often do you check on them?"

"At least three times a week. I take good care of those animals. Keith will vouch for that so don't think about trying to nail me on some phony mistreatment of animals charge to get the goats off the property early. You said you'd let them stay until the end of the year."

"I haven't changed my mind. I was curious because I've never seen you out here."

"Some of us work for a living."

"How do you get into the pasture?"

"My lock's on the gate in the southwest corner. The water and feed troughs along the fence belong to me. I'll be taking them when I move the goats."

"Understood. I spoke to the Sheriff's Department; they'll keep an eye on the gate."

"I don't need nothin' from anyone in the sheriff's department."

Hoping that Dale's phone had survived his slammed disconnect, Darcy took a deep breath. One stir of the pot down, and one to go. While she looked for Keith's number, her phone rang.

"Hello?"

"Darcy, it's Maggie."

"Hi! Too bad you didn't call earlier. Beth and Annie were here, and Annie loves talking with you."

"I'll have to give the munchkin a call this weekend. I like talking to her too. She's as close as I'm going to get to a grandchild. Did you show Beth the sights?"

"I took her to a goat show if you can imagine that. Other than a repair in the fence, it's been a good week."

"Well, a fence repair is better than the dishwasher flood I had yesterday. The maid's still finding water in the darndest places."

"I'm sorry to hear that," Darcy said. "A mass exodus of Dale Anderson's goats into the neighbor's pasture is the worst that could have happened here. Fortunately, they're all there. I let him know. He didn't appreciate my concern."

"Alex mentioned Dale's short temper several times."

"Oh! I've been meaning to ask you if Alex ever told you he was giving me his house and land."

"He never mentioned it. But he was one to keep things private. Shoot! There's the doorbell. I'll call back later to reschedule my visit."

"Bye."

Darcy dialed Keith.

"What can I do for you, darlin'?"

She heard a chair creak and pictured booted feet settling on his desk. "Does your dad ever feed at night?"

"I suppose he would if he hadn't been able to get out during daylight. Why are you asking?"

"This morning, I found where someone had driven either in or out after cutting the wire at the back fence. They repaired the fence, and your dad's goats are all accounted for, by the way."

"Did you call the sheriff's office?"

"I spoke to a deputy. I have one more question."

"This is beginning to sound more like an interrogation than a conversation."

"Sorry, but I need to know who owns the property behind me. I want to ask if they've seen anything. If you don't know, I'll ask at the feed store."

"You remember that friend of Alex's who told me why you'd inherited the property?"

She smiled. "What's his name?"

"You'll owe me. At the least, his name is worth dinner."

"A trip to the feed store is cheaper."

"Lunch then."

"Deal." She poised a pen over a notepad.

"His name is Bob Hughes, and his wife's name is Martha. Hang on, and I'll look up their number for you."

Bob Hughes spat a stream of tobacco onto the ground beyond where he squatted beside Darcy. "It wasn't me, but at least it's a good job. You say the tracks go down into your pasture?"

"Yes, but not far. I followed the trail here then onto your place. I suspect they used your ranch road to access the highway. I apologize for trespassing."

"No need. You're a neighbor."

She rose fluidly; Bob unbent like a folding yardstick.

"Has anyone asked you about selling your land?" she asked.

"That detective asked me the same thing."

"Detective Wainright came to see you?"

"Yep, that was his name; the man smiles with too many teeth. He showed up yesterday."

"Someone tried to buy me out after I inherited. I guess he wondered if anyone around me received the same offer."

"Wouldn't sell if they had made an offer. Ranching's my life, not a hobby."

Darcy pulled a business card from her pocket.

"If you see anything suspicious, Mr. Hughes, I'd appreciate a call. And I'll call you if I find more fence patches."

"Mends," he said, squinting and holding the card at arm's length.

"What?"

"You mend a fence. Patching is for clothes and roads. Lost Creek Bed & Breakfast, huh? Alex said you were a homemaker at heart. How's business?"

She stuck her hands in her back pockets. "I haven't opened yet. But plenty is keeping me busy."

"I read the paper." His faded blue eyes studied her. "Alex said you had gumption and heart. You remember that."

She smiled. "Yes, sir."

"Now that you know where we live don't be a stranger. Martha likes a good visit now and then."

Friday, Darcy placed frozen catfish fillets in the refrigerator to thaw. As she mentally reviewed ingredients for tartar sauce, her phone rang. The caller ID displayed Maggie Williams. She could use a friendly visit.

"Hey, Maggie! How are you?"

"Darcy Cooper, you had better have a good excuse for not telling me what's been going on with you and your house. I spoke with Beth, and she told me everything. Break-ins and the attack at Border's!" Maggie paused for breath.

"I didn't want to worry you, and the sheriff's department is looking for the men involved."

"When can I come down?"

"I'd love to have you, but despite the alarm system I installed, I'm not comfortable having guests until the men are caught."

"You let Beth and Annie stay."

"They brought Hank with them."

"The security hunk," Maggie said, her voice softening. "I wonder if I can pay him to come with me."

"He's in Atlanta for the opening of the new hotel."

"Darn. Regardless, I'll be down to visit you next week to look over your B&B. If I can't stay with you, I'll get a hotel room near the interstate."

Friday evening at the roadhouse, the boisterous band set the rhythm for Darcy's movements as she set up food.

Carl pulled one last beer and joined her. "Hey, girl!" He inhaled appreciatively. "My stomach's growled for hours, what did you fix tonight?"

"Beer-battered catfish nuggets and homemade tartar sauce. The extra sauce is in the bar fridge." She glanced around. Exuberant dancers filled the dance floor. The bar was two-deep, standing room only.

"A lot of folks from the country music festival are wandering in and performing spur-of-the-moment concerts. Why don't you hang out for a while to listen and eat some of that food you brought? You're looking like a good wind would carry you to the next county."

"Thanks, Carl, but I have a deputy escort."

"Things back to normal at your place?"

"As normal as they can be. No more snakes or break-ins. I did find a place where my pasture fence had been cut and mended."

His face sobered. "You tell the sheriff?"

"I told his deputy."

"You mind yourself. Listen, I haven't written your check yet. I hired a second bartender to handle the festival crowd. Give me a minute to slip to the back and get you paid." He turned away, spoke to his assistant bartender, and then leaned towards a silvering-blonde seated at the bar. When he pointed Darcy's way, the woman pushed through the crowd and squeezed in beside her.

"Ms. Cooper, I'm Candice Walker. I tasted some chocolate-raspberry muffins you made for the real estate office next door to my antiques shop and was wondering if you could put together something similar for a tea I want to serve at the shop next Thursday."

"Of course." Darcy leaned in to talk over the band.

By the time they ran out of ideas, and Candice accepted a cowboy's invitation to dance, Darcy had a menu sketched out on a napkin, a deposit check in her purse, and a smile on her face.

"Way to go, young 'un." Carl handed her his check. "Want me to walk you to your car?"

"Thanks." She squeezed his arm, then pointed to the queue at the bar. "But you have business, and I have an escort. I'll be fine."

The sandy-haired, plainclothes deputy met her at the door.

"Ready?" he asked.

"I am. Sorry for the delay, Deputy Cole."

"No problem, I like the band."

Darcy pulled keys from her purse as they walked

outside. The sun had faded to a memory. Time and daylight flew when you were marketing.

She looked right to left as she walked between the shadowed rows of vehicles.

A thud made her spin. The deputy lay on the gravel.

The ghoul's clammy palm clamped her mouth. "Keep quiet and walk like we're headed home."

She made a fist, covered it with her other hand, and drove her elbow back. Her purse got in the way, and her elbow slid off his ribs.

His angry hold tightened over her mouth and nose.

She clawed at his arm until white flashes confused her vision. He eased off as her knees buckled.

His switchblade sprang open, the tip menaced her ribcage.

Darcy dropped her purse as he forced her toward the end of the row. If she got in a car with him, she'd never get out alive.

High beam headlights blinded them. The knife wavered.

Darcy grabbed his wrist and pushed his arm away.

The ghoul stumbled and fell, dragging her with him.

Red and blue lights flashed. Voices shouted.

She scrambled and swung a fist, connecting with his nose. Pain seared her knuckles.

Cursing, he wrapped her braid around his hand and jerked her head back, exposing her throat. He shouted toward the lights.

The knife arced.

The ghoul's body jerked and twisted as the world and its sounds spun away.

CHAPTER TWENTY-FIVE

"You're safe, Darcy."

Eli's familiar scent and voice soothed her.

Believing him, she opened her eyes.

Blue and red flashes bounced wildly; disembodied voices conversed. Eli's warmth surrounded her. Her chest constricted. As she gasped in air, his arms tightened.

"You're all right; you're safe."

She concentrated on his voice. Slowly, her lips regained feeling, and her chattering teeth quieted—soothed by his steady heartbeat. "I've missed you," she whispered.

He tensed.

Horror vied with embarrassment. She'd cried her mascara off all over the front of his shirt and then told him what he didn't want to hear.

She pushed away, but his grip tightened.

"I didn't mean it." The lie choked her.

"Okay, I meant it, but I promised I wouldn't bring it up again. Please let me go, Eli."

A tap sounded on the window. His grip eased as he opened the door.

"Sir, the coroner has finished with Randy Hall. He called a hearse. The EMTs can take a look at Ms. Cooper now."

Something soft brushed her hair before he released her and stepped from the car.

Randy Hall was dead? Darcy eased towards the door, the question on her lips. The paramedics intercepted her. One asked questions while the second blinded her with a penlight.

She looked up at Deputy Carlisle. "How's Deputy Cole?"

Carlisle folded her arms over the top of the door.

"He has a headache and a mild concussion. He'll pull desk duty for a few days, but he'll be all right."

Darcy flinched as EMTs cleaned grit from the scrapes on her hands and knees. They bandaged a few and declared her good to go.

"I thought you were a goner," Carlisle said, handing her a blanket.

"From scrapes and bruises?" Darcy searched the crowd for Eli.

"No, from when that guy tried to open your windpipe. It happened so fast no one got a shot off except the Sheriff, and he put two rounds into him before you'd finished screaming his name. I've never seen anyone shoot so fast and accurately. You two must be living right."

Darcy struggled with memory. She'd called Eli's name, and he'd shot the ghoul? She stared out at the yellow crime-scene tape that cordoned the parking lot like a morbid block party and saw Eli hand his pistol to a deputy.

"Don't worry, there were plenty of witnesses; the shooting was justified." Carlisle straightened. "Stay put while I tell the boss I'm taking you home."

Every muscle in Darcy's body tightened as she shook. Fragments of images formed in her mind. She didn't remember the shots, just a brilliant flash of light in her peripheral vision. And blood. She remembered blood.

She touched her hair, flinched at the sticky places and hastily wiped her fingers on her skirt. She studied her shirt in the faint glow of the dome light. Dark red splotches dotted the material—blood that would have been hers if not for Eli. She wanted to strip her clothes off and burn them. She wanted to shower until her skin was scalded clean. She silently thanked whoever had wiped the blood from her face and arms. Eli?

Deputy Carlisle opened the front door and slid behind the wheel. "Ready to go?"

"What about my car? And my purse?"

"I have your purse; the Sheriff has your keys. He'll see that your car makes it to your place by tomorrow morning."

But he wouldn't be the one driving it.

"That's not necessary, I can drive."

A stupid statement. The EMTs had told her she was suffering mild shock.

Carlisle shot her a casual look.

"Won't be much fun with scraped palms. Besides, if I stay here, they'll make me conduct interviews and fill out paperwork. You don't want me to have to do that, do you?"

"I surrender," Darcy said.

Carlisle started the cruiser. "You might want to wave at

Carl as we drive out. He's worried sick about what happened to you."

Darcy waved and signaled a thumbs up when she spotted Carl. His creased face lit up with an emotional, crooked smile as they passed.

He tossed the baby rattle onto the seat beside the night vision goggles he'd ripped from his face when the headlights had nearly blinded him. Randy was dead. Better dead than wounded—dead men didn't talk.

Raul sat silently beside him. He'd raced unseen from the parking lot like the devil had called his own. He'd worked his way around and up the hill to the truck. Raul possessed more intellect and self-preservation instinct then hotheaded Randy had ever imagined.

The man tapped the steering wheel with his fingers. His ideal operation was now a liability, but he was close to scoring big. He'd locate another staging area and move the drugs as quickly as tonight's debacle, sheriff patrols, and the golden girl's habits allowed. And before he left Lost Creek, he'd settle his debt with her.

After failing to convince herself that she didn't want a nightlight, Darcy left the bathroom light on and the door ajar. Lying in bed, she stared at the ceiling, wondering if Eli would forget what she'd said in the backseat of the patrol car. Deciding her chances weren't good, she prayed for sleep.

He'd just killed a man, but all Eli could think about was Darcy saying she missed him.

His grip tightened on the steering wheel. After all he'd done to discourage her, she still cared. And the truth was, he'd missed her too. Now that he didn't see her every day, it was like a light had gone out in his world. Tonight, her light had almost extinguished for good.

Her near-death had raised his greatest fear's ugly head. Premature loss had destroyed his mother and left his sister to raise her son solo. Darcy had smiled her way past his defenses and lodged like a burr in his heart but watching her almost die reinforced the fact that loving meant eventually losing. There was no future in letting himself love her.

He turned up Darcy's driveway and parked her car under the illuminated security light. Exiting with two cups of coffee, he walked over to Deputy Carlisle who had parked facing the road, in front of the house.

"Any problems?" he asked.

"No, sir. Her lights went out about an hour ago. I sent the deputy at the gate on patrol, like you asked. It's been quiet. Will you need a ride in tomorrow morning?"

"I've already made arrangements." He held out a cup. "I brought extra coffee."

"Thanks, but keep both. I'll pick some up on my rounds. Goodnight, Sheriff."

Eli walked to the oak grove as Carlisle drove off. She

was a good cop, and Darcy had mentioned she had a daughter. He should put her on day-shift. He'd make the change before the election.

He'd stopped dreading the election when he'd prioritized Darcy's safety over his campaign. Would she stay in Lost Creek after almost dying tonight? Add that to her foundering business startup, and she might decide to accept the generous real estate offer and return to the heavily-populated anonymity and random safety of Dallas.

He leaned against a live oak with a good view of the drive and house. His senses adjusted to the darkness and night sounds.

The motion sensor light on the kitchen porch lit up. He set the coffee on the ground and studied the shadows around the house. Had he missed a trespasser?

Light reflected off her bedroom wall. Darcy struggled from beneath the covers feeling like she'd spent the evening in a rock tumbler with some boulders. Knees, hands, neck, and scalp protested every movement. Gritting her teeth, she stood and straightened her nightshirt. A gift from Beth, the copper-colored silk fell to mid-thigh. It took several attempts to grip her bat. Using it as a cane, she limped to the window.

The security light illuminated the front yard. Deputy Carlisle hadn't called her, so she must be expecting the new arrival. Her replacement? No, it was her car, Darcy realized, happy to see it. She froze in place.

The driver was Eli.

Instead of getting in the cruiser with Carlisle, he walked to the oak grove. And Carlisle left.

Her heart skipped several beats as she pleated the front of her nightgown. Eli didn't have a vehicle to sit in while he watched over her in the dark—uncomfortable—alone.

She blew out a long breath and eased the bath towel hanging off the foot of her bed, around her shoulders. She'd invite him inside. If he said no, at least she'd made an effort, and that might help her sleep. She hobbled to the kitchen, unlocked the door, and hobbled outside.

He emerged from the trees and strode towards her when she reached the bottom porch step.

"Why are you out here?" he demanded.

"I came to invite you inside."

She turned for the steps. He took her arm as she climbed.

"Why are you wearing a towel?"

"It was easier to put on than a robe."

"You're shaking. Get inside."

His presence—not the air temperature—triggered her trembling. She leaned on her bat and entered the door he opened.

Eli took her towel, then shrugged out of his jacket and held it open. It was the same coat he'd worn the night he'd invited her to sit down at Border's a lifetime ago. She slipped her arms through the sleeves and clutched the lapels to her chest.

"I'll make hot chocolate," he said.

She sat while he filled the kettle and set it over high heat.

"Why are you here?"

"I returned your car, remember?" His eyes narrowed, and his hand stopped midway between the open cabinet and her mugs. "Were you checked for a concussion?"

"Yes. I don't have one." She watched him set mugs on the counter, then spooned the homemade cocoa mix into each.

The teakettle finally whistled.

Eli poured water into the mugs and set them on the table.

"Do you want a statement?"

"Not unless you can't sleep." He sat.

"I'm having trouble sleeping, but I'd still rather wait until tomorrow." She hesitated. "Why were you at Border's tonight?"

"Ransacking your house signaled an escalation. I happened to be on tonight's rotation for Border's," Eli said.

As he'd done every Friday night since she'd found the heroin. "Your predictable delivery schedule made it a likely place to approach you again."

She shook her head. "I never heard him coming."

He relived the dark moment when Hall had grabbed her. When Hall's arm had risen with intent, Eli hadn't hesitated—just aimed, fired twice, and advanced to haul Randy off her.

There was so much blood he'd thought he'd shot too late—or hit her also. His senses had always sharpened during combat but seeing her lying on the ground had hammered in a spike of despair so sharp he'd nearly gone to his knees. Training and a need to know had kept him moving toward her. It wasn't until Carlisle found Darcy's pulse, that his heart restarted.

He'd scooped Darcy up and carried her to a squad car. Sat and held her, watching the rise and fall of her steady breaths while his deputies secured the scene and tended to the injured deputy.

"You should have gone back to Brooke's. She called when you didn't show up."

"I couldn't. If they try again, I don't want them coming to Brooke's." She looked at him. "Deputy Carlisle said she'd never seen anyone shoot so fast and accurate."

"The Rangers trained me well. I'm even better with a rifle." His humorless smile ended as he picked up his mug and sipped. Grimacing, he set the cup on the table and stirred the steaming liquid.

"I imagine that part of your decision to return to Lost Creek was to leave big-city violence behind," Darcy said. "Given current circumstances, the county should be thankful you're here. I know I am." She met his eyes. "I'm sorry you had to kill someone tonight."

"He left me no choice."

"Do you think they'll try again?"

"They now know we're always watching you. Returning or running will depend on how badly they want revenge. Don't let down your guard, and don't go outside this late again no matter who or what you see."

She cradled her cup between her hands. "When I'm making money again, I'll donate a computer or two to your department. I like to pay my debts."

"You don't owe us anything."

"Once again, we disagree." Setting her cup aside, she stood and walked to the empty fireplace. Her fingertips ran lightly along the red cedar mantle's polished curves and indentations. A small smile lifted her lips.

She'd found a happy thought. He envied her sudden easing of tension. "What are you thinking?" he asked.

"Of you."

"What about me?" Habitual wariness entered his voice and he saw her tense.

"Don't worry, Sheriff. I won't repeat my behavior in the cruiser." She turned toward her room. "Thank you for saving my life. You're welcome to stay in the house until your ride arrives."

Eli stared after her. Her words elicited no relief—only emptiness. She wouldn't turn to him again.

Darcy slept the remainder of the night soundly, surrounded by Eli's jacket and his scent. Waking early to the sound of a car engine, she heard the front door open and shut, and then the sound of the engine receding into the distance.

Walking into the living room, she detected the altered pillow arrangement and the neatly folded chenille throw. Whether it was his original intent or not, Eli had stayed and watched over her.

"That's it." Darcy leaned back in the chair in front of

Detective Wainright's desk.

The detective looked up from his notepad. "If I'd been at Border's, I'd have kept a closer tail on you. We might have a suspect in custody now, instead of a body at the morgue."

"Or I might be dead." She smiled to soften her words. "I saw you in the parking lot after the excitement ended. I presumed you'd been there all along."

He shook his head. "I took a personal day."

"Dispatch found you quickly."

"Dispatch didn't call me, Whitepath did."

"The sheriff is a man of honor."

"He called me because I'm in charge of this case," Wainright said.

"Would you have done the same for him were your positions reversed?"

Wainright switched off the recorder. "Call me if you remember any other details, Ms. Cooper."

"Of course." She stood and walked away, straightening her calf-length skirt. She took the elevator to the second floor and smiled at Eli's secretary.

Janet smiled past her headset. "Yes, sir, I've faxed the request. The DA's office promised a reply as soon as they look over the papers. And Ms. Cooper is here."

Darcy shook her head. She'd planned to hand Eli's jacket over to Janet and then leave. Seconds later, his office door opened. Swallowing, she turned.

"I ran off with your coat last night."

"Come in." Eli stood aside.

She walked past him and stopped in the middle of the room. "I meant to leave the jacket with Janet. I hung it in the bathroom while I showered this morning; I think the steam released most of the wrinkles. Now that I think about it, I slept in it; I should have it cleaned." She turned for the door. Eli stepped in front of her.

"It's fine." He took the jacket. "How are you?"

She licked her lips. "I'm okay unless I stop and think about it." She walked to a window and picked out her car in the parking lot. "Do you still have nightmares from violent experiences in your past?"

"Yes. Time makes some difference."

"But you never forget."

"No. You never forget."

She nodded. "Thank you for the loan of your jacket. I'll let you get back to work."

Monday, Darcy arrived first at the What's Time to a Hog barbecue and sat at an outdoor picnic table. Absently tracing the red and white squares on the paper table cover, she watched blue-black grackles squawk a protest at the lack of food on the ground.

Tires squealed. Her head jerked toward the parking lot as Keith swung into an open slot and exited his truck. He spotted her and hurried over to issue a quick hug and brush a kiss across her cheek.

"Hey, darlin', sorry I'm late. Let's see your hands."

She pulled away. "How did you hear? This week's paper

isn't out yet."

"I got the scoop from an unexpected source."

She extended her hands. He checked the one with bandages then balanced the tops of her hands in his palms. "Girl, at the rate you're going, it's a good thing you heal fast."

"Name your source, cowboy. Is that why you're late?"

"Yep. Sit down, and I'll tell you about my last-minute surgery on a mutt brought in by the woman who hit him."

"How horrible for both. Are they all right?"

Keith straddled the seat opposite her. "They will be. The fender clipped the pooch's hip. He took twenty staples, but nothing broke besides the skin. Two weeks and he'll be fine. I wasn't much inclined to do anything for the driver."

"She did bring the dog in instead of leaving him on the side of the road."

"It was Cheryl Greer, the newspaper reporter making your life public."

"Oh." Darcy frowned. "But still, she did the right thing."

Keith nodded. "I made her feel so bad about the whole incident, she's adopting the mutt. That pup's feet are the size of ping-pong paddles, but he's only a foot tall right now. When she asked, I told her he must have some retriever blood because he had swimming paws."

"You didn't." Darcy tried to sound horrified, but humor ruined the attempt. "At least the dog won't end up at the pound."

"Normally I give a Good Samaritan discount, but I billed

her for all the shots and the surgery. It's time she took responsibility for the consequences of her actions." He grinned. "She had to wait to file the exclusive story she got from the detective-in-charge until I finished with the dog."

Wainright was anxious to get his version—probably minus his after-the-fact appearance—to the voters, Darcy thought.

Keith stood as other vehicles parked.

"This place doesn't have waitresses. I'll get our food; you keep our seats. These tables fill up fast, and it's too nice a day to eat inside."

"My treat, remember?" Darcy handed Keith cash.

He took the money, disappeared inside, and returned minutes later with two plates piled with sliced brisket, sausage, half a chicken, potato salad, onions, pickles, and coleslaw.

"Is a National Guard unit joining us?" she asked.

"Fresh air makes me hungry."

He entertained and teased as they ate. She tried to respond naturally but worried that Keith would take her responses as encouragement. Eventually, he rested his elbows on the table.

"I've seen happier faces on animals I've vaccinated. Am I moving too fast?"

"Right now, everything except my bed-and-breakfast opening is moving too fast." She met his eyes. "You know I value your friendship."

His head fell to his hands. "Not the friendship speech."

"Keith, my life is a mess right now, and I need to concentrate on straightening it out. Are we still friends?"

"I can't be your friend right now." Keith pushed his plate aside, and crossed his forearms on the table. "Circumstances won't permit it."

"I'm sorry," she said, meaning it. Keith had been a better friend to her than she'd been to him.

He looked away. His solemn profile made his face unfamiliar.

"Well, darlin', everything in life can't turn out the way I hope."

Tuesday morning, Darcy sat on her porch swing. Despite her promise to accept Eli's decision not to pursue their relationship, she still pondered the puzzle of his actions. Maybe he'd spent the night because his ride hadn't shown. Or perhaps he'd spent the night out of a sense of duty. But why, after his "no way" speech, had he comforted her in the patrol car?

Standing, she brushed off the seat of her jeans. The barbecue grill looked like a garden feature forgotten amid ankle-high grass. She flexed her hands. They no longer needed Band-Aids, but pushing a mower didn't sound like fun. She'd start another project instead.

She got her SUV keys and drove through the gate nearest the house and into the pasture. Spotting a likely cluster of rocks, she parked and donned a pair of work gloves.

Using a crowbar, she pried future stepping-stones from the caliche. Most came up easily. She checked the stones for scorpions and sang along with the Texas Rebel Radio station as she loaded the smaller ones into the SUV's cargo space.

She spotted a Styrofoam cup and picked it up, raising an eyebrow at the "Don't Mess with Texas" logo printed on the side. Whoever tossed it wasn't sympathetic to the Lone Star state's anti-littering campaign.

She flipped a stone and uncovered a dull glint of olive-green metal. Dropping the crowbar, she knelt to brush the dirt off the flat surface. A handle on top of the box made it easy to lift out.

She rested the ammo box on the ground. It looked relatively new.

She opened the lid.

The packages filled with a black substance sent a chill up her spine.

"I'll take that," a harsh voice said behind her.

CHAPTER TWENTY-SIX

Darcy shielded her eyes with one hand. It took her a minute to place the man's vaguely familiar features.

The blood rushed from her face. The sketch!

The rattler.

"Can I help you?" she bluffed, standing.

"You've already saved me the trouble of hunting you down."

She spun.

He shoved her to the ground before she made it to her car.

Pulling both hands behind her, he tugged her gloves off and quickly wound a length of twine around her wrists.

She screamed.

He pulled the bandana from her neck, stuffed it in her mouth, then yanked her to her feet. She stumbled onto the passenger seat of her Explorer.

Fear froze her as Raul approached. They were working together.

"Bring the truck in and finish digging up the rest of the boxes," the rattler said.

Raul's angry gaze promised her he'd take his pound of flesh for Randy's death soon.

The rattler drove to her house, dragged her out of the car, and forced her towards the storm cellar. He lifted the door.

"Get in."

She barely made it down the steps before he dropped the door in place. She heard the latch slide closed. The cellar lacked electricity, but a meager measure of light seeped through the ventilation slats.

She eased up the steps and pushed with her back and shoulders against the metal door. It didn't budge.

She'd cleaned the cellar too thoroughly and left nothing to cut the rough twine binding her wrists. No matter how she worked her jaw and tongue, she couldn't spit out the gag. Sweat trickled down her spine. She sat on the concrete steps, knees tucked to her chest, forehead on her knees.

How long had the heroin been buried in the pasture? The rattler appeared to be Raul's boss. She felt like she should know him, and not from the sketch.

What seemed like hours later, the door swung open. Light entered at a dramatic angle. The rattler filled the opening.

"Get up. We're going to the kitchen."

Staggering on stiff legs, she stomped her feet to encourage circulation. Her wrists burned from her attempts to work the twine loose. She walked up the concrete stairs. When she reached the top step, he grabbed her arm and hauled her across her yard.

Fresh air cleared her head and chilled her body as they approached her house. In her field, four men dug with pickaxes while two others loaded metal boxes into a midnight blue pickup. How much heroin was out there?

At the screen door, the rattler jerked the gag from her

mouth and pushed her inside. She stumbled forward then leaned against the kitchen sink.

A woman entered from the dining room.

"Maggie? You shouldn't have come!" Panic hit her.

Maggie Williams moved to stand beside the rattler. Darcy immediately recognized the similarities. "Hello, Darcy. I hope you've enjoyed your stay in Lost Creek."

Maggie had used past tense. "It's had its moments," Darcy answered faintly.

"You've met my son, Todd."

Todd, the rattler, laid a snub-nosed revolver on her kitchen table. The muzzle targeted her belly. Maggie continued. "I appreciate your mentioning the alarm system. Raul disabled it—in case you were expecting help."

Todd hadn't left her in the storm cellar. They wanted her to know they were involved. They wanted to hurt her.

Todd sat. Maggie sat beside him. "Todd says you're responsible for turning our short-term investment into a long-term venture. We've decided we can't postpone retirement any longer—or yours."

"Was Alex involved?" Darcy asked.

Maggie's smile didn't reach her eyes. "Indirectly. Meeting Alex again started Todd and me thinking about this land. Todd used to spend summers with my parents. And he spent quite a bit of time out here with Alex's brother, Dale. This isolated ranch and Lost Creek's provincial airport suited our needs."

Eyes on Darcy, Todd pulled a cigar from his pocket. He

deliberately clipped one end of the cigar with a silver guillotine cutter. Her fingers curled, and her knuckles scraped the jagged counter lip.

Slowly, she tested the twine against the counter's rough edge while shifting from foot to foot. A few strands severed. She moved her feet again, pretending to work circulation back into her legs. More strands separated as she looked at the clock. The sheriff's deputy should drive by soon.

"Alex complicated things by dying and leaving you the land," Maggie continued. "And you moved right in without considering my generous offers to buy the property. If you'd sold when we started the rumors, or when Randy left the snakes, or even after Raul and Randy vandalized the house, you'd be safe now. Was the house worth your life?"

"No," Darcy said. But sharing two and a half months of her life with Eli had been worth staying. Seeing him again was worth staying alive.

Darcy relished a spike of resolve that grew with each strand of twine that gave way. The deputy on patrol must have reported the activity in the field by now. When she ran, she might make it to the safety of the patrol car.

"Have you smuggled long?"

Maggie laughed. "Todd's father and I started out importing produce from Mexico. Along the way, we imported a few artifacts and people, and more than doubled our income." She paused to admire her rings.

"When a Mexican drug cartel suggested we include their product with our produce, we agreed. To refuse would have proved unhealthy to our business and us."

A garbled voice interrupted. Todd pulled a walkie-talkie from his pocket, picked up his revolver, and walked outside.

Maggie pulled a pistol from her purse. "In case you get any ideas," she said.

Both women looked at the ringing phone. The machine picked up after the fourth ring.

"Dar-cy." Beth's voice sing-songed then paused. "Darcy, I know you're there, you told me to call tonight." Another pause. "I'm counting to ten. Answer or I'm calling the sheriff."

Darcy knew Beth meant her threat as humor—Maggie didn't.

Maggie stood and pressed the gun to Darcy's ribs.

"Make an excuse and say goodbye."

She placed the receiver against Darcy's ear and leaned in to listen.

"Seven, eight—"

"I'm here, Beth." Darcy's voice echoed back from the answering machine.

"What kept you? Can you turn the machine off?"

Maggie shook her head.

"No, I'm baking. I'm up to my elbows in dough."

"Darcy, you're a wonderful cook, but there's more to life."

Metal dug into her side. "Beth, can I call you back tomorrow? I need to finish these pastries before I have to resort to drinking a pot of coffee to make it through the next three batches."

"Of course, you never were one for an all-nighter. I love you too, Darcy. Take care."

"I love you too; talk to you tomorrow."

Maggie hung up. Darcy hoped Beth remembered their college code for trouble. Maggie wouldn't talk this much unless she knew Darcy wouldn't be around to share the details.

She returned to the counter and continued to rock and saw. Outside, a car door slammed. She sucked in a breath as Raul entered the kitchen.

"It took longer than planned to deal with the deputy," he told Maggie.

"What did you do to the deputy?" Darcy asked, frantic.

Dark eyes locked on her, assessing. Darcy's courage faltered. He walked to the kitchen door.

Her legs went weak. Had Raul killed the deputy?

Todd walked in. "The truck's loaded, Juan's driving. I'll ride with Raul." He glanced at Darcy then back to Maggie. "Let's finish this; we've stayed too long."

"Use the storm cellar. It will take them longer to find her. We'll wait at the airport."

Raul gripped Darcy's arm, and she felt the twine give. Heart racing, she linked her fingers.

"If we had more time, I'd make this memorable for you," he hissed.

Todd led the way outside. Darcy dragged her feet with little effect as Raul hauled her into the twilight and towards the cellar.

She searched the horizon. No red and blue lights

approached. Why couldn't Todd or Raul have gone with Maggie? Against one, she had a chance, but two? She might as well wish the dusk would immediately morph into a starless, moonless night. Behind them, two vehicles receded down the driveway.

Todd heaved the cellar door open. She deliberately stumbled against Raul. The twine fell to the grass as he pulled her against his chest. "Guess what I have for you," he snarled.

When his secretary Janet walked in, Eli looked up at the clock over his office door.

"It's after five. Why are you still here?" he asked.

"I waited on these." Janet handed him papers. "I left the originals on Detective Wainright's desk. A fax from the Dallas realtor; and Margaret Williams' DMV photo, license plate, address, and phone number."

He skimmed the fax. The potential buyer, listed as MEX/TEX Importers, sounded familiar. He dug a DEA report from one of the stacks in front of him. Running a finger down the list, he stopped at MEX/TEX Importers. The owners were listed as Margaret and Todd Williams. He lifted the receiver and punched in Maggie's number.

"Williams residence." A heavily accented voice answered.

"I'd like to speak with Margaret Williams."

"Missus Williams is not home."

"When do you expect her?"

"It will be several days."

"Is Todd around?"

"He left two days ago."

He hung up and looked at Janet. "Take a little more overtime and contact the DMV. I want a photo of Todd Williams, and a BOLO issued for any vehicles registered to either Todd or Margaret Williams. If they're in the county, I want to know."

"Yes, sir." Janet pivoted for the door as the phone rang. Turning back, she picked up his handset. "Sheriff Whitepath's office." She listened then put a hand over the mouthpiece.

"It's a Beth Thompson. She says it's an emergency."

Eli took the phone. "Yes, Beth?"

"You have to go to Darcy's house now! I called her, and she used our college code for trouble. Something is wrong. Please hurry!"

"I'm on my way."

Eli palmed his cell phone as he and his deputies sped toward Darcy's house. "Whitepath," he answered.

"Sheriff, Todd Williams' DMV photo came through. He strongly resembles the sketch of the man Deputy Carlisle saw with the rattle," Janet said.

"Have you contacted Wainright or Price?" he asked.

"Wainright's en route from Merritt. The dispatcher is still trying to raise Deputy Price. Ms. Cooper's answering machine picked up when I called."

"Keep me posted."

Where was Price? The deputy was supposed to be watching Darcy's place.

Price's voice came on the radio. Eli quickly cut off the answering dispatcher. "What's your situation, and where is Ms. Cooper?"

"A nicely dressed woman in a red Cadillac flagged me down and asked for directions. Someone hit me from behind. I woke up, handcuffed, in the backseat of my patrol car. I'm loose now. The same Cadillac is now following a pickup truck. The truck cab held three men."

"Was Ms. Cooper in either vehicle?"

"I didn't see her in the truck, but someone's sitting in the Cadillac's back seat. I ducked so they wouldn't realize I was awake, so I didn't see the passenger. I used my spare keys to get out of the 'cuffs. I'm following with lights off at a good distance. They might be heading for the airport."

"I'll set up a roadblock." Eli activated his lights and positioned his deputies via radio. Five minutes later, Deputy Carlisle crouched beside him behind their cruisers. Wainright was closing in on Price.

A dark blue pickup rounded the curve. The driver skidded to a halt and attempted a U-turn that the full-sized truck couldn't hope to achieve on the narrow, two-lane blacktop. The Cadillac, following too close, broadsided the truck, shoving it toward the ditch paralleling the road. Price and Wainright skidded to stops, blocking both vehicles.

Men jumped from the pickup cab like a flushed covey of

quail. The deputies gave chase, tackled, and aligned the runners face down on the side of the road. Once searched and handcuffed, they hustled the runners into the patrol cars.

Eli read the Cadillac's license plate as a silver-blonde woman struggled from behind the deployed driver-side airbag. He checked the back seat and saw a man cowering. The woman clutched his arm; a golf ball-sized knot marred her forehead.

"I hope you're writing an accident report. I couldn't avoid the truck."

"Keep your hands where I can see them." Eli pried her grip loose. "Deputy, cuff the man in the back and add him to the others."

Carlisle motioned for the man to step out.

"You have the right to remain silent." Stomach twisting, Eli recited Miranda. "Where is Darcy Cooper?" he ended.

"I'm sorry, who?" The woman smiled as she opened her purse. "This is a mistake. I'm not at fault here. Let me get my driver's license."

"Keep your hands where I can see them, Mrs. Williams."

Her smile faltered.

"Where is Darcy Cooper?" he repeated.

Deputy Carlisle returned and bumped Maggie Williams with all the finesse of a defensive end stripping a football from a receiver. "Sorry, ma'am."

Maggie's purse fell to the ground revealing a revolver.

"Oh, look there, sir," Carlisle said.

Eli lifted the pistol by its trigger guard and sniffed. The gun hadn't been fired recently.

He called another deputy over to bag the gun. He turned to Carlisle. "Check the car."

Carlisle pulled the interior latch that opened the Cadillac's trunk. She sorted through the luggage. "Ms. Cooper isn't in the car, sir."

Deputy Price approached. "Sheriff, the truck is loaded with enough heroin to put everyone in Texas in rehab. Ms. Cooper's not in the truck, but I heard the driver tell his amigo to keep quiet about the gringa. He might mean this lady," he inclined his head toward Maggie, "or Ms. Cooper. He's not willing to clarify his statement at this time."

Deputy Carlisle snapped handcuffs on Maggie's wrists.

"What are you doing?" Maggie sputtered. "I'm the victim of a traffic accident caused by your vehicles blocking the road."

"You're under arrest for carrying a concealed weapon," Eli said.

"I'm a Texas resident. I'm allowed to carry a weapon in my vehicle without a concealed carry license if I'm traveling in Texas."

"In your vehicle, yes. When you stepped out of the car and revealed the gun, you broke the law." Eli paused.

"Where's Todd, Mrs. Williams?" When she remained silent, he rested a palm on the roof of her car. "I imagine soil samples on those boxes in the truck are going to match the soil in Ms. Cooper's pasture. If anything has happened to her, I'll do everything in my power to see that the only way you ever get out of prison is by lethal injection."

"Raul shot her, Todd and I had nothing to do with it," Maggie blurted.

Eli's breath fled his body.

CHAPTER TWENTY-SEVEN

Eli sped through the darkness, picturing his hands circling Raul's neck and squeezing until death extinguished life from the drug dealer's eyes. The irony mocked him. He'd forfeit his freedom to avenge Darcy's death, but he hadn't been willing to let her into his life.

Uncle John had called it right—by cutting himself off, by not allowing Darcy in—he'd let fear win. He could have told her he loved her last Friday and built two days of memories. Instead, he'd spend a lifetime with regrets.

She would never smile her blinding smile at him again. Never tease him, kiss him, soothe or excite him. He'd rejected the happiness and love she'd offered.

Death permitted no second chances.

Neither would he when he found Raul.

Eli cut his lights, turned up Darcy's driveway, and rolled to a stop. Deputy Carlisle's cruiser pulled in behind his.

Raul's tan sedan sat in front of Darcy's house. Were they destroying evidence?

Eli stepped from his cruiser. Carlisle crept up beside him.

"Take the front. I'll check the back," he said.

He circled stealthily, looking through windows into empty rooms. When they met up at the kitchen door, she shook her head no.

As he reached for the doorknob, raised voices came from behind. He signaled a direction change.

Moonlight illuminated the bullet holes perforating the cellar door. The sound of pounding fists mixed with cursing.

"The door's built to withstand a tornado," a male voice complained.

"If you hadn't shot her, we'd of had enough bullets to shoot the hinges or bolt off," an accented voice answered.

"The plane can't leave without me; I'm the pilot. Mother will send Juan to look for us. Now get up here and help me."

Eli squatted to peer through the ventilation slats. A lighter flared then guttered. He couldn't see if Darcy was inside. Why was the door locked?

He signaled Carlisle to kneel. She drew her automatic and thumbed the safety off.

Eli moved to the door and quietly worked the bolt free as one of the men in the cellar counted to three.

The door flew open. The men's momentum carried them onto the grass.

Eli and Carlisle yelled.

"Sheriff's Department! Stay down!"

"Keep your hands where I can see them!"

Raul spread his arms and legs. Eli covered both men while Carlisle cuffed their hands behind their backs and recited their rights.

"This is the man I saw at the diner, sir," she said,

pointing at Todd Williams.

Eli went down the cellar steps. The smell of gunpowder hung heavy. He played his flashlight beam around the floor. No Darcy.

Climbing out, he aimed the flashlight beam in ever-widening circles, working away from the cellar. No visible blood but he'd need a stronger light to be sure.

"Darcy!" He switched off the light and listened.

No answer. Was she bleeding somewhere in the dark?

He shouted again. No answer.

He stood in front of the men. "Where is Darcy Cooper?"

Neither man answered.

Carlisle had confiscated two pistols. She checked clips and chambers. "Both weapons have been fired and are empty, Sheriff."

"Call dispatch and get the crime scene team out here. We need dogs and lights."

"Yes, sir."

When Carlisle trotted out of earshot, Eli turned to the men on the ground. "Mrs. Williams says you shot Ms. Cooper, Raul."

"She lied. It was Todd. I never pointed a gun at her."

"Shut up!" When Todd attempted to roll face up, Eli planted a boot on his back and aimed his pistol at Todd's head.

"Where is Darcy Cooper?"

Two patrol cars roared into Darcy's driveway.

"Sir!" Carlisle ran toward him. "Ms. Cooper called in to report the men in her cellar. She's at the Hughes' place."

Headlights illuminated the cellar and yard. Light also flooded his soul.

Bob Hughes answered Eli's knock with a shotgun cradled in his arm.

"She's in the kitchen; we got her warm. Martha's getting the first aid kit."

"She's hurt?" Eli asked, entering the house.

"Just scratches. Did you catch them?"

"Yes. You won't need that." Eli nodded at the shotgun. "Thank you for protecting her."

Hughes set the shotgun in a corner. Eli followed him through the living room along a well-worn traffic pattern in the medium brown carpet. Bob pointed. "Kitchen's that way. I'll tell Martha you're here."

Eli hurried down the hall and stopped in the doorway. Relief flowed through him.

Darcy stood at the sink. Her long-sleeved, pale blue T-shirt bore a line of small rips across the back; dirt streaked her jeans. He hadn't made a sound, but she swung to face him.

"Did you get them?" she asked, her face a mixture of fear and hope.

He nodded. The old Darcy would have launched herself at him after hearing the news of a capture. He wanted to catch her up in his arms, but she remained at the sink.

"Todd and Raul will join Maggie and the others in jail. We grounded a private plane at the airport. It seems Todd has a pilot's license. Also, a collection of metal boxes is headed for the evidence lockup."

The overhead light revealed blue shadows beneath her eyes. She turned and soaped up her arms and hands.

"They won't hurt you again."

"Thank you."

"Thank Beth."

He pulled a handful of paper towels and carefully blotted her arms dry. He saw the ligature marks on her wrists. They'd tied her. She stood still while he used the damp towels on her face and neck. What would she do if he kissed her?

Martha Hughes entered. Her lined face revealed disdain for sunscreen.

"Sheriff."

She retrieved a bottle from the first aid kit and poured peroxide over Darcy's wrists and hands. Darcy flinched but kept her hands under the stream.

"We'll let them dry then do bandages. Meantime, let me clean where the barbed wire caught you." Martha rolled Darcy's shirt to expose her nicked back. "This isn't bad. Sheriff, hold her shirt while I use the peroxide and antibiotic ointment."

Placing one hand on Darcy's rigid back, Eli held the soft turquoise cotton shirt out of the way while Martha dabbed at angry, red scratches. A quick shiver shook Darcy.

"That takes care of that." Martha capped the bottle and looked Darcy over. "I want a peek at your knees; there's dirt mixed with the blood."

Darcy looked down. "Some scabs have reopened. It feels like the blood has dried the denim to my scrapes."

"Then we'll soak them off," Martha said. "The shower is this way."

"Can we use the garden hose outside?" Darcy asked. "I don't want to rinse all this dirt in your shower and I'd like to sit."

"The water outside is cold," Martha said. "We'll carry out warm water."

Darcy sat on the lawn chair Eli carried to the porch. He removed her shoes and socks.

Bob supplied pitchers of warm water that Eli poured over Darcy's knees while Martha loosely bandaged Darcy's hands.

"You said Beth called?" Darcy asked him. "She recognized our trouble code. Oh!"

She jerked with his experimental tug on her jeans. He nearly dropped the water pitcher. "Did I pull a scab loose?"

"No! Raul said he'd taken care of one of your deputies. Someone needs to look for him."

Eli put a hand on her shoulder as she tried to stand. She'd narrowly escaped death a second time, yet still worried about his deputy. God, he loved this woman.

"Stay put. Deputy Price is fine. Raul cold-cocked him then handcuffed him in the back seat of the cruiser. Fortunately, Price is flexible and carries spare keys."

"I'm glad he's safe," she said, adding, "The jeans are loose."

He gave a gentle tug. The material pulled away from her knees. Martha returned to the porch holding a towel and a scrap of denim.

"Our teenage granddaughter left these shorts from her last stay. They should just about fit you."

Eli and Bob turned their backs while Martha helped Darcy out of wet jeans and into shorts.

"How old is your granddaughter?" he heard Darcy ask. She sounded like she was holding her breath.

"Sixteen," Martha answered with a grunt.

"What a difference ten years makes," Darcy gasped.

"The difference is you have hips. Deep breath," Martha instructed.

The women's laughter made Eli smile. Tension drained from his body.

Five minutes later, bandages covered Darcy's knees. She leaned toward her shoes, groaned, and leaned again. Eli knelt to help her back into her socks and shoes. He sat Darcy on the front passenger seat then circled the cruiser and slid behind the wheel.

"Thank you both," Darcy called to the Hughes. "I'll invite you over for dinner in a week or two."

Eli laid an arm across the seatback and reversed until he could turn around. Their route to the station took them past her house. She leaned forward to glimpse the activity. He slowed.

"Wainright and the crime scene team are going through your house and the cellar. Deputies will watch the field until a team can search for leftovers in the morning." He increased their speed. "Maggie said that Raul shot you. Raul thinks Todd shot you." He paused. "Raul wasn't walking very well; he said you were responsible for his discomfort."

A faint grin lifted her lips. "I was fighting for my life—he got in the way."

"You haven't lost your sense of humor."

"It was a near thing. When Raul doubled over, I shoved him into Todd, and they fell down the cellar stairs. I slammed the door and slid the bolt. It was pure Divine intervention. I ran, and they started shooting."

He felt her watching him.

"What happens now?"

"You identify Maggie and her crew and give a statement. Are you up for that?"

"Yes. But first I need to call Beth and let her know I'm OK."

He handed her his cell phone. She dialed Beth's number and spent an emotional seven minutes reassuring Beth and finally passing the phone to Eli so he could confirm her condition.

He ended the call. "Can you breathe in those shorts?"

"Barely. My real concern is how I'm going to get them off." She looked away. "I'm not suggesting that you help. My hands are stiff. Maybe Deputy Carlisle could lend me another pair of sweat pants."

He nodded. His constant rebuffs had made her defensive. "Darcy, I'm sorry that I couldn't keep you safe."

Confusion entered her eyes. "You aren't my shadow, as handy as that might have proved tonight. Things could have gone better, but cuts and bruises aren't bad considering the people involved. I'd say everything turned out okay."

Not quite everything. Not yet. He pulled into the station lot. "We'll talk later," he said.

Later. Darcy leaned against the couch in Eli's office and closed her eyes. The word promised another opportunity or another rejection because saying he was sorry didn't mean he'd changed his mind about relationships. She wouldn't risk misreading his feelings again—her own were too tightly strung to risk.

She'd identified Maggie, Todd, and Raul from behind one-way glass. Now, she was finishing her statement to a subdued Detective Wainright. She looked at the wall clock. Midnight. Thank goodness for Deputy Carlisle's sweatpants and her help getting out of the breath-restricting denim.

She picked up where she'd left off. "I jogged the mile and a half of pasture to the Hughes house. I was afraid Raul and Todd would shoot their way out and come after me. I was also afraid they'd all escape with the drugs."

The interview took place in Eli's office with Eli present. He stood with his attention focused on something outside his window. His ramrod posture and crossed arms reminded her of when he'd commandeered a cubicle in the emergency room after the first attack. He was as protective—and distant—as before.

She shook the last cashew from the packet Eli had bought for her. Her stomach had stopped growling.

"Thank you, Ms. Cooper, that's all for now." Wainright closed his notebook. He faced Eli. "I'm talking to Mrs. Williams again. Her lawyer should be here. You want to sit in?"

"I'll make arrangements for Ms. Cooper, then join you."

He closed the door behind Wainright before facing her. "The next few days will be busy for me."

She crumpled the empty snack package. "The election is two weeks away. I imagine you have a few speeches to make. Especially now that you've caught Maggie's gang and ended the heroin trafficking in Tell County and other parts of Texas. This story needs to hit the newspaper and the local radio first thing in the morning. I know you're not a political animal, but the people in this county deserve the best sheriff they can get. That's you."

"You can say that after I failed to protect you?"

His harsh tone surprised her.

"Sheriff, if you were psychic, you'd have a valid argument. Since you're human like the rest of us, you'll have to accept that you can't predict or prevent bad things from happening. I could die next week in a car crash. But there's an equal or greater chance that I'll live to spoil lots of grandchildren."

"Would you stay with Brooke tonight?"

His change of subject meant he probably wouldn't heed her life's-a-risk lecture. She stifled a sigh.

"Have your people finished at my house?"

"Except for the field, yes."

"Then I'll go home."

He opened the door. She walked out.

The talk he'd promised hadn't happened. Later hadn't arrived. She still didn't know what his apology meant.

CHAPTER TWENTY-EIGHT

Wednesday morning, Darcy stood on her porch and watched her pasture where deputies continued to search with metal detectors and a drug dog. A few more ammo boxes, presumably filled with black tar heroin, were added to the stash already collected.

She glanced at the county road. No red pickup approached to join the patrol cars in her driveway.

Was this what her future held? Looking for Eli on the road, in the grocery store, in a crowd?

Sighing, she checked the coffee and tea urns, added ice to the cooler of water bottles, and replenished the bin of chocolate chip cookies. Inside, the timer went off. She pulled banana-nut muffins from the oven. Catering orders had picked up, and every one of her new customers wanted details of her ordeal. She complied happily, emphasizing Eli's involvement in keeping her alive.

Friday night, Darcy looked over Border's parking lot like trouble lurked between every vehicle. She probably would for a while. She parked her Explorer and stepped into the crisp late-October evening. Leaves were dropping and grass was turning brown.

As she stuffed her purse under the seat, a flash of yellow caught her eye. Reaching, she wiggled the manila envelope from between her seat and the console and read the return address. Laughing, she tossed the package onto the passenger seat. Her insurance policy—Maggie's real estate offer—had expired with Maggie's arrest.

New catering bookings were edging her bank account from anorexic to recovering. If catering jobs continued to increase, she could earn a living without making her home a full-time bed-and-breakfast. She didn't like admitting it, but she wasn't as ready to let strangers into her home as she had once been.

Some of the jobs came from unexpected clients. When she'd missed showing up last week, the independent living residents had taken turns leaving messages on her machine to alternately convey get-well wishes and inquire if she was a quitter. The last message was from the home's director, asking Darcy to cater an eighty-eighth birthday party for a resident that had requested a Nerf ball shooter as a gift since she was abandoning impromptu food pitching.

Sunday, Darcy watched a car come up the driveway. Cheryl Greer exited and was nearly knocked over by the yellow dog that followed her out, leash attached to his collar. The puppy stood as tall as the goats in the pasture, and he headed towards them at a gallop. Cheryl braced herself as the retractable leash reached its limit. The pup jerked to a halt and commenced barking.

Spotting her, Cheryl said, "Thanks for letting me bring Sulfur along. I can't leave him alone. He's already eaten my favorite shoes."

"Tie his leash to the light pole in the yard. He can entertain himself while you're inside."

Darcy brought a bowl of water for Sulfur. Cheryl followed her back inside.

"I'm surprised you called me," Cheryl said.

Darcy poured two cups of hot pumpkin-spice tea.

"I'm doing it because coverage in your paper is slanted toward one candidate for sheriff." Darcy sat at the kitchen table. Cheryl sat across from her; a pink flush highlighted her cheeks.

"That was brought to my attention recently. Do you know Lisa Lantz? She gave me an earful, and I had to admit her points were justified. I let my excitement over cultivating certain people as sources override my journalistic ethics. Now I wonder who was cultivating who. I was lazy about corroborating and checking facts, and I wound up pushing an agenda instead of reporting facts." Her shoulders slumped. "I'm not a very good journalist."

Darcy smiled. "Cheryl, I think you're on your way to becoming one."

Two cups of tea later, Cheryl closed her notebook and turned off her mini-recorder. "You are one brave lady. I don't think I could have put up with a fifth of what you went through. I'd probably have sold out and run as fast as I could away from Lost Creek."

"Are you a local?" Darcy asked.

"Born and raised here. My dream was to work for one of the bigger papers, but I like living here. The only downside is meeting someone I'd like to date." She looked out the window. Sulfur had barked himself out and lay panting, still watching the goats. "Off the record, what can you tell me about Keith Anderson? I've heard a lot of stories, but he's all business when I bring Sulfur in for his checkups."

"Keith is a good guy. Maybe you could do a local color piece about him. He's told me some hilarious stories about animals he's treated."

She walked Cheryl outside and waved her down the driveway.

"Thank You, Lord, for the gift of life," Darcy said for the fourth time that day. It was good to be a survivor.

Those who'd wished her harm were in jail. Their heroin was locked up and would be destroyed after their trials. That Maggie had used her and Alex still made her mad, but if she'd never met Alex, she'd never have come to Lost Creek or met Eli.

Eli. She suddenly knew what she was going to do with her second chance.

Monday, Darcy rolled her food carriers into the independent living community. Someone had covered a central table with orange and black tablecloths and set out serving trays and napkins.

"Thanks to whoever did this!" she said.

A woman stepped forward. "After what happened to you, we weren't sure you'd be here. But Burt said, 'If we set it up, she will come.' He watched some baseball movie last night and said it worked for the folks in the film."

Several residents came closer.

"I can help you arrange food," one said.

"Do you have time to stay and visit?"

"Would you share your carrot cake recipe with the kitchen staff?"

"Thank you, yes, and yes," Darcy said.

She smiled and handed a container to a resident. The woman removed the lid.

"Well, aren't these cute!" She arranged the Halloween-themed pumpkin muffins on a tray.

Another resident opened another container. "Cookies!" She squinted. "Vote?"

"Local and state elections are coming up on Tuesday," Darcy said. "I'm encouraging everyone I see to go to the polls."

"We're all registered," a man said. "We take our civic duty seriously."

The woman with red-framed glasses opened a third container. "What are these?"

"Nerf balls," Darcy said.

The woman grinned.

The room filled as residents picked up cookies and muffins and sat at the tables.

"Ted's daughter is running for county clerk," a man said. "She comes by to visit regularly. She's a good girl. I plan to vote for her."

"The newspaper has run quite a few articles mentioning that detective who wants to be sheriff."

"Okay," Darcy said. "I'll take questions now."

When the room ran out of questions, Darcy left some of Eli's campaign flyers on the serving table. She stacked her containers and rolled them toward the door.

"Now!" someone shouted.

She smiled as Nerf balls softly bounced off her back.

Tuesday afternoon, Darcy stood and stretched. If she had to spend any more time looking at Eli's face on the campaign postcards—well, there was only so much a volunteer could take. He wasn't smiling in the picture, but his relaxed pose and direct stare worked for marketing purposes. He made you want to stare back.

Darcy tapped the last bundle of postcards by their edges until they aligned. "This is the last of them; all addressed. I'll leave them at the bulk mail drop-off on my way home."

"You have to leave?" Lisa checked her wristwatch. "Why don't you hang around for another half-hour."

Darcy tilted her head. "What's happening in the next half-hour?"

"Dan said Eli was stopping by. Don't you want to say hello?"

Darcy raised an eyebrow.

"Okay," Lisa said. "I was hoping a casual encounter

might give you two a chance to talk. Eli is quieter than usual. And you put on a good front, but your smile needs exercise. The only genuine smile I've seen from you is when you talk to Jared. But who wouldn't have a genuine smile for Jared? He's such a handsome and good baby."

"Yes, he is," Darcy agreed, lifting him from his playpen to tickle his cheek and press a kiss to his forehead. She set him back down. "But I need to leave. I'm making treats for a tea party at the antiques store. Which reminds me, I need forty flyers to leave there tomorrow."

Lisa handed them over. Darcy hugged her then picked up the boxes of postcards. "If you need another volunteer before next Tuesday, call me."

She settled the boxes in her SUV and then started the car. A red truck pulled up behind her. Eli's face looked thinner than usual. Either he'd lost weight, or her rearview mirror was distorting his image.

She raised her hand in what she hoped passed for a casual wave while driving away.

Eli let his window down as Dan walked up to his truck.

"Did Darcy stop by to visit Jared?" Eli asked, watching her turn the corner.

"That, and she's a volunteer for your campaign."

Eli looked at Dan. "Volunteer?"

"Yep. Making phone calls, creating address labels, sending postcards, and handing out flyers. She's been a big help to Lisa."

Dan crossed his arms. "Darcy is safe now. I know the election is taking up your time, but when it's over, you might consider giving her a call to see how she's adjusting."

"Lisa has trained you well, Dan. You're becoming a matchmaker too."

"Nah. I'm commenting on what my eyes see, and what my gut tells me."

Eli got out of his truck. "What can I do to help?"

CHAPTER TWENTY-NINE

On the second Tuesday in November, Darcy drove to the community center to vote. The independent living community van was pulling out of the parking lot as she arrived. Familiar faces looked out the windows as the residents inside waved. She waved back, then turned toward the building. An orange Nerf ball flew past her head. She spun and glimpsed red-framed glasses before the window closed.

Smiling, she picked up the ball and walked inside.

That afternoon, her home phone rang. Lisa's number displayed on the caller ID.

"Darcy, are you sure you won't come to the election-watch party tonight? You've worked so hard for Eli, you deserve to be here."

"Is Eli coming?"

"Yes, but so are lots of other people like Brooke and Jeremy and Deputy Carlisle."

"Thanks, but I'll pass."

Lisa sighed. "You and Eli are the most stubborn people I know."

"I love you too, Lisa. Bye."

Eli walked into the party at eight PM. Dan jumped up from his recliner and handed Eli a beer. "You're ahead!"

The big-screen TV displayed poll results on a slow scroll across the bottom of the regular programming.

He accepted a plate of appetizers from Lisa as he scanned the room and then glanced towards the kitchen.

"She's not here," Lisa said.

Eli nodded and took a seat. He hadn't expected Darcy to be here. But he realized that he'd hoped she would be here. Now that she was no longer in danger, he wasn't seeing her often. He missed her. Oddly, the thought didn't aggravate or surprise him—it was just the truth. Since they'd met, he had done his best to run her off physically and emotionally. He'd hurt her. And that made him hurt.

An hour and a half later, the newscaster said, "We can call the Tell County sheriff's race for incumbent Elias Whitepath."

Dan whooped and pounded him on the back.

Brooke hugged him. "Congratulations, brother." She nodded at Jeremy, asleep on the sofa. "Can you carry him to the car for me?"

He picked up his nephew, settled him into Brooke's car, and waved her off. Dan walked outside and joined him.

"In all the excitement, I forgot to tell you that the District Attorney and Wainright are finishing up the case. Darcy may not even have to testify, and you're out of the loop. What you do now with your personal life is up to you. See you at the office tomorrow."

Eli stood, staring at his truck. Instead of feeling

victorious, he felt defeated. Instead of enjoying the win, he mourned the loss of Darcy. He'd won the election but felt like he'd lost much more.

Darcy smiled as the San Antonio station called the Tell County sheriff's race for Eli by a landslide.

Brooke and Jeremy would be ecstatic that Eli wouldn't be leaving Lost Creek to look for a new job. She was happy for them all.

She'd be okay, she told herself. Eventually, seeing Eli and thinking about him wouldn't hurt so bad, right? She wasn't going to be another Nurse Ellison—looking for crumbs when the table had already been wiped clean.

Searching for a happy thought, she turned off the TV and headed for bed.

The cougar from her dream in Colorado stared intently at Darcy like he was trying to tell her something. She stared back, unwilling to put words in his mouth—words of her own making. Frustrated, she turned away for a moment. When she turned back, he was gone.

Eli sat up in bed, his heart pounding. The white hawk with brown eyes had circled him twice. He'd held out his arm, inviting her to land. But she'd circled again and flown away. He felt like she was saying goodbye.

CHAPTER THIRTY

Friday night, Darcy hefted a brimming picnic basket from the back seat of her SUV and carried it into Border's. She lit the chafers and filled them with spring rolls. Carl appeared at her side; a smile stretched his broad face.

"Young'un, you sure perk up the place when you walk in. That's a pretty dress you're wearing."

"What, this old thing?" She flared the moss green skirt of her long-sleeved shirtwaist dress. "And I mean that literally. But thanks; you're good for my ego. I made spring rolls and dipping sauces."

Carl inhaled. "Smells great." His smile disappeared. "I read your interview in the paper. That's quite an ordeal you survived."

"I decided it was time for Cheryl Greer to give Eli direct credit for the drug bust. I couldn't talk about everything because of the pending trial, but I hoped the interview would win the sheriff some reelection votes."

"He won, so I'd say it helped. If you liked beer, I'd buy you one."

"I'll take water."

"How about wine?"

She widened her eyes. "Grape juice in a roadhouse?

Since when do you serve wine?"

"Since a smart blonde told me tourists drink the stuff."

"In that case, I'll take a chardonnay."

"That's white, right?" Carl winked then glanced down the bar. "Have a seat; there's one left there at the end."

Darcy claimed the last stool. Shirley set a coaster in front of her as she exchanged a tray of empty beer bottles for full bottles.

"What can I get for you, Darcy?"

"Carl's taking care of me, thanks."

"Then it's back to the wildlife." Shirley balanced her tray and headed for the tables.

Darcy smiled. Friendship was a good feeling. When she'd inherited Alex's house, she'd tried to make her new home feel permanent with inanimate things like photographs, Gramma's baskets, and new rugs. Those things brought her pleasure, but love endured in relationships and memories, not in belongings.

"Here you go, young'un."

Carl set a wine glass in front of her then left to fill another order. Darcy sipped then frowned. Her chardonnay tasted suspiciously like Chablis. She'd have to put together a wine list for Carl.

"Can I join you?"

The familiar voice made her catch her breath.

"Of course." She inhaled Eli's pine scent as he squeezed in beside her and put his back to the wall.

"Congratulations on your reelection," she said.

"Your interview in the paper helped a great deal."

"That was my intention." She looked up at him. The lines beside his mouth had deepened since she'd seen him last. She squashed the urge to smooth them away. "Did you need to ask me something about the case?"

"No, not about the case."

He continued to look at her. "In the patrol car, you said you missed me. I've missed you too."

Her pulse quickened. "Is this the later you mentioned?"

"This is later."

The band started playing again.

"My truck's outside," he said.

She left a tip beside her wine glass and walked to the door. Eli followed her closely through the crowd, but he didn't try to touch her. Outside, he seated her in his truck before sitting behind the steering wheel. On the western horizon, the sun ignited a blazing end to the day.

Eli looked at her. "I had a vision in Colorado—a white hawk with brown eyes was mortally wounded before I could help her. And you had a vision too."

Darcy watched the sunset and nodded as he continued.

"Our visions prophesied a danger I couldn't react to in time because you distracted me." His voice softened. "You fill my senses when we're together. I needed detachment to help you."

"I think my vision was telling me I had to rely on myself to survive. You distract me too." She looked at him. "So, you were put off by our visions, not me?"

"Not entirely. I didn't want an emotional commitment to you or anyone. I was protecting myself from you, and you from me." He paused.

"I saw your spirit guide in my dreams Tuesday night."

"I saw yours Tuesday night, too." She looked down and untangled her fingers. Too bad life didn't untangle as easily. "So we're back where we started. You don't want commitment, and I want more than an affair."

Eli gripped the steering wheel like he was trying to control his response.

"I've known since we met that I wanted you, Darcy but I denied that my growing attraction for you was the real reason I couldn't put you out of my mind. Seeing you almost die was like dying myself. I came within a blade stroke of existing in a meaningless world."

He caressed her cheek with a finger.

"I can't," she said.

She hated the pain that clouded his eyes. "Eli, I don't want an affair. My body would survive the eventual breakup, but my spirit wouldn't. I don't want to become a woman afraid to tell you I love you because you might decide it's time to move on."

He faced her. "I enjoy your spirit and our disagreements. I hope to be arguing with you sixty years from now."

She frowned. "You want to date until we're in a nursing home?"

"I want to date until you decide if you want to marry me."

The air in the cab seemed to vanish. She fought for breath.

"You want 'for as long as we both shall live'?"

"Yes. For as long as we both shall live. I want your tenacity, your heart, your loyalty, your passion, and your love. Unless after all I've done to discourage you, you no longer want me."

She cupped his face with her hands and smoothed the knotted muscles in his jaw. She searched his eyes and found her answer. "I love you, Eli."

Eli swept her hair from her face, nuzzled her neck, then found her mouth.

"You even taste like honeysuckle," he murmured. His arms closed around her.

When she surfaced, she nestled against his shoulder, her eyes closed, her lips parted.

She smiled. She'd finally realized what Alex had meant about discovering what she really sought—and what Eli had implied about recreating her past. Having a permanent home with her grandparents for four years straight wasn't what had made her happy with them. Loving them, and knowing they loved her back, was what had made her high-school years so happy.

"You found a happy thought?" Eli asked. She met his eyes.

"My happiest thought ever. You."

Read on for a preview of

INHERITING REDEMPTION

available at Amazon in paperback and ebook.

INHERITING REDEMPTION

DAWN SMITH

Sixteen days after Lyssa Eastin's sister marries into a wealthy Scottish family, she and her husband are dead, and Lyssa is flying to Scotland. When Lyssa is named as the beneficiary of her brother-in-law's half of the family business, the horrified family immediately tries to nullify her influence in the company. When the authorities tell Lyssa her sister's and brother-in-law's deaths are now a homicide case, she begins investigating and uncovers a hornet's nest of conflicting interests, jilted lovers, and a shadowy adversary. If only things stayed that simple...